Anna King was born in the East End of London and grew up in Hackney. Now married, she lives in Kent with her husband and two children.

A HANDFUL OF SOVEREIGNS

Anna King

WARNER BOOKS

A *Warner* Book

First published in Great Britain by
Warner in 1994
Reprinted 1998

A CIP catalogue record for this book
is available from the British Library

ISBN 0 7515 0749 0

Typeset by M Rules
Printed in England by Clays Ltd, St Ives plc

Warner Books
A Division of
Little, Brown and Company (UK)
Brettenham House
Lancaster Place
London WC2E 7EN

Dedicated to
My sister Helen Midson (née Masterson)
My brother-in-law Stuart
and nephews Craig and Sean Midson

CHAPTER ONE

'Will we have to go to the workhouse, Maggie?'

Fifteen year old Maggie Paige shot a startled look at her younger brother before answering quickly, 'Of course not, Charlie, whatever gave you that idea?'

The young boy shrugged his thin shoulders, his white, pinched face giving him the appearance of a boy much older than his eight years. The sight of the desolation in her brother's eyes caused Maggie's heart to lurch painfully inside her breast. Putting out her hand she said softly, 'Come here, love. Come and give me a cuddle.'

When the small arms wrapped themselves around her neck she swallowed hard, warning herself not to break down. The tears she had been holding in check all morning would have to wait a little longer, for now she had to be strong. Looking over his shoulder to where her sister stood by the door, she said gently, 'Put the kettle on, Liz, and when the tea's ready we can make a start on those sandwiches I made this morning.'

Lizzie Paige looked across the room at her sister, her eyes still red from crying and shook her head slowly.

'I'm not hungry, Maggie.'

Fighting down a feeling of irritation Maggie strove to keep her voice steady.

'I know you're not, Liz, but we have to eat. We've had nothing since last night, and the last thing we need right now is for one of us to get ill.'

For a moment Maggie thought that Lizzie was going to start an argument, and prayed silently. 'Not today, please God, not today.' She felt her body slacken with relief as Lizzie walked slowly past her and into the scullery.

Shifting her weight slightly she leaned back against the horsehair sofa pulling Charlie with her. Stroking his hair gently she closed her eyes and thought back over the past week. Was it only a week? Could their carefree, happy lives have been so drastically changed in such a short space of time? She felt the tears begin to seep between her closed eyelids and swallowed noisily.

The first victim of the diphtheria epidemic that was running rife in the East End streets had been old Mr Blackstone in the basement flat. His sudden death had caused no more than slight ripples of alarm to run through the four-storey house in Bethnal Green, where they lived in the top two rooms. There was always some disease breaking out due to the blocked-up, overflowing sewers that were part and parcel of living in this area of London. Illness and disease were common occurrences that the people accepted with resigned endurance. Apart from taking the precaution of boiling their drinking water, her mother hadn't taken any notice of the danger in their midst.

Then, a week after Mr Blackstone's death, ten-year-old Billy Simms from the second floor came home from school complaining of feeling unwell, and within twenty-four hours he was dead. The other residents in the building had felt the first stirring of panic at the news of the young boy's death, and their fears had soon become justified. Like a fire out of control, the disease had caught hold and swept through the large, over-crowded house, indiscriminate in its choice of victims.

Maggie hadn't been surprised when the fever had claimed her Dad, for he had always been sickly, spending more time at home than he did at the docks. Nor had it come as any surprise when her four younger brothers had succumbed to the sickness, for like their Dad they had no constitution. But when her Mum, that strong, single-minded woman that they had all looked to for guidance and strength had taken to her bed and quietly died, the shock had nearly been the end for the three of them. They had all loved their Dad and brothers, but not with the fierce, almost worshipping feeling they'd had for their Mum. Without her presence they were like a ship without its helm, floundering helplessly and without direction in a sea of pain and grief.

'Tea's ready,' Lizzie muttered sullenly as she walked past Maggie and Charlie. Banging the teapot down on the green cotton tablecloth she pulled out a chair and slumped onto it dejectedly. Maggie looked at her sister's dispirited face and felt the weight of responsibility bearing down heavily on her shoulders. Although Lizzie was two years older than her, Maggie knew that it would fall to her to see that the three of them stayed together.

Giving Charlie a gentle nudge she said kindly, 'Come on, love, let's get some grub down us, it'll make us all feel better.'

Charlie hesitated for a moment. He wasn't hungry, in fact he felt sick, but he must do as Maggie told him. From now on he must be very good, because if he was bad, then his sisters might send him to the workhouse. The very thought of that grim building was enough to send the bile rushing up into his throat. He felt the sweat break out on his forehead as he fought to keep from being sick, but it was no good. The days of grief and nights of fear he had endured this past week had accumulated until his nerve-racked system could take no more; when his stomach lurched he cast a beseeching look at Maggie before jumping down from the table and rushing into the scullery.

'Well, so much for making us feel better,' Lizzie said, her voice scathing as she watched the retreating figure of her brother.

Maggie looked up swiftly, her hackles rising at the tone of her sister's voice. Her eyes raked over the small, plump figure dressed in the navy skirt and blouse with their mother's black fringed shawl draped round the hunched shoulders and she felt her anger abating. Getting to her feet she asked mildly, 'Pour me out a cup of tea, would you, Liz? I'd better see if Charlie's all right, then we'll have to talk about what we plan to do now that Mum and Dad have gone.'

'What do you mean, have a talk? There's nothing to talk about that I can see. We'll just have to carry on like before but on less money, that's all there is to it.'

Maggie stared at her elder sister in amazement. Was she being deliberately obtuse, or did she really think that their lives wouldn't be affected by the death of their parents. But then hadn't Liz always been the same? As far back as Maggie could remember, her sister had seemed to glide through life with her eyes closed to the problems of those around her. Only when she herself was directly affected, did she make an effort to stir herself, and it was this attitude that had been the cause of many a row between the two of them. With a resigned sigh she pushed back her chair and went in search of her brother.

Charlie heard her coming and tried valiantly to get to his feet, but the effort was too much and with a quiet groan he slumped back down onto the cold stone floor.

'Oh, Charlie, oh you poor love,' Maggie cried, her heart wrenching at the sight of the crumpled figure.

5

Bending down she put her arms under the thin legs and lifted him from the floor. Holding him tight against her breast she carried him into the front room and laid him down on the mattress in the far corner, then, kneeling by his side she took hold of his clammy hands and said urgently, 'Charlie, you won't end up in the workhouse, I promise. I'd never let that happen to you. I love you, you silly ha'pence, and I'm going to look after you. Now try and get some sleep, there's a good lad.' Pushing back a tendril of damp hair from his forehead she took one last look at his ashen face before pulling the thin blanket over his trembling body.

'What's the matter with him?' Lizzie asked as Maggie sat down at the table. Picking up a sandwich from the plate in front of her Maggie made a studious effort at eating in order to play for time before answering. Glancing sideways to where Lizzie sat, her fingers drumming impatiently on the table, Maggie was alarmed at the feeling of dislike that rose inside her at the sight of her sister. They had never been close – they didn't even bear any resemblance to each other. Whereas Maggie was tall and slender with dark brown hair and eyes, Lizzie had always been on the plump side with fair, mousy hair and pale blue eyes, the image of her late father, while Maggie and Charlie had in-herited their mother's striking looks. This fact had been a bone of contention with Lizzie since the day she had started to take an interest in herself; and that interest had started very early in her life. The two girls had

fought and argued as children, and growing into adulthood hadn't softened their attitude towards each other.
Maggie's mind ran swiftly down the years, recalling all
the petty grievances and squabbles, and felt a growing
sense of dismay. There was no loving, understanding
Mum now to intervene between them and restore order.
Maggie had to admit to herself that she didn't like her
sister; she loved her, but she didn't like her. She also
knew that if it wasn't for Charlie they would probably
go their separate ways, but until he was old enough to
look after himself they would have to bury their differences and try to create a stable environment for him to
grow up in.

Pushing away the half-eaten sandwich she took a deep
breath and said quietly, 'What's wrong with you, Lizzie?
How can you sit there and ask what's the matter with
him? He's only eight years old and he's just seen his
Mum and Dad and brothers buried. How do you expect
him to act? The poor little sod thinks we're going to put
him in the workhouse, he's half out of his mind with
fear and if you weren't so wrapped up in yourself you
would have noticed before now.'

Maggie heard her voice rising and saw the flash of
anger cross Lizzie's face. Anxious to avoid an argument
she reached out and grabbed the plump hand tightly,
saying, 'I'm sorry, Liz, I shouldn't have said that. Please,
don't let's fight, I know we haven't always got on, but
we have to forget the past and pull together now. If only
for Charlie's sake, let's try and be friends, eh?'

Lizzie squirmed uncomfortably on the chair, her face a mixture of confused emotions while Maggie held her breath waiting for an answer. When she felt the hand within hers tighten she expelled a silent sigh of relief.

Lizzie remained silent for a few moments, then clearing her throat loudly she said awkwardly, 'All right, I'm prepared to try to if you are. So what do you suggest we do now? How are we going to manage without Mum and Dad's wages? I know Dad was more out of work than in it, but he did bring some money into the house, and Mum could sometimes earn as much as fifteen shillings from the washing and ironing she did for the big houses up Hackney and Aldgate way. I know I just said we could carry on like before, but I was just talking for the sake of it. We're never going to be able to manage on our wages, are we?'

Maggie shook her head despondently. 'Not while we stay on living where we are. The first thing we have to do is find somewhere smaller, we can't afford to pay the rent here. First thing tomorrow I'll start looking for another place. Mr Abrahams said I could have a few more days off while I sort things out; he's been very good.' As the image of her kindly employer appeared in her mind she found herself smiling fondly. Her Mum had got her the job in the dusty, overcrowded book shop when she was thirteen, and for the past two years she had happily run the dilapidated, untidy shop whilst old Mr Abrahams had whiled his time away sitting outside the front of the shop in his wicker chair, puffing

8

contentedly on his smelly pipe and chatting with anyone who happened to pass by.

Maggie knew she had been lucky to get such an easy, pleasant job, and had often felt guilty about Lizzie having to work in the matchbox factory in Bow. Conditions had improved slightly since the massive walk-out at Bryant and May in July, when 672 women had downed tools in support of a young girl unjustly sacked. This unbelievable action had led to an all-out strike, during which time Lizzie had been in her element. Every day she had gone down to the factory and taken her place in the picket line holding aloft her makeshift banner, retailing with relish the horrific conditions to the throng of curious bystanders who gathered to witness the historic event. For the first time in her life she had felt important, and although her wages had been sorely missed until strike pay had been organised, it had been almost worth the extra hardship to see her happy for a change.

'What do you mean, somewhere smaller?' Lizzie's voice shrilled loudly, cutting into Maggie's reverie. 'How much smaller were you thinking of? We've only got two rooms and a scullery as it is, if you think I'm moving into something even smaller you've got another think coming. Now you listen to me, Maggie, I. . . .'

'No, you listen,' Maggie hissed back. 'You earn nine shillings a week, I only get five and sixpence. The rent here alone is twelve bob, and that's without food, coal and money for clothes and shoes; you work it out. And as for this place being too small, it was big enough for the nine of us for years, wasn't it?'

The two girls glared at each other, their short-lived friendship gone, swept away on the tide of anger engulfing them both. An uneasy silence settled on the room, and then, her body heaving with rage and frustration, Lizzie leant towards Maggie and said savagely, 'Oh, yes, it was big enough for nine of us, with Mum, Dad, Harry, Johnny, Jimmy and Ken packed into one bedroom and you, me and Charlie huddled together on a mattress hardly big enough for two people in the same room we use as a kitchen and sitting room. Huh.' She was on her feet now, her hands resting on the table, her face inches away from Maggie's.

'And as for the money we bring home, you could help there by giving up the bookshop and getting a real job. It's not fair that I should have to slog my guts out in that stinking factory while you ponce around dusting old books pretending you're someone special. But then Mum thought you were, didn't she? She didn't drag you down to the factory when you left school like she did me, oh, no, not her precious Maggie, she wanted something better for you. Never mind that I've risked having the jaws eaten out of my head by phosphorus for the past four years working in that hell hole. As long as I brought my wages home that's all that mattered to Mum.'

Maggie sat rooted to her chair, her eyes wide with pity and sudden understanding of her sister's animosity towards her over the years. If the positions had been reversed, wouldn't she have felt the same?

'Liz, I'm sorry,' she murmured softly, 'I had no idea, I just never thought about it – you've never said anything before.'

'What good would it have done to complain?' Lizzie replied bitterly. 'The factory's bad enough, but there are worse places so I kept quiet. But there's hardly been a day gone by when I haven't thought of you working in that bookshop while I've stood at my bench pasting strips of magenta paper and thin pieces of wood together. I've become fast over the years, that's why I can earn up to nine bob a week. But when I first started my fingers used to be rubbed raw trying to fill my quota, some days, when the foreman was breathing down my neck and I was scared I'd lose my job, I'd work even faster until my fingers bled. I . . . oh, what the hell.' Her voice broke, and when Maggie saw the tears spring into her sister's eyes she pushed back her chair, and going to Lizzie's side she placed an arm around the heaving shoulders. Gently turning the sobbing girl around, Maggie led her to the sofa and together they slumped down onto the worn cushions. As they sat side by side, their arms closely entwined, Maggie felt a sense of peace and well-being steal over her. But the moment was short lived, as Lizzie, recovered now from her crying spasm and feeling awkward at being in such close proximity with her young sister, quickly disentangled herself from Maggie's grasp.

'Well now,' she said gruffly, 'I'd better get back to work. If I hurry, I can still get an afternoon's work in. Like you said, we're going to need all the money we can get now.'

'But, Liz, we haven't had a proper talk yet,' Maggie's voice rose in alarm. 'There's such a lot to be sorted out – can't you take the rest of the day off?'

Lizzie was already pulling on her heavy black shawl, her face impassive as she made for the door. 'We need the money,' she repeated dully. Maggie stood watching her for a moment, then with a quick bound she was across the room, her hand clutching at the plump arm.

'I'm going to go and see Mr Abrahams tomorrow and tell him I won't be able to work for him any more.' The words tumbled out breathlessly while her mind reeled in shock at the enormity of what she had said.

Shaking her head impatiently she carried on, 'You're right, it isn't fair to expect you to carry on in a job you hate when I'm so happy in mine. I thought maybe I could take over Mum's job. Her customers will still want their washing and ironing done, and that way I can stay at home and keep an eye on Charlie. He needs one of us to be around right now. You know how nervous he is, and he'd hate coming home from school to an empty house. And . . . and if I can persuade Mum's customers to let me do their laundry for them, then maybe we can stay here after all. What do you think, Liz?' Her hand tightened on Lizzie's arm, her voice pleading for some kind word, however small – but she was disappointed.

Shrugging her arm free, Lizzie opened the door, then turning her head slightly she said tersely, 'If you're waiting for a pat on the back, you're out of luck. It's about time you found out what hard work's really like, you've had it easy for far too long. Now if you'll excuse me, I'm late for work.'

When the door was slammed in her face Maggie stood for a long moment staring in hurt silence at the stained wooden panels, and then her mood changed swiftly to anger. Her fists clenched into tight balls, she stormed across the cracked, lino-covered floor and into the bedroom that had belonged to her parents and younger brothers. Ignoring the brass bedstead and the bare, stained mattress she sat instead on the long wooden ottoman at the foot of the bed. Placing her fists between her knees she rocked her body back and forth all the while muttering, 'The cow, the nasty, spiteful cow. How could she know how hard I've worked?' What about all the times she had had to carry heavy boxes of books from the big houses down to the shop? And how about when she'd had to haggle a price for the books, some of which were fit only for the rubbish tip, while the so-called better-classed ladies and gentlemen had treated her as if they were bestowing a great favour in allowing her to take their prized possessions away.

As for the shop itself, why, she had run it single handed since she started. Her duties included serving the customers, keeping some kind of order among the thousands of old, dusty books, making sure the accounts were kept up to date as well as making Mr Abrahams countless cups of tea and cooking his meals for him. Then when she came home, she'd always helped Mum with the never-ending pile of sheets and soiled under-garments that littered the tiny scullery.

Liz had never helped at home, nor had she ever looked after the children or cooked a meal. Once she had finished her day at the factory she had considered her work done for the rest of the day and had spent the evenings lolling about on the sofa reading some cheap magazine.

Raising her eyes she looked at the bed and whispered, 'I tried, Mum, I tried to be friends with her, but without you here to help us it's impossible. I thought for a while back there when she was upset that maybe we could bury our differences, but the truth is we don't like each other and we never will.'

'Who are you talking to, Maggie?' Charlie stood in the doorway rubbing his eyes, his Sunday shorts and pullover rumpled where he had been sleeping in them.

'No-one, love, just thinking out loud. You'd better get out of your good clothes and then if you're feeling better you can have something to eat.'

'Has Liz gone out?' he asked, his eyes moving around the room, and Maggie was quick to note the relief in his voice as he realised his elder sister was obviously not at home. Getting up from the ottoman Maggie took his hand and led him from the room. Later, when he had finished a bowl of soup and a sandwich, she ordered

14

him back to bed, and he went without a murmur.

When she was sure Charlie was asleep she settled herself on the sofa, her elbows resting on her long faded serge dress, her hands cupping her face as she stared into space. All of a sudden she felt deathly tired, and would have liked nothing better than to crawl under the thin blanket with Charlie, but if she slept now she would be awake half the night. Also she was determined to make Liz sit down and talk about their future. There was such a lot to be sorted out. The brass bedstead would have to be disposed of. It seemed a waste, but six people had died in it. Although Maggie knew that if the diphtheria had been going to get the three of them, it should have done so by now, she wasn't about to take any chances. She had already burned all of her Dad's clothes and those belonging to her brothers, but her Mum's clothes she had boiled thoroughly and packed away in the ottoman. There had been nothing sentimental about her decision to keep her mother's clothing – she had done so for purely practical reasons. Who knew when she or Liz would be able to afford any new clothes? And by new she meant the second-hand garments her Mum had bought them off the stall down the market, as not one of the family had ever owned anything brand new. The only thing she had to get rid of now was the bed, and that shouldn't prove too difficult. There was many a family who would take it off her hands, even when they knew her reasons for getting rid of it.

Glancing at the mantel clock she was surprised to see that it was nearly six o'clock. Liz would be home in a couple of hours, and then the battle would resume where it had left off. Knowing if she stayed on the sofa she would probably fall asleep, she dragged herself to her feet. Clearing the table quickly, she carried the dirty crockery into the scullery and placed them in the wooden sink. Taking her time she began to wash each item, and when that was done she got down on her knees and slowly scrubbed the floor in an effort to pass the time until Lizzie came home.

CHAPTER TWO

By ten o'clock Lizzie still hadn't returned home. Maggie's mood had changed from fear for her sister's safety to anger at what she thought to be inconsiderate behaviour, then back to fear. She didn't know what time she had finally fallen asleep on the worn sofa, but when she awoke, cold and cramped, her first instinct was to hurry over to the bed, praying to see the short, plump body lying beside Charlie. Peering into the gloom her heart sank at the sight of the empty space beside the inert, silent form of her brother. Biting her lower lip anxiously she pulled her brown woollen shawl from the peg behind the scullery door and, careful not to wake Charlie, she crept from the room and down to the communal lavatory. Holding her breath against the stench of the tiny closet she quickly relieved herself and hurried back up the bare, wooden stairway.

Once back in the flat she stripped herself to the waist and lathered the top half of her body with the thin bar of carbolic soap. Her teeth chattering wildly, she swiftly dried herself on the threadbare grey towel before setting about the business of getting a fire going in the living room grate. Ten minutes later, with a bright roaring fire heating the still dark room she reluctantly pulled herself away from the warmth of the flames to make the morning pot of tea.

'Charlie, Charlie, come on, wake up, love,' she said softly, her free hand shaking the thin shoulder. Charlie woke slowly, his eyes opening with a supreme effort. Blinking rapidly he gave a huge yawn before asking tiredly, 'Is it time to get up already, Maggie?'

'No, no, it's all right, love,' she reassured him, 'but I have to get to the shop, and I didn't want to go without telling you. Here, sit up and drink this tea while it's hot. I'm sorry there's no milk, I'll bring some home with me tonight.'

Placing the tin mug carefully in his hand she stood up, adding, 'You can stay in bed if you want, you might as well have the rest of the week off school, but you'll have to go back on Monday.'

Without waiting for an answer, she picked up her own mug of steaming black tea from the table and between quick gulps, she spread a thick layer of pork fat on two slices of bread for Charlie's breakfast.

'There's a piece of paper on the floor, Maggie.'

Holding the thin blanket over his shoulders, Charlie bent down to retrieve the small scrap of paper. Laying it on the table, he asked timidly, 'Can I use the pot this morning, Maggie? I'll empty it when I'm dressed.'

Maggie nodded absently, then walked over to the fire so that she could read the short note by the light of the leaping flames. Quickly scanning the page she felt her face relax and a smile come to her lips.

Dear Maggie

Sorry I was so late home last night. I stayed late at work to earn some extra money, and I'm leaving early so I can walk instead of getting the horse-bus, every little bit helps. See you later.

Liz

'What is it, Maggie?' Charlie asked curiously as he came back to the table.

'Nothing important, love. Just a note from Liz. Now look.' She waved a finger under his nose, 'I've got to go now. You bring your breakfast over to the fire and keep yourself warm. And don't forget to empty that pot, mind.'

Charlie moved over to the fire, his eyes following his sister as she wrapped her shawl over her head and around the top half of her body, her fingers deftly tying the edges into a small knot at the back of her waist. He wished she didn't have to go back to work, he didn't like being on his own, but he mustn't say anything. Remembering how he had felt yesterday he swallowed hard and looked into the fire. The fear of the workhouse was still with him and he had to make a conscious effort not to plead with Maggie to stay home. He knew she loved him now, but she might change her mind if he became a nuisance.

Stretching his lips into a smile he said loudly, 'I'll be all right, I can look after meself.'

Maggie smiled fondly at him, then bending over she kissed him lightly on the cheek, saying, 'I know you can, love. See you later.'

When she had gone, he sat for a long while, his breakfast forgotten as he stared at the tall, black shadows that seemed to dance on the walls from the reflection of the fire. He wished that Maggie had lit the gas-lamp before leaving, even though he knew it would soon be light. Closing his eyes tightly he leant his head against his knees and waited for the dawn to break.

When Maggie reached the second floor she hesitated a moment before knocking on the door where the Simms family lived. Within minutes Ethel Simms, a slovenly but amiable woman in her mid-forties stood before her, a broad smile spreading over her grimy face at the sight of her young neighbour.

'Why, 'ello, Maggie, you off back to work then?'

'Good morning, Mrs Simms, yes, I am. That's why I knocked. You see I've left Charlie on his own and I was wondering if you'd keep an eye on him. I don't like leaving him just now, you know, after what's happened, but I don't have any choice.'

Ethel Simms looked closely at the young girl and sighed heavily. Then folding her arms across her ample chest she said sadly, 'I know, love, I know. We've all suffered, and you're not the only ones who'll miss yer Mum. She always 'ad time to stop and 'ave a chat wiv me, and many's a time she 'elped me out when money was short, even though she didn't 'ave much 'erself. She was well-liked was yer Mum, but Maggie, love, I know it's none of me business, but Charlie ain't a baby no more. My Billy, God rest him, 'e took care of 'imself almost from the time 'e could walk, and 'e was more 'elp to me than that lazy bugger I married. Went up West every day after school 'e did to clear the 'orse's muck from the roads, 'and 'e 'anded over every penny wivout me 'aving to ask him.'

Stopping for a moment to wipe her nose on her sleeve, she gave a loud sniff before adding sombrely, 'I still can't believe 'e's gorn. Strong as a bull my Billy, it don't make sense that a boy like that could be taken while some like . . .'

Maggie bowed her head for a brief second before raising her eyes to meet the woman's anguished gaze.

'Like my Charlie you mean? Oh, it's all right, Mrs Simms, there's no need to feel embarrassed, I've wondered the same thing myself. Look at my Mum, she never had a day's illness in her life, but it never did her any good, did it? But if it's too much trouble, about Charlie I mean, just say – I won't be offended.'

She watched as Mrs Simms gave her nose another swipe at her sleeve, trying to keep the disgust from her face.

'Don't you worry, love, I'll keep me eye out for 'im. You get off to work and if . . .' Her words were cut off by the sound of a child's piercing wail coming from somewhere inside the room. Maggie used the distraction to make her escape. With a last shout of thanks to the already retreating figure, she carefully concentrated on descending the darkened stairway, her mind thinking over what Ethel Simms had said.

It was true that some children of Charlie's age worked after school. There were plenty of the poor mites working at the matchbox factory where Liz worked, sometimes until ten or eleven at night, and Maggie knew that if it wasn't compulsory to send children to school, many parents wouldn't bother. Not like her Mum. She had been very strict on education, refusing to let any of her children work before they left school, even though she had been sorely in need of the extra money they could have brought in before her two daughters had finally left school. She'd made them speak properly too, always pulling them up if they dropped their aitches, much to the amusement of their father. As he'd often pointed out, schooling hadn't done much for Lizzie when the time had come for her to start work. His remarks had always been made without malice, he being perfectly content to leave the upbringing of his children in his wife's capable hands.

The blast of cold air from the open porch made Maggie pull her shawl even tighter around her slender body. Before stepping out onto the pavement she looked up at the dark stairway, her mind picturing Charlie already counting the hours until she returned home.

'Oh, stop it,' she told herself sternly, 'Mrs Simms is right. He's not a baby, and he's going to have to toughen up sooner or later. It might as well be now.' Pushing aside the feeling of guilt that threatened to overcome her, she bent her head against the cold and left the building.

A slight flurry of snow was just beginning to fall as Maggie hurried down Old Ford Road. If she kept up this pace she should reach Petticoat Lane in another twenty minutes. For some unknown reason she was anxious to reach the shop and see Mr Abrahams. A nagging feeling of disquiet had been tormenting her since she'd woken up this morning, and even the cheery note from Liz hadn't been able to dispel it. It was nearly eight o'clock when she finally turned the corner into the Lane, and hugging her arms around her chest she quickened her steps. It had only been two days since she had been here, but it seemed like a lifetime A few minutes later she was standing outside the shop, her eyes wide in disbelief at the sight that greeted her. Black boards covered the grimy windows, and the pavement outside that was normally covered with dozens of books packed tightly into wooden boxes was startlingly empty. She could feel her jaw drop in amazement as she stood rooted to the spot unable to move. Then with a startled cry she sprang forward and began to knock furiously on the shuttered door, but it remained firmly closed in her face.

'It's no good you banging, love, no-one's gonna answer. The old boy dropped dead two days ago.'

Maggie spun round to face the woman who had come up behind her. She recognised her vaguely as one of the stallholders in the market, a small, untidy looking woman who sold old clothes from a barrow.

'But . . . but he can't be dead,' Maggie stuttered nervously, 'I saw him two days ago . . . he was all right then. What happened?'

The woman looked keenly at the distraught young girl, then cocking her head to one side asked, 'You the girl that worked for 'im?'

'Yes . . . yes, I am. Look, are you sure. I mean . . . Are you sure he's dead? Maybe he's been taken ill or something?' The words tumbled out from between Maggie's dry lips. Clutching the woman's arm she cried desperately, 'Please, you must be mistaken, you must.'

Removing her arm from Maggie's grasp, the woman hitched up her bust and laughed loudly, 'Well, I 'ope for 'is sake I ain't, love. They're burying 'im tomorrow.'

Maggie let her hands fall to her side. She couldn't take

it in, she just couldn't. Shaking her head from side to side she whispered, 'But I saw him two days ago, he was fine. He told me he was going to collect some new books from a house in Stepney.'

'Ah, well, 'e never got there. 'Eart attack it was, so the doctor says. Still, 'e was getting on, must 'ave been over seventy. Anyway ducks, can't stand 'ere chatting, I've left me youngest setting up me barra. If I don't keep an eye on 'im, 'e'll let people rob 'im blind. What ya gonna do now, love? Not much work abaht – well, not cushy work like you've been used to.' When she received no answer, she gave another hitch to her bust and with a last look at the forlorn girl standing outside the shop, she went on her way.

The snow had started to fall harder, but Maggie, wrapped up in her misery, didn't notice. It was only when two women on their way to the market bumped into her that she reluctantly moved away from where she had worked for over two years. Fighting down the panic that was gnawing at her insides she began the long walk home. What was she going to do now? She had been banking on her wages from the shop to keep her going until she'd established herself with her Mum's old customers. And what would Liz say when she found out? She had always begrudged handing over her wages to her Mum, so how would she react when she discovered that she was now the sole breadwinner? Maggie shuddered at the thought of the confrontation to come. Hot on the heels of this thought came another, more frightening notion. What if Liz decided to leave home and get a place of her own? There was no binding love to keep them together, no reason for Liz to stay and support her and Charlie, even if it was only for a short time until Maggie found work.

Half-blinded by the falling snow she stumbled on, her mind working furiously, trying to decide the best course of action to take. She could go to the house in Hackney where her Mum had gotten most of the work that had brought in the bulk of the laundry money. Many a Monday morning had seen her accompanying her Mum up to the big house to collect the piles of sheets and towels that could only have been used a couple of times before being thrown into the dirty linen hamper. That was another reason she'd had cause to be grateful to Mr Abrahams. How many other employers would let their staff have time off to help their mothers? Stopping for a moment to get her bearings she leant against a wall and whispered, 'Oh, Mr Abrahams, you were so kind to me, and I never even had the chance to say goodbye.'

The sound of the town hall clock brought her head up sharply. Ten o'clock! Good God – she had been wandering around for nearly two hours. Brushing the snow and tears from her eyes she straightened up, her chin thrust out resolutely. This wasn't getting anything done, and if her Mum could have seen her moping around she'd have boxed her ears. The thought of her dead mother gave her the strength needed to set her on her way.

Pushing herself away from the wall she began to walk towards Hackney.

Mare Street was situated in the heart of Hackney. A long, sprawling thoroughfare, it contained a few select shops and public houses amidst the rows of imposing, pillar-flanked houses that stood grandly side by side – a million miles away from the dirty, back-to-back tenement buildings only a short horse-ride away.

The street was busy at this time of day, and Maggie hurriedly stepped off the pavement to allow a smartly dressed couple to pass by. Her footsteps slowing down she made her way to number seventeen, rehearsing in her mind what she was going to say to Mrs Biggins, the elderly housekeeper. Raising her eyes warily, she saw as if for the first time how grandiose the house in front of her was, and felt her heart quail at the task ahead of her. She had been here more times than she could remember, but never had she felt as she did now. When she had been before it had been under the protection and strength of her mother, and without that self-assured presence she felt awkward and shabby, and dreadfully vunerable. If it hadn't been for the fear of facing Lizzie without a job she would have turned tail and run back home, but the fear that her sister would leave her and Charlie to fend for themselves if she didn't find some kind of work gave her the courage to push back the black iron gate and descend the stone steps to the basement.

27

Swallowing hard she took a deep breath, then raised the brass knocker on the brown-painted door and banged it down hard. As the metallic sound rang in her ears she stepped back in alarm, amazed at her temerity. When the door was pulled open she caught a glimpse of the small, white face belonging to the scullery maid, her eyes widening at the sight of the figure before her.

'Hello,' Maggie started nervously. 'I wonder if I could speak to Mrs Biggins, please. My name's Maggie Paige, my Mum used to do the laundry here and . . .' The words died in her throat as the door was pushed to. Then she heard the sound of the maid's voice calling urgently, 'Mrs Biggins, Mrs Biggins, it's that girl, the one whose Mum used to do the washing.'

Within minutes the door was pulled open again to reveal the short, plump body of the housekeeper, her face wild with fury. Maggie saw the look and felt her stomach turn over at the undisguised hostility on the woman's face. Summoning all of her courage she tried again.

'Hello, my name's Maggie Paige, my mother used to . . .' She got no further.

'I know who you are, madam,' the woman growled at her, 'and how you've the nerve to come here after what's happened, I don't know.'

'What . . . what are you talking about, Mrs Biggins? My Mum always did a good job for you, didn't she? And . . . and I wondered if I could take over now that she's . . .' Again she faltered, unable to say the dreadful word.

'Yes, she did a good job, and I liked her. She was a nice woman, but that doesn't change the fact that she died of the diphtheria, and most of your family so I heard. And you've got the cheek to bring the disease here. What are you thinking of, girl? Do you want all of us here to catch it as well? Now get off with you before the mistress finds out you've been.'

Her voice cracking with anxiety Maggie stepped forward, her hands outstretched as she made one final plea.

'Please, Mrs Biggins, I haven't got it, I wouldn't have come here if I thought there was any chance of passing it on, and I need a job, please, don't turn me away.'

Already the door was being closed in her face.

'I'm sorry, I can't take the chance, and neither will any of your Mum's other customers, so save yourself shoe leather. You'd better try for work in your own neck of the woods.'

'Oh, no, please, Mrs Biggins, I haven't got it, I haven't.' But it was no good – the door was shut firmly against her entreaties, leaving her no alternative but to leave. Her shoulders slumped in despair, she mounted the three stone steps and after giving one last beseeching look at the cold, grey house she moved her tired, aching legs once again out onto the slippery, cobbled pavement.

What was she to do now? The thought of waiting at the flat for Liz to come home caused her to shiver. Even remembering the warm, friendly note from this morning didn't hearten her. She knew her sister, and her frequent changes of mood. No, better she went now and met her from work to get it over with quickly than spend the rest of the day worrying herself sick with only Charlie for company. Trying to ignore the sinking feeling in the pit of her stomach, she set off briskly in the direction of Bow.

CHAPTER THREE

'ʹEre, ain't that yer sister waiting at the gate?'

Lizzie followed the pointing finger of her companion and nodded, her eyes narrowing in surprise at the unexpected appearance of her sister.

'Yes, yes it is, I wonder what she's doing here. Hey, Maggie over here,' she called out, her voice rising over the babble of noise from her workmates as they made their way across the yard towards the black iron gate. Maggie heard Liz's voice calling to her, but when she tried to turn her body round she nearly toppled over. She had been standing here for hours and her legs and feet were frozen with the cold. Lifting first one foot then the other, she stamped them as hard as she could to try and bring the circulation back into her stiff limbs.

'Hello, Liz. I thought you were never coming out,' she said, her teeth chattering violently as she tried to maintain a calm image. Lizzie eyed her sister warily. She was supposed to have gone to the bookshop, then home to look after Charlie. What was she doing here?

' 'Allo, yer Lizzie's sister, ain't yer? I seen yer down the market wiv Liz.'

Maggie switched her gaze from Liz to the young girl standing by her side. She judged her to be about her own age, and as her eyes took in the threadbare clothes and dirty, bare feet blue with the cold she forgot for a moment her own troubles. The left side of the girl's face was badly bruised and swollen, and when she suddenly smiled, revealing a large empty gap in her upper teeth, Maggie felt an irrational urge to cry.

'What are you doing here? Has something happened?'

Maggie tore her eyes away from the girl's battered face, her heart racing at the sound of Lizzie's sharp voice. All the rehearsing she'd done on how to tell her sister what had happened vanished and, bowing her head slightly she answered. 'Mr Abraham's dead.'

'Dead?' Lizzie echoed, her face stretched wide with surprise. 'How? I mean, what happened? Was it the diphtheria?'

'No, no not that,' Maggie continued, stamping her feet. 'A woman from the market told me he'd had a heart attack two days ago. The shop is all boarded up, I don't know what's going to happen to it now.'

'Christ! That's all we need.'

Maggie winced at the vehemence of Lizzie's words, but before she could make any rejoinder she felt her arm being seized roughly as Lizzie steered her away from the gate.

'Bye, Teresa,' she called to the girl who had been watching the scene with avid curiosity, 'I'll see you tomorrow.'

They had walked some distance from the factory before Liz spoke. Pulling Maggie none too gently to a stop she said harshly, 'Don't think you're going to laze about at home while I slog my guts out. I'll bet you've been swanning round the shops all day instead of looking for another job.'

'I haven't,' Maggie replied hotly, 'and let go of my arm, Liz, else I'll shove you back.'

The two girls stood glaring at each other, the cold puffs of air pouring from their mouths forming a barrier of steam between them. Then Liz, her voice slightly mollified asked, 'Well, what have you been doing all day then?' They had started to walk on, and as they walked, Maggie recounted the events of the day. When she had finished, a silence settled on them. It wasn't until they had reached Bethnal Green Road that Maggie, unable to bear the strained silence any longer asked, 'That girl, you know, the one you were with at the factory, what happened to her face? And how can she walk about in this weather without any boots on? My feet are frozen and I've got thick stockings under my boots. How does she bear it? I mean, it must be bad enough walking barefoot in any weather, but on a day like today, with the snow settling, it's a wonder she can feel her feet at all.' Liz shrugged her shoulders, and then as if explaining a difficult question to a child she answered, 'She doesn't have any choice. There are twelve of them at home, and only two pairs of boots between them all. If her Mum and Dad are working they get the use of the boots. When they're not, Teresa gets to wear a pair. Either way she can't win, because if they're out of work she doesn't eat, and given the choice she'd rather have a full belly than boots on her feet.'

'Oh,' Maggie's voice sank to a whisper, 'but what about her face? Did she have an accident?'

Liz gave a mirthless laugh. 'You could say that. She ran into a fist – I don't know whose. Her Mum and Dad both knock her about, so it could have been either of them.'

'But that's terrible,' Maggie cried. 'Can't she tell someone?'

'Oh, for God's sake, who's she going to tell? Besides, she's used to it, it's a way of life to her, she doesn't know any different. She had a baby when she was thirteen, probably by her Dad, but it could have been one of her brothers – she's not sure. The kid died two days after it was born, and Teresa nearly joined it. The old midwife who delivered it was so drunk she made a right muck up of Teresa's insides. She probably won't ever be able to have any more children, which is a blessing in disguise considering her circumstances.'

Maggie walked on, her eyes firmly on the slippery pavement, her whole being horrified at what she had just heard. Bowing her head against the cold wind she protested, 'There must be something she can do, someone she can go to for help.'

'Oh, grow up, Maggie,' Liz said impatiently. 'It happens all the time. The trouble with you is Mum always protected you from the seamier side of life. That's probably one of the reasons she got you that job with Mr Abrahams. If you'd started with me, you'd soon have had your eyes opened to what goes on in the real world. Anyway, forget about Teresa, we've got our own troubles to worry about without taking on anyone else's.'

They were nearly home, and when Liz marched off, Maggie made no attempt to catch up with her. Instead she walked slowly behind, her mind going over what Liz had said, realising for the first time just how lucky they had been to had parents like theirs. Despite the fact that they lived in an area known as a slum, Mum had always kept the flat and the children spotless. None of them had ever gone without food, even when times had been very hard with her Dad out of work. And as for any of them going without boots, why, her Mum would have sold the last stick of furniture rather than let that happen. She felt the tears spring to her eyes and quickly wiped them away in case Liz saw her crying and started on her again.

'Come on,' Liz called out impatiently, 'I want to get home. I hope Charlie's kept the fire going, I'm freezing.'

At the mention of her brother's name Maggie's head jerked back in alarm. With all that had happened, she had forgotten all about him. Her concern for Charlie pushed all other thoughts from her mind. Heedless of the strong wind and biting cold she pushed her aching legs into a run, ignoring the muffled shouts of Liz to wait for her. Ten minutes later she was inside the building, her breath coming in short gasps, her mind visualising all manner of terrible things that could have happened to Charlie while she'd been out. She was halfway up the stairs when Liz caught up with her.

'What the hell did you run off like that for?' Liz demanded angrily, her face red with exertion.

'It's Charlie, he's been on his own all day.' The words tumbled out breathlessly. 'I hope he's all right.'

A look of irritation crossed Liz's face, and with her lips drawn tightly together she muttered, 'Bloody hell, you make a right pair. Neither of you know you're born. Well, all I can say is you've both got a few shocks coming to you.'

As Liz went to pass her, Maggie's hand shot out and gripped her arm.

'Maybe you're right, maybe we have had it soft, but I'll tell you this much for nothing, Liz, after today I'm learning fast.' Her voice was soft but the look in her eyes warned Liz to keep quiet. Releasing her hold on Liz's arm, Maggie pushed her aside and carefully made her way up the darkened stairway to the flat.

*

Charlie lay on his side, his knees drawn up to his chin as he listened to the familiar sound of his sisters arguing. The row didn't frighten him, for after spending the day alone the sound of the raised voices was like balm to his frayed nerves. Hugging the blanket tighter around his body, he turned over on the mattress, letting the noise from the far end of the room wash over him.

'We don't have any choice, we can't afford to stay here,' Maggie was yelling. 'I don't care what you say, when Mr Bates comes for the rent on Friday, I'm going to ask him about the basement.'

'And I'm telling you there's no way I'm going to live in one room under the ground. Mum sent me down there once with a bowl of soup for Mr Blackstone when he was ill, and I couldn't wait to get out. The room was filthy, and the smell nearly knocked me over. And another thing, there's no windows down there, the only way to get any light or air into the room is to leave the door open. Can you imagine what it would be like in this weather? And once the door is closed it'd be like being buried alive, so think again. Maggie, I'm not going down there and that's final.'

Maggie looked at Liz's set, determined face and closed her eyes wearily.

'All right, Liz,' she said quietly, 'I'm too tired to argue any more. I'm going to make something to eat, and while I'm doing that maybe you can come up with a better solution.'

Once in the scullery she gripped the side of the sink as

she tried to control the turmoil that was raging inside her taut body. What she really wanted to do was to return to the living room and smack Lizzie hard. Her hands curled into fists as she imagined herself doing just that. It wouldn't achieve anything, and she'd probably end up getting her own face bashed in, for Liz was well able to look after herself – but oh what a blessed relief it would be to land that first blow.

Turning from the sink she began to cut the loaf of stale bread into thick slices, her active mind trying to work out what course of action to take next. The situation facing her was partly her own fault. She should have known that Liz would oppose any idea that she came up with, and that there was no way she would let herself be seen to be taking orders from her younger sister. Placing a lump of cheese next to the plate of bread Maggie took a deep breath. As much as it went against the grain, she was going to have to swallow her pride and try to placate Liz, make her think that she was in charge of their destiny. It shouldn't be too hard, for if there was one thing guaranteed to soften Liz, it was feeling important. Taking another deep breath she walked back into the living room, her face subdued, her body slumped in an attitude of one who has accepted defeat.

'I'm afraid that's all there is, Liz,' she murmured as she laid the plate on the table. 'I hope it's all right.'

Liz looked sharply at her sister. 'You can cut out the sarcasm, Maggie, it won't wash with me.'

Maggie quickly bent her head. Careful, she warned herself, don't overdo it.

'I wasn't being sarky, Liz, I meant it. After all, you're the one who's bringing in the money, you should have something decent to eat.'

Before Liz could answer, Maggie left the room to fetch the teapot and mugs. When she returned Liz was already tucking into the bread and cheese, her strong teeth tearing at the hard crust.

'I'll let Charlie have his tea in bed, shall I? It'll be warmer for him, and it'll save having to put more coal on the fire.'

'Oh, don't matter if we freeze, as long as Charlie's warm,' Liz answered, her mouth crammed with food.

'I just thought it would save us some money. I'll build the fire up if you want, but let me give Charlie his tea first.'

Charlie was sitting up in bed waiting for her, and as she put the mug of tea on the floor he leaned towards her, his face worried.

'What's up, Maggie? Why are you crawling to Liz?' he asked, his voice barely above a whisper. 'Is she going to leave us, is that why you're sucking up to her?'

'Shush, she might hear you,' Maggie admonished gently. 'Eat your supper and go to sleep, there's nothing for you to worry about.'

'But Maggie, I don't like to hear you talk like that – it makes me feel sort of funny inside.'

Putting the plate on his lap she ruffled his hair, saying,

'I know what I'm doing, love, now do as I say, there's a good boy.' Then she left him, to join Liz at the table.

As she helped herself to a piece of bread she thought about what Charlie had said about feeling funny inside. She knew exactly how he felt, for every fibre in her body was crying out at the servile attitude she was being forced to assume. The dry bread stuck in her throat, and with a sad sigh she pushed her plate away.

'What's the matter, not hungry?' Liz enquired, her face still filled with suspicion at the sudden change in her sister.

'I can't eat, I'm too worried about what's going to happen to us. What if I can't find another job, what are we going to do then? We can't live on just your money. What are we going to do, Liz? I'm scared, really scared. Oh, Liz, how are we going to manage.'

With a loud moan, Maggie slumped over the table, her head resting on her arms, and when the first tears started to fall she realised she wasn't play-acting any more. The long, traumatic day had finally taken its toll. She felt so tired, tired and worn out, and afraid, desperately afraid of the long days that lay ahead. Work was scarce, and the only kind of job a young girl like her could hope to find wouldn't pay half what she'd been earning in the bookshop. She'd thought it would be so easy, just a matter of knocking on a few doors and offering her services. Well, she'd learnt the hard way. How could she have imagined that she could step into her mother's shoes and earn the money Mum had? Even if she had been given the chance, she would never have been able to manage all that washing and ironing on her own, because she couldn't see Liz offering to help after work like she herself had done with her Mum.

When she felt the hand stroking her hair she raised her head wearily, expecting to find Charlie standing beside her. When she saw Liz by her side, her plump face filled with concern, the surprise was so great she immediately stopped crying.

'Here, take this and wipe your face before Charlie comes over to see what's going on,' she said gruffly handing over a large square piece of cloth.

Maggie took the makeshift handkerchief gratefully and began to rub her tear-stained cheeks. Minutes later a steaming mug of tea was deposited in front of her, and wrapping her hands around it she said shakily, 'Thanks, Liz, just what I needed.'

But Liz was no longer listening. Her body fidgeting from side to side, she swept her gaze around the room as if seeking a solution from the four walls. The silence in the room lengthened, and just when Maggie thought she could take no more, Lizzie spoke.

'I'll ask round the factory tomorrow – maybe someone knows of a job going. But in the meantime, you get out and have a look around.'

Gulping down the last of her tea Maggie laid the mug on the table and asked, 'What about the factory, aren't there any jobs going. . . .' Before she could finish Liz leapt to her feet, her face red with anger.

'No, it's bad enough I have to work there, I'm not having you risk your health and maybe your life as well, so you can put that idea out of your mind right now.' Her voice had risen, and Maggie watched in alarm as the irate figure paced the room.

'But, Liz, you've worked there for years and you're all right. I know there's a danger working with matches, but if you can do it then so can I.'

Lizzie looked down into the wide brown eyes and shook her head sorrowfully. 'You don't know the half of it, Maggie.' She was sitting down again, her hands laid out flat on the table.

'If you're lucky enough not to get 'phossy jaw' there's still the sulphur. It can rot your chest and throat if you inhale too much of it.' Her eyes were staring over Maggie's head and when she spoke again it was as if she were talking to herself.

'The first week I was there, the woman next to me dropped at her bench. The lower part of her face was horribly disfigured and she could hardly breathe. She was carried out and dumped outside the gates with as much compassion as you'd show a pile of rags, and within the hour another woman had taken her place. I cried all day for that woman, and got docked three-pence for falling behind on my work. I've lost count of the women and girls I've seen go the same way. But I don't cry any more, I just pray, and thank God it wasn't me.'

Maggie felt a lump settle in her throat. By refusing to

let her work at the factory, Liz had shown how much she cared for her. This alone made Maggie more determined than ever to share the work load, no matter how dangerous it was. Jutting her chin out she said firmly, 'It's good of you to worry about me, but we don't have a lot of choice in the matter, do we? I'll come with you tomorrow and . . .'

'And what?' Liz asked, her voice flat. 'You think you can just walk in and be given a job. There must be a couple of dozen women waiting for someone to drop so they can take their place. They're outside the gates every morning waiting on the off chance that a vacancy will come up. There's always plenty of jobs for home workers, but the pay is awful, tuppence farthing for every gross of matchboxes you finish. But it's not just that the pay is so bad, you'd be bringing the same danger I face every day into the house, and you can't do that – it wouldn't be fair to Charlie.'

Maggie stared down at her lap, a feeling of hopelessness sweeping over her. Liz was right, she couldn't put Charlie at risk, but there must be something she could do, there must be.

Fighting down a rising feeling of panic she answered, 'Perhaps I could get another job in a shop, I've got the experience, and I could get an evening job as well. If I earned enough money, you could give up the factory and . . .'

'And maybe one day a lord or duke will come riding by and whisk us off to his castle and we'll all live happily ever after,' Liz's voice cut in sardonically. 'Grow up, Maggie, for God's sake. You were damned lucky to get that job with Mr Abrahams – you won't get another chance like that. Now be quiet a minute and let me think.'

Drumming her fingers impatiently on the table, she suddenly gave a short laugh, 'We could always ply our wares up West. Teresa's forever telling me I'm sitting on a fortune.'

'What!' Maggie's face screwed up in bewilderment. 'I don't understand . . . Oh.' The import of Lizzie's words suddenly became clear, and Maggie felt her lips stretching into a wide grin. The next moment both girls were laughing freely, united together in a rare moment of comradeship.

'Oh, Liz, I didn't think I'd laugh today,' Maggie hiccuped loudly. 'In fact I didn't think I'd ever laugh again.'

'Well, there hasn't been much to laugh about lately, has there?' Liz was wiping her eyes with the back of her hand. 'Anyway, we'd better get to bed, we've both got to get up early in the morning.'

Still chuckling they undressed and climbed in beside Charlie who was snoring softly on the edge of the mattress. 'Goodnight, Liz.'

'Goodnight.'

Turning over on her side Maggie smiled into the darkness as she recalled what Liz had said. Then remembering her earlier fears, she rolled over on her back and whispered tentatively, 'You wouldn't leave us, would you, Liz? I mean, I wouldn't blame you if you did, but I will get a job, I promise. You won't have to look after me and Charlie for long.'

When no answer came she thought Liz had fallen asleep and was about to turn back on her side when Lizzie spoke.

'Thanks, Maggie, thanks a bunch,' she said, her voice filled with bitterness. 'It just shows what you really think of me if you could imagine I would walk out and leave you and Charlie without any money coming in. And there was me thinking you really cared about me, when all you're worried about is losing my wages.'

Shocked at the hurt in Lizzie's voice Maggie propped herself up on her elbow crying, 'That's not true, Liz, I . . . I love you, honest I do, even if we are always fighting. And I do care about you working in the factory. I'd give anything to be able to get you out of there. Please, Liz, don't be angry with me. I shouldn't have said anything, it's just that I feel so useless. Please say something, Liz, I feel terrible.'

'All right, all right, don't get yourself into a state,' the voice came back at her. 'I believe you. And . . . and I'll probably never say this again, but I love you too. Now go to sleep before we get too soppy, we've a long day ahead of us tomorrow.'

Heaving a sigh of relief Maggie settled down once more, and when she moved close to Liz for warmth she felt the body stiffen for a moment before relaxing against her. Snuggling down under the blanket she closed her eyes, and just before sleep overcame her she heard Liz mutter softly, 'When Mr Bates comes on Friday, you'd better ask him about the basement. It won't hurt to have another look.'

CHAPTER FOUR

The small, overcrowded room was stifling, the smell from last night's dinner of herrings and cabbage lingering heavily in the dim, airless basement. In the middle of the room stood the table and four chairs, only inches separating them from the horsehair sofa and armchair. Resting in the recess by the door was the wooden dresser, its shelves crammed with crockery, pots and pans and ornaments in an effort to conserve space. Behind the sofa lay the mattress piled high with pillows, blankets and clothing, and as Maggie looked despairingly around her new home, the familiar feeling of depression threatened to overwhelm her. They had been here for nearly six months, and during that time the relationship between her and Lizzie had deteriorated to such an extent that they now rarely spoke unless they had to. Poor Charlie, caught in the middle, had retreated even further into his shell, causing Maggie further worry. Despite her assurances that she would find another job, it had been over a month before the vacancy in the chocolate factory had come up, and then it had been only temporary. Within three weeks she had found herself once more dependent on Liz's money. Since then she had managed to find a few part-time jobs, but nothing permanent. The lack of employment wasn't due to want of trying, for each day after Charlie left for school she would tramp the streets enquiring at factories and shops only to return tired and dispirited, the feeling of desperation growing inside her until she thought she would explode with worry.

It wasn't only the lack of work that was getting her down, but rather the responsibility she had taken on of running the household. The fact that she only had to manage one room didn't make the problem any easier; if anything it made her task more difficult. There was no scullery now in which they could wash in private, but what seemed worse to her was the fact that there was no stove to cook on. Instead she had to light the fire every time they needed hot water, so that even the simplest task of making a cup of tea had turned into a chore, for the burning coal gave off thick black dust which settled all around the room. She was constantly washing down the walls and sweeping the bare floorboards in a futile effort to keep the place clean. Then there were the bedbugs to contend with, tiny almost invisible parasites that had invaded the mattress they slept on. She had tried valiantly to rid their makeshift bed of the verminous creatures by banging and shaking the mattress every morning but all to no avail until finally she had accepted defeat. She couldn't even get any air into the room, for opening the door meant admitting the hordes of house-flies and bluebottles that hovered outside in the street. She'd tried hanging flytraps from the ceiling; but the foul-smelling, sticky paper had soon become dark with the swarm of writhing bodies, which had turned all their stomachs and she had been forced to take them down.

Added to all these hardships there remained the prob-lem of lighting. With no window the room was in permanent darkness, and the use of the gas lamp was necessary even in the daytime. This was yet another rea-son she got out of the basement as much as possible – she just couldn't afford to use too much gas.' All of Lizzie's wages went on rent and food, so there was no money left over for any luxuries. In a way it was fortu-nate that the strained atmosphere caused them to go to bed early to avoid more confrontations. If the relation-ship between her and Liz wasn't so fraught they would probably stay up late talking and using up the precious gas supply.

Running her fingers wearily through her hair she tidied the clothes and bedding into a neat pile on the floor then heaved the mattress up against the wall, won-dering as she did so why she bothered. Charlie always wanted to go to bed straight after his dinner, and this she could understand, for she too would go to bed as early as possible rather than endure the deathly silence that now existed between them all. Every evening she would mumble a curt 'goodnight' to Liz, then climb in beside Charlie in an effort to blot out yet another cheerless, depressing day, always hoping that tomorrow would bring something good, something, anything, that would lift her out of the drab, boring and frightening existence that was now her life.

The room tidied, she was about to leave, when a knock came on the door.

'Why, hello, Mrs Casey,' she exclaimed in surprise when she saw who her visitor was. Joyce Casey had lived in the third floor flat for as long as Maggie could remember; a quiet, reticent woman in her mid-fifties who had always kept herself apart from her neighbours, preferring her own company. But when the disease had swept the house, she had been at the forefront, running errands and helping to nurse the sick despite the risk to her own health. She had sat with Maggie's mother during her last days, sponging the sick woman down and encouraging her to drink the hot broth that Maggie had made. Since the funerals, though, she had retreated to her flat, never intruding upon the other occupants' lives until now.

'Hello, Maggie, how are you?' she enquired kindly.

'Oh, not too bad, Mrs Casey,' Maggie answered lightly, not wishing to burden the woman with her troubles.

Joyce Casey looked at the young girl valiantly trying to maintain a brave front, knowing full well the plight she was in. Well, maybe she could help. Shifting her canvas shopping bag further up her arm, she adjusted her black woollen shawl more firmly across her chest before saying, 'I hope you don't think I'm interfering, Maggie, but I might know of a job going if you're interested.'

'Oh, Mrs Casey,' Maggie cried out in delight, 'nobody could ever accuse you of interfering, and yes, I would be interested, very interested. Please, won't you come in for a minute?'

After refusing the offer of a drink, the tall, sparsely built woman concentrated her attention on the excited girl, trying not to let her dismay show at the sight of the crowded, poky room the three young Paiges now occupied. It was a lot cleaner than she had imagined, and for that she silently applauded Maggie. She couldn't help but notice that the dirty old patterned wallpaper had vanished to be replaced by white-wash, through which the damp was already beginning to show. But none of these improvements could hide the sickening sweet-odoured presence of bed bugs that pervaded the room.

Out of the corner of her eye she spotted a cockroach running across the floor and shuddered.

Drawing herself up to her full height, she said briskly, 'Now, don't get too excited, love, it may already be gone.' She saw the look of startled dismay cross Maggie's face and added quickly, 'I'm not saying it will be, just preparing you for the worst. It's like this; you

51

know I've got a cleaning job at the hospital?' Maggie nodded silently, her eyes never leaving the thin face.

'Well, one of the women I work with, her friend does some outdoor work making knickerbockers – that is, she did. She died yesterday, just popped off in her sleep. Anyway, my friend says there's a chance the factory owners haven't had time to replace her yet. She'd go herself, 'cos it can pay up to six bob a week if you work hard, and an extra four or five bob if you can find someone to do the finishing on them. But as she says, she's happy at the hospital and piece-work's always a bit dodgy; anyway, you'd better get moving, because like I said, somebody else might get there before you.'

'I'm ready now, Mrs Casey,' Maggie answered eagerly. 'I was on my way out when you knocked.'

'You've left the lamp burning, and you'd better put on your bonnet, it's going to be hot today.'

Laughing gaily, Maggie hurriedly did as she was bidden, while her neighbour watched the excited figure twirling round the room. Once outside the building Mrs Casey handed Maggie a slip of paper.

'Here's the address, love. It's somewhere in Shoreditch, so you've a bit of a walk ahead of you.'

'I don't mind, and thank you again, Mrs Casey. It was good of you to think of me.'

'Don't thank me until you've got the job. Now get going before someone beats you to it.'

The woman stood on the pavement waving until the slim figure disappeared from view, her face solemn, hoping that her young neighbour's journey wouldn't be in vain. Then with a heavy sigh she set off for work.

Maggie walked unsteadily over the cobbled pavement, her arms piled high with bundles of material as she tried to peer over the top of the bulky packets to see where she was going. Sweat poured down her face and her arms felt as if they were being pulled out of their sockets, but she didn't care. She had work, lots of it, enough for the week and a promise of more to come. Carefully picking her way down the basement steps she lowered the parcels to the floor while she opened the door. The blast of hot air hit her as soon as she walked into the room, making her catch her breath sharply. Leaving the door open to get some light into the room she carried the packages into the flat before lighting the lamp. Pouring some tepid water from the jug into the basin, she sluiced her face and hands before turning her attention to the pile of material on the table. Taking a note of the time from the mantel clock she began to unwrap the parcels, smiling all the while.

'Coo, Maggie, it's hotter in here than it is outside,' Charlie breathed tiredly as he flopped into the armchair.

'Here, get that down you,' Maggie said, handing him a mug of lemonade. She waited until he had drained the tin mug, then gesturing towards the table she asked airily, 'Haven't you noticed anything, Charlie?'

Wiping the back of his mouth with his hand, Charlie

turned his head, his face lighting up as he surveyed the mountain of material piled high on the table.

'You got some work, Maggie?'

'What does it look like?' she answered happily. 'And the man said there's plenty more where that came from.'

'Wait till Liz sees that lot – that'll cheer her up, won't it, Maggie?'

The question was couched in the form of a plea, bringing home to Maggie just how much her brother was suffering because of the strained relationship between her and Liz. Placing her hand on his head she ruffled his hair fondly.

'Well, we can't expect miracles, but it should make life easier for us. And don't be too hard on Liz, you can't blame her for being so miserable. If it wasn't for her we'd be out on the street by now, so try and be a bit kinder to her, eh, Charlie.'

'I do try, honest, but she ignores me most of the time. I don't think she likes me very much.'

'Now, don't say that,' she came back at him. 'If she didn't care she wouldn't still be here. She could have walked out months ago, but she's stayed, so it must mean she loves us.'

'I suppose so.' The small voice carried no conviction, and Maggie, anxious not to put a blight on the day, said briskly, 'There's no "suppose" about it, now get yourself out of that chair and start getting the dinner ready. There's some potatoes and cabbage to boil up, and there should be enough bread left to go with it. Come on, get moving, lad, it's all hands to the pump. I can't be expected to make dinner, I'm a wage earner now you know.' The jocular words had the desired effect as Charlie reluctantly left the comfort of the armchair to do as he was bid.

The potatoes peeled and deposited with the cabbage in a large copper pot, he carried it over to where Maggie was busily sewing and smiling wanly he asked, 'I'm so hot, Maggie, do we have to light the fire?'

Biting off a piece of thread Maggie looked at him over the pile of garments.

'Don't be daft, how can we cook without lighting the fire? We haven't got an oven any more, now stop being so silly and get it going, or would you rather go hungry?'

'But it's too hot for a fire and . . .'

'Now stop it, Charlie,' she snapped impatiently. 'I'm hot too, you know, there's nothing I can do about it so stop your moaning and get it lit.'

His shoulders hunched, Charlie turned away and walked slowly over to the grate. Putting the pot on the floor he began placing the cinders a few inches apart at the bottom of the grate and covered them with a sheet of newspaper and a few crossbars of wood. When this was done he took a handful of rubbly coal and slack from the scuttle, scattering them on top and set light to the paper with a lucifer match. Almost immediately a billow of smoke covered him causing him to cough violently.

'Oh, sodding hell!' Maggie exclaimed in alarm as the smoke began to waft her way, the black soot settling lightly on the uncovered knickerbockers. Shaking the garments one by one, she pulled the brown paper wrapping over her precious work.

'I forgot about the smoke.' Her eyes raked over the white material searching for any trace of soot. Satisfied that she had saved them from permanent damage, she turned her attention to the forlorn figure crouched by the grate.

'I'm sorry, Maggie, it wasn't my fault.'

'I didn't say it was, did I, you soppy ha'pence? It's my own fault, I should have realised, never mind, I'll have to be more careful in future, though.' Moving away from the table she dusted Charlie down and gave him a drink of water from the pewter jug.

'Leave the dinner, love, I'll see to it, you go and sit down.'

'I'll do it, Maggie, you have to get on with your work,' Charlie said, his face anxious, wondering if he'd upset his sister.

'I've done enough for now, I can do some more later on after we've had our dinner. And Charlie,' she added, smiling, 'how would you like it if I bought a chicken for tomorrow.'

'Ooh, Maggie, will you?' he breathed excitedly. 'We haven't had chicken for a long time, I've forgotten what it tastes like. Did they pay you already? I thought you had to finish them first.'

Placing her finger to her lips she whispered in a conspiratorial manner.

'There's two bob in the tin for the gas. I'll borrow that for now and put it back when I get paid, but don't tell Liz, mind – I don't want to give her any excuse to start a row.'

At the mention of his elder sister Charlie's face fell. Seeing the change in his expression, Maggie cried, 'Don't look like that, love, I was only teasing you. Look, come here.'

Turning him round to face her she took his hands and said earnestly, 'Things are going to be different from now on, I promise. Now I'm earning too, Liz won't feel so pressured, and like I said, we've a lot to be grateful to her for. She's not the ogre she makes out to be – she's just tired and unhappy, so be patient with her, eh, Charlie, for my sake.'

'If you say so.' Already he was walking away from her towards the sofa and within minutes of lying down he was asleep.

Maggie stood over Charlie, her face thoughtful. All he seemed to do lately was eat and sleep, but then what else was there for him to do? He was too timid to play out in the street with the other children and for this she partly blamed herself. He had always been this way, but since their parents' deaths he had clung to her more than he had ever done with his mother. She knew she should have encouraged him to go out, but the truth was she preferred to keep him by her side. The youngsters in this area were a rough lot, more like miniature men and women than the children they were, which wasn't surprising considering their upbringing. Most of them worked after school and had done from an early age, and the girls usually had the added burden of looking after their baby siblings while the mothers worked. With each passing day the realisation of the easy, comfortable life they'd enjoyed was pushed home more forcibly, especially for Charlie. She could only hope that he would grow stronger with the years, but however his character developed, she would always be there for him.

Giving herself a mental shake, she set the pot full of vegetables over the fire and returned to the table. Pulling the lamp nearer to her she resumed work, her nimble fingers expertly threading the cotton through the soft material. The next hour flew by, and when the front door banged she gave a nervous start.

'You made me jump, I didn't realise it was that late.'

Maggie smiled at the figure standing by the doorway, only to receive a stony glance in return. Laying down the needle and cotton she waited for her sister to notice the jumble of cloth that littered the table: she didn't have to wait long.

'Where did you get that lot from?' Liz asked, her hands pulling at the strings of her straw bonnet. Without waiting for an answer she walked past Maggie and poured herself a drink of water. She grimaced as she tasted the tepid, soot-covered fluid, but she was too thirsty to be fastidious. The heat from the fire seared through her blue-checked cotton dress, and she quickly moved away. The once plump figure, now as slim as her sister, walked over to the sofa only to give an impatient 'tut' when she saw the supine figure sprawled there.

'Doesn't he ever do anything else but sleep?' she demanded crossly, her hand pushing back a strand of limp, blond hair from her perspiring face.

Ignoring the angry tone Maggie said plaintively, 'Liz, I've got work. Look, Mrs Casey came down this morning and told me there was some out-work going in a factory in Shoreditch, and I went straight away. What's the matter with you? I thought you'd be over the moon instead of acting like nothing's changed.'

Flopping into the armchair Liz stared hard at the earnest face and felt her heart begin to race. Of course she was pleased that her sister had at long last managed to find some work, but for how long? When she'd come in the door and seen Maggie bent over the disordered array of clothing she had experienced a surge of excitement, a feeling that had abated as quickly as it had come. Maggie's last two jobs hadn't lasted longer than a couple of weeks, so she wasn't going to get her hopes up thinking their luck had changed. Closing her eyes she sighed deeply. God, she was tired, tired and depressed. She knew her surly attitude was adding to the misery of their already dismal life, but she couldn't help it. She didn't possess Maggie's cheerful, optimistic view of life, always thinking that something good was just around the corner. Instead she preferred to look on the black side, at least that way she could never be disappointed. A sudden loud snort from Charlie brought her eyes open and cautiously she looked over to where Maggie sat, her face mirroring her disappointment at the way her good news had been received. Swallowing hard Liz fought with her troubled emotions. Maybe this time the work would last, maybe the worry of providing for them all was finally going to be shared – maybe. Clearing her throat she asked nonchalantly, 'So how long is this lot going to last for? I suppose it's too much to hope that it's permanent.'

Maggie felt her body relax and the smile return to her lips.

'The foreman said there's plenty more – they've got a standing order with most of the big stores up the West End.' She knew she was gabbling, but she couldn't stop herself, desperate to bring a smile to Liz's face.

They remained staring at each other across the room, their eyes locked, and then to Maggie's horror Liz began to cry. Softly at first, and then gathering momentum until her thin shoulders began to heave with loud, heartwrenching sobs. Thoroughly shaken Maggie hurried to her sister's side.

Falling to her knees she took hold of the trembling fingers crying, 'What's the matter, Liz? Has something happened at work? Tell me, please, I've never seen you so upset, and I thought you'd be so happy to come home and find I'd found work. Come on, Liz, tell me what's wrong, you're frightening me.'

Pulling her hands free from Maggie's grasp, Liz searched in the pocket of her dress for a handkerchief, and wiping her face she answered shakily, 'I am pleased, oh, Maggie, you don't know how pleased I am. It's the relief I suppose, that and the knowledge that we'll be able to move out of this dreadful place and get ourselves somewhere decent to live.'

Maggie felt her body stiffen in alarm, her mouth opening and closing as she tried to think of what to say. The thought of moving hadn't crossed her mind, for although she hated the basement as much as Liz and Charlie did, she was wise enough to know that despite what the foreman had told her, out-work was unpredictable; knowing this, it would be foolhardy to think of moving. They were only paying five shillings a week here, as opposed to the twelve shillings they would need to find every week for a larger flat. If they took the chance and she lost her new-found job they would be back where they started from. Raising her eyes she looked at Liz and saw the tremulous smile hovering on the thin lips and the look of hope, long since dead come back into the blue eyes. Knowing that what she was about to say would wipe the smile from the face before her, she swallowed painfully and stuttered.

'I think it would be better if . . . if we waited a while, Liz, just in case. I mean, I know I was told there's plenty of work, but . . . but we can't take the chance, not yet. Look, what if we carry on living on your wages for the time being and save mine. That way we can build up a little nest egg, and if the worst comes to the worst and I lose this job, at least that way we'd have something to fall back on while I looked for something else.'

Liz sat motionless, her body churning with disappointment. What Maggie said made sense and yet . . . oh, God, how much longer would they have to live in this ghastly place, how much longer could she bear it without going mad? 'Liz? What do you think? Don't you agree it's better to wait for a while before making a decision. It won't be forever, and I won't stop looking for a permanent job, somewhere where I'll be guaranteed a regular wage, and when that happens we can leave here and find somewhere decent to live.'

Her voice filled with pleading she waited for an answer, and when Liz moved forward in the chair she jumped back, bracing herself for the outburst she was sure was forthcoming.

'You're right as usual,' Liz said gruffly, her voice thick with disappointment, 'but I hope something turns up soon, 'cos, I'm telling you, Maggie, I don't know how much longer I can go on. I hate it here so much my stomach turns every time I walk through that door.'

Getting to her feet she turned towards the bed adding, 'I think I'll have a bit of a sleep before dinner, wake me when it's ready.'

Maggie watched as Liz pulled the mattress from the wall and laid it on the floor. A few minutes later, as she lifted the pot of vegetables over the fire to warm up, she heard the faint sound of weeping coming from the far corner of the room. She would have felt better if Liz had gone for her – that reaction she could have coped with. But this attitude of acceptance and defeatism, so unlike her normally argumentative sister, had left her feeling out of her depth. All her earlier happiness evaporated, and with a heavy heart she turned towards the fire. Her head bowed over the evening meal she began stirring the contents with a large wooden spoon, and when the first tear dropped into the meagre stew she made no attempt to stop herself from crying, but continued stirring.

CHAPTER FIVE

'Here, Maggie, what do you think?'

Maggie lifted her head, her lips breaking into a wide grin at the sight of Charlie posing in a pair of white knickerbockers, his hand resting coyly on his hip.

'Very nice, they suit you. Tell you what, I'll buy you a pair for school, how would you like that?'

Charlie's smile faltered for a moment, then seeing the glint of laughter in his sister's eyes he chuckled loudly.

'Eh, you frightened me for a minute, Maggie. If I went out in these, I wouldn't get as far as the corner before getting knocked black and blue.' Carefully stepping out of the frilly garment, he put it back on the table and picked up another pair that Maggie had laid to one side. Pulling his chair nearer to the lamp he began the process of tidying up the loose threads and checking to see that the seams were straight and the tiny stitches unbroken. This was termed 'finishing' and for this Maggie received an extra penny per pair, making their total earnings twelve and sixpence a week.

The sight of her brother hunched over the table, his eyes screwed up in concentration, his tongue protruding slightly between pursed lips, brought a feeling of warmth and well-being to Maggie's body. It was good to see him so content and happy, and the knowledge that he was earning a wage had instilled a sense of pride in him and finally dispelled his fear of being sent to the workhouse.

Her fingers moving rapidly, Maggie once again blessed the day Mrs Casey had knocked on the door, for without her intervention and the ensuing work that had followed the timely visit, Maggie doubted if the three of them would still be together today. In spite of what Liz had said about not leaving them, the constant strain and worry of providing for a family would eventually have proven too much for her. Thank God that worry had now passed.

Humming a tuneless song under her breath Maggie let her mind wander back over the past six months, her facial expressions changing from solemnity to happiness as her thoughts leapt back and forth. As she had feared, the work hadn't been as constant as the foreman had promised. Sometimes she had gone days without any work at all, and even when it was available she lost two hours a day going to fetch it and bring it home. She also had to provide her own cotton and needles, and although these items weren't expensive, it was still money she could have used for other things. Then there were the days she'd had to stand for three hours or more waiting in line with a crowd of other girls and women to get her bundle of cloth, not knowing if she would be sent away empty handed. Those times had been the hardest to bear. But now at long last their luck was beginning to change. Hugging herself in silent glee she thought back to the events of that morning. She had stood in the line as usual, but when she'd handed over her completed work, instead of the foreman allotting her another bundle, he'd told her to stand to one side until he'd seen to the remainder of the queue. Her heart thumping wildly, she had complied.

When the last of the women had left and the foreman had asked her if she'd be interested in working full-time in the factory, the relief had been so great her legs had nearly given way under her. His complimentary remarks on the neatness of her work had washed over her, and when he'd asked if she knew of anyone who could sew as well as she did her excitement had known no bounds. Jabbering like an idiot just released from Bedlam, she had put Liz's name forward and watched in a fever of agitation while the man wrote both their names down in a large, black ledger. It didn't matter that she would be losing Charlie's money – the wage for a factory worker was two shillings more than an out-worker. What was more important was the peace of mind, knowing that starting from next week she would be earning a regular wage. That was worth more to her than the few extra bob that Charlie had been earning.

It seemed ironic that the handsewing skills that had brought the foreman's attention upon her would no longer be required, as the factory workers all used sewing machines, but what odds? Her dexterity with a needle had served its purpose, and she'd soon get used to the machines as she was a quick learner. More important was that once she was safely installed at the factory she would be able to keep her ears open for any vacancy that was going. For no matter how many times Liz told her she was all right where she was, Maggie would never rest easy until her sister was out of the matchbox workshop, and the dangers it entailed.

During the time she had spent working at home, she'd managed to save nearly six pounds. There hadn't been a week gone by that Liz and Charlie hadn't begged her to use the money to get them out of the dark, cramped, smelly flat they refused to call home, but she had remained firm. She'd come back empty handed too many times to risk spending her precious savings, but now that worry had been lifted, hopefully for good.

Now she was waiting for the front door to open, to see Liz's face when she told her the good news. With Christmas only six weeks away, it couldn't have happened at a better time; and if their luck held, they might be able to find another place to live before then. Laying down her needle she stared over Charlie's bent head, her eyes focusing on the blazing fire. Oh, if only they could, it would put the seal of happiness on the events of the day. Picking up her needle once more she resumed work, her mind spinning with plans. If she worked late tonight, she would be able to start looking for a place tomorrow. It would have to be somewhere nearby as she didn't want to take Charlie out of his school. There were plenty of big houses divided into flats in this area; the problem would be in finding one that was both clean and reasonably cheap.

For a moment doubts began to creep into her mind – maybe it wouldn't be that easy finding somewhere else? The flat they had once occupied on the top floor had been taken over the same day they'd moved down here, the new occupants expressing relief at having found two clean rooms that suited their pockets. A niggle of fear crept up her spine and impatiently she shrugged it off. She'd find somewhere, if she had to knock on every door in the neighbourhood. She wasn't about to be knocked back now. The first thing she would do once they were installed in their new home would be to buy a Christmas tree and decorate it with the coloured balls and baubles she'd kept stored in a cardboard box under the dresser. She'd also make sure it was placed so that it was the first sight they saw when they came through the door, just like her Mum had always done.

So wrapped up in her thoughts was she that she didn't hear the front door opening until Charlie, lifting his head from the piece of white material, his fist rubbing at his red eyes said tiredly, 'Hello, Liz.'

Maggie sat still for a moment, her face wreathed in smiles, silently hugging herself with glee as she anticipated Liz's reaction when she heard the news. Turning slightly she made to rise from her chair, only to freeze in shock at the sight of her sister leaning against the door, her face ashen, her eyes screwed up tightly as if in pain.

The smile slipping from her face Maggie ran to the distraught figure, crying in alarm, 'What's the matter, Liz? You look awful, come on, put your arm round my shoulder, that's it.'

Taking the weight of the limp body against her own she looked to where Charlie still sat at the table, his eyes wide with surprise and shouted crossly, 'Don't just sit there, help me get her on the sofa.'

Startled into action he came to his sister's aid, and taking hold of Liz's other arm he helped Maggie lead the trembling figure the short distance to the sofa. With a soft moan Liz slid down onto the worn cushions, her head lolling to one side. Dropping to her knees Maggie took hold of the ice cold hands and began to rub them vigorously, her eyes never leaving the white face.

'Say something, Liz,' she pleaded urgently. 'Aren't you feeling well?'

Immediately she cursed herself for her stupidity, and placing her hand gently on the pale forehead she said, 'That was a silly question, wasn't it? Look, you lie quiet while I fix you a hot drink, I won't be a minute.'

Leaving the prostrate figure, she picked up the ladle from beside the grate and poured two generous scoops of soup from the pot hanging over the fire into a tin mug. Holding Liz's head gently she placed the steaming liquid to the blue lips.

'Here you are, love, try and drink this. It'll make you feel better.'

Propping herself up on one elbow Liz tried to do as Maggie said, but after only one small sip she weakly pushed Maggie's hand away crying piteously, 'I can't, it's too hot, and I feel sick.'

Maggie sat back on her heels, not knowing what to do next. She'd never known Liz to be ill. Oh, God, no; her head jerked on her shoulders – not the diphtheria, it couldn't be, there hadn't been a case since the epidemic. No, of course it wasn't, she chided herself, you're panicking over nothing. Just calm down for a minute, it's probably only a cold. But her silent protestations did nothing to ease her mind.

When Liz started to shiver, she raced over to the far side of the room, quickly returning with two blankets. Wrapping them tightly round the trembling body she said earnestly, 'You'll be all right, Liz. Don't worry, I'll look after you. Look, you rest, you'll feel better after a few hours sleep, wait and see.'

Liz heard the voice, but it seemed to be coming from a long way away. She wanted to answer, to hear her own voice, but the effort was too much. It was so much easier to lie here, not talking, not doing anything. She'd known for days she was coming down with something, colds and flu were common at this time of the year. But she'd never had a cold like this before. Every bone in her body ached, her throat was sore and her chest felt tight. Every time she breathed deeply, she experienced a sharp pain below her ribs as if someone was stabbing at her with a knife. A sudden fit of coughing brought her body doubled over, a harsh, racking sound that tore at her chest.

'Oh, Liz, Liz, shall I fetch Mrs Simms, she might know what to do.'

With all the effort she could muster Liz opened her eyes and stared bleakly into the frightened face leaning over her.

'Just leave me alone for a while, Maggie. Please, just leave me alone.' Her head dropped back on the arm of the sofa, her breathing laboured as she sank into an uneasy sleep.

Maggie and Charlie stood side by side, their faces as pale as the one lying restlessly before them. Swallowing hard, Maggie squeezed Charlie's hand, muttering thickly, 'Don't worry, she'll be all right, it's just a cold, that's all; just a cold.' The words hung heavily in the air, bringing no comfort to herself or the young boy by her side. Giving his hand another squeeze she left him and began to clear the table in preparation for their dinner.

By the following morning Liz was in a high fever, her body thrashing from side to side, her hands trying to throw off the blankets that covered her. Maggie had dragged the sofa nearer the fire, her own body drenched with sweat from the searing heat as she bathed Liz's face and hands in an effort to keep the agitated figure comfortable. Laying a wet cloth on Liz's forehead she slumped to the floor, her head resting wearily on the edge of the sofa. She'd been up all night, afraid to leave her sister alone even for a moment, but she couldn't keep her eyes open any longer. Her eyelids felt like stone, and within seconds of laying her head down she was asleep.

'No, no, stop it, go away, stop it, no, no, no!'

Maggie's head jerked back painfully on her neck, her eyes springing open at the hoarse sound of Liz's voice.

'It's all right, love, I'm here, I'm here. I won't leave you, Liz, don't worry,' she said soothingly, gripping the trembling hands, but Liz seemed unaware of her sister's presence.

Her eyelids fluttered open, her blue eyes sweeping sightlessly over Maggie as she moaned. 'I'm scared, don't let me die, I don't want to die.'

'You're not going to die, Liz, I promise. Do you think you could manage a drink? It'll ease your throat.'

But the eyes had already closed again, leaving Maggie staring fearfully down on the sister she'd spent her whole life fighting with. She could feel her throat swelling with tears, but before she could give vent to her feelings the door opened and Charlie came into the room, his footsteps dragging as he walked over to the table and sat down heavily on the wooden chair. Maggie had sent him down to the factory early this morning with the bundle of work she'd finished during the night, along with a scrawled note explaining her absence. Her eyes flickered nervously. Why had he come back empty handed? She'd asked in the note for more work, so where was it?

Her voice shaking with apprehension, she asked quietly, 'What did the foreman say?'

Charlie lifted his eyes reluctantly – he'd been dreading this moment since he'd left the factory gates.

'He wasn't best pleased, Maggie,' he stuttered. 'He said if you want the work, you'll have to go and get it yourself. And, Maggie, he . . . said that if you didn't go today, then not to bother going back. He gave me your money, look.' Eagerly Charlie plunged his hand into his pocket, bringing out a small handful of silver and coppers, a tremulous smile hovering on his lips. Maggie looked down at the outstretched palm for a moment, then taking the money she counted it carefully. Four and threepence. God, that wouldn't even pay the rent. For a second she thought she was going to fall, and quickly took hold of herself.

'Didn't you explain what had happened, Charlie? Did you remember to give him the note?' Her voice crackled with alarm, while her stomach tightened painfully.

'Of course I did, Maggie, what do you take me for? But he said it wasn't his worry. And if you don't want the work, there's plenty more that do.'

A sudden bout of coughing bought Maggie's attention

back to Liz. Turning quickly on her heel she called over her shoulder.

'Go and get Mrs Simms. She might know what's the matter with Liz. Hurry, Charlie.' The boy needed no second bidding to leave the room, and within seconds the door banged behind him.

Taking the cloth from Liz's forehead she soaked it thoroughly in the pitcher, then returned to the sofa. While she waited for Mrs Simms to appear she thought about what had happened. How could the foreman be so unfeeling? It wasn't her fault Liz was ill, and she couldn't leave her, not like this. Another thought suddenly struck her; what if Liz lost her job as well? Oh, God, no, that prospect didn't bear thinking about. Thank heavens she had held onto her savings – if the worst did happen at least they'd have some money to live on. Shaking her head in despair she clenched her fists tightly.

She'd see what Mrs Simms had to say. Maybe her neighbour could sit with Liz while she went to the factory and collected more work. And Liz wouldn't lose her job because of a few days off sick. No, she was worrying over nothing. What she needed was a good night's sleep, she couldn't think straight at the moment. Nodding to herself she watched the door, her ears listening out for the footsteps on the stairs.

CHAPTER SIX

'I don't want to frighten you, ducks, but it looks like pneumonia to me,' Mrs Simms said solemnly. 'My Jim 'ad it a couple a years back. You know my Jim? The one that went orf and joined the Navy. Me eldest 'e is, but never got on wiv 'is Dad, that's why 'e left 'ome. Can't say as I blame 'im for going, I don't like the old bugger meself, but I don't fink the navy would 'ave taken me.' She chuckled softly, then seeing the frightened look on the young girl's face she shuffled her feet awkwardly, her fingers scratching at the soiled, damp patch under her armpit.

'Is she going to die, Mrs Simms?' The question was barely above a whisper, and when the kindly woman looked into the white face, the brown eyes seeming to

75

grow larger by the minute she drew her shoulders back and answered briskly.

'Well now, my Jim pulled through it, so I don't see why Liz can't, it all depends on the constitution, like. Now then, you get that pot of water boiling, we're gonna need plenty of steam to sweat it out of 'er. Charlie 'ere can 'elp by fetching the water from the yard, can't you, love?' she asked, directing her attention to the small boy who was still standing mutely by the door, bewildered at the sudden turn of events.

'You heard what Mrs Simms said,' Maggie said sharply, the fear inside her body making her angry. 'Get as many pots and buckets as you can find and start filling them up, and don't take all day about it.'

'Yeah, all right, Maggie, I'm going,' he answered quickly, pleased to be doing something to help. Gathering up three saucepans under his arm he made for the standpipe in the yard.

'Right now, you 'elp me move the sofa nearer the fire. We're gonna 'ave to get 'er as close as we can wivout setting the sofa alight.' When that was done, Mrs Simms stood back, her round, homely face flushed with exertion.

'That's it, love, now all we can do is keep the pots boiling; plenty of steam, that's wot's needed, plenty of steam.'

'Thanks, Mrs Simms, it was good of you to come down so quickly. I didn't know what else to do.'

The round face broke into a wide smile. 'Don't be daft,

love, that's wot neighbours are for, ain't it. Now look, Maggie, I can stay wiv yer for abaht an hour, then I'll 'ave to be orf. I've got a cleaning job on today. Lottie's off school wiv a cold, so she can look after the rest of 'em until I get back. And I'll pop back later when I've given 'em their tea.'

Maggie's heart dropped. She'd been trying to pluck up courage to ask her friend if she'd stay with Liz while she went to the factory to pick up some work, but now that avenue of help was closed. The only other person she knew to ask was Mrs Casey, but she too was at work. That left only Charlie, and she couldn't leave him to care for Liz. If only it didn't take so long to get to the factory and back she might have chanced it. With a resigned shrug of her shoulders she poured more water into the pot and stoked up the fire.

The heat in the room was almost unbearable. Maggie had taken off her patched brown skirt and pink cotton blouse. She was now clothed only in her thin shift and drawers, and they were both sticking to her skin. She'd been on her knees for most of the day, holding steaming pans close to Liz's body in an effort to draw out the fever that was racking the tormented figure. Mrs Simms had returned as promised, and with her help they had stripped the unconscious form and rubbed the sweat-soaked body with warm towels. Mrs Casey had also come down, and the two elder women had stood to one side of the room, their faces grave as they'd discussed the situation, their faces breaking into false smiles of assurance whenever Maggie looked their way. They were both gone now, Mrs Simms back to her brood of children, and Mrs Casey to her evening stint at the hospital.

Now it was getting on for eleven o'clock, with a long night to look forward to, and Liz seemed to be getting worse every minute. Charlie was asleep on the mattress, exhausted by the constant trips to the yard carrying back heavy pots of water. She'd turned out the gas lamp and lit a few candles, placing them on the mantelpiece. Her eyes burnt with fatigue, her teeth biting hard into her bottom lip as she listened to the tortured sound of Liz's breathing. The urgent pressure on her bladder forced her to rise, only to fall back on the floor, her cramped legs refusing to support her. Gritting her teeth she got to her feet, grimacing with distaste as she relieved herself in the chamber pot, but she was too tired to get dressed and go outside to the yard.

'Thirsty, so thirsty,' Liz called out weakly.

Maggie was quickly by Liz's side, holding a mug full of water to the parched lips, only to have it knocked out of her grasp. Maggie looked down at the pool of water spilling over the floor, her eyes bleak, and even when she felt the wetness spread around her legs she didn't make any move to wipe it up. Leaning back on her heels she put her face in her hands and began to rock back and forth. There was nothing else she could do. Liz was going to die, and she was powerless to do anything about it. She thought back down the years; her mind reliving every fight, every unkind word that had passed between them and groaned inwardly. The only time she could remember them being close was the night they'd admitted their love for each other. She also recalled the embarrassment they'd both felt the following morning; neither of them had ever referred to that night again.

And now she'd never have the chance to repeat those words – she had left it too late. Her shoulders began to heave as the first tears trickled between her closed fingers, then as if a dam had broken her whole body shook with grief, the torrent of tears gushing from her eyes. Adding to her grief was an overwhelming sense of guilt. She could have tried harder to make friends with Liz. Maybe if she'd been kinder, or a bit more understanding the rift between them wouldn't have grown so big. If only she could take back some of the things she'd said, the hurtful words spoken in anger often followed by days of silence, both of them wanting to make up, but neither of them prepared to be the first one to say sorry. If only, if only: the most futile words in the world.

The height of the crisis came at three o'clock in the morning. Opening her eyes briefly Liz spoke, her voice racked with pain as she struggled to utter the words she needed to say.

'Ma . . . Maggie, sorry, so . . . sorry.' Her hand came up weakly and stroked the tear-stained cheeks of her sister, and Maggie, too full with grief and exhaustion, could only grip the hand and hold it tight against her breast, gathering the hot body close to her own. When the coughing started again Maggie screwed her eyes up in pain at the sound. She could feel Liz's heart racing wildly as the sweat oozed out of every pore in her body, soaking them both. Maggie began to pray, her lips uttering every prayer she had ever learnt, the mumbled words scarcely audible against the rasping, choking sounds coming from Liz's throat.

Time passed, and when she felt a hand on her shoulder and turned to see Joyce Casey standing by her side she showed no surprise at the unexpected presence but said simply, 'She's not going to make it, Mrs Casey.'

When she felt herself being pulled away from Liz's body she made no protest, but rolled over on the floor drawing her cramped legs up to her chin. Wrapping her numb arms around her knees, she lay still.

Cradling Liz's head in her arms the woman gazed down on the inert body, her eyes filled with sadness, and when she felt her shudder she thought for a moment Liz had gone. Then a soft sound came from Liz's throat followed by a trickle of mucus from her mouth, and carefully removing her arm Joyce Casey laid the head back on the pillow. 'Maggie, Maggie, love,' she whispered. 'It's all over, she's going to be all right, it's all over.'

But Maggie was past hearing. Stepping over the sleeping form, the tall figure removed her shawl then settled down in the armchair and waited for the girls to awake.

'Come on, Liz, try and drink your soup, please, you need to get your strength back,' Maggie pleaded, then sighed with relief as the mug was taken from her hand and Liz began to sip at the hot beverage. When she had finished she handed the mug back wordlessly, her blue eyes looking out vacantly from the pinched, white face.

'There, that's better, we'll soon have you on your feet again,' Maggie said, trying hard to keep her voice cheerful. Leaving the silent figure she put the mug in a large pot of water for washing later, then leant her arm on the mantelpiece, her hand idly wiping away the deposits of soot that rested on the top. The silence in the room bore down on her, making her feel both restless and angry. It had been three days since Liz had taken a turn for the better, yet to all outward appearances she might as well have died. Oh no, don't think that; she shook her head quickly, ashamed at her thoughts. But if only Liz would say something, do something, instead of just sitting in the chair expecting to be waited on hand and foot. Maggie didn't expect her sister to jump up suddenly and run round the room, she knew only too well how ill she'd been, but it wouldn't hurt her to try and make some kind of effort, however small. Maggie didn't begrudge the time she spent looking after Liz, she just wished she'd meet her half way.

Well, no matter how Liz was tomorrow, Maggie would have to leave her on her own. She'd already lost her job at the knickerbocker factory, a fact that had been driven home forcibly yesterday when she'd made the journey to Shoreditch, leaving Liz in the care of Mrs Simms. She had tried to explain to the foreman the reason for her absence, and when that had failed she had resorted to pleading, but all to no avail. The job she had been offered was no longer available to her, and all because she'd committed the unpardonable sin of putting family before work. That sort of behaviour was frowned upon by employers, who looked upon their workforce as objects to be used solely for their own benefit, objects that could be cast aside when they were no longer of any use. Working conditions were still poorly paid at best, and hazardous at worst, and Maggie couldn't see the order of things changing in her lifetime.

When she heard the soft knock on the door she smiled, glad of the prospect of company. Both Mrs Simms and Mrs Casey had been marvellous over the past few days – she didn't know what she would have done without their help and support. Smoothing down her grey corded dress she called out, 'Come in, it's open.'

When the door was pushed open and Teresa walked timidly into the room, Maggie's mouth opened in surprise.

'Why, hello, Teresa,' she stuttered awkwardly. 'I didn't expect to see you. Liz, Liz, look who's here,' she said loudly, her mind whirling in alarm. Although Liz worked with Teresa, she wasn't the sort of girl her sister would choose for a personal friend, and certainly not the kind of person she would encourage to visit whatever the reason.

Forcing a smile to her lips she said lightly, 'Can I get you a drink, Teresa, something hot? You must be frozen.' Her eyes dropped to the dirty, bare feet and Maggie felt again a surge of pity at the life this young girl was forced to endure.

'No fanks, Maggie, I can't stop, me muvver's waiting for me to get 'ome. 'Ello, Liz, 'ow you feeling?' she called out to the figure silently sitting in the armchair, her fingers nervously plucking at the filthy, tattered piece of black cloth that passed for a shawl as she studiously tried to avoid meeting Maggie's anxious gaze.

Maggie saw the furtive actions, and trying to stem the tide of alarm that was rising in her chest she asked quietly, 'What is it, Teresa, is it about Liz's job? Is that why you've come?' She watched as a deep flush rose over the girl's face, and put her hand to her throat waiting for the words she knew were coming.

'I'm sorry, Maggie, I didn't want to come,' she answered, her embarrassment making her head bounce wildly on her shoulders. 'But the fing is, well . . .' She broke off for a moment. Then, hanging her head, she whispered, 'She's been given 'er notice, Maggie, the gaffer sent me round to tell 'er and give 'er wot's owing to 'er. We all 'ad a go at 'im, 'onest, but . . . but 'e only got nasty and said if we didn't mind our own business we would join 'er. I'm sorry, Maggie, reely I am, but there's nuffink we can do.'

Gulping twice Maggie tried to keep calm. Taking a deep breath she said, 'I thought you had a union now, I remember Liz telling me about it after the strike.'

'We 'ave . . . well, sort of, and like I said, we all tried to keep Liz's job for 'er, but the union don't want anovver strike, a lot of the women are still trying to make up the money they lost in the last one.'

Seeing the girl's evident distress and knowing it couldn't have been easy for her coming here, Maggie said gently, 'It's all right, Teresa, don't upset yourself, it was good of you to come.'

Her mission over, Teresa turned to leave, anxious to get away, only to turn back suddenly, her hand flying to her mouth as she exclaimed worriedly, 'Eh, I nearly forgot to give you Liz's money, 'ere it is, Maggie.'

'Thanks, Teresa.' The money lay on the table, and Maggie didn't even look at it.

Taking her leave, Teresa glanced over her shoulder to the huddled figure in the armchair. Eh, she looked stuffed, nothing like the girl she had worked with for so long, it was scarey. She wouldn't fancy being shut up with her all day, not like she was now; poor Maggie. Still, couldn't spend your life feeling too sorry for other people, it was hard enough work living your own. Just before the door shut behind her she caught a glimpse of Maggie's face. The look of desolation in the large brown eyes sent a shiver down her back and hurriedly pulling the black shawl up and round her face she walked up the basement steps.

'I'm hungry, Maggie.'

Charlie sat at the table, his hands splayed out in front of him and stared into the brown eyes so like his own.

'I know you are, love, we all are,' Maggie answered patiently. 'But you know how things are. I've only got enough potatoes and cabbage for one more meal and I'm saving that for tomorrow.'

'But I'm hungry now, Maggie,' came the plaintive reply. 'I feel sick, and my stomach hurts. Please, Maggie.'

'Oh, for goodness sake, let's eat it now. Things aren't going to be any better tomorrow or the next day, so why bother saving it?' Liz had joined her brother at the table and as Maggie looked down at the pair of them she felt a rush of anger rising in her breast. Tearing her gaze away she stared down at the empty grate, the sight of the bare, iron slates yet another reminder of the plight they were in. It was nearly eight weeks since Liz had lost her job, and she still showed no signs of looking for another one despite Maggie's urging. Every time she brought the subject up, Liz complained that she needed more time to recover from her illness, professing herself too ill to work. She was quite content to let Maggie take on any menial work she could find in order to support them all. The fact that her sister hadn't been able to find any work for the past two weeks didn't seem to bother her. Even when Maggie had told her all the savings were gone and they were two weeks behind on the rent the cloud of detachment stayed in her eyes. It was as if the illness had drained all the life and feeling from her body and mind.

Tucking a strand of hair behind her ear Maggie reflected on the ironies of life. Less than two months ago she had knelt in this room praying and begging for the life of her sister to be spared, now it was all she could do to stop herself from jumping on Liz and pummelling her to the floor.

'Well, are we going to eat now or not?' Liz's petulant voice cut into her thoughts and with an impatient toss of her head Maggie picked up the pot containing the left-over stew and banged it down on the table.

'There, have it,' she shouted angrily, 'but you'll have to eat it cold. There's no more coal for the fire, just a few pieces of wood left to boil a kettle for a hot drink later.'

'I'll go down the market before school tomorrow and see if I can scrounge some wooden crates off the stalls, all right, Maggie?' Charlie piped up timidly.

'You're not going to school tomorrow,' she yelled back at him. 'You can't last all day on an empty stomach, you'll likely pass out and you know what'll happen then? Probably have some nosy parker from the author-ities come snooping round here, and that's the last thing I need right now.'

Charlie lowered his head so that his sisters wouldn't see the tears that had sprung to his eyes. He had only been trying to help, and he'd still got it wrong. His hand trembling he picked up a spoon and began to eat the congealed mess in front of him. It didn't taste very nice cold, but he didn't dare make any comment for fear of a further outburst from his favourite sister. Peeking out from under his eyelids he made sure Maggie wasn't watching him and quickly wiped his nose with the back of his sleeve. He would go down the market tomorrow, and when he came back with a pile of wood and maybe some bruised fruit and vegetables that had fallen off the stalls and rolled into the kerb, then Maggie would be pleased with him again. 'I don't know why you're making such a fuss,' Liz was saying as she picked over the food on her plate. 'Mrs Simms and Mrs Casey always help out, you've only got to ask.'

Maggie rounded on her furiously, 'That's right, Liz, I only have to ask; me, not you, me. I'm sick of asking for handouts, and especially from people who aren't much better off than we are. There's such a thing as abusing friendship, Liz, and I think we've just about used up our quota of favours from the neighbours.' Pulling up a chair she sat down beside Liz, and placing a hand on her arm she asked urgently, 'Don't you have any pride left, Liz? How long are you going to sit around expecting other people to support you without lifting a finger to help yourself?'

For one brief instant, a spark of anger flared in Liz's eyes and then vanished, leaving Maggie to wonder if she'd imagined it.

Maggie let her hand drop to the table and said bitterly, 'All right, I've done all I can, and I'll go on trying, but the bits of work I've been getting are barely enough to keep us in food. Unless you get up off your backside and help, the next step is the workhouse, and I'm not joking, Liz. Right now I can't see any other way out.'

She had saved the threat of the workhouse as a last

resort, thinking that if all else failed the mention of the grim building would spur her sister back to life, but Liz merely shrugged her shoulders listlessly and carried on eating.

Frustrated beyond endurance Maggie leapt to her feet crying, 'Right then, the workhouse it is. You'd better get your things ready, because when Mr Bates comes on Friday and there's no money to give him we're all going to be out in the streets.'

'Oh, no, Maggie, not the workhouse,' Charlie screamed, his eyes wide with terror. Jumping from his chair he rushed to Maggie's side and threw his arms round her waist, his big brown eyes staring up at her in mute pleading. Her throat swelling with emotion Maggie could only draw him closer to her. She wished with all her heart she could say something to take the fear from his face, but it would be cruel of her to fill him with false hope. Picking him up in her arms, she walked unsteadily to the mattress and laid him down gently. And when he tried to plead with her once more, she placed a finger to her lips and shook her head sadly.

The sound of his sobs tore at her heart as she slumped down into the armchair and closed her eyes wearily. How could things have gone so terribly wrong? Just a short time ago life had seemed so bright. Now the darkness was closing in on her, pressing down relentlessly so that her very breath seemed to have been stilled. She would go out again tomorrow like she did every day, and maybe she'd be lucky and find a morning's work, or even a couple of days' work. But even if she did what good would it do? The few shillings she could expect to earn wouldn't pay the rent and keep them in food. Then there was the coal to buy – they hadn't had a proper fire for days. She had managed to find enough bits of wood and old newspapers lying in the streets to start a blaze in the grate just long enough to cook a meagre meal or boil a kettle, but it wasn't enough. They were in the midst of winter, and had so far managed to keep warm by wearing two lots of clothing day and night, but they couldn't go on like this. It would be different if Liz was helping her, but as things stood she was only putting off the inevitable by trying to keep them all together. There was no way she could get enough money together to pay Mr Bates on Friday, no way. Yes, there is, the voice in the back of her mind whispered to her.

The thought that had sprung unbidden to her mind caused Maggie to jump forward in the chair. Running a hand over her face she shook her head in denial. No, dear God, no. She couldn't do that, she couldn't. Despite the coldness of the room she found herself sweating as she listened to the voice in her head. It's either that or the workhouse, which would you prefer? the insidious little voice taunted her. Once you're inside that building you might never get out, and Charlie will be taken away to the children's section, you'll never see him again. All you have to do is go to the nearest pub and wait outside, it's easy. You're young and pretty, you won't have any trouble finding a customer, and it won't be forever, just a few nights till you get enough to tide you over. She remembered vividly the night when Liz had said jokingly that they were sitting on a fortune. How they had laughed. . . .

The candle flickered and went out, plunging the room into total darkness. She heard Liz say goodnight, and mumbled a reply as she tried to gather her jumbled, confused thoughts into some kind of order. For weeks now she had tried everything she knew to keep them from being thrown onto the streets. Every ornament and knick-knack had been sold; even their treasured clock had found its way into the pawn shop in an effort to keep body and soul together. There was nothing left to pawn – except herself. Rising slowly from the armchair she walked through the pitch darkness of the room and opened the door. A gust of icy wind blasted her body, lifting the top of her shawl from her head, but she scarcely noticed. Keeping a tight rein on her emotions she let her mind go blank and slowly climbed the stone steps. A passing carriage drove over a large puddle, splashing her boots and the bottom of her dress, but she kept on walking, her eyes firmly on the street ahead. Nothing could touch her now; she was past caring.

CHAPTER SEVEN

Judge Edward Stewart sat at the head of the long, heavily laden dining table, his thick lips pursed with impatience as he waited for his family to finish their dessert. The dinner had been an unusually long one. It had started with game soup, followed by turbot, then a fricassee of chicken and a large side of beef accompanied by an enormous plate of roast potatoes and vegetables. The penultimate course of gooseberry fool and thick cream lay untouched in front of him. The sound of silver cutlery being replaced against glass brought a smile of satisfaction to his lips. There only remained the cheese and biscuit board to be placed on the table, and then he would be free to indulge in a glass of port along with a Havana cigar. While he waited for the servants to clear the dessert dishes, he thought of the reason for the sumptuous meal he had just partaken of and felt a rush of pride sweep over him. It wasn't every day a man's son qualified as a doctor, no indeed it wasn't; and a youngest son at that. Leaning slightly back in his chair he placed his broad hands over an even broader stomach and smiled benevolently.

Edward Stewart was a stout man of medium height in his late fifties. The grey streaked hair seemed to match perfectly the heavy features of his face, a face that was both feared and respected by the people he came into contact with. Respected by his friends and family, he was feared by the never-ending stream of criminals who were brought daily before him. Many a miserable wretch had taken one look into those deep, black commanding eyes and declared himself guilty of all charges, thus saving precious time in the overcrowded, hard-pressed courtroom. Yet for all his sternness, he was considered to be a fair man, willing to hear out any man or woman he thought to be innocent.

Happily married for over thirty years and the father of three children, he considered himself a fortunate man, and a wealthy one. When his father, a prosperous landowner, had died some ten years ago, he had left his vast estate to be equally divided between his only son and his two grandsons; of his granddaughter there had been no mention. The generous legacy had enabled Edward to move his family to the imposing four-storey house in Hackney where they now resided, and had also removed the necessity to work for a living. This option he had scornfully rejected, however. He enjoyed his work, and knew himself to be good at the profession he had chosen. Always an active man, he could never have been happy living the life of the idle rich, and he was proud that his youngest son had taken after him in this respect. Lifting his head he let his eyes settle on the two young men seated at the left-hand side of the table and shook his head indulgently.

Nobody seeing the two men together would have taken them for brothers. Hugh Stewart, newly appointed doctor of medicine, was a quiet, almost painfully shy man who had the unfortunate habit of blushing and stammering on any occasion where he felt out of his depth. Not so his elder brother Harry, who always seemed to be at ease with himself regardless of circumstance. People meeting him for the first time were instantly won over by his friendly, outgoing personality, and he could always be relied on to smooth out any awkward situations wherever they might arise. Unlike his brother, Harry had so far shown no inclination to pursue a career, and at the age of twenty-five, a year older than Hugh, it seemed unlikely he would change at this stage in his life.

Edward let his eyes linger on his eldest son. He felt it impossible to believe that a man of Harry's depth could waste his life away in trivial pursuits. His irregular lifestyle had caused Edward some concern over the years. At one point he had even imagined Harry to be involved in shady activities, such was his reluctance to talk about his interests and friends. This notion had been firmly rejected by his wife who had scolded him for his lack of trust in his son. She had gone on to say that Harry would find his own purpose in life in good time. Her words had hung heavily on his anxious mind. He loved both of his sons, but he had to admit that Harry had always been his favourite. Maybe Beatrice was right, but the latter years had found Edward's pride in his eldest son being tempered with impatience at Harry's nonchalant attitude to life.

Not only were the two brothers totally different in character, they also bore no resemblance to each other. Harry was tall and slim with dark brown hair and deep blue eyes. With features too rugged to be termed handsome, his attractiveness came from a forceful personality and casual charm that drew women to his side with no effort on his part. Men too were eager for his company, but his male counterparts saw past the engaging smile and casual manner to the firm jaw and eyes that could turn cold if their owner thought himself slighted. Men didn't take liberties with Harry Stewart any more than they would have done with his father.

Sadly, Hugh had inherited none of his father's strength. He had, however, inherited his mother's delicate features and his late grandfather's pale auburn hair, attributes that would have been better served upon a woman. With this thought in mind, Edward Stewart turned his attention to his right and looked at his daughter, his eyes clouding over with pity at the sight of the round, painfully plain face, her heavy mannish features framed by a mass of black hair parted in the middle and falling in two bunches of thick ringlets on either side of her ears. On a younger woman the style would have been complimentary, but on Bella it merely served to make her resemble an ageing spaniel. Even the expensive white evening dress cut low across her shoulders and the sparkling emerald necklace she wore did nothing to alleviate the plainness of her face. As if aware of his scrutiny, Bella Stewart raised her head and Edward found himself staring into a pair of small, black eyes. Almost imperceptibly he shuddered: God she was ugly. The moment the thought flashed across his mind he felt ashamed, but feeling guilty didn't alter the facts. Not only was his daughter ugly, she was also sly and often unpleasant. She had never forgiven her grandfather for leaving her out of his will. Strangely enough, however, she had never shown any rancour towards her brothers, preferring instead to take her anger and bitterness out on her long-suffering parents – parents who had long since given up hope of ridding themselves of their disagreeable daughter through marriage; at the age of thirty, Bella was long past the marrying stage. Five years ago, Edward had put aside a large proportion of his wealth for a dowry, but even this tempting enticement hadn't been enough to lure a prospective suitor to their door. The black eyes continued to stare at him, causing him to drop his gaze. Poor Bella. He could understand her bitterness towards him, for it was his features he had passed on to her, features that on a man like himself portrayed character, had doomed her to a life of spinsterhood.

A gentle hand rested on his, and pulling himself from his reverie he looked at his wife and smiled tenderly.

'Would you like to say a few words, dear?' Beatrice Stewart asked, her soft blue eyes shining with pride, the pale pink dress she wore bringing out the colour in her heart-shaped face.

'Yes, yes, of course.' Clearing his throat, he pushed back his chair and rose to his feet.

Picking up a crystal glass filled with sherry he held it aloft for a moment, then pointing it towards his son said, 'To Hugh, newly appointed doctor of medicine. Congratulations, we are all very proud of you.'

'To Hugh,' Harry echoed, standing alongside his father, his glass held high above his brother's flushed face.

'Thank you, Father, Harry,' Hugh replied awkwardly, clearly embarrassed by the attention he was receiving. The toast delivered, the men sat down.

While the servants cleared away the last remnants of the meal, Harry leaned back in his chair and asked. 'What are you planning to do to celebrate, Hugh? I suppose you'll be going out with your friends from the hospital this evening to let off some steam after all those years of studying. Lord knows how you stuck it out for so long. I couldn't have done it, but then I don't possess your dedication. It must be a wonderful feeling to have a purpose in life – I'm still searching for mine.'

Hugh looked up sharply, his eyes searching his brother's face for signs of ridicule, but found only an open, frank look of admiration. He felt his already red cheeks burning hotly and stammered, 'It was no hardship for me, Harry. I . . . I've always wanted to be a . . . a doctor, ever since I was a young boy and we both had the measles. Do you remember, Harry?' His voice was eager now as he recalled his childhood dream.

'We were both lying in bed thinking we were going to die and scratching ourselves to pieces. We couldn't even see each other because mother had closed the curtains and turned off all the lights so that the room would remain in total darkness. And then the doctor came, dressed in his morning suit and high silk hat, carrying a shiny black bag, and after a thorough examination declared that we would be up and running about the house in a week's time. He sounded so confident, so utterly sure of himself, that I began to feel better straight away. It was then I decided what I wanted to do with my life. Don't you remember, Harry? I told you as soon as he'd gone.'

'Can't say as I do, old chap,' Harry replied, smiling. 'I was much too busy feeling sorry for myself to take in any earth shattering revelations about your future role in life.'

Again Hugh looked for some sign that he was being made fun of but could find none.

'Well now, if we have finished in here, Bella and I will

take our leave and let you men enjoy your port. Come, Bella.'

Beatrice was already walking towards the dining-room door, and after a moment's hesitation Bella slowly followed her mother, her displeasure at having to leave the room highly evident. The room to themselves, the men lounged back casually in their chairs and waited for their glasses to be filled from the port decanter.

'Thank you, Burrows, that will be all,' Judge Stewart said to the elderly butler hovering by his side.

'Very good, sir.' The man bowed stiffly, then leaving the decanter within easy reach of his master, he left the room.

'So, where are you going this evening, Hugh, or is it a dark secret?' Harry laughed good-naturedly, his long legs clad in tight beige trousers sprawled under the table. Hugh jumped nervously, spilling some of the dark red wine onto the white tablecloth.

'Of course it isn't,' he answered sharply. 'I'm going to meet a few friends in a club in Piccadilly, nothing exciting I can assure you.'

'Steady on, old chap,' Harry exclaimed in surprise, 'I was merely expressing an interest. I had thought you might care to accompany me to my club, but seeing as you've already made plans. . . .' He shrugged his shoulders and turned his attention to the glass of port in his hand.

'Sorry, Harry, I didn't mean to speak so sharply,' Hugh mumbled apologetically, 'nerves, I expect. I still can't get used to the fact that I'm now a fully qualified doctor. It'll take some time for the realisation to sink in.'

Harry stared at his brother, his keen eyes taking in the nervous trembling of the long, elegant fingers beating out a steady tattoo on the table, wondering at the real reason behind his brother's agitation. Still, if Hugh did have something on his mind he would tell him in his own good time. Lifting his glass to his lips Harry downed his drink and stood up. 'Well, if you'll both excuse me I'll be off to my club; and once again, Hugh, my deepest congratulations, you put me to shame.'

Hugh smiled weakly. He couldn't imagine anyone or anything putting his elder brother to shame. Not like himself. God, if Harry or his father knew of his real plans for tonight . . . he gave an involuntary shudder. He waited a few more minutes after Harry had left the room before taking his own leave.

Alone at last Edward Stewart poured himself another liberal helping of port and lit a cigar, then settled himself more comfortably in his chair, happy to enjoy the luxury of a few more minutes' solitude before joining his wife and daughter in the parlour.

Harry had just finished buttoning a clean shirt when his bedroom door burst open and Bella entered the room. Whirling round quickly he snatched up his brown coat from the back of a chair and shouted angrily, 'Damn it, Bella, how many times have I asked you to knock before coming into my room.'

Taking no notice of his anger Bella sidled past him and sat down on the double bed. Then, as if she had all the time in the world, she smoothed and arranged the voluminous skirt of the white dress evenly over the bed. Fighting down his irritation at her presence, Harry pulled on his coat and snatched his black high hat from the dresser.

'Well?' he snapped impatiently. 'If you've something you want to talk to me about, you'd better make it quick. I'm on my way out.'

Still unmoved by Harry's open hostility, Bella beat her closed fan against the folds of her skirt. Then, her voice petulant, she answered, 'Oh, you're always on your way out; what about me? I never get to go anywhere except to church fêtes and visiting Mother's tiresome friends. I'm so bored. Harry, you've no idea what it's like being a girl, we never have any fun.'

Harry shook his head despairingly. It was true he had no idea what it was like to be a girl, but by the same token, it had been many a long year since Bella could lay claim to that knowledge.

'Can't I come with you, Harry? Just this once, I promise not to be a bother.' She was leaning forward, her hands clasped as if in prayer, the black eyes silently begging him to say yes. Harry looked hard into the plain face and turned away before she saw the distaste in his eyes. She wasn't natural. She was his own sister, and up until a few years ago he had had a certain fondness for her, but now he had to admit she wasn't normal. What sort of woman was she to burst into her brother's room unannounced, and not just tonight, but many times. On one such occasion she had found him dressed only in his underclothes, a few minutes earlier and he would have been standing naked. Yet even then she had shown no embarrassment and would have entered the room if he hadn't bundled her unceremoniously out of the door. And this business of wanting to accompany him on his evening jaunts was getting to be a habit. This was the fifth time this month she had made the same plea. He felt sorry for her, of course; it must be hell to be a woman and look like she did. But it wasn't only her looks that had prevented her from marrying. Many an ugly woman had managed to find a husband, but their looks had been compensated for by pleasant personalities and kind natures; his sister possessed none of these attributes. Sighing heavily he turned to face her.

'Now look, Bella, we've been over this before,' he said tiredly. 'The places I visit don't allow women in, and even if they did I wouldn't take you. Now please, go back downstairs and leave me in peace.'

Harry watched her lips tighten into a thin line and braced himself for an outburst, but she continued to stare at him until with an exasperated sigh he nearly threw himself around and made for the door.

'I wonder what Father would say if he knew how you spent your days.' The soft words hit him in the back and he felt himself stiffen in surprise. 'That stopped you, didn't it?' Her voice still soft, she rose from the bed, her

101

skirts crackling as she walked towards him. Placing her back against the door she faced him, all signs of pleading gone. In their place was a face contorted with pain and malice.

'I followed you one day. I was curious to know where you disappeared to every day, so I waited until you'd left the house and then I followed you in a cab.' Her eyes were pinned to his, and when she saw his startled look she experienced a feeling of excitement.

Unable to keep the gloating tone from her voice she continued, 'I don't think much of the company you keep, brother dear. Why, even the cab driver was reluctant to enter the street you were obviously so familiar with. I must admit I was expecting some rendezvous with either a married woman or one of ill repute – that is the correct term isn't it? Well, never mind, it isn't important now.' She waved her hand airily in his face. 'But you see, Harry, you've placed me in an awkward position. I mean, do I tell Mother and Father that their son is on intimate terms with thieves, murderers and prostitutes? I haven't left anyone out, have I? No? Very well then, let's lump them all together and give them the collective term of degenerates; that just about sums up the description of your companions, doesn't it?'

Harry stared down into the upturned face, his stomach churning at the undisguised malevolence in the glittering black eyes.

Then very deliberately and without a trace of anger he said calmly, 'You're not normal, Bella. I came to that conclusion quite some time ago when you first started to come into my room at all odd hours hoping to catch me in a state of undress. And it's not just me, is it? You've been trying the same tricks with Hugh, haven't you?' The colour flooded her pasty skin, but he felt not the slightest trace of pity for her. She had gone too far this time. Taking hold of her arm he pulled her away from the door roughly, the action causing her to stumble on the hem of her dress. Before she could recover her balance, she found herself sprawled lengthwise on the thick-carpeted floor.

Ignoring her plight Harry opened the door. 'If you feel it your duty to acquaint Mother and Father of my nefarious ways then do so by all means. I wouldn't want your conscience to be troubled on my account. But before you go running with your tales, you'd best have a good story ready to explain how you came by the knowledge. And now my dear sister, I'll bid you a good night, although I doubt very much if you will ever experience such an event.' Doffing his hat to her he strode from the room. When she heard his carefree whistling as he ran lightly down the stairway she gritted her teeth in frustration. It wasn't fair, it just wasn't fair. Both her brothers and parents enjoyed an active social life, even the servants had somewhere to go or someone to visit on their days off; what did she herself have? Nothing, absolutely nothing. She had no friends, no outside interests, no life at all beyond the four walls of the house. It had always been that way, even as a child, yet she hadn't realised she was different until Harry had been born. Her mind ran back down the years.

Bella had been so excited when her baby brother had been placed in her small, awkward arms, her parents hovering on either side of her. As she had gazed down at the tiny, puckered face, she had seen his arrival as an end to her loneliness. Instead the presence of the infant had brought home to her for the first time her own inadequacies. Even at such a young age she had known she wasn't pretty and had felt an affinity to the ugly baby in her arms. She had watched him take his first, faltering steps, his small, pudgy hands angrily waving away any offer of help. It was about that time she had begun to notice how visitors to the house always found an excuse to pick him up and make a fuss of him, while she was patted absently on the head, much as one would treat a pet dog, and then ignored. Even her parents had seemed unable to keep their hands off him. She could remember her father coming home and her waiting to greet him, only to receive a perfunctory hug before he hurried to the nursery to play with his son.

When Hugh had arrived the following year she found herself being pushed even further into the background, leaving her hurt and bewildered. Her mother had always included her daughter in the family pastimes, careful not to let the little girl be overshadowed by her baby siblings. Then one summer afternoon she had overheard a conversation in the drawing-room. Two of her mother's friends had come to visit, and as usual Harry and Hugh were the centre of attention. Bella had left the room to fetch some toys; on her return she had heard her name mentioned and stood outside the door waiting to hear what was being said.

The woman holding Hugh had announced loudly, 'He's gorgeous, Beatrice, simply gorgeous, I can hardly bring myself to hand him back to you. He's going to break a few hearts when he gets older, and Harry too I've no doubt.'

Beatrice had laughed gaily. 'Oh, come now, Anne, I've no illusions about Harry. Even my mother's biased eyes can see Harry is no beauty.'

'No, I'll agree he isn't handsome in the conventional sense,' the woman had replied, 'but he has charm and an engaging personality even at his tender years. Besides, it doesn't seem to matter so much if a man is ugly as long as he has charm, not like Bella, poor soul.'

The casual words had pierced Bella's heart like a knife. Even her mother's heated words in her defence hadn't helped to ease the pain. She had returned to her room, her small body trembling with hurt and confusion, wondering why she was different from her brothers.

As she had grown older she had renewed her efforts to be liked, but without success. The two boys had very early forged a bond, and although they tolerated her presence, it was painfully clear they didn't want her to join in their games. Made to feel like an interloper, she had resorted to bullying and telling tales in a desperate attempt to gain attention, her reward being several hard smacks to her bottom administered by her father while her mother turned away, her hands covering her eyes, unable to witness it.

To be fair to her parents, they had tried their best to make her feel loved and a part of the family, but her childish resentment had prevented her from accepting their affection. After a while, her father had given up trying to placate her surly moods and left her to her own devices. If it hadn't been for her mother, who refused to give up on her only daughter, Bella's childhood would have been unbearable.

She had kept her spirits high, thinking that once she reached womanhood her life would change, but here too she was cruelly disappointed. When Bella turned eighteen her mother had entered into a whirl of social engagements hoping to find a husband for her only daughter. At first Bella had been excited, delighting in the new clothes and jewellery that filled her wardrobe and trinket box. Then the inward humiliation had begun all over again.

At first she had been hopeful, even gay, at the prospect of meeting someone with whom she could spend the rest of her life with. Her nights were filled with images of walking down a church aisle, dressed in a flowing white gown, a faceless man by her side – but the faceless man never materialised. Over the years she watched women of her own age being swept around a dance floor, while she sat on the side, her mother always close by. Each time she scanned the wedding announcements in *The*

Times and saw yet another acquaintance's name printed, she felt the bitterness grow. When her twenty-fifth birthday came around she announced that she would no longer be attending any balls or parties, proclaiming herself weary of such events. But when, three months later, her father had settled a substantial dowry upon her, Bella had been furious, seeing such an action as the final humiliation; she had done nothing to stop the news being spread, though telling herself that a bought husband was better than no husband at all. The ultimate humiliation, however, was the absence of any man willing to accept the bribe, for bribe was what it amounted to.

In a last, frantic effort to make a life for herself she had begun to try and inveigle herself into her brothers' lives, hoping to find a prospective groom among their many friends, but here too her hopes had been dashed. Hugh was malleable enough, being too weak-willed to protest at her intrusions into his life, but Harry had steadfastly refused to pander to her wishes. Still she had persevered, driven by a desperate need to be included in their lives. The young medical students that had visited Hugh had shown clearly their lack of interest in the ageing woman who hovered round them trying to join in their conversations, until Hugh, deeply embarrassed by his sister's constant presence, had stopped inviting his friends home. She had then switched her attentions back to Harry, prepared to swallow what little pride she had left in order to penetrate his circle of friends. Now she would try no more. Her brother's sneering words and obvious dislike of her had left her with no more illusions. Lying on the floor, her head resting against the four-poster bed, she felt the bitterness and resentment flood over her. Why had she been born like this? Why hadn't God bestowed upon her a sunny nature, a natural wit or a vibrant personality to compensate her for her ugliness? Again her mind screamed, that it wasn't fair, it wasn't bloody fair.

Bella's thoughts turned again to Harry. He was so sure of himself, so confident. He would never know the misery of rejection or uncertainty for the future. Lifting her head she stared at the window. If she couldn't find happiness then she would do all in her power to prevent Harry from finding any. A rush of pure hatred swept through her. 'I'll get even with you, you bastard,' she whispered, her throat thick with tears. 'You wait and see, you'll be sorry you spoke to me like that.' Anxious to share her misery she rose awkwardly to her feet and stumbled from the room in search of Hugh.

Hugh sat nervously on his bed listening to his sister's soft entreaties to let her in, his eyes glued to the twisting door handle, praying that the chair he had placed beneath it would remain firm. When he heard the muffled footsteps walking away from the door he heaved a sigh of relief and rose unsteadily to his feet. Walking over to the full-length mirror he looked at his perspiring face and felt a deep sense of self-disgust at the way he had behaved. God! What a pitiful specimen of a man he was. He had heard the raised voices and could only guess at the reason behind the heated argument. When he had heard Harry leaving the house, followed quickly by the sound of Bella's footsteps heading in his direction, he had barricaded himself in his room rather than face his sister's fury. Waves of self-loathing swept over him, and with a muffled moan he sank back onto the bed.

Putting his head in his hands, he thought back to the conversation he'd had with Harry at dinner about his reasons for becoming a doctor, and laughed mirthlessly. Rubbing his hands over his face he dropped them into his lap and stared sightlessly at the far wall. He hadn't worked and studied for over four years out of any noble calling; the reason was much simpler than that. From the time he was old enough to reason for himself, he had known that he would have to do something special with his life if he ever wanted to command respect and comradeship outside his immediate family.

Hugh was painfully aware of his lack of personality and character. He had decided at an early age to make something of himself, to be somebody, somebody that people would look up to and come to for advice – like they did with Harry. As the image of his brother came to mind Hugh shook his head sorrowfully. It wasn't fair, Harry had never had to try to make people like him – in fact he could be downright rude at times. Yet in spite of his sometimes disinterested attitude, anyone who came into contact with him eagerly sought his company, whereas he himself didn't have one single person, man or woman, that he could honestly call a friend. Colleagues yes, but friends, real friends that he could call upon at any time day or night, no. Shaking his head sadly he reflected on his life and the profession he had chosen. He had imagined that the status of a doctor would automatically bring forth respect; but he was honest enough to admit that a title alone wouldn't bring about the recognition he craved so desperately, for the more he chased respect, the more it eluded him.

Getting heavily to his feet he reached for his pearl-grey jacket and slipped it on over the dark blue straight trousers, his reflection in the oval mirror giving him a much-needed boost of confidence. As he picked up his hat another fragment of conversation floated into his mind. He could see Harry clearly as he'd lounged casually in the chair and asked the question, 'So where are you going tonight, Hugh, or is it a dark secret?'

How close to the truth Harry had come. And the truth was that Hugh Stewart, twenty-four years old and newly qualified doctor of medicine, was still a virgin. It seemed impossible that a man of his age had never known a woman, and yet, was it so unusual? How many men would admit to such a state? Certainly not himself. He had done his fair share of story telling among his fellow students, drawing on an active imagination to make his tales of conquests more plausible. Now he wondered how many of the hair-raising exploits he had listened to had been fact, and how many simply wishful thinking on the part of the story teller?

Drawing himself up to his full height he pulled his shoulders back and drew a deep breath. There was nothing he could do about his weak character or lack of personality, but there was a simple remedy to his virginal status. He knew where to find plenty of girls and women who would be only too happy to help rid him of this particular handicap, but until recently he had lacked the courage to seek them out.

Even now as he prepared to set out on his mission he wondered if he would back out at the last minute, but quickly put the thought from his mind. It was no longer something he had to do to make him feel more of a man; his body needed relief, and it was his natural urges, suppressed for so long, that had finally made up his mind. Checking his wallet to make sure he had enough money on him, he counted the four five-pound notes and nodded. He had no idea of the going rate, but even in his ignorance he knew the money he had would be ample for his needs. Slipping the leather wallet inside his breast pocket, he carefully pulled the chair away from the door and peered out. The sight of the deserted corridor gave him the impetus he needed. Shutting the door softly behind him he made for the stairway and a new phase in his life.

CHAPTER EIGHT

Harry walked briskly over the cobbled pavement, his mind seething at the confrontation he had had with Bella. God damn the woman for sticking her nose into his business. Even the knowledge that her interference stemmed from loneliness didn't make him feel any more charitable towards her. A passing hansom cab slowed hopefully alongside him and soon he was seated comfortably on the red leather seat, leaving his mind free to wander back into the past.

It had been four years since his first excursion into the East End of London. Together with a crowd of young men friends he had entered the dimly lit back streets searching for adventure, but instead had met grim poverty and dire distress. The alleys and culs-de-sac packed tight with houses three storeys high and hardly six feet apart, the obnoxious smells wafting from the open doorways causing the smartly dressed men to cover their faces with white linen handkerchiefs had created in Harry a deep, over-riding sense of shame. They had moved swiftly past the depressing sights and into the nearest tavern where they had ordered whiskeys and then stood uncomfortably in their new surroundings, their voices over-loud and hearty as they'd tried to disguise their unease amidst the hostile company that milled around them. They had nearly choked in their haste to finish their drinks, then with a great show of false bravado they had sauntered casually out of the pub and into the street.

Once outside they had run pell-mell down the narrow, winding alleyways until reaching the safety of the brightly lit high street. It was then that two of Harry's companions found that they had been the victims of pick-pockets, and although they had tried to put a brave face on, the evening had soured. The party had broken up amid assurances that they must 'do it again sometime'.

Harry had spent an uneasy night, the memories of the sights he had witnessed refusing to let him sleep. A week later he had found himself once more in the same pub, his heart racing nervously as he'd sipped his pint of beer. The evening had passed without incident, encouraging him to return the following night, and the night after that. For the first few weeks he had drunk his one glass of beer and left, not wishing to tempt fate by over-staying his welcome. Then the one pint of beer had given way to two, then three, until gradually he had felt himself becoming more and more at ease with his unlikely new companions. They in turn came to accept his presence, and once they had assured themselves he was neither ranter, reformer nor plain-clothed policeman, had taken to sitting with him and pouring out their troubles to the sympathetic young man who seemed genuinely concerned with their lives.

Many a guinea found its way into a dirty palm, but Harry was no fool and only gave to those he deemed to be genuinely in need of help. This in turn had led to bad feeling among some of the other clientele, in particular a man called Frankie Fields, a well known pick-pocket and ruffian of the highest order. He had swaggered into the Black Swan one night, knocking all who stood in his path out of his way, his unsteady gait taking him towards Harry's table. Resting fists as big as hams on the table, he had at first wheedled and then demanded ten pounds, only to be met by a steely gaze. Infuriated by the toffee-nosed interloper's lack of fear, the huge bull of a man had heaved over the table spilling Harry's drink and sending the nearby occupants scuttling for the safety of the far end of the bar. Holding the man's gaze, Harry had slowly risen to his feet. Without a word his arm had shot out, the iron fist connecting with the bullish jaw and felling the man to the floor. Stunned by the unexpected attack, Frankie Fields had lain prone on the floor while the rest of the room had held its breath. The last man to tackle Big Frank was now lying at rest in Highbury Cemetery. Shaking his head as if to clear it, the enraged man had let out a mighty bellow and charged the tall, slim man only to stop short at the sight of the dagger protruding from the end of the gold-tipped walking cane. His face red with fury he had stared hard into the cold blue eyes, then letting loose a barrage of curses he had stormed from the bar.

An astonished silence had settled on the room, then with a concerted rush the men and women of the East End had crowded round Harry, slapping him soundly on the back, their admiration for his courage shining from their grime-streaked faces. From that moment on he had become a part of their lives, his action earning him their respect and the affectionate nick-name 'The Toff'.

In the years he had been among them, many a family had been saved from being thrown out into the street when they could no longer pay their rent by the intervention of 'The Toff'. The calls upon his purse had been great over the years, but he was careful to temper his generosity, and was quick to send packing the loafers and street scavengers who thought him to be an easy touch. Word soon travelled round the tightly knit community. Generous he might be; a fool he was not. For his part, Harry had the greatest admiration for the indomitable spirit that kept the people of the East End going. They accepted their lot with fortitude, their attitude for the most part cheerful and optimistic. There were of course those who didn't try to help themselves, resorting to thievery from laziness rather than necessity, and these Harry avoided wherever possible.

Harry had been content with his life until recently. For some months now he had been growing increasingly discontented with his day-to-day existence, experiencing a growing desire to make something of himself, to do something worthwhile with his days. It was all very well to help his friends on occasion, but his monetary aid was merely a temporary solution to their many problems. If only he could think of a way in which he could alleviate their poverty-stricken way of life – not only for them, but for himself too.

At twenty-five years of age, it was time he stopped his carefree, casual lifestyle, combined his sharp intellect and wealth and put both to good use. He had never imagined he would feel envious of his younger brother, not poor Hugh with his painful shyness and lack of confidence. Not the small boy who had looked up to his elder brother, obeying his every command without question, his eyes shining with adoration and respect. As for Harry, he had taken the fair-haired boy under his wing from the moment he could walk and talk. He had protected him from the playground bullies, collecting many a bruised eye and cut lip for his pains, while a wailing Hugh had looked on as his dark-haired brother received a beating meant for him.

But Hugh was a boy no longer. He would always need someone to lean on, to make life easier for him, yet in spite of his shortcomings, Hugh had done something with his life, he had achieved his goal, carving out a niche for himself in the arduous medical world. In doing so he had forced Harry to take a long, hard look at his own affairs. He remembered the undisguised look of pride on his parents' faces as they had toasted the red-faced Hugh, and felt again a twinge of envy. The hansom cab jolted to a stop, jerking Harry out of his reverie. Alighting quickly he paid the cabbie, smiling reassuringly at the man's worried face as he watched his passenger walk cheerfully into the dark warren of houses where even the police only went *en masse*.

Harry pushed open the heavy pub doors and was immediately enveloped in a sea of noise, smoke and loud music and smiled broadly. Here was life – roaring, teeming vibrant life that made his nerve ends tingle. Walking briskly to the bar he was greeted cheerfully by the people that thronged the tightly packed tap-room. A tall glass of ale on the bar-top in front of him, he took a deep swallow and glanced around the room. Over in the corner sat the dilapidated piano, its well-worn keys being thrashed unmercifully by an old dock worker named Bob who earned a few extra shillings a week for entertaining the customers.

As he surveyed the boisterous scene an image of Bella's spiteful face flashed before his eyes, and he gave a short laugh. What if he had given in to her entreaties and brought her along with him? He could imagine the reception she would have received, for if there was one thing the people of the East End wouldn't tolerate, it was disdain, or worse still, well-meaning pity from people who were ill-prepared to do anything constructive to alleviate their plight.

The smile slipped from his face as he visualised his parents' reactions if they ever found out about his twice weekly visits to this now familiar place. Yet would they be so horrified? His mother had spent many a day helping out in the many soup-kitchens of London. She deplored snobbery, and often shed tears when reading of the numerous, poverty related incidents retailed eagerly in the daily papers. His father too, had no time for people who considered themselves better than others, but would he understand his son's need to align himself with the very people who stood before him in the dock every day?

Harry took another swig of his ale. Many of the crowd present had probably been up before the Honourable Judge Stewart at one time or another, and it was the one fear in his otherwise carefree life that his friends would discover his parentage. He loved his father dearly, and respected him more than any other man he had ever known, but he doubted if the people here would share his view. Nobody knew his full name. He was known as Harry 'The Toff', and he hoped they would never learn his true identity. Finishing his drink, he beckoned to the bartender to replenish his glass, then leant his elbow on the stained bar-top, his eyes sweeping the packed room. His glass half-way to his lips he noticed a new face among the familiar crowd and paused. She sat alone in a corner, her face defiant and pinched, her small fists clenched in her lap as her eyes moved restlessly round the room. Placing his glass back on the bar-top Harry looked more closely at her and felt a stirring of pity swell inside his chest. God; she couldn't be more than fifteen, and judging from the scared look on her face this was her first outing. Shaking his head sadly he turned away. There was only so much he could do, yet no matter how many times he witnessed such a scene, the feeling of helplessness never lessened.

It was on occasions such as these that he wished he had never entered this world. A world that could turn the old and the sick onto the streets and force the young, girls and boys, to trade their bodies for money to buy food for their starving bellies.

Still there were hundreds like her, and within a month the scared look would be replaced by a world-weary expression. If she was lucky she would be picked up by a costermonger, or some other such man willing to house her in a small room for his pleasures until he tired of her. But this happened rarely. At best she could hope for a few years before her looks faded and the light died in her eyes from the constant attacks on her body, at worst she would contact a venereal disease that would eventually kill her. His eyes bleak he stared at his empty glass, wondering whether to order another beer or take his leave. The sight of the young, vulnerable girl had put a blight on his evening.

Before he could make up his mind he heard a commotion break out over the raised voices gathered around the piano. Turning his head in the direction of the corner he felt his body stiffen at the sight of three heavily painted women crowding in on the girl.

Hesitating for only a moment, he pushed his way to the table, and laying his hand on the arm of the woman nearest to him, he said cheerfully. 'Here, what's going on, Clara? Leave the girl alone, she's not doing any harm.'

'What the . . . Oh it's you, 'Arry.' The woman addressed as Clara faced him, her hands planted firmly on her ample hips.

'Now, stay out of it, 'Arry. You knows the rules round 'ere. We all got our own little patch to work, and we can't 'ave outsiders coming in and pinching our trade. 'Specially little bits of girls like 'er.'

Turning her attention back to the girl she shook her fist in the startled face, shouting fiercely, 'Go on, git out of 'ere afore yer gits yer pretty face bashed in. I ain't gonna tell yer twice; get going.'

The girl got to her feet, her face set in defiance, the trembling of her bottom lip the only sign of her fear. Without uttering a word she walked through the jeering women, and as she passed Harry she stumbled and reached out blindly, her hand catching hold of his coat sleeve. Harry caught a fleeting glimpse of a pair of large brown eyes glazed with unshed tears and then she was gone, leaving him shaken by the encounter. For one wild moment he was tempted to follow her, but he quickly quashed the idea. In all the years he had been coming here, he had never availed himself of the services so readily offered by the steady stream of prostitutes that touted their wares openly in the bar; he wasn't about to start now. He had a mistress tucked away in a comfortable house in Bow whom he visited every Wednesday and Sunday. In return for her favours he paid the rent on the house and left a 'gift' on her bedside table after every visit. There was no romance between them, simply a convenient arrangement that suited them both.

'Fancy a couple hours of bliss, 'Arry?' Clara was back by his side, her eager painted face garish in the bright, over-hanging gas-lamp.

Laughing loudly, Harry disentangled her arm. 'Now then Clara, you know me better than that,' he answered good naturedly. 'I come here merely for the pleasure of the company, nothing more.'

' 'Ere, you ain't one of them nancy boys are yer, 'Arry? Be a crying shame if yer was, a fine figure of a gentleman like yerself.'

'Clara, how could you think such a thing?' Harry said reproachfully, his eyes twinkling as he enjoyed the familiar repartee. Edging closer to his side the woman stood on tiptoe and whispered in his ear, 'I could make yer 'appy, 'Arry. I knows what men like, and I wouldn't charge yer, and yer'd be doing me a favour as well. It's years since I 'ad a real man in me bed.'

'Sorry, Clara, thanks all the same, but it's time for me to leave. I'll see you next week. Be good.'

The woman's face fell, her eyes turning hard at the all too familiar rejection, then pulling her arm away she smiled tiredly, 'Go on then, but I'll get yer upstairs one of these days, 'Arry, I don't give up easily.' With a toss of her head she walked back to her friends.

Weaving his way through the tap-room Harry made for the door. He normally stayed longer, but the incident with the young girl had left a sour taste in his mouth. He wondered briefly where she would go, then dismissed her from his mind. Taking out his pocket watch he saw that it was nearly ten o'clock, plenty of time to get to his club and play a few hands of cards in the back room before returning home. His mind decided, he buttoned up his thick woollen coat and set off for the club.

Maggie walked along the cobbled road, her head hung dejectedly as she fought a silent war within herself. How could she have been so stupid? What on earth had possessed her to come here tonight when she knew deep down that she would never have gone through with it? The idea had seemed so easy back in the basement, but faced with the reality her nerve had quickly vanished. Her bolstered-up courage had lasted no longer than it had taken her to walk into the pub; it had only been the spectre of the workhouse that had enabled her to order a glass of ale and sit at the table by the wall. As she'd sipped the strange-tasting liquid she'd tried to keep her resolve, her mind forming questions such as how much should she ask? Where would she go to accomplish the deed, and most fearful of all, what was she supposed to do while the act was being performed? Would she be expected to participate or simply let the man get on with it? The more she thought about what she had planned to do, the more frightened she had become. And when those horrible women had ganged up on her she'd needed no second bidding to abandon her plans and flee.

God, she must had have a brainstorm to have even thought of such an idea. Things were desperate, but she could always apply for parish relief, even though it was next to nothing. Then there were the soup kitchens run by the Sally Army; this thought caused her to shiver with shame and quickly she pulled herself upright. Neither she nor her family could afford the luxury of pride, and when Mr Bates came for the rent tomorrow, she would make one last attempt and plead with him for an extra week, even though she knew it wasn't up to him, but instead the faceless man or woman who owned the house she lived in. Hugging her shawl tighter around her chest she hurried on, ignoring the tears that were stinging her eyes. It was hopeless, there was no way they could survive without a wage coming into the house. The workhouse loomed before her eyes, causing her to stop in her tracks. The streets were her only chance of keeping herself and her family out of the grim building, but she couldn't do it; she just couldn't. The tears were falling freely now and as she stumbled into the darkness of the alleyway she failed to see the man waiting by the wall. The first she knew of his presence was a rough hand on her arm, and then she was being pulled into a narrow alley and thrown roughly against the brick wall.

'How much?' the man's voice whispered urgently, his hands tugging at the buttons of her blouse. Stunned by the attack Maggie could only pull at the strange hands that were invading her breasts, her mouth opening and closing futilely as she tried to find her voice.

'No, no, you've made a mistake, I'm not a pr . . .'

She got no further. Her skirt was suddenly pulled up and over her face muffling any sound she might have made. When the cold hands came into contact with her bare stomach she froze for a moment, then as if coming out of a stupor she began to fight the unknown stranger. Her hands clenched into tight fists she pounded the man's head and shoulders while trying to move her legs in an attempt to kick out at the man's shins, but he had her pinned firmly against the wall. The cold night air hit her exposed body and then she felt the pain as the man invaded her body. She tried to scream but the heavy skirt muffled any sound she may have made. As the pain became more intense she thrashed about wildly, but the more she struggled the more excited the man became. And then mercifully it was over, and with a soft moan she slid silently down the wall and onto the cold, dirty pathway. She sensed rather than saw the man bend down towards her, then her fingers were prised apart and the unmistakeable feel of money pressed into her palm.

'I'm sorry . . . I didn't mean to hurt you. I thought . . . I thought you were looking for . . . for a customer. Oh, God, I'm sorry . . .'

Maggie heard the mumbled apology through a mist of pain, but kept her eyes firmly shut. Only when she heard the footsteps hurry away did she open them, her gaze concentrating on the dim coins nestling in her outstretched hand. The coldness of the ground was seeping through her clothes and with all the effort she could muster she rose shakily to her feet.

The sound of footsteps approaching hastened her effort, and when she felt her arm grabbed for the second time that night she didn't hesitate. Opening her mouth wide she went to let out a loud scream, a scream that was cut off by a hand being placed gently but firmly over her lips.

'Shush, it's all right, don't be frightened. I'm not going to hurt you.'

The alley was situated between the two lamp-posts that lined both ends of the street, their pale light showing the dim outline of the man beside her. Her heart was beating so wildly she thought it must surely burst from her chest. The man was still talking although his head was turned in the direction of her assailant.

Harry peered into the gloom. He had seen the man run off and had wondered at his haste. Now he squinted as if to see him better. As the man reached the lamp-post at the end of the road Harry felt his breath catch in his throat. It couldn't be, not Hugh. No, of course it wasn't, there must be hundreds of men with that colour hair, his mind was playing tricks on him.

Turning his attention back to the girl he gently removed his hand, and his voice pitched low, he said kindly, 'He's gone, are you all right? Did he hurt you?' The violent trembling of the slight body answered his question, and moving away, he screwed up his eyes as if to see her better.

'You were in the pub, weren't you? Just a little while back, before Clara and her cronies set about you.' He saw the head nod silently and wondered what to do now. He had assured himself she was all right; there was nothing more he could do for her – by the look of it the damage had already been done. Yet he was loath to leave her standing here alone. That maniac the papers had daubed 'The Ripper' was still at large, and even though he hadn't struck for over a year, who could tell when he might return to the back streets of the East End. Knowing he wouldn't be able to sleep tonight unless he knew she had reached home safely, he took hold of her arm, his face twisting with compassion as he felt her flinch under his touch.

'It's all right, I intend you no harm, I just want to see you get home safely. Now come along, I'll find you a cab.'

'I don't have money to waste on a cab.' The words were spoken so low he had to strain in order to hear her properly.

'Don't worry about the money. I'm on my way to

Piccadilly, you can ride with me. If you tell me where you live, I can get the cab driver to let you off on the way.'

Maggie looked at the man in astonishment. Why on earth would a gentleman like him be worried about her welfare unless he was after something?

Moving away from him she answered stiffly, 'Bethnal Green, but I can make my own way home, thanks all the same.'

'Don't be a fool!' The man's voice had risen. 'You don't know who may be waiting to jump out on you. You don't want another repetition, do you?'

Did she want a repetition? God, no. She never wanted to feel a man's hand on her ever again. Anxious to get away she began to walk on, then stopped as her foot came into contact with something lying in her path, and without thinking she stooped to pick it up.

'What have you found?' Harry asked curiously.

Not trusting herself to speak she held out her hand, revealing the brown leather wallet she held between her fingers. Even in the gloom of the street Harry recognised the wallet, and felt his stomach contract painfully. It was the one he had given Hugh for Christmas; he could just make out the fancy initials set in gold lettering on the flap of the wallet. So it had been Hugh he'd seen running away. But why? What in God's name had brought his young brother to this part of London. Had he taken a leaf out of Bella's book and taken to following him. No, he shook his head, that wasn't it; then why?

The girl was walking away from him, her movements stiff as if she were in pain and again he shook his head. Hugh would never deliberately hurt anyone. Oh, Lord, Lord, what should he do? His first impulse was to race home and confront his brother, but he dismissed this idea. Firstly he would have to explain what he himself had been doing in the area, and secondly, his brother was no longer a young boy to be chastised for his actions. And it wasn't as if he had pounced on some unsuspecting young lady out for a stroll in Hyde Park. Quickening his step he caught up with the girl as she passed under the lamp-post, the bright light illuminating the warm brown colour of her hair as it fell in curls over her shoulders and back. Careful not to alarm her, he gently placed his hands on both her arms and pulled her round to face him. The warm brown eyes he had first seen in the pub stared up at him, still defiant in spite of the tears that glistened on the black eyelashes.

Clearing his throat he said softly, 'I'm sorry for what happened to you, but you must have known what you were walking into when you came down here; why did you come if you weren't prepared to . . . to. . . .' His voice trailed off, not knowing quite what to say next.

Maggie gulped noisily, then dashing away the tears with the back of her hand, she shouted angrily, 'Look, mister, I don't know who you are or why you're so bothered about me but seeing as you're so interested I'll tell you. I've got a brother and sister at home depending on me to look after them, but I can't look after them any more because I can't find any work. We're cold and hungry and behind with the rent. If I don't pay it by tomorrow we'll be thrown out into the street, and from there it's only a short step to the workhouse.' Her chest heaving with anger, she glared at the well-dressed man who looked as if he'd never done a day's work in his life.

'But what would you know about being hungry and cold,' she carried on bitterly. 'You come here from your big houses to do a bit of slumming, and once you've had your fill you go back to your comfy beds with servants to wait on you hand and foot. People like you never have to worry about where the next meal is coming from, or if you'll have enough coal to keep you warm – you just take it all for granted. Well, some of us aren't that lucky, some of us have to sell whatever we can just to keep alive for one more day, and when there's nothing left to sell we end up in a place like this. So, now you know why I came here, only, only I changed my mind, I . . . I couldn't go through with it. I was about to leave the pub when those horrible women started on me, and then, just when I thought things couldn't get any worse, that man grabbed me. I tried to . . . to tell him I wasn't on the game, but he wouldn't listen to me.'

Her voice broke, and she would have fallen if Harry hadn't grabbed hold of her.

Fighting down the impulse to gather her into his arms he carefully held her away from him and said soothingly, 'I'm sorry, truly I am, but what's done is done. Now, please let me see you home safely, your family will be waiting for you.' Her body totally drained, Maggie allowed herself to be led from the alley and into the main road.

Minutes later she was sitting for the first time in a hansom cab, but the experience meant nothing to her. Her body rigid, she sat stiffly on the edge of the red leather seat, her eyes averted from the man sitting opposite her. Watching her, Harry wondered how much Hugh had paid the girl. Whatever the amount, it wasn't enough. Opening the flap of the wallet he held in his hand he extracted the four white five-pound notes and folded them in a small square. When the cab drew up outside the address she had given him, he alighted quickly and helped her down from the carriage.

'It's none of my business, but I hope you'll never find it necessary to visit The Black Swan again,' he said quietly. His gaze dropped to her tightly clenched fist and taking hold of her other hand he pressed the wad of notes into her palm together with a gold-printed card.

'This is my card. If ever you need a friend, please don't hesitate to call upon me.' The moment the words were out of his mouth he cursed himself for a fool. He didn't know the girl; for all he knew she could be the sort who would cause trouble – but he didn't think so. Also he felt in a way responsible for her, seeing it was his brother who had brought her to this pass. Bowing slightly from the waist he left her standing on the pavement and climbed back into the carriage.

Lord, what a night, and how he was going to face

Hugh knowing what he did he couldn't imagine. Closing his eyes wearily he tried to rest but the image of a pair of brown eyes kept floating in front of his eyelids. With an impatient 'tut' he sat upright and shook his head. The girl had made an impression on him, but now he must put her out of his mind. Their paths would never cross again; it had been mere chance that they had met tonight. The knowledge that he had seen the last of the girl should have been met with relief; so why then did he feel so despondent? All at once the prospect of an evening spent playing cards lost its appeal, and banging on the roof of the cab he ordered the cab driver to change direction and take him to the house in Bow.

CHAPTER NINE

Maggie stood and watched until the hansom cab disappeared from sight, then turning slowly she walked stiffly to the basement railings and leant against the black iron bars. Her initial shock had faded to be replaced by a feeling of lethargy and a curious sense of unreality. It was as if she had somehow climbed out of her body and was looking down at herself from a great height. She knew she should make an effort to move, but the cocoon her mind had created to block out the events of the evening was so comforting she was reluctant to break free from its grasp. The icy February wind swirled round her body, cutting through her clothes, and with an involuntary shiver she came back to her senses. As if coming out of a deep sleep she shuddered, wondering if she had imagined the whole thing. Then she felt the dull ache between her legs and the warmth of the coins in her palm and knew with shameful certainty that it had been no dream.

The card she held in her other hand was scratching her skin, and her first instinct was to throw it into the gutter along with the wad of paper that accompanied it. The man, whoever he was, was probably already regretting his rash impulse, but what was the wad of paper for? Maybe he had written her a love letter on the journey home. She gave a soft hiccup of a laugh and thrust the card and paper into her pocket, she couldn't be bothered to look at it now, all she wanted to do at the moment was to crawl into bed and try to lose all memory of the past hours in sleep. But she couldn't get into bed with Liz and Charlie, not now, not after what she'd done. She felt dirty, inside and out, she felt dirty. If only she could climb into a hot, soapy bath and stay there indefinitely, but no amount of scrubbing would ever make her feel clean again. Another shudder shook her body, and pulling her shawl tighter she reluctantly descended the basement stairs. Careful not to make any noise she crept across the darkened room towards the sofa but before she could reach her goal the sound of a match being struck brought her to a startled halt, the flickering light revealing Liz sitting in the armchair, her face set and accusing.

'Where the hell have you been?' she demanded. 'You've been gone for over two hours. What've you been up to?'

'L . . . Liz, what are you doing up. I . . . I thought you were asleep.' Maggie stuttered nervously as she frantically sought a plausible excuse for her absence.

'Never mind about me, I asked you a question,' Liz shot back sharply. The match she was holding went out, plunging the room once more into total darkness. Cursing softly she groped for the matchbox on the floor giving Maggie a few precious moments to compose herself. She heard Liz move from the chair and when the half-used candle on the mantelshelf spurted a weak flame she was ready with her story.

'I couldn't settle so I went for a walk, you know, to try and sort things out in my head. And . . . and while I was out, I asked in a couple of pubs to see if they needed any help. I didn't have any luck around here, so I went down to Whitechapel and I got set on for a couple of hours. One of the barmaids hadn't come into work and . . . and the landlord, he said I could stand in for her. Just for tonight, like. That's where I've been, and look, Liz, he paid me straight away, see . . .' Her whole body was trembling now as she stumbled over the lie, and without stopping to think she opened her shaking hand to show Liz the money.

Too late she realised her mistake, for there nestling in her palm lay three golden guineas. The shock at seeing such a vast amount knocked the wind from her body. Since the moment the money had been placed there, she had kept her hand tightly shut, not wanting to look at the price she'd paid for the degrading act she'd been forced to endure. A far corner of her mind had imagined the coins to be florins, or maybe half-crowns, but never guineas. In normal circumstances she would have recognised the contents of her hand simply by the feel of the coins, but the money hadn't been put there in normal circumstances. She felt the colour drain from her face and tried to close her hand, but she was too late.

'Liar,' Liz spat at her, her face working furiously. 'What do you take me for, Maggie? You stand there and tell me you've been working for a couple of hours in a pub in Whitechapel and expect me to believe you. The pneumonia may have left me weak, it didn't make me daft. For a start, it would have taken you nearly an hour just to get there and back, that's without the time spent asking in the other pubs for work, like you say you did. Now I know we don't have the clock any more so I can't be positive about the time, but I do know you haven't had time to do all you say you've been doing.'

'Liz, please listen to me . . .' Maggie pleaded desperately.

'Shut up, Maggie,' Liz hissed between clenched teeth. 'Just shut up until I've finished and then you can tell me where exactly this pub is, you know, the one that pays girls three guineas for supposedly two hours' work. Well! I'm waiting.' Liz glared at Maggie, her chest heaving with agitation at the look of fear and guilt that passed over her young sister's face. Then with an enraged cry she sprang forward, the sudden action causing Maggie to stagger back in alarm.

The raised voices penetrated Charlie's light slumber. Lifting himself up on to his elbows, he was about to call out to Maggie when an inner instinct warned him to remain silent. He was used to the sound of his sisters arguing and had no wish to be dragged into another fight. Putting his fingers tightly into his ears, he burrowed as far beneath the blanket as he could.

'You stole it, didn't you?' Lizzie's voice rose higher. 'There's no other way you could have got hold of money like that without thieving; or worse.'

Steadying herself on the arm of the sofa, Maggie felt a surge of relief rush through her body. Liz thought she had stolen the money, thank God. Well she wouldn't contradict her, she'd far rather be thought of as a thief than admit to the truth. Raising her head she returned Liz's wrathful gaze, but the look of hurt reflected in the thin face forced her to turn away.

Lord, what a mess she had landed herself in, and what a time for Liz to choose to return to the land of the living. For months now, Maggie had been praying for Liz to snap out of the apathetic state she'd wallowed in since her illness. Now she wished fervently that her sister had remained in the twilight world where she'd been living for so long. At least then she, Maggie, wouldn't have had to faced this barrage of questions that were being fired at her. Then again, if Liz had tried harder to get well, then she wouldn't have had to take to the streets in the first place.

Oh, hell! hell! hell! What was done was done. She

couldn't undo the events of the evening, and apportioning blame wasn't going to help either. She'd just have to brazen it out as best she could for now, and hope that Liz wouldn't continue to press her for details about the money. But that forlorn hope was quickly quashed.

'Well, I'm still waiting. I want to know everything you did tonight, and neither of us is getting any sleep until you tell me exactly what happened.'

'Give it a rest, Liz, please,' Maggie answered wearily. 'You know what happened, it's like you said, I stole it; happy now? So if you don't mind, I'd like to get some sleep, you can carry on where you left off in the morning.'

'Oh, no you don't, you're not getting off that easy,' Liz cried determinedly. Her arm shot out, her hand grabbing at the woollen shawl draped across Maggie's shoulders. Caught off guard, Maggie felt the protective covering pulled from her upper body. With a frantic effort she tried to hide her torn blouse with her hands, but the damage had already been done.

'My God, Maggie, what have you done?' Liz stood as if turned to stone, her voice dropping to a whisper as she watched Maggie valiantly try to pull the ripped pink material together. 'It's not what you think, Liz,' Maggie gabbled, her eyes wide with fear as she saw the look of horror cross Liz's face.

'Honest, I know what it looks like, but if you'll just let me ex . . .'

'You've been on the streets, haven't you? That's where you got the money from, you've gone on the game.'

The shawl dropped from her lifeless fingers as the full enormity of what her sister had done seared through her shocked mind. Mental images of Maggie and a faceless man floated before her eyes and she shook her head violently as if to clear the disgusting scenes from her mind. Then, her face filled with contempt and loathing she advanced upon the trembling figure.

'Liz, Liz, please, listen to me, it wasn't my fault. If you'll just li . . .' Maggie implored, her eyes widening as Liz's arm swept up towards her face.

'Whore!' The upstretched arm swung outwards, the back of the hand catching Maggie viciously across the face spinning her round and over the arm of the sofa head first onto the cold, hard floor. Maggie felt the world go black as her head collided with the stone floor, the impact jolting her entire body. The blackness lasted only a few seconds and when she gingerly opened her eyes, tiny specks of red spots seemed to be dancing in front of her. Through a mist of pain she thought ruefully that for someone supposedly too ill to work, Liz was surprisingly strong. She tried to lift her head and was rewarded for her effort by a sharp, excruciating pain knifing through her forehead.

'Come on, get up, I haven't finished with you yet.' Maggie felt hands tugging at her arm and weakly tried to pull away.

'Don't pretend you're hurt, you're going to get a lot more than that before I'm finished with you.' Liz muttered, her voice filled with righteous indignation.

It was the tone of moral outrage that penetrated Maggie's fogged brain, and the unjustice of Liz's behaviour acted like a spur to Maggie. The fear left her, to be replaced by a smouldering anger, and pushing away the groping hands she staggered to her feet. When she saw Liz raise her arm again she said evenly, 'Don't you dare touch me, Liz. Not now, not ever again, or I swear I'll do for you.' Her voice pitched dangerously low, she continued to hold Liz's gaze, but not until she saw the threatening arm lowered did she move to the settee. Dropping heavily onto the worn cushions she closed her eyes, the pain in her temples making her feel sick.

'Don't get too comfortable, 'cos you're not stopping here, not after what you've done, I just hope the neighbours never find out, that's all, I couldn't bear the shame.' Liz had gone back to stand by the mantelpiece, the flickering candle throwing her shadow onto the wall as she pulled at her fingers in agitation while keeping her eyes fixed firmly on the blackened iron bars surrounding the empty fire grate. When the soft laughter filled the silence she felt her back stiffen, and when the sound grew louder she turned her head warily in its direction.

'Oh, you're priceless, Liz, you really are.' Maggie sat on the edge of the settee, her elbows resting on her knees. 'In case you've forgotten, we're due to be evicted tomorrow, and then there won't be any neighbours to worry about, will there? Of course, we could always use the money I "earned" tonight, but I wouldn't insult you by suggesting that option. I mean, you'd rather be thrown out into the street than take dirty money, wouldn't you, Liz?' She saw the look of uncertainty cross Liz's face and felt the anger and hurt rise in her breast. She knew her sister well enough to know that now the first rush of anger had passed, she'd be weighing up the situation and wondering at what to do for her own best interest.

This was proved when Liz, licking her lips, blustered, 'Well, now you've disgraced yourself, we might as well make use of the money. I mean, there's no point in letting ourselves be thrown out when we can pay what's owing, is there?'

For a moment Maggie thought she was going to be sick. She'd known all along that Liz would take the money, but what really stuck in her throat was the blatant hypocrisy her sister had displayed. Her stomach churning with anger, her voice filled with anguish, she cried, 'You hypocrite, you bloody hypocrite, standing there so full of moral indignation, sitting in judgement on me when what happened tonight was partly your fault.'

'My fault! Now don't you try and shift the blame onto me, Maggie, I didn't force you onto the streets, you thought of that idea all by yourself,' Liz answered back uneasily. 'I didn't . . .'

'I didn't, I didn't, that's all you can say, and you're right, you didn't. You didn't bloody do anything, did you? You haven't done anything for the past two months except sit around pretending to be an invalid. If you'd got up off your arse and helped me look for work, I wouldn't have had to take to the streets in order to keep a roof over our heads and food in our bellies. Well, don't worry about being sullied by my presence. Come tomorrow I'm not waiting for Mr Bates to chuck us out – I'm leaving before he comes, and I'm taking Charlie with me.'

'Oh no you're not,' Liz shouted wildly. 'You're not fit to look after him, he's staying with me.'

'Why? So you can push him out to work for you, you lazy cow. You don't care for him any more than you do for me, you've proved that tonight. Anyway, he's old enough to decide for himself, but we both know who he'll choose given the chance, don't we?'

They stared at each other across the dimly lit room, each one knowing the situation had gotten out of their control but neither of them knowing how to get things back to normal.

The silence lengthened until Maggie, her voice bitter, said, 'You were so quick to judge, weren't you? You immediately thought the worst of me, even though I've never given you cause to. Well, I was telling the truth, believe it or not. It's true I went out intending to earn some money any way I could, but when it came down to it I lost my nerve. I was on my way home when it happened, but I wasn't to blame. A man grabbed me and forced me into an alley. I was raped, Liz, I didn't go on the game, I was raped, and it was the most terrible thing

141

that's ever happened to me, and . . . and it hurt . . . it hurt so bad . . .'

Liz could feel her heart racing, and a part of her urged her to go to Maggie and comfort her, but she couldn't. Ever since the death of their parents when they'd been forced down into this rathole, a slow anger had been burning inside her. An anger that had continued building at each new blow that life dealt them. The burden of knowing that Maggie and Charlie were dependent on the wage she brought home had weighed heavily on her mind. When Maggie had found a job, the onus of responsibility had been lifted from her, and for a while she'd imagined that they would someday be able to leave this place and go somewhere where they'd be happy again; be a family again. And then she'd fallen ill, and her whole world had once again been turned upside down. With both of them out of a job and the workhouse looming before them, she had made no effort to get better. Every day as she'd watched Maggie leave the basement in search of work, a feeling of guilt had attacked her, a feeling she had dampened down, telling herself that if Maggie couldn't find work there wasn't any point in her tramping the streets as well.

Then this evening, when Maggie had told her that they would be out on the street the next day, the anger had returned. It had lain inside her chest, smouldering quietly while she'd waited for Maggie to return home. And when she'd seen the money in the outstretched palm, and then the further evidence of the torn blouse, the guilt and anger had merged into one explosive, tearing emotion. The blow she had felled Maggie with hadn't been directed at her, but at life itself.

Liz knew Maggie was waiting for her to speak, to offer some words of comfort and understanding, but her own feeling of guilt prevented her from uttering the much-needed words. She needed to hit out, to inflict hurt on somebody, and who better than the girl sitting across the room? Her mouth curling cruelly, she heard the words leave her lips before she could stop them.

'That's a new one, I've never heard of a rapist paying for it before.'

The sneering words hit Maggie in the face, causing her as much pain as the blow had done. With a low scream she was across the room knocking Liz to the floor. Kicking and screaming, the two girls rolled back and forth, their fingers pulling unmercifully at each other's hair, both of them grateful to have found an outlet for their anger.

'Stop it, stop it, Liz, let go of Maggie, let go, stop it . . .!' Unable to keep quiet any longer, Charlie had leapt from his bed and run across the room. Now he danced around the thrashing figures, his terrified entreaties unheard above the screeching of the combatants locked in mortal battle.

'Give over, please, oh please,' he sobbed pitifully as his small hands tried futilely to prise the girls apart. Not knowing what else to do, he threw himself into the *mêlée*,

143

collecting a blow to his head for his troubles. His loud howl of pain acted like a bucket of cold water on the girls, as they stopped fighting to comfort the figure rolling on the floor.

'Oh, Charlie, oh you poor thing, are you all right?' Maggie cried anxiously, worried in case he was really hurt, yet grateful for an excuse to stop the fight.

'No, I ain't, my head hurts, one of you kicked me.' His doleful expression looked from one to the other, and both girls bowed their heads in shame. The three figures remained huddled close, none wanting to be the first to move. And when Liz moved her body slightly to ease the pressure on her leg, Maggie thought for moment she was going to start the fight again and raised her arms protectively. They were both trying not to cry, and when Liz put a tentative hand out Maggie grabbed at it grate-fully. Then they were in each other's arms, sobbing as they told each other how sorry they were, stumbling over their words in an effort to make things right between them again. Squashed between them lay a bemused Charlie, forgotten for the moment as his sisters tried to bury their differences.

Maggie was the first to rise, holding out her hand to Liz to help her from the floor. Charlie peered up at the two figures, wondering what this row had been over. It must have been a bad one as they'd never come to blows before.

'Upsadaisy, Charlie,' Maggie said, her voice trembling with relief. Then, turning to Liz, she asked tremulously,

'How about if we go out and get some food, and maybe a bit of wood to build a fire?'

Liz looked at her in surprise, then sniffing loudly she said, 'What, now, at this time of night?'

'Why not?' Maggie replied shakily. 'We could get some pies and peas from outside The George. The stall never closes until the pub empties, and old Fred sleeps with his barrow of firewood.'

The thought of hot food and a blazing fire won over Liz's reservations at setting out at such a late hour.

'Well, all right then.' Her voice still held a tremor as she wrapped her shawl around her shoulders.

When they were ready, they stood by the door smiling wanly at each other. Promising Charlie they wouldn't be long, they set off before he could make any protest at being left on his own.

'This man, you know, the one that brought you home, what's he like?'

They were sitting in front of a roaring fire, the hot pies and peas resting comfortably in their stomachs. Charlie had been put back to bed with a happy smile on his face, and now the girls sat curled up at either end of the sofa ready to talk. Resting her elbow on the arm of the sofa, Maggie cupped the side of her face in her hand as she pondered the question. She could see him clearly in her mind as they'd stood under the gas lamp, but how could she describe him to Liz? Could she tell her about the way his dark, wavy hair curled out from beneath his shiny black hat, hair that sat above a face that was neither handsome or ugly. Or maybe she could attempt to describe his eyes, those deep blue eyes that had gazed down at her, their look filled with compassion and concern. No; she could say none of these things to Liz, they were her memories, memories she wanted to keep to herself for reasons she couldn't fully understand. Yet she had to give some kind of answer.

So, speaking softly, she replied, 'He was kind to me. I don't know why he stopped to help me, not a gentleman like him, but he did, and I didn't even thank him. I thought he was after something, like the . . . the other one, and I was rude to him, and suspicious. But he never even tried to touch me, not even when we were alone in the cab. And then when we got here, he helped me down and told me if ever I needed help to get in touch with him. Not that I would, of course, but it was nice of him to say it.'

'Well, it's easy enough to say, isn't it?' Liz said lazily. 'I mean, he was safe enough telling you that seeing as you wouldn't be able to find him again anyway.'

'Oh, no, you're wrong there, Liz, he gave me his card,' Maggie said, quickly jumping to the unknown man's defence. 'He's probably wishing he hadn't now, but he wouldn't have given it to me if he hadn't meant what he said at the time, would he?'

Liz swivelled round to face her, her eyes wide with disbelief. 'He gave you his card? You must be joking, Maggie. Either that or he was making fun of you – let's have a look at it.'

For a moment, Maggie toyed with the idea of pretending she'd thrown it away, but her own curiosity and a desire to prove Liz wrong overcame her misgivings. Moving her legs to one side, she delved deep into her pocket, her fingers closing around the stiff card. For a brief second she held onto it, then with a triumphant gesture she handed it over to Liz.

'There, have a look if you don't believe me.'

Liz took the card, then leaning forward on her knees she held it out towards the fire to see it better.

Her eyes scanned the gold lettering quickly, then turning to look at Maggie she said blithely, 'How do you know it's his? This could belong to anybody, I wouldn't set much stock by it if I were you.'

Putting her hand out, Maggie snatched it back angrily.

'It is his, I'm sure of it, and that's not all, he gave me something else as well.' Plunging her hand back into her pocket she searched for the wad of paper and felt a moment's panic when she couldn't find it. Standing up swiftly she dug deeper then sighed with relief as her fingers found what she was searching for.

'I forgot about that hole in my pocket. Here it is. I think it's a note of some sort, although what cou . . .' She broke off, her face screwing up in puzzlement as she unfolded the crinkly paper. Then, as she realised what she was holding in her hand she sank back onto the sofa, her mouth opening and closing in bewilderment.

'What is it? What does it say?' Liz edged closer, her

eyes widening at the sight of the five-pound notes now in Maggie's lap.

'Oh, my God,' she whispered breathlessly. 'Are they real? I've never seen a five-pound note before.' Then, her voice changing she added sharply, 'Are you sure you've told me everything, Maggie? Men don't go round giving fivers away for nothing.'

The accusing tone brought Maggie out of her reverie. 'I didn't do anything, Liz, I've told you the truth,' she cried desperately. 'Please believe me, I didn't do anything.'

Picking up the notes Liz stared down at them, her face filled with awe. 'There's twenty pounds here; Lord Almighty, twenty pounds.' She turned to Maggie and seeing the stricken look on the pale face she smiled reassuringly, 'Don't worry, I believe you. You'd have had to sleep with the entire Household Cavalry to earn this kind of money, and you weren't gone that long.'

'It's not funny, Liz.' Maggie twisted her fingers nervously. 'Why would he give me twenty pounds? It must be a mistake, there's no other explanation, I'll have to take it back.'

'Are you mad?' Liz jumped from the sofa, the money held firmly in her hand. 'Think, Maggie, think. With this we can get out of here and live comfortably for months, maybe longer. And what if you go to his house, who's to say you won't be accused of stealing it? And anyway, he can afford it. People like that spend money like water; he won't miss it, but it's a fortune to the likes of us. Come on, Maggie, be sensible.'

Wetting her lips Maggie looked into the animated face then quickly turned away. She had been struck across the face and called a whore for the sake of three guineas, and she still wasn't quite sure Liz believed her. Now, with so much money at stake, she didn't think Liz would really care where it had come from, or how it had been earned.

The pie and peas she'd eaten earlier rose in her throat and gulping noisily she stuttered, 'But how can we spend them? People round here aren't used to taking five-pound notes, they'll ask questions.'

Her face relaxing Liz carefully folded the notes into a small square before tucking them into the inside of her boot.

'Don't you worry about that, I'll see to it.' She was all solicitude now. 'I'll get a tram up to the West End and change them up in the shops, they're used to handling this kind of money.'

Bustling round excitedly she suddenly cried, 'Eh, and we went out with all that money in your pocket. It's lucky that hole wasn't any bigger – you could have dropped it and never known what you'd lost.'

Maggie leaned back against the sofa as she listened to Liz drone on. She knew only too well what she'd lost this night, but Liz had forgotten about her ordeal, so intent was she on their new-found wealth. Closing her eyes she conjured up the man's image in her mind and silently she asked, Why, why, why?

CHAPTER TEN

The August sun beat down as the two figures pushed their wooden cart over the cobbled pavement, careful not to collide with the oncoming pedestrians that surged around them on the narrow pathway. Maggie, dressed in a red-checked cotton dress, held onto the side of the cart to balance it, while Charlie, gripping the wooden handles, steered the ramshackle vehicle expertly through the crowd.

'How many more houses are we going to, Maggie?' he panted heavily, the sweat running in rivulets down his red face.

'Just a few more, love,' Maggie answered cheerfully, her free hand pulling down the brim of her wide straw hat. 'We've hardly collected anything this morning so far. Look, tell you what, when we get to the bottom of the road, you know, where that little park is, I'll look after the cart while you go and get something to eat from the pie shop, and maybe some lemonade, if you can carry it all without dropping anything.'

The promise of food and drink acted like a spur to Charlie. With a whoop of delight he grabbed the handles tighter and broke into a run, leaving Maggie to hold onto the cart as best she could as the wooden wheels bounced over the cobbles at an alarming speed. When they reached the iron benches surrounding the park, Maggie took the two tin mugs that were hanging on the side of the cart and handed them to the waiting Charlie.

'Now, don't fill them to the brim like you normally do – you only lose half of it on the way back.'

'All right, Maggie.' Charlie grinned at her while holding his hand out for the money.

Maggie looked at him, smiling fondly. He now almost reached her shoulder, and in his navy, ribbed sleeveless jersey and flat cap, he looked every inch a barrow boy. Reaching into her pocket she extracted a florin.

'Thanks, Maggie. I won't be long,' he said cheerfully, taking the silver coin and putting it into the pocket of his long, grey trousers. With a wave of his hand he set off at a run.

Making sure the cart was lodged firmly against the black iron railings, Maggie sat down on a bench giving a sigh of contentment at the feel of the warm sun seeping through her thin clothing. Behind her she could hear the sounds of children laughing as they ran along the narrow pathway to the small pond, their home-made boats held tightly in sweaty palms, eager to try out their new toys. Mixed with their laughter was the piercing wail of a fretful baby, its plaintive cries filling the air despite the fact that the pram it was lying in was being rocked violently by a tired, harrassed mother.

The sound attracted Maggie's attention and, turning her head slightly, she peered through the wrought-iron railing and smiled in sympathy at the young woman. Poor cow, she thought idly, rather her than me. Three youths ran past her shouting and punching each other, playfully leaving in their wake crumpled up grease-stained newspaper that had contained their dinner. Maggie glared after them, then blowing out her cheeks she stooped down to retrieve the litter they had left behind.

Depositing the rubbish in a nearby bin she strolled back to the park gate and let her gaze wander over the enclosed area. It had originally been planned for the people living in the surrounding square, but over the years had attracted more and more people looking for somewhere to rest during their lunch breaks, or simply parents who brought their children here for picnics, seeing it as a cheap way to spend a day out. Maggie looked on enviously at the figures sprawled out on the inviting lawn, wishing she could join them. Shrugging her shoulders she walked back to the bench, her mind busy.

They had done the Aldgate rounds and were now in

Dalston. After they had finished their dinner she planned to walk up to Bow before making her way back home. Hopefully they would be more successful there than they had been this morning.

Tilting her head back slightly she lifted her face to the sky and closed her eyes. She loved the summer, somehow life always seemed to be brighter when the sun was shining, especially when she was in, or near a park. The smell of newly cut grass and blossoming flowers never failed to lift her spirits, no matter how down she was feeling. Not that she had any cause for complaint these days. It was over two years now since she had taken that fateful walk in a last-ditch attempt to save herself and her small family from the workhouse; she had succeeded in her effort, succeeded beyond her wildest dreams.

That night had marked the beginning of a whole new way of life for her, Lizzie and Charlie. For weeks afterwards though, she had suffered the torment of the damned, fearful lest she may have picked up some dreadful disease or found herself pregnant. It was only when she finally realised that neither of these fates had befallen her that she had begun to take an interest in life again. It was Lizzie who had moved them out of the basement and into the two rooms they now occupied just a few minutes walk away from their old home, and it was Lizzie who had thought of setting up a stall in the market selling second-hand clothes. Yet true to form, Liz had opted to run the stall while Maggie and Charlie made the rounds of the big houses in search of cast-offs from the gentry. Maggie had made no objection to the arrangement. She had her own private reasons for wanting an excuse to keep returning to a certain house in Hackney. Although the gold-printed card had long since been destroyed, the memory of the name and address had remained firmly in her mind. Not that she went there too often; as Liz had pointed out, even the toffs with all their money didn't throw out clothing on a weekly basis. Heedful of Liz's words, Maggie had carefully spaced out her visits to once every six weeks; although she had so far not caught as much as a glimpse of her benefactor, she had managed to make friends with Mrs Sheldon, the cook, and the two young housemaids, Gertie and Annie.

With skilful, gentle probing, Maggie had soon learned all about the members of the Stewart family. Her first instinct on learning that the head of the household was a judge had been one of panic, and it had taken all of her courage not to take to her heels and flee from the house. Then common sense had prevailed as she'd silently berated herself for a fool. Even if Harry Stewart had confided in his father, which given the circumstances was highly unlikely, she had been the victim, and that being the case she had nothing to fear from the Law. Even so, she had let two months elapse before returning to the house.

Now sixteen months later, she felt as if she knew each one of the Stewart family personally. She'd heard all about the youngest son who had astounded everyone by becoming a doctor, and the spinster daughter who was disliked both above and below stairs, but it was only when the talk turned to Harry Stewart that she gave her full attention, her mind devouring every word to be stored away in her memory and recounted to herself at night when she lay unable to sleep in the double bed she shared with Lizzie.

''Ello, darlin', want some company?' Her eyes flew open, then narrowed in distaste at the sight of the shabbily dressed man who was inching his way along the bench towards her, a leering grin on his unshaven face.

Not wanting to make a scene, Maggie moved away, saying quietly, 'Please go away, I'm waiting for a gentleman friend.'

'Well now, girlie, I've been watching you a while now and I don't fink your gentleman friend is coming, so how's about you and me take a little walk, eh?'

The smell from his unwashed body assailed her nostrils and turning her head away she looked desperately down the road to see if Charlie was coming. The man saw the look and edged closer.

' 'E ain't gonna turn up, darlin'. Look, how'd you like ter come back to my place for a while? You won't regret it, I can promise you that.' He grinned, his hand grasping the top of her leg.

Knowing that polite reasoning would be a waste of time, Maggie looked first at the offending hand, then lifting her eyes to his, she said icily. 'How would you like a kick in the balls?'

The man jumped back quickly, his hand falling to his side. He was about to speak again, but the cold look in the girl's blue eyes and the sight of the small hands bunched into fists stopped him. Getting to his feet he looked down at her for a moment, then spat at her feet, growling 'slag' before slouching off towards the park. Maggie watched him go with relief. She was used to being accosted when on her own, but it never failed to make her angry. Why couldn't a woman go out on her own without being pestered by some man, and why was there never a bobby around at such times? Shaking her head slightly she wondered how Liz would fare out on the streets, but she'd have to go on wondering, for her sister had made sure from the start that she would be safely installed behind the wooden bench piled high with clothes in the market, surrounded by hefty stall-holders ready to see off any trouble makers. Oh, yes, her sister was no fool.

During the first few weeks of their new venture it had been decided that Maggie would take the cart out on a Wednesday, and on Saturdays Charlie would accompany her and keep a watchful eye on the cart while she completed her business inside the houses. Of course whatever items the owners had discarded would have been checked over first by the staff, and anything they didn't want would then be sold to people like herself who made a living from cast-off clothing.

Maggie had felt awkward and embarrassed at first, knocking on strange doors and asking if they had anything to sell, but she was used to it now. She also enjoyed her days spent running the stall with Liz, and had become quite expert at bargaining with potential customers, all of whom seemed determined to get themselves a bargain at the expense of the two young women. Maggie had been surprised at how easily Liz had slipped into her new occupation. Within a month of setting up their stall in Bethnal Green Road, Liz had been haggling and shouting her wares with the rest of the stallholders. More important still, they now had a comfortable nest-egg carefully hidden in an iron box beneath a loose floorboard in the scullery, ensuring a secure future.

There were only two things that worried Maggie now. The first was to give back the twenty pounds to Harold Stewart; how she was going to accomplish this she didn't know, but she wouldn't rest until she'd returned the money that had enabled them to start a new life. The second worry was Jimmy Simms. Their old neighbour's son had returned from sea over eight months ago, and upon learning of his father's death had decided to stay ashore for good. Mrs Simms had brought him round on one of her frequent visits, her pride in her tall, blond son oozing from every pore, but Maggie had taken an instant dislike to the young man. Why, she didn't know – there was just something about him that made her move away whenever he came close to her. Liz, on the other hand, couldn't get enough of his company, openly flirting with him at every given opportunity. Her coy antics made

Maggie and Charlie cringe with embarrassment. It was only the long-standing friendship between them and Mrs Simms that prevented her from making her feelings known. She owed the kindly woman too much to take the chance of hurting her in any way, not only for the way she had helped them when they were down on their luck, but also because she had never asked any questions about their new-found wealth even though she must have been dying of curiosity.

Pulling her hat down further over her eyes she gave a deep sigh. She could only wait and hope that Jimmy Simms would tire of his visits and take his attentions elsewhere. The moment the thought entered her head she felt ashamed. Liz obviously liked him and would be bitterly upset if he stopped coming round.

'You'll just have to lump it, my girl,' she told herself silently. 'It's as much Lizzie's home as it is yours. Stop being selfish, and think yourself fortunate things turned out so well for all of us, because there are plenty of young women who haven't been so lucky; like poor Teresa Deere.'

Her mood became sombre as she recalled the unfortunate wretch that had worked alongside Liz at the matchbox factory. Neither herself nor Liz had given the young girl much thought after the night she had brought news of Lizzie's dismissal. After all, it wasn't as if she had been a close friend, and they'd had enough troubles of their own to occupy their minds. Then, about a year ago, another woman who had worked at the factory had stopped by the stall, and, upon recognising Liz had promptly brought her up to date with all the news of her former workmates. The woman had stayed chatting for over an hour. Despite her fulsome praise for Lizzie's new lifestyle, she had been unable to hide her envy, much to the delight of Liz, who already saw herself as a cut above her old friend.

As the woman had made to leave them, she had added by way of an afterthought. 'By the way, did you hear about poor Teresa? Got the phossy jaw she did, poor little cow, and copped a bellyful from her dad, the dirty old bastard; well it was either 'im or one of those brothers of 'er's, 'cos she never 'ad time for any boyfriends.' With that she had waved and disappeared into the crowd. Maggie had been appalled, but Liz, who should have been more affected by the news, hadn't seemed unduly upset. But then loyalty had never been one of her sister's strong points. Out of sight, out of mind, was Lizzie's motto, especially if the person concerned might need some help or a sympathetic shoulder to cry on. A friend to Liz was someone to have a laugh and a night out with. As soon as they found themselves in trouble she dumped them as quick as possible. But this time Maggie had refused to let her sister take the easy way out. It had been simple enough to find out where the young girl lived. Carrying a basket of food between them, they had made their way to the run-down tenement in Whitechapel, with Liz moaning every step of the way.

Once inside the evil-smelling building even Maggie

had had second thoughts. She had thought her old home in the basement had been bad, but compared to the rat-infested building with its walls running alive with cockroaches, they had been living in luxury. Spurred on by an inner strength, she had ignored Lizzie's protests and after knocking on several doors had finally found Teresa's home . . . home! She gave a mirthless laugh. God, but she would never forget the sights that had met her eyes. Ushered into the filthy room by an equally filthy woman they assumed was Teresa's mother, they had stood warily, intimidated by the leering looks of the three drunken men sitting on upturned boxes by an empty fire grate.

Marshalling all of her courage, Maggie had asked to see Teresa and when the eldest of the men, presumably the father, had jerked his head towards the farthest corner of the room, she had tightened her grip on Lizzie's hand, pulling her over to a pile of dirt-encrusted, thread-bare blankets. Even though Maggie had steeled herself to expect the worst, she was unprepared for the sight of Teresa's horribly disfigured face. The young girl's eyes were dulled with pain and showed no sign of recognition. Beneath the motley assortment of blankets her swollen stomach was clearly evident, and it took all of Maggie's will power to stop her from screaming abuse at the grinning men watching their every move.

To compare them to animals would have been an insult to the animal kingdom. How could any man commit such an act with their own flesh and blood? And according to Liz it had been going on since Teresa was little more than a child. And what of the mother who had allowed this to happen? To Maggie's way of thinking the woman was more repulsive than the men. She had shown more interest in the basket of food than the terrible plight of her daughter. Even now Maggie couldn't remember leaving the squalid room, what she could remember was holding Lizzie's head as she had thrown up her breakfast in a quiet alley, while struggling to retain her own.

All the way home, Liz had held onto Maggie's arm saying over and over again. 'It could have been me . . . it could have been me,' referring to the phossy jaw, but not once had she mentioned Teresa's pregnancy. Once over the initial shock, Maggie had intended to go back to the tenement and offer what little comfort she could but even her considerable strength of character hadn't been sufficient to enable her to make the journey again. Now Teresa was dead, buried in a pauper's grave along with the child she had died giving birth to. She hadn't had a chance, for if she had survived the birth she would have died as a result of the phossy jaw. She had been just sixteen years old.

Tears of recrimination stung Maggie's eyes. Here she was thinking herself badly off just because Liz had found a boyfriend that she herself couldn't stand the sight of. Shaking her head she sat up straighter on the bench, telling herself to count her blessings. As her Mum used to say, 'You don't know when you're well off'.

A bee flew past her ear making her start and without stopping to think she lashed out at it. When she felt the sharp pain in her hand she jumped to her feet in alarm. 'Oh, sod it, the bloody thing's stung me.' Her angry cries caught the attention of the passers-by who smiled in amusement at the young girl's evident discomfort. Ignoring their presence she peered down at her hand wondering what to do; she'd never been stung before, but she knew she'd have to get the sting out of her palm. The sharp pain had subsided, and she glanced quickly down the street to see if Charlie was anywhere in sight. He might know what to do, but there was no sign of him.

'Damn and blast, Charlie, what's taking you so long?' she muttered under her breath. Sitting back down on the bench she again looked at her palm and the small black sting protruding from the inflamed skin. Just as she was about to go in search of her brother she became aware of someone standing beside her.

'May I be of any assistance?' a deep, cultured voice asked. Peering up from under her straw hat she saw the tall figure of a man bending over her.

Screwing up her eyes against the glare of the sun she answered quickly, 'Oh, no thank you, sir, it's just a bee sting, my brother will be back soon, he'll get it out for me.'

'Well now, it just so happens I'm an expert at removing stings. If you'll allow me?'

Without giving her the chance to answer he sat down

and taking hold of her hand he deftly removed the offending object.

'There, that wasn't so bad, was it?' he asked, while wrapping a white handkerchief around her palm.

'It will probably swell up, they normally do. When you get home, soak it in cold water – that usually does the trick.'

During the delicate operation Maggie had kept her eyes firmly on her hand, now, remembering her manners she started to thank the stranger.

'Thank you, sir, it was very kind of . . . Oh, my God, it's you!' she exclaimed fearfully as she looked into the face that had been haunting her dreams for the past two years.

'Please, don't be afraid, I mean you no harm,' Harry said earnestly, anxious to dispel the look of fear from the girl's face. Pulling her hand free, Maggie inched her way along the bench, her eyes never leaving Harry's face.

'That's what you said to me that night,' she whispered, her bandaged hand gripping the front of her dress.

'I remember.' Harry's voice was gentle. 'And I kept my word, didn't I? I never harmed you then, and I'm not going to harm you now. Won't you trust me, please?'

He had moved closer to her and this time Maggie didn't draw away. She had dreamt of this moment hundreds of times, and had rehearsed what she would say to him if ever they came face to face again. But that had been in the comfortable world of make believe where she could let fly with her imagination. This was reality, and for the life of her she couldn't think of a thing to say.

'Won't you even tell me your name?' Harry was speaking again. Looking into the kind blue eyes, Maggie answered shakily, 'Ma . . . Maggie, sir. Maggie Paige.'

'Maggie,' he repeated softly. 'It's a nice name, and it suits you perfectly. My name is Harry. Now that we've dispensed with the formalities maybe you can tell me what you've been doing since we last met.'

The banal remark caused Maggie's lower lip to drop in amazement. Anybody listening would think their last encounter had been a tea-party instead of a dark, filthy alleyway. Now that the initial shock at seeing him had passed, Maggie could feel her composure returning, and with it her courage.

Drawing her shoulders back she stared him straight in the eyes and said quietly, 'You mean since the night you found me sprawled in an alley after being raped?' The brutal words made Harry flinch, followed swiftly by a growing admiration for the girl seated beside him. Here was someone who wasn't afraid to face up to the truth, however unpleasant it may be. When he had first seen her sitting on the bench he had been unsure if it was the same girl he had aided that night. He had stood on the opposite side of the street trying to make up his mind whether to approach her when she'd jumped from the bench in obvious distress. Without stopping to think he had once again come to her aid. Knowing that small talk would only aggravate her further he decided to be frank.

Inclining his head towards her he said, 'You are very direct, Miss Paige, and yes, that is what I meant, although I would never have had the courage to put it so bluntly.'

Hearing the obvious sincerity in his voice Maggie bowed her head in confusion, then swallowing noisily she began to tell him about her new livelihood. He listened intently, his head nodding from time to time, and when she had finished her story he smiled warmly.

'That's splendid, Miss Paige, simply splendid. You know, I've often thought about you and wondered how you were faring. Now I see that my first impressions of you were accurate. You're a fighter, Miss Paige. You also possess a rare honesty that is refreshing to find in one so young. I'm delighted that things have worked out so well for you and your family.'

'Thank you, sir,' Maggie murmured, while her mind shouted at her to say something interesting instead of sitting like a stuffed dummy.

When he reached into his waistcoat pocket and extracted a gold watch, she said quickly, 'Please don't let me keep you from your business, sir. You must have been on your way somewhere before you stopped to help me.'

Harry looked up at the flushed face, and anxious to put her at her ease he replied, 'Actually, I'm supposed to be meeting my brother and sister here. It's my sister's birthday, you see, and my brother and I are taking her to the Cafe Royal in Regent Street to celebrate,' he said by way of explanation. He omitted the fact that he had tried his level best to get out of the afternoon excursion, without success.

Knowing that at any moment Charlie would be back, the question that had been tormenting her for over two years hovered on her tongue.

Then without any preamble she burst out suddenly, 'Why did you help me that night? I was nothing to you, and people of your class don't normally have anything to do with the likes of me. And why did you give me all that money? Not that I'm not grateful, because without it we could have ended up in the workhouse, but I still want to know why.'

Harry shifted uncomfortably on the bench, wondering how best to answer. He couldn't very well tell her the origin of the money he had so generously handed over, yet he owed her some kind of explanation. And so, lifting his shoulders slightly he answered simply, 'I wanted to help you. As for the money . . .' Again he shrugged. 'I have more than enough, but I very rarely have the opportunity to put it to good use.'

Unable to meet his gaze, Maggie glanced over her shoulder and felt her body slump with relief at the sight of Charlie hurrying towards them. Harry followed her gaze and realising that the running figure was the brother, rose to his feet.

Bowing from the waist he took hold of her bandaged hand and said, 'I'm glad we had this opportunity to talk,

Miss Paige, and at the risk of repeating myself from our first meeting, if you ever need my help, please don't hesitate to contact me.'

'But the money,' Maggie stammered, 'I want to return it. I always looked upon it as a loan. I never intended to keep it.'

Now it was Harry's turn to look amazed. He knew better than most of his class just how much twenty pounds would mean to someone like Maggie, yet here she was offering to give back what must seem a fortune to her. The enormity of the gesture made him feel very humble.

'I see you are a woman of principle, Miss Paige and I respect that, but please believe me when I say that you would be doing me a great service if you looked upon the money as a gift.'

'You all right, Maggie?' Charlie had appeared by the bench, his face set beneath the flat cap he always wore. Hampered as he was by the newspaper-wrapped parcel from which emanated an appetizing smell, and the two tin mugs filled with lemonade, he nevertheless assumed a menacing stance, ready to forfeit his dinner if need be to rush to his sister's defence.

Harry saw the threatening gesture of the boy, who couldn't have been more than ten or eleven, and fought down the impulse to smile. Clearly the Paige family were a force to be reckoned with. Placing his high hat back on his head, he once again bowed to Maggie.

'I see your luncheon has arrived, so I'll bid you good

day, Miss Paige, and you too, young sir. I hope we'll meet again in the not too distant future.'

Slightly mollified by the stranger's friendly manner, Charlie relaxed somewhat, his eyes darting from Maggie to the tall, well-dressed man as if seeking an explanation.

'What on earth kept you so long, Charlie?' Maggie's voice was unusually high, 'I thought you'd got lost.'

'It wasn't my fault, Maggie,' Charlie answered defensively. 'There was a queue, and when it got to my turn I had to wait for the next lot out of the oven.'

Harry turned to leave, and seeing him about to walk off, Maggie said quickly, 'I won't be a minute, Charlie. You start on your dinner.'

Looking to where Harry stood waiting, she said, 'Would you mind if I walked with you, Mr Stewart? There is something I'd like to discuss with you.' Without waiting for him to answer she fell into step beside him; when she was certain they were out of earshot she spoke again.

'I can't possibly accept your kind offer, but at the same time I can't afford to pay the money back all at once. Would it be all right if I sent you, say five pounds now and the rest at regular intervals?'

'My dear, Miss Paige, I've already told you . . .'

'Yes, I know what you told me,' Maggie interrupted, 'and I told you I couldn't keep it. To be perfectly honest, I could pay it all back now, but I don't think my sister would be very pleased if I raided our nest-egg.'

Harry gazed down at her earnest face and felt his

heartbeat quicken. Lord, she was pretty; it was a shame she was also highly principled, else he might have been tempted to . . . No, no, put that idea out of your head, Harry boy, he told himself sternly, she deserves better than a quick tumble. She had moved closer to his side and he quickly stepped back a pace, his hands clasped tightly behind his back. 'If you are determined to return the money I won't insult you by refusing.' His voice sounded hoarse, and he had to clear his throat before continuing. 'However, five pounds seems a great deal, so shall we say a pound a week until the debt is cleared?' Maggie nodded her head, glad that the matter had been settled.

'I have your address. I'll send you the first payment on Monday, and sir,' she wet her lips nervously, 'can I just say again how grateful I am for all your kindness, and that goes for my brother and sister.'

'Tell me,' he asked, nodding in the direction of where Charlie was now seated on the bench, his watchful eyes on the couple, 'does your brother know . . .'

'Oh, no, sir,' Maggie cried, horrified at the thought. 'He was only nine when it happened. We told him, that is, my sister and I told him, that we had found jobs. We pretended to be at work while he was at school, and then after a couple of weeks, we told him we had saved enough to buy a stall. He didn't ask any questions. As I said, he was only nine at the time.'

'And your sister, what does she have to say about returning the twenty pounds?'

A smile flitted across Maggie's face as she remembered the arguments they'd had every time the subject was mentioned.

'She thinks I'm barmy, sir,' she replied, her voice filled with laughter.

The sight of Maggie's smiling face nearly proved to be Harry's undoing. The temptation to reach out and pull her into his arms was becoming unbearable. Gripping his hands even tighter he returned her smile.

'I have to say I'm inclined to agree with her, Miss Paige, Ah, I believe my errant brother and sister have arrived at last,' he said, glancing over her shoulder. 'Shall we say the same time next week? I think it would be wiser if we conducted our business in private rather than trust in the mail service. Good day to you, Miss Paige.'

'Oh, but, sir, wait a . . .' Maggie cried in bewilderment, but he had already joined the approaching couple, leaving her no choice but to return to the bench where Charlie was waiting anxiously for her.

'Who was that, Maggie?' Charlie asked, his mouth crammed with pastry.

'I don't know his name,' she lied. 'I got stung by a bee, and he helped me get the sting out, that's all.'

'You looked friendly to me.'

'Well we're not,' she snapped irritably, taking the warm parcel from Charlie's lap. The sight of the golden pies and mushy peas caused her stomach to lurch and with an impatient sigh she passed them back. 'Here you can have mine. I'm not hungry.'

'Ain't you feeling well, Maggie? We can always go home if you like,' Charlie said hopefully.

Was she feeling well? No, she wasn't. Her legs felt like jelly and her heart was beating so fast she was sure Charlie must hear it. But she couldn't afford the luxury of rest – she had a living to earn.

'Eat up, Charlie. We've still got another few hours of work to do,' she replied, her eyes staring after the retreating trio.

'Really, Harry, we are all painfully aware of your empathy with the common people, but must you mix with them in public? What if someone had seen you?' Bella was saying, her voice pettish.

'Why, then I would have introduced them to the lady in question,' Harry replied lazily. 'I'm sure they would have been as charmed by her as I was.'

'Oh, you're impossible, Harry, but I refuse to let you spoil my day, after all it is my birthday, don't forget.'

Harry's eyes flickered briefly over his sister, his mind trying to visualise how Maggie would look in the square-necked, blue silk dress Bella was wearing. It was a beautiful creation, and had looked delightful laid out in the cardboard box it had arrived in. Sadly, as soon as Bella had donned it, the dress seemed to have lost interest.

'I haven't forgotten, Bella, else I wouldn't be here now,' he said heavily. Then, unable to resist the temptation to torment his sister further, he added, smiling. 'It's your thirty-fourth, isn't it?'

'No it isn't,' Bella snapped back angrily. 'I'm thirty-two, as you well know, you spiteful swine.' The small hands encased in white lace gloves spun the handle of her parasol round violently, her thin lips pursed into a tight line of anger.

'Careful, Bella, if you twirl that parasol any harder it'll take off.'

'Bugger you!' The words were spat at him, then turning sharply on her heel she marched off, her back stiff with outrage at the sound of Harry's loud laughter following her.

'I say, Harry, there was no need for that.' Hugh was standing in front of him, his face filled with discomfort. 'She is our sister after all, and you could make an effort to be nice to her, even if it is only for one day.'

The sound of misery in his brother's voice curbed Harry's mirth, and it was with a mixture of pity and exasperation that he turned his attention to the figure by his side. Poor Hugh; always willing to put up with anything rather than risk confrontation. How he managed at the hospital, heaven only knew. Yet by all accounts, his brother was very adept in his profession. Harry could only assume that when Hugh donned the mantle of 'Doctor' that he also took on a different personality.

Shaking his head he said soberly, 'I know, Hugh, I know, but I can't seem to help myself where Bella's concerned. She's such a self-opinionated little snob, and vindictive to boot. I'm afraid she brings out the worst in me. I only came today because Mother asked me to, but that doesn't mean I have to enjoy myself.'

Bella had been joined at the corner by two women friends, her face now wreathed in smiles as she engaged in a few minutes of pleasurable gossip. There was no trace now of the surly demeanour she had displayed only moments earlier.

'Cheer up, old man,' Harry said cheerfully to the forlorn looking face. 'I promise to be on my best behaviour for the rest of the day.'

Hugh shuffled uncomfortably before blurting out. 'You think I'm a poor stick, don't you, Harry? I mean the way I'll put up with anything for the sake of a bit of peace. I wish to God I was more like you, but I'm not and never will be.' Looking into his brother's self-assured face he added miserably, 'You know what's worse than having nobody like you? No, of course you don't. Well I'll tell you. It's not liking yourself, and I don't like myself, Harry, I don't like myself at all.' Seeing that Harry was about to protest he held up his hand.

'No, don't say anything, Harry, I know what I'm talking about. I did something a long time ago that I've never been able to forget, and seeing you talking to that young girl brought back painful memories I've been trying to bury ever since.'

Harry looked at Hugh sharply, 'Do you know that girl, Hugh?' he demanded.

Hugh looked up in surprise.

'No, I've never seen her before, but I once knew

173

someone just like her. Maybe I'll tell you about it one day, because you know, Harry, if there's one person in this world I could talk to, it's you.'

The look on Hugh's face came near to hero worship and Harry lowered his eyes as a strong feeling of shame washed over him. When he had returned home that night he had gone to Hugh's room, fully intending to throw the wallet in his face and wait for his reaction. But when he'd entered the room and found his brother sitting on the bed, his face a picture of misery and guilt, he had changed his mind. Startled by his brother's entry, Hugh had stammered something about having had his pocket picked while out with his friends, in an effort to explain his distraught attitude. Pretending to accept his story, Harry had mumbled something about informing the police in the morning and quickly left the room. The wallet was now lying hidden beneath a pile of Harry's undergarments. He knew he should have thrown it away, but for some reason he was loath to part with it.

'Hugh, Harry, coo'ee,' Bella called out, her voice sounding happy for the benefit of her companions.

Harry grimaced at the unfamiliar tone, then, resigning himself to a boring afternoon, said lightly, 'I suppose we'd better join our charming sister before the strain of acting pleasant causes her an injury.'

Before walking on, Harry turned Hugh to face him, and in a rare demonstrative gesture he placed both hands on Hugh's shoulders and said softly. 'If ever you need me, Hugh, I'm here for you and always will be.

Nothing you do or have done could ever lessen my feeling for you. Remember that, will you? Any time, night or day, my door is always open for you. And now,' he added briskly, 'our sister awaits our company. Thank God it's only once a year.'

Dropping his hands from Hugh's shoulders he called out sweetly, 'We're coming, Bella, dear.' Then with a broad wink to Hugh, the two men strode towards the waiting figure.

CHAPTER ELEVEN

Maggie lay on her back listening to the sound of Liz's soft snoring coupled with the insistent ticking of the clock on the table by the bed and sighed heavily. She had been trying to get to sleep for hours now, but the harder she tried the more awake she'd become. Flouncing over onto her side she drew her knees up to her stomach and closed her eyes once more. She felt herself begin to drift away, the sound of Liz's snores became fainter as the elusive sleep took hold. Then, from the other room a loud grunt, followed by a crescendo of nasal snores brought her eyes wide open.

'Damn and blast,' she cursed softly, rolling onto her back. Charlie was certainly driving the pigs home tonight. Beside her, Liz turned over smacking her lips noisily, while managing to whistle through her nostrils and scratch vigorously at some unknown spot below her waist. Giving up all hope of sleep, she threw back the blankets and grabbed the old woollen coat that served as a dressing gown from the foot of the bed. She wrapped it around the upper part of her body and padded over to the armchair by the window. Tucking her feet under her bottom, she pulled back the curtain slightly to allow the light from the street lamp to enter the room. Resting her chin in her hand she stared morosely at the deserted street. It had been raining earlier in the evening, and the wet cobbled pavement glistened brightly beneath the lamp-post. Laying her head against the wing of the chair she let her mind wander back over the past five months.

Her first arranged meeting with Harry had proved awkward and fraught with embarrassment. She had told herself before setting out that she would simply meet him, hand over the first instalment of the debt and then go on her way. But it hadn't worked out like that. When she had arrived at the designated place by the park railings, he had been waiting for her, a welcoming smile on his craggy face. Despite her feeble protests, he had insisted that she sit with him and share the lunch he had brought with him from the wicker hamper by his side on the bench. She felt a smile come to her lips as she recalled Charlie's face at the sight of the dainty sandwiches and small cakes that had been offered to him.

When asked by Harry if he'd enjoyed his lunch he'd replied truthfully, 'I'd rather have pie and peas, sir,' at which Harry had thrown back his head and roared with laughter. She had found herself enjoying his company, and it was only when it was time to leave and she hadn't given him his money that the embarrassment had returned. Her hand trembling, she had proffered the bank-note, and he, after a moment's hesitation, had taken the money from her, his face sad as if she had insulted him in some way. Then, just as they were saying goodbye, a maid from one of the houses bordering the other side of the park had approached them, asking Maggie if she'd like to call at the house as the mistress had some clothing she wished to sell.

That encounter had been the ultimate humiliation for Maggie, clearly defining the stark difference between her and the man she had been chatting to so comfortably for the past hour. He was evidently of the upper class, and she, in spite of the effort she'd made with her appearance, was simply a common totter. If Harry had felt any embarrassment he had shown no sign, but she had been mortified.

On the following Saturday she had been tempted to leave the cart at home and go alone to the park, but she knew what Liz's reaction would have been, as Liz was already far from pleased at having to give up their hard-earned money to somebody who had no need of it. So she had continued to do her rounds with Charlie in tow, and then, just over a month ago, Harry had turned up with a fair-haired young man whom he had introduced as his brother. She had taken an immediate liking to the shy, introverted man, and had marvelled at the fact that he could be related to Harry. They were so different in every way, yet beneath the light-hearted banter they displayed, she had sensed from the start the strong bond that existed between them.

Was it possible to be in love with two men at the same time? Well, maybe not love, exactly, but she was certainly strongly attracted to both men, and she was sure they felt the same way. A gentle rivalry had sprung up between the two men over the past few weeks as they'd vied for her attention, making her feel as if she were someone special. It was only the presence of Charlie and the cart that served as a constant reminder of just how far apart she was from the smartly dressed men.

And now it was all coming to an end. Today was the last time she would have the excuse to go to the park. The final instalment of her debt would be paid today, and unless she happened to meet them on one of her visits to the houses in their street, it was unlikely she would ever see either of them again. Could she bear it? She shook her head sadly. It didn't matter if she could or not, she would have to. Despite the heavy coat she shivered and, unravelling her feet from beneath her body she walked slowly back to the bed. She wished now she hadn't agreed to pay a pound a week. If she'd offered to pay back ten shillings at a time, then she would still have had another five months to look forward to. But sooner or later her new-found world would have had to come to an end, so maybe it was best it happened now. Lizzie and Charlie were still snoring loudly, but Maggie no longer heard. Closing her eyes she lay down, and her eyelashes wet with tears, she finally fell asleep.

'It's half past six, Maggie, time to get up.' Charlie shook his sister's shoulder gently. 'Here's your tea – don't let it get cold.'

Maggie opened her eyes slowly, then hitching herself up onto her elbow she reached out for the steaming mug that Charlie had placed on the bedside table.

'Thanks, love,' she murmured, her voice thick with sleep.

'I'll start the breakfast, shall I, Maggie?'

'What? Oh, all right, just give me a few minutes to come round, will you? I, oh . . .' A loud yawn smothered the rest of her words.

'And I've put some hot water in the pitcher for you and Liz,' the young boy added proudly.

'Oh, ta, Charlie, that was thoughtful of you.' Placing her hand over her mouth to stifle another yawn she swung her legs over the side of the bed, her feet searching for and finding her slippers.

'Come on, Liz, wake up,' she said prodding the figure lying on the other side of the double bed. A muffled grunt came from beneath the blankets.

'It's gone half past six, Liz,' Maggie said loudly, giving the prone form another nudge.

'All right, all right, I'm getting up,' Liz muttered irritably, her arm shrugging away the insistent hand.

Wrapping her woollen coat across her shoulders, Maggie left the bedroom and made her way to the yard, thinking as she did every morning how wonderful it would be to have an indoor toilet.

When she returned a few minutes later, she was surprised to find Lizzie up and already dressed.

'Bloody hell!' Maggie exclaimed. 'You were quick. I hope you've left me some hot water, it was freezing out in the yard.'

'It's not exactly warm in here,' Liz retorted, her body shivering in spite of the thick brown dress she was wearing. 'Anyway, I didn't use any of the water, it's too cold to stand around washing.'

'You dirty cow,' Maggie replied good naturedly. 'You're getting as bad as Charlie.'

'Well, I don't have to be so particular, do I? I don't have a fancy gentleman to meet for lunch like some I could mention. Still, it's the last day today, isn't it? I don't suppose you'll see him again once you've handed over the last of the money, or his brother for that matter. Will he be there today, or is it just you and . . .'

'Don't start, Liz. I'm warning you, I've had about enough of your spiteful remarks.' Maggie had finished washing, and was now buttoning up the front of a dark blue woollen dress. 'You've already made your feelings painfully clear, and I'm sick of hearing you griping on about it. I know you didn't want to give back the money, but you were quick enough to take it, weren't you?'

'Maybe I was,' Liz answered sullenly, 'but like I said at

the time, the likes of him wouldn't miss twenty pounds, and I still think you've made a mistake. There might come a time when we'll be grateful for that money.'

Maggie sat down heavily on the bed, her head shaking from side to side. 'You don't understand, do you, Liz?' she said sadly. 'It wouldn't matter to me if he had millions, it still doesn't mean we're entitled to any of it. But if you don't understand that, then there's no point in me trying to explain. Anyway, as you just said, today's the last time I'll be handing over any money, so there'll be no more cause for arguments.'

Rising from the bed she threw back the blankets to let the sheets air while they had breakfast, then walked past Liz and sat down at the scarred walnut dressing table to brush her hair. She waited until Liz had left the room, then laid down the brush and gazed at her reflection in the mirror. One more day, one last chance to see them, and then it would be back to the same mundane life with nothing to look forward to from one week to the next; how would she be able to bear it? She felt the tears spring to her eyes, and quickly picked up the brush and began to pull the bristles through her long, wavy hair.

'You nearly ready, Maggie? Your breakfast will be cold if you don't hurry up,' Liz's voice called from the adjoining room.

'Yes, all right, I'm just coming,' she shouted back. Pushing back the stool she stood up, then taking a deep breath she stretched her lips into a smile and walked into the sitting-room.

It was a large room, serving as both dining-room and bedroom for Charlie. The brown, horsehair sofa and armchair stood in the middle of the room opposite the open fire range and the door leading off into the scullery. The table and four chairs they used for their meals were placed a couple of feet further on, giving the impression of two separate rooms. At the far end, where the room narrowed into a corner, lay Charlie's bed and tallboy hidden from view by the dark, grey curtain Maggie had hung between the two opposite walls.

The long floorboards were partly covered by an assortment of brightly coloured mats that blended in with the pale pink flowered wallpaper that Maggie had painstakingly pasted over the whitewashed walls. It was the room Maggie had dreamed of during the long, dark days of the basement, but today it held no joy for her.

Liz and Charlie were already half-way through their breakfast as she sat down at the square, wooden table and the plate of sausages and egg that Charlie had set for her. Aware they were both watching her, she began to eat, each mouthful sticking painfully in her throat as she endeavoured to swallow the food past the lump lodged in her throat.

When she had finished she laid down her knife and fork and looking round the table said brightly, 'Well, I suppose we'd better be making a move. I'll just put these plates in the sink before we go.'

'I'll bring the cart round to the front, Maggie,' Charlie said, springing to his feet.

'Wrap up warm, love, it's bitter out today,' Maggie called after him.

Left alone, a silence fell on the two young women until Liz said awkwardly, 'I'm sorry, Maggie, I mean about what I said before. I suppose I'm a bit jealous about you being so friendly with someone from the gentry. But it's not just that, I've been worrying about you ever since you started meeting him. I've seen the way you look on Saturdays, and I don't want you getting hurt. You know what I'm talking about, don't you?' Maggie opened her mouth to protest but the look of concern on Liz's face silenced the words of denial hovering on her lips.

'You don't have to worry about me, Liz,' she said lightly. 'I know my place, and I know that men like Harry and Doctor Stewart aren't for the likes of me. I won't deny that I'll miss their company, even if it was only for an hour a week.'

They were in the scullery now, and as Maggie took down their coats from the wooden rack, Liz once again felt a surge of resentment and envy towards her younger sister. Maggie had paid five shillings for the olive green fitted coat and matching bonnet trimmed with sable, but it had been money well spent. It isn't fair, Liz cried silently as she gazed at the well-dressed trim figure, miserably aware of her own bulky form crammed into a dull grey coat. Yet she was honest enough to admit that even if their attire was reversed, Maggie would still look smarter than she ever could.

'That really suits you,' she said with grudging admiration. 'But then anything you wear looks good on you. Not like me, I wish I had a figure like yours, but I only have to look at food and I put on weight.'

Maggie looked up in surprise, it wasn't like Liz to hand out compliments. Resisting the temptation to say that if all she did was look at food instead of eating it, then she wouldn't be so plump, she smiled broadly. 'It wouldn't suit you to be thin, anyway, men like a woman with a bit of meat on them, ask your Jimmy.' At the mention of his name, Liz jumped, her cheeks colouring in confusion.

Then, her fingers pulling nervously at the front of her brown coat, she said hesitantly, 'About Jimmy, Maggie, I've been meaning to talk to you about him. I think he might be going to ask me to . . . well, you know, to marry him. He hasn't said it in so many words, but I've just got an idea he's leading up to it, and I wondered if he did . . . ask me, I mean, well, would you mind? I know you don't like him very much, but if you could try and get to know him a bit better, I'm sure you'd change your mind.'

Maggie felt a cold chill settle on her chest at Lizzie's halting words, yet why was she surprised? Hadn't she been waiting for something like this to happen? Good Lord, the man had hardly been off their doorstep for the past few months. But the thought of him wangling his way into her family made her blood run cold. Still, if it was what Liz wanted then she wouldn't put any obstacles in her way.

Forcing a smile to her lips she said cheerfully, 'It's nothing to do with me, Liz, I won't have to live with him. Besides, you're a grown woman, you don't need my permission or approval. If you think you'll be happy with him, well then . . .' She shrugged her shoulders, not knowing what else to say.

'That's just it, Maggie,' Liz licked her lips nervously. 'You know Jim hasn't got a job at the moment, he only gets a bit of casual now and then down at the docks. What I mean is . . . well, we wouldn't be able to afford a place of our own to start with, and I wondered if maybe . . .'

Maggie looked at her in horror. 'You don't mean you'd want to move in here surely? Is that what you're getting at?'

Seeing the pleading look in Liz's face she backed away, crying loudly, 'Oh, no, definitely not, even if I did get on with him, which I don't, where the hell would we all sleep? We've only got the one bedroom, unless you think I'd be willing to doss down in the sitting-room alongside of Charlie. Oh, no, Liz, you can get that idea out of your mind straight away.'

'But Jim says, that if we . . .' Liz began, her voice faltering.

'Jim says, Jim says,' Maggie interrupted angrily, 'so you've talked it over then. Wait a minute.' She pulled at Liz's arm. 'He's already asked you, hasn't he? That's what this is all about, you're trying to butter me up so you can both move in here, well, forget it, Liz. There's no way I'm living under the same roof as Jimmy Simms, not even for your sake, and you can tell him that from me.'

'Maggie, please hear me out.' Liz followed Maggie from the scullery into the sitting room. 'He's got plans, has Jimmy, he's very clever you know. And he says that if we all work together, we could set up another stall in a different market and double what we're earning now. Please, Maggie, give him a chance,' she entreated, but Maggie remained unmoved.

'Jimmy seems to have it all worked out, doesn't he?' she said, her face set. 'And as you say, he's very clever. How many men could find a woman with her own business and able to provide him with a roof over his head. God!' she laughed derisively, 'he must think Christmas has come early this year.'

Hearing the scornful words brought Liz's back straight, and seeing she wouldn't be able to persuade Maggie she swiftly changed her tack. 'If you hadn't given away twenty pounds of our money, we could have afforded our own place, but seeing as you have, it's only fair that we live here for a while, just until we see how things work out.'

Maggie felt her hackles rise but determined to keep calm she said evenly, 'For the last time, Liz, it wasn't our money, and I'm not making any more apologies for giving it back. As for us all living here, the answer's still no. If your Jimmy's so clever, he won't have any trouble finding a place for the two of you, especially if you set up another stall to help pay for it. Now, I don't want to talk about it any more, we're late as it is and I . . .'

'Oh no, mustn't be late, must you?' Liz cut in, her voice sneering. 'Mustn't be late meeting your fancy friends, they might decide not to wait, and that would never do, would it?'

Refusing to be drawn further into a row, Maggie calmly pulled her gloves on, saying lightly, 'I'm not arguing with you, Liz, the matter's closed. Although why you'd want to live here with me and Charlie is beyond me. You could use the money from our nest-egg to start you off, surely that would be a better idea.' But even as she said the words she knew the reason behind Jimmy's planning. From the start he had made it plain he wanted her, and when she had made it equally plain she wasn't interested, he had switched his attentions to Liz. But still he tried to get close to Maggie at every given opportunity. She had long since given up sitting on the sofa when he was in the room, and had taken to using the armchair to stop him from getting next to her. But that hadn't deterred him. Now he simply sat on the arm of her chair, his arm accidently brushing across her chest at every opportunity. Even if she remained standing she would feel his eyes boring into her wherever she went, his gaze seeming to strip the clothes from her body. She shuddered at the thought. Surely Liz must have noticed, or was her sister so besotted she was turning a blind eye to what went on under her nose? Jimmy reminded her of a dog following a bitch in heat, and again she shuddered. The envelope containing the bank-note was lying on the table, and putting it into her bag she walked towards the door. She had decided on this course of action early on; it saved embarrassment if the money was concealed and gave an air of respectability to the meetings.

She was about to open the door when Liz's voice stopped her in her tracks. 'It's all right for you,' Liz said bitterly, 'you'll never have to worry about getting a man. You've already got two eating out of your hand. You attract everything in trousers without even trying; the stallholders, customers, even my . . .' She broke off, turning her back so that Maggie couldn't see the tears that had sprang to her eyes. Maggie looked at the rigid back, her mouth open in amazement at the outburst, then her eyes clouded over with pity. So Liz knew about Jimmy, and was still prepared to marry him and bring him here to live rather than take the chance of losing him. Poor Liz, poor, poor Liz.

Putting out her hand she touched Liz's arm and her voice gentle now, she asked, 'Why, Liz? Why marry him if you know he's only . . .' She couldn't finish what she had started to say, but Liz did it for her. Wiping her eyes with the back of her hand she turned to face Maggie.

'Using me? That's what you were going to say, wasn't it? Well, I'll tell you why. I'm plain and fat, and he's the only man ever to take any interest in me, let alone ask me to marry him. It's probably the only chance I'll ever get to have a husband and family of my own. Women like me can't afford to be too particular.'

'No, oh, no, Liz, you're being too hard on yourself. You're not plain, no you're not,' she repeated loudly, refusing to let Liz contradict her. 'As for being fat, well, you lost weight before, didn't you? You can do it again. You're worth more than the likes of Jimmy Simms. Liz, don't throw your life away. There'll be other men, men who'll want you for yourself, not for what you can give them, please, Liz, think about it.'

'I have thought about it, Maggie, and I've made up my mind.' Liz's voice was sombre. 'I'm twenty-one years old, and until Jimmy came along, I thought I'd spend the rest of my days alone. Because, let's face it, sooner or later you'll meet someone, that's if you haven't already.' She glanced sharply at Maggie. Seeing the frown that passed over her sister's face she added good-humouredly, 'And as for me losing weight, well, I didn't have much choice, did I? We were all bloody starving if you remember.

'Maggie . . .' the pleading note was back in her voice. 'Please, do this for me. I know I could use the money we've saved to tide us over, but . . . but Jimmy says he doesn't want to use our money, he'd rather earn it for himself. He's got his pride, has Jim, all he wants is a chance to make a living. We could move in with Mrs Simms, I know she'd have us, but, oh, Maggie I'd much rather stay here with you.' Her eyes gazed at Maggie imploringly. 'Please, do this for me. It won't be for long, a year at the most. Once me and Jimmy have got a few bob saved we'll move out, I promise you.'

Maggie looked into the pleading face and sighed heavily. What could she say? Even the thought of living under the same roof as Jimmy Simms caused her stomach to tighten. Yet if she refused and he moved on, Liz would never forgive her. Furthermore, if Liz didn't meet anyone else then she, Maggie, would feel obliged to remain with her sister for the rest of their lives. Still, if they did move in here at least she could keep an eye on her elder sister. Maggie had a strong feeling that if Liz went ahead with her plans to marry Jimmy Simms, she would need a friend – and what better friend than her own sister? She'd just have to make sure she was never alone with her future brother-in-law.

Tying the ribbons of her bonnet under her chin she looked steadily at the anxious face in front of her and said quietly, 'Just for a year, Liz, no longer. Charlie's getting too big to have to share a bed with me, he's . . .'

'Oh, thank you, Maggie, thank you.' Liz was ecstatic, her round face beaming with gratitude and relief. 'You won't regret it, I promise you, you won't regret it.'

Twirling around gaily she picked up one of the bundles of clothing that lay by the door, leaving the smallest one for Maggie to carry. Their arms full, they left the house. The sun was just beginning to rise as they joined the waiting Charlie on the pavement, and without a word they began to pile the clothes onto the cart.

'Gawd, I thought you two were never coming out,' Charlie exclaimed, stamping his feet to keep warm.

'Would you mind walking on ahead of me, Maggie?' Liz asked self-consciously. 'I thought maybe I'd go and see if Jimmy's awake, you know, to tell him about . . .'

'Yes, all right, but don't take all day about it. I don't

want to have to hang round the market waiting for you, I've got my own work to do.' Maggie cut her off impatiently. She was already regretting her decision, but the sight of Liz hurrying down the street bursting with happiness created in her a feeling of helplessness. She couldn't go back on her word now, yet the need to release the tension that seemed to be consuming her entire body was overpowering.

Turning to the unfortunate Charlie she snapped, 'Well, don't just stand there gawping, we're late enough as it is.' Charlie shot his sister a startled glance. It wasn't like Maggie to be bad tempered, and why was Lizzie going to see Jim this early? He was tempted to ask what the matter was, then seeing the set look on her face he decided against it. His shoulders hunched, he pushed the laden barrow over the bumpy cobbles, his eyes flickering every so often to the dejected figure by his side. Then suddenly comprehension dawned. Of course, the two gentlemen were going away tomorrow, somewhere abroad so Maggie had said, and they wouldn't be back for months. His face cleared. So that's why Maggie looked so miserable, this was the last time she was going to see them. Whistling under his breath Charlie concentrated on the street ahead. He felt sorry for Maggie, for he knew how much she enjoyed her Saturdays outside the park, but he wouldn't be sorry to see an end to them. Even though the two men had always tried to make him feel at ease, he had never quite managed to feel comfortable in their presence. It still didn't explain why Liz had dashed off to see Jim, but he wasn't bothered about what his eldest sister did. Maggie was the only one who mattered to him.

Maggie trailed alongside the barrow, her forehead furrowed with thought. She had planned to make the most of today, to try and cram as much as possible into the precious hour that would be her last. And now the entire day was ruined. She wouldn't be at all surprised if Liz left her to set up the stall while she dallied with her precious Jim. She felt her lips tighten in anger and despair. Damn Liz, and damn Jimmy Simms. Why couldn't he have remained at sea instead of intruding into their lives? And all that tripe about him being too proud to use their money to set him and Liz up was a load of rubbish. Maggie couldn't see him putting himself out to start a business of his own; more likely he was planning to live off their savings for as long as possible, while she and Liz carried on working. And the way he drank the money they had worked so hard for would soon be gone, and him along with it, if she was any judge of character.

Well, one thing was for sure, the day they got married she was going to take half of the money from the tin box beneath the floorboards and hide it somewhere safe. If Liz was happy to give her share of their nest-egg to him that was up to her, but she'd be damned if she was going to let him get his grubby hands on hers.

So lost in her thoughts was she, she didn't realise they had arrived at the market until the sounds and smells assailed her ears and nostrils. Keeping her eyes skinned for an opening, she walked down the middle of the road careful to avoid stepping on the squashed tomatoes and fruit that littered the cobbles. Both sides of the road were already filled with stalls and barrows displaying their wares, their owners ready and waiting for the first customers of the day. Some of the more established market traders had canopies placed high over their stalls to protect their wares from the elements, but these were few and far between.

Behind the stalls on the pavement stood rows of open-fronted shops where goods of finer quality could be purchased by those fortunate enough to afford it. Because of the vast selection, Whitechapel Road was one of the busiest markets in London. Passing by a stall piled high with boots and shoes, Maggie made a mental note to get Charlie another pair of boots – he could do with a spare pair. Holding onto the side of the cart, they continued to make their way down the road, their noses wrinkling at the overpowering smell of fish and stale cabbage that seemed to fill the air, while answering greetings from the many friends who called out to them.

Just as Maggie was beginning to panic, Charlie shouted, 'Over there, Maggie, between Fred an' Ma Jenkins.' Quickly they pushed the barrow into the empty space, their cheeks puffed out in relief.

'Wot ya, Mags, no Liz today, ain't she well or summfink?'

Fred Thompson grinned at her over the top of his fruit and vegetable laden barrow, a battered cap set on the back of his head and the inevitable cigarette dangling from his lips. Old Fred was a man of indeterminate age, his lined face always cheerful and his voice never seeming to grow hoarse, despite his constant yelling to the crowds that thronged the long, winding street. In spite of her bad mood, Maggie felt herself returning his grin.

'She'll be along later, Fred. I'm just going to get the stall ready for her – she shouldn't be long.'

While Charlie went to fetch the thick plank of wood and four orange crates that served for their stall from the grocery store a few shops down the road, Maggie began to fold the clothing into a tidy pile.

'Don't know why yer bothering wiv that, love,' Ma Jenkins called out to her. 'They won't stay that way fer long. Most a the buggers just rummage through the lot fer summfink ter do. Got no respect fer ovver people's fings, some a them. Lizzie just bungs the 'ole lot on the stall and lets 'em 'elp themselves.'

Maggie's mouth settled into a grim line. That lazy cow. Liz had promised to lay out the clothes neatly to make a better impression. She might have known her sister wouldn't put herself out if she didn't have to.

'Ere, don't look like that, love. It ain't worth the effort trying ter arrange 'em nice. The people wot come down 'ere ain't looking fer fancy displays, they just want a bargain.'

'She's right, Mags,' Fred chimed in. 'And Liz don't do too bad, yer know. She can shout and 'aggle wiv the customers as well as any of us. She works 'ard, Mags, so don't be too 'ard on 'er when she gets 'ere, eh? After all, yer wouldn't like it if she told yer 'ow ter run your part of the business, now would yer?'

The muscles in Maggie's face relaxed. 'No, you're right there, Fred. And look, could you remind Liz to bring home some potatoes and a bit of fruit, we're running low.'

'Don't yer worry, Mags, I'll put 'em aside now. And it'll be me best, no rubbish fer me two favourite girls. Yes, missus, an' what can I get fer yer? I got some lovely Cox's, came up from Kent this mornin' they did. Oh, oranges is it? Well now, love, yer won't find any better than ole Fred's.' Fred had turned to a customer, his nimble hands tipping four large oranges into the woman's basket.

Maggie turned to face Ma Jenkins, her eyes twinkling with laughter. 'Up from Kent this morning,' she whispered to the old woman. 'They must have been travelling all night.'

'Ah, yer can laugh, Maggie, but 'e's the best in the business is Fred. Why, 'e could sell a pair a frilly drawers ter a nun if 'e put 'is mind ter it.' The wrinkly face stared up at the young girl as if daring her to contradict her words.

Smothering a laugh with the back of her hand, Maggie leant towards the old woman. 'And where did your cakes and biscuits come from, Ma – Harrods?' she teased the indignant woman.

'I'll give yer 'Arrods, yer sarky little cow. I bakes me own, an' well you know it.' The black, crochet shawl she always wore over her head and shoulders slipped, revealing wispy white hair. With a swift movement the elderly woman pulled the edge of the shawl back into place over her head. Maggie looked at the stall laid out with cakes and biscuits of every description, her eyes lingering on a box of chocolate-covered cakes.

'Sorry, Ma, only joking, I wish I could bake, it would save me having to buy them.'

'Listen ter her. First she insults me, then tries ter do me out of a living,' Ma retorted quickly, her natural good humour coming to the fore. The two women were still laughing when Charlie returned, the wooden plank held awkwardly under one arm, while manoeuvring the four stacked boxes along with his foot.

'Mr Ball says he's putting 'is price up ter a shilling a week. He says 'is back yard's getting too crowded, an' if we want ter leave the stall there in future, we'll 'ave ter pay more.'

'A shilling a week!' Maggie and Ma exclaimed in unison.

'Why that old skinflint, yer bit a wood and boxes can't take up that much room. Yer ain't gonna pay it, are yer, Maggie?'

Maggie shook her head angrily. 'No I'm not. We'll load them on the barrow in future and take them home with us. It was handy having them stored – it's awkward loading them onto the barrow with the clothing, it makes the barrow harder to push. I didn't mind paying sixpence a week, but I'm definitely not paying a shilling. It's daylight robbery, the tight old sod.'

Another outburst from Ma was interrupted by the arrival of two woman at her stall. Giving Maggie's arm a reassuring squeeze she turned to her customers.

Ten minutes later the makeshift stall was covered with an assortment of dresses, blouses and skirts and still there was no sign of Liz.

'Where the hell has she got to? She promised she wouldn't be long. If I have to stay here all . . .'

'Ere she comes now, Maggie. You ain't gonna start a row, are yer?' Charlie asked anxiously.

'No, I won't start a row,' Maggie muttered, her teeth clenched.

'Sorry, Maggie, I didn't mean to be so long. You'd better get started or you won't get much work done today.' Liz was standing by the stall, her face dreamy as she remembered the time spent with her Jimmy. Charlie looked at Maggie's face and quickly grabbed hold of her arm, steering her away from Liz.

'Come on, Maggie, we'd better get going,' he pleaded, knowing that if he didn't put some distance between his sisters there would be an argument. Darting a baleful glance at Liz's back, Maggie called out her goodbyes to Ma and Fred before striding off down the road. Gripping the handles of the now empty barrow a relieved Charlie followed the retreating figure.

CHAPTER TWELVE

In sharp contrast to Maggie's mood, Harry was feeling positively euphoric as he studied the contents of the letter before him.

'Good news I trust, sir?' enquired Benson who was standing by his side, a large silver coffee pot in his hand.

'Indeed it is', Harry replied happily, the smile on his lips almost splitting his face into two. Putting down the letter he pointed to a small document lying on the table and said, 'You see before you a man of property, Benson. What do you think of that, eh?'

'I'm very pleased for you, sir', the old man answered gravely, his looks belying his words. 'Will you be requiring breakfast, sir?' he added solemnly. Looking into the weathered face, Harry contained the urge to burst into laughter. The lack of enthusiasm in the butler's face and voice came as no surprise to Harry. Compared to a judge and a doctor, a man of property must appear to Benson a very lowly trade indeed. For a moment Harry felt his spirits dampened, then he shook his head and smiled. Every man had his calling, and he had never been destined to spend his days enclosed between four walls, no matter how exciting or worthy the occupation. He was very proud of his father's and Hugh's profession, but their kind of life wasn't for him. Now, finally, he had found his own niche, and he knew there would be many eyes on him waiting to see how he handled his new-found responsibility.

'Shall I serve breakfast, sir, or will you be helping yourself?' Benson's voice cut into his thoughts.

Harry glanced over to where the elderly man was standing patiently by the sideboard, the surface of which was covered in silver trays and platters, and said gaily, 'I think I'll be pampered today, Benson. Just put a bit of everything on a plate – I've suddenly found I'm ravenous.'

When the laden plate of kidneys, bacon, sausages and scrambled eggs was placed before him he picked up his napkin saying, 'Am I the first one down today? The house seems extraordinarily quiet for a Saturday morning.'

'Your father and Master Hugh left over an hour ago, sir, I believe they have some business to attend to in the City. Your mother and Mistress Bella have yet to come down. Will that be all, sir?'

'What? Oh yes, thank you, Benson. I'll ring if I need you.'

Left alone he quickly devoured his meal, then made his way to the study. Sitting down in a black-leather winged chair he read through the letter once more, then picked up the deeds to the houses he had become the owner of. Again he felt a surge of satisfaction run through his body. No more would he have to keep his friendship with the people of the East End a secret, and it was all thanks to Bella.

Ever since the night she had confronted him with her knowledge of his activities she had used it as a weapon against him. Never openly saying anything, she had preferred instead to drop sly hints and innuendos whenever the family were gathered for a meal. It had taken all of his strength and endurance to refuse to rise to the bait, and continue to ignore her veiled remarks. He wasn't and never had been afraid of his father's wrath, but had been concerned that his relationship with his new-found friends might in some way injure his father professionally. And of course there had been his mother to consider. Although Harry was sure of her full support in whatever he chose to do with his life, her influential ladyfriends might not be so tolerant of his activities, and so he had held his tongue until the night of Bella's birthday.

Bella had refused her mother's offer to hold a celebration, probably due to the fact that she had so few friends she could have invited, and instead had settled for a special dinner. The evening had progressed pleasantly enough, and then the sly remarks had begun to fly. Having almost consumed an entire bottle of port, Bella had become more and more voluble, her eyes challenging him to retaliate while the rest of the family had looked on in bewilderment. Unable to tolerate any more he had stood up and out of courtesy to his mother had asked permission to leave the table pleading a headache. He had been half-way across the room when Bella, her voice almost screeching with spite, had asked him if he was intending to sneak out to meet his latest slut. It had been the final straw. Striding back to where she sat, a gloating look on her flushed face, he had stared down into those glittering, black eyes until she had been forced to drop her gaze. Turning to where his father was now standing at the head of the table, he had told him everything, from his first excursion into the East End to his present-day friendship with Maggie. He had of course omitted the encounter that had led to their first meeting, saying only that she was a very dear friend, and one that he intended to keep on seeing despite her humble origins. The room had fallen deathly quiet, and Harry, already regretting his rash outburst, had let his eyes sweep the room. Bella had sat looking as if she'd been slapped in the face, while his mother, bless her, despite her ashen face had remained calm, her quiet dignity acting as a balm upon the heavy atmosphere. Rising to her feet she had dismissed the goggle-eyed servants and ordered Bella to her room. When the red-faced, indignant woman had started to protest, the men had watched in amazement as the normally placid Beatrice Stewart had forcibly grabbed her daughter's arm and pushed her from the room. The moment the women had left, Hugh had tried to follow them, only to be ordered back to his seat by the formidable Edward Stewart. Obeying his father's command, the hapless figure had slumped back in his chair, his face a picture of misery and embarrassment. Harry too, had experienced a strong desire to flee, but the presence of the stoutly built man had held him rooted to the spot.

Looking into those steely black eyes, Harry had seen not his father, but Judge Stewart, and like the thousands who had stood before this impressive man he had felt a shudder of apprehension run through his body. Steeling himself for the backlash he had brought upon himself, Harry waited for his father to speak. When he did, the shock at what Harry heard was so great he had to put out his hand to grab the back of the nearest chair to stop himself from falling.

For instead of the strong reprimand he had been expecting, his father had said quietly, 'If you really intend to help the people of the East End, then do something constructive. Friendship is all very well in its place, but these people need more than an occasional guinea and a sympathetic ear. If you are sincere in your wish to help them, then do something constructive. I for one can think of nothing better than to provide decent accommodation for the poor wretches, most of them live in conditions unfit for animals, let alone human beings.

And the landlords fleece the poor beggars for every penny they can get out of them. So put your money where it will do the most good, into property. I'll help you all I can. I have contacts, and I'll start asking around first thing Monday morning. Now, let's open another bottle of port, I don't know about you two, but I could do with a bloody drink.'

It had taken all of Harry's will power to stop himself from running across the room and throwing his arms around the stout figure. His father had been as good as his word, as the letter and deeds he held in his hand proved. The property in question comprised a row of three-storey houses, six in all, with a total of nine rooms per house. He had been shown around the houses by the former owner, a grasping, odious little man, and had been appalled by the stench and dilapidation of the interior of the once grand houses. But he, Harry Stewart, was going to change all that. His first priority would be to have all the houses fumigated and the vermin-infested furniture thrown onto a bonfire. Then he intended to have all the rooms whitewashed and linoleum fitted throughout. He also intended to furnish the rooms with good, sturdy furniture and decent second-hand beds. He didn't want his good work undone by somebody bringing in their own flea-ridden possessions and run the risk of the vermin spreading throughout the rest of the houses. Then there was the task of installing plumbing and indoor water closets to be dealt with. Oh, he had plans, so many plans he could feel his head begin to reel at the task he had undertaken, but he would succeed, of that he had no doubts whatsoever.

He put the letter and deeds back into the envelope and then into the inside pocket of his grey jacket, a slow grin spreading across his face. He walked out into the hall, and taking the staircase steps two at a time, he knocked on Bella's door and without waiting for an answer burst into the room.

Bella was sitting up in bed, a silver tray containing the remnants of her breakfast across her knees, her eyes widening at the unexpected appearance of her brother. Her black hair above the heavily cream laden face was encased with curling rags, and Harry taking in the scene could barely repress a shudder. Lord, what a sight to be greeted with first thing in the morning.

'Really, Harry, what do you mean by bursting into my bedroom unannounced?' Bella cried indignantly. 'I might have been in a state of undress.'

Grimacing at the thought, Harry smiled broadly and said, 'Why, it's very considerate of you to consider my feelings, Bella, but you needn't concern yourself, I have a strong stomach, and besides, I've already eaten.'

'Why you . . .'

'Now, now, Bella, I haven't come for an argument. On the contrary, I've come to thank you.'

Bella's eyes narrowed with suspicion as she waited for Harry to continue.

Still smiling, he took the envelope from his pocket and waved it in front of her face, saying, 'These are the deeds

I've been waiting for. I am now the proud owner of six houses, houses I intend to renovate to let to those people you so pompously look down your nose at. And when I've finished, I intend to buy more, and more. Who knows but that I may end up running an empire, and it's all thanks to you, Bella, dear.' Suddenly the smile slipped from his face, and his voice sombre now, he said softly, 'You couldn't stop yourself, could you? You couldn't rest until you'd brought me down, but you underestimated Father, you imagined he was as big a snob as you are. Well, maybe we were both guilty of that assumption, for if I had had more faith in him I would never have let you torment me for so long. But it's finished now, you no longer have any power over me. My life from now on will be an open book, so I ask you, let me get on with it and have done with these childish arguments, if only for the sake of Mother. You know how upset she gets at the antagonism that exists between us. What do you say, Bella?'

'You think you're so clever, don't you?' She was glaring at him, the muscles on her face working furiously. 'But I'll see my day with you, Harry. You've ridiculed and humiliated me all our lives, and now you've got what you want you expect me to forgive and forget: never, do you hear me, never. I'll find a way yet to wipe that stupid smile off your face, and when I do it will be permanently.' Her voice was rising, and fearful his mother would hear the commotion, Harry backed from the room shaking his head sorrowfully.

In spite of her rantings, Bella had been right when she'd said he'd always found fault with her. Maybe if he'd been a bit more understanding . . . No, that attitude would have done no good, she would simply have taken advantage of any kindness shown to her, like she did with Hugh. There could never be any harmony between the two of them, so maybe it was time to leave this house and find a place of his own. Again he shook his head. His mother would be deeply hurt if he announced his decision to leave. If he were leaving to get married, that would be different, but what reason could he give other than he couldn't stand the sight of his own sister? Then there was Hugh. How could he leave his younger brother to the mercies of that vindictive harridan upstairs? Without him acting as a buffer, Bella would latch onto Hugh even tighter, controlling and perhaps eventually ruining his life. Sighing deeply he walked slowly down the stairway, his mind thoughtful.

Thinking of Hugh had awoken another painful subject. Why had he ever asked him to accompany him on his Saturday visits to the park? Had he subconsciously wanted to punish his brother by bringing him face to face with the girl he had raped so long ago? If so, it had been a fruitless exercise, for neither had recognised the other, and as the months had passed he had noticed a growing attraction between the two people he cared most about. He didn't like it, he didn't like it at all. By the time he had realised how fond of Maggie Hugh was becoming, it was too late. Now he tried to discourage

Hugh from accompanying him on his weekly visits, but without much success. Still, he wouldn't be able to make it today, so he, Harry would have Maggie all to himself. His face brightening, he ran down the remainder of the stairs, and donning his long, heavy coat and gloves he left the house.

Bella watched from her window as the tall figure sauntered down the road, his long legs eating up the pavement until he disappeared from view. Letting the curtain drop she walked slowly back to her bed. So, he thought he'd bested her, did he? Well, she still had a trick up her sleeve, namely the unknown little slut he and Hugh had become so friendly with. Oh, she'd seen them, laughing and talking as if they hadn't a care in the world. They hadn't seen her of course, she'd made sure of that. Picking up a piece of toast from the tray she began to chew the hard bread, a cruel smile playing about her lips. Yes indeed, there was more than one way to skin a cat, and that common little guttersnipe might be just the tool she was looking for.

Harry alighted from a hansom cab and hurried towards the park, his face falling at the sight of a nanny and her charge sitting in Maggie's customary spot. Taking out his pocket watch he looked at the large gold hands that were pointing to one o'clock, then held it to his ear to make sure it hadn't stopped. The familiar soft ticking assuring him he wasn't late, he let his eyes sweep the long row of benches before transferring his gaze towards the park. Despite the coldness of the day the square was bustling with activity. Men and women from all walks of life strolled arm in arm, the brightness of the gentry's clothing contrasting sharply with the drab dullness of the working classes' garb as they mingled together on the dry, brittle grass. The air was filled with the sound of mothers and nannies calling out to their children, and the children themselves whooping with laughter as they played their games of football and leapfrog, studiously ignoring their mothers' warnings to 'be careful'. Harry watched the scenes with amusement, remembering days gone by when he and Hugh had played the same games and listened unheedingly to the same warnings.

The sound of a woman's footsteps approaching caused his head to swivel round, the smile on his lips dying when he saw it wasn't Maggie. Taking his watch once more from his pocket he saw that the time was now fifteen minutes past one, and felt a gnawing feeling of anxiety begin to grow. What if she wasn't coming? No, that was ridiculous. She would have sent word if she'd been unable to keep their appointment. But what if she were ill? Surely if that was the case, she would send Charlie to let him know. He began to pace up and down the pavement, his face furrowed in thought. He didn't even know where she lived except that it was somewhere in Whitechapel. Gripping the handle of his walking cane, he strode towards an empty bench and sat down heavily. There was nothing he could do except wait, even if he had to sit here all afternoon, and if she didn't come today then he would go to the market on Monday and enquire among the stallholders as to her whereabouts. Feeling easier in his mind he relaxed his body against the hard bench and settled down to wait. In an effort to dispel his anxiety he let his mind drift to other matters and found himself thinking once more of Hugh. Was it wrong of him to try and stop what was for Hugh the one bright spot of the week? It had been foolhardy of him to bring them together in the first place, for if ever either of them discovered the reason behind his action the consequences would be unthinkable. And if he were to be honest, he had to admit that he was jealous of the friendship that had developed so quickly between them. Any further thoughts were interrupted by Maggie's arrival.

Looking harrassed and out of breath she flopped down beside him on the bench saying, 'I'm sorry I'm late, I wasn't sure you'd still be here.'

Harry looked at the heart-shaped face framed by a band of brown fur on the dark green bonnet and felt his heart begin to race. Without the presence of Hugh maybe now would be the time to pose the question that had been nagging at his mind since the first time he'd met her. But before he could utter a word she launched into the events of that morning in an effort to explain why she had been late.

She finished with, 'And to cap it all, when she did show up two hours later all smiles and bursting with apologies for leaving me to run the stall, she had the cheek to bring "him" with her, when she knew he was the last person I'd want to see today. And if that wasn't bad enough, the smarmy sod grabbed hold of me and kissed me, knowing full well I wouldn't make a scene in front of the other stallholders. Ugh, it makes me feel sick just thinking about it.'

Harry stared at her in concern. 'But this is outrageous. You can't seriously be thinking of sharing a house with a man who so clearly has designs on you – you'll have to find somewhere else to live. Look, I've been meaning to talk to . . .'

But Maggie wasn't listening. Now that she was here she was anxious to hand over the last payment and leave. There was no use in prolonging the moment, and the way she was feeling right now she couldn't trust herself not to break down and cry. Above all else, she wanted to hang onto her dignity. The absence of Hugh had come as a great relief, for it meant that she could have these last precious moments alone with Harry. Oh, she had grown very fond of Hugh – she had even wondered last night if she could be in love with him – but now, sitting so close to the craggy-faced man who had changed her life she realised that the thought of never seeing Harry again was unbearable. A moment of panic assailed her, beads of sweat broke out on her forehead, and she thought for a frantic moment she would slide off the bench into a heap at his feet. Her hand trembling, she took the small envelope from her bag and held it out to him.

'Well, here it is, the last payment, and I know I've said it a dozen times before, but thank you once again. I don't know what would have become of us if I hadn't met you that night. Now I really must be off, Charlie's waiting for me at the café – I thought we'd eat in the warm today.'

She could feel the tears begin to gather, and quickly held out her hand. 'Goodbye Harry. Please give my regards to Hugh, and if you ever need any second-hand clothing, you know where to find me.' The attempt at humour was wasted on Harry, who was staring at her in bewilderment.

'Wha . . . what are you talking about?' he cried hoarsely. 'You're talking as if we're never going to see each other again.'

Avoiding his gaze she rose unsteadily to her feet, and in a voice near to breaking she whispered, 'It's the best way, Harry. Nothing can ever come of our meetings. We come from different worlds, and if we continue meeting I'm going to end up getting hurt, and I've had enough pain in my life.'

'Maggie, Maggie, you can't go like this. The thought of never seeing you again is unbearable, I simply can't imagine life without you. You must know how very dear you are to me.' Suddenly conscious that they were in a public place he took hold of her arm and, finding little resistance, led her further into the park until they were standing alone under an oak tree, their bodies almost concealed by the large trunk.

Satisfied that they couldn't be seen, Harry gently

pulled her body close to his, his arms encircling her waist. The nearness of him sent Maggie's heart thumping. Her stomach churned with excitement as his face grew nearer and nearer her own. Her eyelids fluttered then closed as she gave herself up to the wonderment of her first real kiss. All her dreams of this moment paled against the breathtaking reality. As if from a great distance, she could hear the birds singing and faint voices of families walking near by, but caught up in a world of her own, she wouldn't have noticed if the entire Coldstream Guard had marched by. She had never imagined she would welcome a man's hands on her body, but this feeling, this marvellous feeling that was sending a tingle along the length of her spine and building to a delicious warmness in the pit of her stomach was proof that she hadn't been emotionally damaged by that dreadful experience at the hands of her unknown assailant. For over two years she had felt dirty and spoiled, and the recent unwelcome attentions of Jimmy Simms hadn't helped her self-esteem. But now, safely held in Harry's arms, knowing she was loved and was capable of loving in return, she felt as if her body had finally been cleansed.

When at last their lips parted, she gazed up into Harry's face, her eyes glistening with happiness. Smiling down at her, Harry gently cupped her face in his hands, the tender action causing Maggie's heart to leap with hope, a hope that was cruelly crushed by his next words.

'I can look after you, Maggie, darling. Just say the word and I'll take you out of that home you'll soon be sharing with a man you despise, and find you a decent place to live. We could be happy together, my dearest, and you need never worry about dragging that barrow around the streets and haggling with servants for cast-off clothing ever again. What do you say, Maggie? Will you let me take care of you?'

Maggie slowly pulled herself free from his embrace, her happiness evaporating as the full import of his words penetrated her dulled senses. Fighting to regain her dignity she stepped away from him, her eyes regarding him coldly.

'Are you asking me to marry you, Harry?'

Harry felt his body jerk at the harshness of her voice, and sought desperately for the right words to say. But Maggie had already seen the startled look her words had evoked. What a fool she'd been, to imagine for one minute that a man of his class and breeding would ever consider a girl of her background as a wife.

With all the self-control she could muster, she said icily, 'I thought not. Well, let me tell you, Harry Stewart, I'll be no man's mistress, and I'm insulted that you could think so little of me as to suggest such a thing. Goodbye sir. We won't be meeting again.'

Caught off guard, there was nothing Harry could do except watch her walk out of his life. The thought of marriage had never entered his head, and now by his blundering he had ruined any chance of keeping in contact with her. The only consolation he had was the fact that she obviously cared more for him than she did for

Hugh, but not enough it seemed to agree to become his mistress. A deep sense of shame swept over him. If anyone deserved the sanctity of marriage, Maggie did.

Sitting back down on the bench he bit his lip in agitation. His father he knew was a fair man, but he wasn't so liberal that he would welcome a street trader as a daughter-in-law, and his mother . . . Good lord, the shock could very well send her into a decline. Oh, face up to it, man, he rebuked himself sternly, you could easily find a place to set up home with Maggie, but you're afraid to make the commitment. Admit it, everything is just starting to go right for you, and you're afraid to do anything that might spoil your new life. His face set and drawn, he rose to his feet, his mind still bitterly attacking himself. How many times had he accused Hugh of having no back-bone? Now he had been tried and found wanting, and for the first time in his life he found himself looking at the selfish side of his nature – and the picture it presented wasn't a pleasant one. With dragging feet he walked from the square. How could a day start so brightly and end so miserably? He hadn't even had the chance to tell her about his good fortune. Oh, damn it to hell. What was he going to do, what in God's name was he going to do?

CHAPTER THIRTEEN

'They're at it again, Maggie,' Charlie moaned sleepily, 'can't you bang on their door or summfink? I can't sleep properly with that racket going on, you'd fink they were doing it on purpose.'

Raising herself onto her elbow, Maggie leaned on the long, grey bolster that separated her from her fourteen-year-old brother and whispered, 'That's just what he wants us to do. He's like a big kid showing off, and I'm not going to give him the satisfaction of letting him know we can hear them. Now, listen, Charlie, it won't be for much longer. Just another few months until Liz has the baby and then we'll be off, I promise. I don't like it here any more than you do, but I gave Liz my word we'd stay until she was safely over the birth. Now go back to sleep, and mind, not a word to Jimmy about you know what. It would make his day, and I can't bear to see him happy.'

With a resigned sigh, Charlie answered glumly, 'All right, Maggie, I won't say nothing, but I feel sorry for that poor little perisher having 'is head bashed in every night.'

Suppressing a smile Maggie whispered sternly, 'That's enough. Now go to sleep, they can't keep it up much longer. There, what did I tell you?' she added as the noises from the bedroom suddenly ceased. Getting no answer she lay back on her pillow, listening to the sound of Charlie's regular breathing, and closed her eyes thankfully.

Charlie was right of course, the situation was becoming intolerable, but what could she do? Liz and Jimmy had been married for over a year now, and she had been all set to leave. She'd even found two rooms for her and Charlie in a house the other side of Whitechapel, and then Liz had found out she was pregnant and had begged Maggie to stay on until the baby was born. Like a fool she'd reluctantly agreed, a decision she'd regretted the moment the words were out of her mouth. For fifteen months she had endured the presence of her brother-in-law, fifteen months of trying to keep out of the way of his 'brotherly' kisses and straying hands. As for his grandiose plans for expanding their business, huh, the lazy sod hadn't even tried to set up another stall. All he'd done since the day he'd moved in was sleep, eat and give the rest of them tips on how to improve business. Yet in spite of it all, Liz still stoutly defended her husband, declaring that he was just biding his time until the right pitch became available.

There was one area, however, where Liz had remained prudent, and that was keeping a tight rein on the money that came into the house. True to her promise to herself, Maggie had taken half of the money from the tin box and hidden it behind a loose brick in the scullery, adding an extra guinea to her hoard whenever she could. Surprisingly Liz had made no argument when Maggie had told her what she'd done; it seemed as if she'd almost been expecting such an action. Maybe she didn't trust Jimmy to stay if he got his hands on a large sum of money, but whatever the reason she had continued to give her erstwhile husband just enough to keep him in beer money and a little extra to indulge in a bit of gambling when the mood took him. There had been blazing rows at the start of the marriage when Jimmy had found out his new wife wasn't as pliable as he'd imagined her to be, but now he seemed to have accepted the situation and was happy enough to be housed and fed without lifting a finger. The only thing Maggie could say in his favour was that he made Liz happy, especially these last few months. For as her pregnancy had progressed her once plain sister had become positively radiant.

Pulling the bolster more firmly into place, Maggie turned over onto her side. Just a few more months, she told herself, and then no matter what entreaties Liz made, she and Charlie were moving out. It wasn't right for a boy of his age to be sharing a bed with his sister, even with the bolster separating them. It had already been agreed that the business would be passed over to Liz, leaving Maggie and Charlie to set up somewhere else. Liz had offered to pay half of her savings to them, but this Maggie had stoutly refused. She had over thirty pounds hidden behind the brick in the scullery, and that was more than they'd had when they had first started. Besides, the poor cow was going to need all the money she could get. And once they'd gone, Jimmy would have to get off his backside and help. Even he wouldn't expect his wife to run a stall, walk the streets with a barrow collecting the necessary clothing and look after a child – would he?

Flouncing over onto her back she stared grimly into the darkness. She couldn't spend the rest of her life worrying about Liz. She'd known what she was taking on when she'd married Jimmy Simms, and there was Charlie to consider. He didn't like his brother-in-law any more than Maggie did, and she didn't see why he should have to work twice as hard to help support a man who was perfectly able to work for himself.

Proof of his ability to work was soon evident at the sound of the bedsprings twanging and creaking once more. Poor Liz, how did she put up with it, especially in her condition? The man was a thoughtless pig. If he had to get up and go to work in a few hours he wouldn't be so keen on using up all his strength. Still, let him enjoy it while he could. A few weeks being on his feet from six in the morning until early evening and he'd be lucky to be able to raise a smile, let alone anything else. The thought brought a smile to her lips. Ignoring the familiar sounds she closed her eyes and immediately Harry's face floated before her. 'Go away, please, leave me alone' she murmured silently. 'I've enough on my plate without you plaguing me. Leave me in peace, Harry, leave me in peace.'

'Will his lordship be joining us for breakfast, or are you going to bring him his breakfast in bed?'

Ignoring the sarcasm in Maggie's voice, Liz placed a bowl of steaming porridge on the table, saying, 'As a matter of fact he's getting up early today. He's going to help Charlie on the stall while me and you go shopping for some baby clothes, that's if you don't mind.'

The spoon Maggie had been holding clattered back onto the table, her mind not believing what her ears had heard.

'You mean he's actually going to do some work! Why, what's he after?'

'He's not after anything,' Liz replied calmly as she poured out the tea into four tin mugs. 'It's my idea – I haven't told him yet. Like you keep telling me, he's going to have to do it when you and Charlie leave and I've got the baby to look after, and today's as good a day as any. Anyway, you two eat your breakfast while I bring him in his tea. I've put extra sugar in it – I've heard it's good for shock.' Winking broadly, she walked into the bedroom shutting the door behind her, leaving Maggie and Charlie staring at each other in stunned surprise.

'Eh, Maggie, he's not gonna like it,' Charlie breathed excitedly. 'I bet he won't do it, Liz must 'ave gone soft in the 'ead, what do you think?' Before Maggie could answer, the sound of raised voices came clearly from the bedroom.

Her face splitting into a wide grin, Maggie bounced her head towards the bedroom and said gleefully, 'I think Liz is finally showing some spunk, and about time too. Because you know, Charlie, I don't think he really believes we're going to leave when the baby's born and set up on our own. He probably thought we'd change our minds when the time came, but Liz knows I'm serious about going. I expect that's why she's decided to get him working now – you know, sort of break him in gently. Well, good for her. I won't feel so guilty about leaving now I know she'll be all right.'

'What exactly are we going to do, Maggie?' Charlie asked, his eyes still on the bedroom door. 'You never really said. Are we going to get another stall, or do something different?' Maggie sipped at the hot tea, her face still smiling.

'I'm not sure yet, love, but don't you worry, I'll think of something.'

Seeing she was in such a good mood, Charlie shifted

221

awkwardly in his chair then, his voice hesitant, he said, 'I saw Harry last week, he asked how you were.'

The smile slid from her face and gripping the handle of the tin mug she said tightly, 'I told you I wasn't interested in what Mr Stewart was doing, and what were you doing down there again anyway?'

'Aw, Maggie, don't be cross. You know I have to go past where he's working to get the pies for our dinner. I can't very well ignore him, can I?' he muttered, wishing he hadn't said anything now. Looking at his miserable face Maggie felt a qualm of guilt. What had happened between her and Harry wasn't Charlie's fault, and she had no right to take her unhappiness out on him.

It was over a year since she'd last seen Harry, but she'd heard about him and the houses he was renovating. By all accounts there was a waiting list as long as Bethnal Green Road for a chance to move into the rooms in the once derelict houses. The rents were reasonable too, so whatever the reason behind his decision to go into property, it certainly wasn't for profit. The row he was working on now was only ten minutes away from the market, so it wasn't surprising that Charlie had met up with him again. And although she had sworn she never wanted to see him again, part of her was still hurt that he had made no effort to come to the market and see her.

Clearing her throat she said gently, 'Sorry, love, I didn't mean to snap at you.' Endeavouring to keep her voice nonchalant she added, 'How is he?'

Charlie's face brightened. 'He's fine, Maggie. I nearly

didn't recognise him when I first saw him. He wasn't wearing his fancy togs, I thought he was one of the workmen until he called out to me. Eh, you should have seen him, stripped to the waist he was, chucking old furniture onto a bonfire and laughing and chatting with the other men like he was one of them. They think a lot of him, his men. Most of them have been with him since he started, and they're hoping to stay with him when he moves on to the next lot of houses down Aldgate way.'

'You seem to have heard a lot, seeing as you told me you only spoke to him for a few minutes.'

Charlie bowed his head, a dull flush creeping up and over his neck and face while he fidgeted with his spoon.

'Well, you were so cross the first time I mentioned I'd seen him, I thought I'd better keep quiet in future. But when I told him we were leaving here soon, he said we could have a couple of rooms as soon as they're ready. They're really nice, Maggie. He showed me round one of the houses, and they're not dear either. He's only asking the same rent as we pay for this place, and his are a lot nicer – they've even got indoor lavs. Shall I tell him to keep us . . .'

'No,' Maggie interrupted him. 'I'm sorry, love, I know you're only trying to help, but I've already got my eye on a place for us when the time comes.' The blatant lie stuck in her throat, and coughing loudly she said, 'Now finish your tea, and when you're at the market today, keep an eye on Jimmy – make sure no money goes into his pockets instead of the box.'

'All right, Maggie.' Charlie rose from the table, his shoulders hunched as he made his way to the door.

Biting her lower lip Maggie watched the dejected figure walk across the room and called after him, 'When you see him again, thank him for the offer, but explain I've already made arrangements.'

Nodding solemnly, he left the room to fetch the cart from the courtyard.

'Charlie gone already?' Liz had come up behind her, the now empty tin mug dangling from her finger. 'We've got another half hour before we have to leave.'

Moving back to the table Maggie began stacking the bowls and mugs onto a tray. Careful to keep her voice steady she answered, 'You know what he's like, he's afraid there's going to be an argument so he's getting out of the way.' She was already walking towards the scullery with Liz close behind her.

'Well, he wasn't far wrong was he? Don't tell me you couldn't hear him shouting? Still, I've told him from now on, no work, no beer money. He'll come round, he doesn't have any choice.'

Maggie looked at her sister in amazement. 'What's come over you, Liz? I've never heard you talk like this before, especially where Jimmy's concerned. Why the sudden change?'

The question hung unanswered for a long moment before Liz spoke. 'Maybe I want this child and any future children to have a father they can respect, or maybe I've just got fed up with being walked all over and taken for a mug.' The words were spoken softly as if she were talking to herself. Then, hearing the bedroom door opening she put a finger to her lips whispering, 'Shush, here he comes, we'll talk more later.'

Jimmy Simms stood in the opening of the scullery, his face sullen. Some women would find him attractive, for he wasn't unpleasant to look at. It was his character that made him so obnoxious, at least as far as Maggie was concerned. His thick blond hair was standing on end, his blue eyes surly as he surveyed the two women. He was wearing a pair of cast-off brown corduroy trousers held up by a pair of black braces. The off-white shirt was unbuttoned, showing off his hairless chest and bulging waistline that hung over the open band of his trousers.

'Where's me breakfast then?' he demanded of Liz. 'And I don't want no porridge muck. If I'm gonna do a day's work I want a real meal, so get the frying pan out sharpish.'

Bristling with anger Maggie made to speak, but the warning pressure of Liz's hand on her arm stopped her.

'It's all ready, love,' Liz answered him evenly. 'I put it in the oven to keep it hot. You go and sit down and I'll bring it to you.'

Grunting loudly he swung round and stomped his way to the table.

'How can you let him talk to you like that?' Maggie hissed as Liz bent down to take the plate of bacon and eggs from the oven. 'I'd give him frying pan, right over the bleeding head.'

'Oh, take no notice of him, Maggie. It's his masculine pride talking. I've got the better of him already, so I can afford to be generous. Look, go easy on him today, will you? And could you make a fresh pot of tea while I get ready?'

Too angry to speak, Maggie could only nod her head. Minutes later, still fuming at the way he had spoken to Liz, she banged the tin mug down in front of him.

'Oh, ta, Maggie,' he looked up at her smiling, happy now he was stuffing his face. ' 'Ere, don't run off. Sit down and 'ave a cuppa wiv me, I want to talk to yer about our Liz.' About to refuse, Maggie sighed and sat down opposite him.

'There, that wasn't so bad, was it? All family together, eh Maggie?'

She watched in silence as he wiped his plate clean with a thick slice of bread and waited for him to speak.

'Ah, that's better,' he sighed, pushing the plate away from him. Then, hitching his thumbs in his braces he leaned back on his chair.

'I've been meaning ter have a chat wiv yer, about Liz. I don't fink she should be working for much longer, that's why I'm gonna start helping out. It's a nuisance though, 'cos between you and me, Maggie, I got a deal going wiv some old mates of mine. I can't say too much at the moment, you know 'ow it is, but once it's settled we'll all be better off. Fing is, Maggie, it might take some time to get started, you know 'ow these fings are, and what wiv you and Charlie going as soon as the nipper's born, well . . .' He spread his hands wide. 'I'll 'elp Liz all I can, 'course I will, but there'll be some days when I won't be 'ere, and I'm worried that it's gonna be too much for her. You can see the spot I'm in, can't yer, Maggie, love? I can't let me mates down, and I can't be in two places at once, now can I?'

Maggie gazed at him steadily, then with a mirthless laugh she rose to her feet. 'Good God, Jimmy, you must think I came down in the last shower. There's no "deal", never was, and the only mates you have are those cronies you meet down the pub. If you think you can blackmail me into staying on, you've got another think coming. I got your measure the first time I met you, and now at last Liz has come to her senses. But even knowing what a lazy, artful slob you are, she still loves you. Thankfully I don't, but you know that already, don't you, so let's not play any more games. I don't like you, never have, and after what's happened this morning, maybe I won't stay until the baby's born. I don't think Liz needs me any more, so maybe I'll be going sooner than you think, and Charlie alongside me.'

'All right, all right, there's no need ter shout,' he muttered, his eyes darting towards the bedroom. And Maggie, watching him, felt her eyes widen in surprise. He was afraid of Liz hearing, this big, blustering hulk of a man was actually afraid of his wife. Relief flooded through her body. Liz was going to manage very well without her, in fact she might even manage better without her presence in the house. Feeling more light-hearted than she had done for months she sat down again and poured herself a mug of tea while she waited for Liz.

Jimmy sat silently, his face downcast as he considered his future. He'd played his last hand and lost, but he could still have some fun with the snooty little bitch sitting opposite him. Burping loudly he leered across at her.

'I 'ope we didn't keep yer awake last night, but yer know 'ow it is wiv married couples.' Maggie felt her stomach tighten with distaste, but refused to rise to the bait.

Still smiling she said sweetly, 'Oh, I wouldn't worry about that, Jimmy. Liz has always snored, even before she got married. I've got used to it over the years, so you needn't worry about disturbing me, I can sleep through anything.'

His eyes clouded with anger and scowling furiously, he scraped back his chair and marched towards the bedroom just as Liz was coming out. Brushing her aside he slammed the door after him.

'You two been at it again?' Liz asked wearily.

'Sorry, Liz, but he gets my back up,' Maggie replied, a little shame-faced.

'Oh forget it and let's get going before there's any more arguments.'

Pulling down a pale blue coat from the back of the door, Lizzie struggled with the buttons before giving up with a resigned sigh.

'We'd better look for another coat for me while we're out – I seem to grow bigger by the day.'

'Is it worth it? I mean we're in March now, the days are getting warmer, and besides, we don't want to give our trade to the opposition, do we?'

'No, I suppose not,' Liz agreed gloomily. 'But wouldn't it be nice, just for once to have something brand new? Something no-one else has ever worn? Still, my baby isn't going to be dressed in someone else's cast-offs. He or she is going to have everything spanking new. Jim doesn't understand, that's one of the reasons he's in such a bad mood. He can't see the point in paying for new clothes when we could pick up the same for a fraction of the cost.'

'Well, men don't, do they?' Maggie was dressed for the outdoors in a lightweight beige coat with matching bonnet. She was well aware that although still in good condition, both the coat and hat were out of date and for a moment she shared in Liz's wish for something brand new. One day, girl, one day, she told herself. Comforted by the thought she followed Liz from the room.

CHAPTER FOURTEEN

'Oxford Street next stop,' the conductor's sonorous voice boomed above the chatter of the passengers on his horse-bus. Maggie jumped to her feet, almost forgetting Liz, who appeared to be stuck in the long seat.

'Come on, Liz, hurry up, it'll be moving off again in a minute,' Maggie cried agitatedly.

'Hang on, will you, I'm not as quick on me feet as I used to be.'

Holding Lizzie's elbow, Maggie assisted her heavily pregnant sister down the curving stairway, not breathing easily until they were safely on the platform.

'Yer shouldn't 'ave gorn upstairs, Missus, not in your condition,' the cheerful conductor admonished them both.

'We wanted to see the view from the top – we've never been up this way before,' Maggie replied by way of explanation.

'Yes, well, sit downstairs on yer way back 'ome. Yer don't want the little 'un being born on a bus now, do yer?'

They had barely set foot on the pavement when the vehicle started up again.

'Bloody 'ell, they don't hang about, do they?' Liz grabbed at Maggie's arm to steady herself. 'We could have walked quicker, the time it's taken us to get here.'

Maggie nodded in agreement. The roads were packed solid with horse-buses, hansom cabs, private carriages and delivery vans. She had thought the roads in the East End were congested, but they were nothing compared to this.

'Oh, blast,' Lizzie cried in disgust.

'What's the matter?' Maggie turned to the cumbersome figure by her side, her voice filled with alarm.

Leaning heavily on Maggie's arm, Liz lifted her foot, her eyes glaring at the brown mess on the bottom of her boot.

'Whoever said the streets of London were paved with gold obviously never came up this way,' she said grinning up at her sister.

Minutes later they were standing in front of a large department store, their noses practically touching the enormous plate-glass window, their eyes wide at the sight of the colourful collection of gowns and costumes on display. At the front of the window stood a wooden mannequin clothed in a brilliant, sky-blue gown. Lying on the floor close to the frilled hem was a wide-brimmed straw hat trimmed with silk flowers and a wide ribbon in the same matching colour. Alongside was another mannequin draped in a white tulle dress with a scarlet band round the waist. Again a matching hat lay at its feet, together with a white lace pair of gloves. The rest of the window was filled with smart skirts and blouses with gaily printed scarves pinned to the wooden display board.

'Makes our stall look sick, doesn't it,' Liz said wistfully, before moving on to the next store. The next two hours were spent leisurely wandering up and down the narrow road, stopping every now and then to look into yet another bright and colourful window display. Finally they found a smaller shop that catered for babies and children's wear. After much debating, they emerged carrying three wrapped parcels.

'I don't know about you, Maggie, but I could do with a cup of tea and something to eat,' Liz said longingly.

'Me an' all, but we can't go into a restaurant, we've spent enough already. Not that I begrudge the baby its new things,' she added hastily, 'after all it's your money, but I bet some of those places cost a guinea just to walk through the door. Besides, I'd feel awkward going into a posh restaurant. They're probably filled with lords and ladies – we'd be out of place.'

Lizzie was about to make a reference to Harry, then

changed her mind; she didn't want to take the risk of spoiling their day out. Linking arms they set off in search of a modest place where they could eat in comfort. Walking slowly they mingled with the gentlemen and ladies of the upper class, their heads held high, refusing to be intimidated by their fellow pedestrians.

'Here, look at them.' Lizzie nudged Maggie in the side, her head nodding towards a group of city gentlemen dressed in pin-striped trousers, black morning coats and bowler hats. 'Look like a load of penguins, don't they?'

Giggling like two school girls, they turned off the main street and found themselves in a cul-de-sac. There were only four small shops set back into the right hand of the road, and it was with enormous relief they saw that one of them was a coffee shop. Clutching their purchases tightly, they peered at the gold-printed menu attached to the frosted-glass window.

'Bloody hell,' Liz exclaimed loudly. 'Half a crown for a pot of tea and a couple of scones, that's daylight robbery. We went into the wrong business, Maggie.'

'Keep your voice down, Liz,' Maggie pleaded. 'They'll hear you inside. Anyway, it was your idea to come up the West End – what did you expect?'

The tinkling of a bell announced the departure of a young couple leaving the shop, and Maggie, looking at her sister, said excitedly, 'Come on, Liz, let's splash out. It might be a very long time before we get another chance.'

Liz gazed into the sparkling eyes and grinned. 'Oh, what the hell, why not. After you, Madam,' she said, sweeping her hand in a grand fashion.

Once inside the shop, however, they found their confidence wavering at the sight of the throng of smartly dressed people seated around the white lace-covered tables. Swallowing nervously Maggie shot a startled look at Liz who immediately inclined her head indicating that they should leave. But before they could make their exit, a tall, elderly man dressed in the same mode as a butler was standing at their side.

'Good afternoon, ladies,' he smiled pleasantly. 'Will you be requiring a table for two?'

The friendliness of his tone acted as a balm upon the two young women, and it was Liz, who recovering her composure first, said grandly, 'Thank you, that would be most agreeable.'

When they were seated and their parcels pushed safely out of the way beneath the table, Liz scanned the menu before grandly ordering a pot of coffee and two large slices of chocolate gateau. When the waiter had gone the two young women gazed at each other for a moment, then burst into muffled laughter.

'Gawd, if my Jimmy could see me now, he'd have a blue fit. Speaking of which, I hope he's behaving himself. I wouldn't put it past him to slope off and leave Charlie to do all the work.'

Maggie shook her head in wonderment. 'I can't get over the change in you, Liz, but I'm glad to see it. I've been worried sick at the thought of leaving you, but not any more. In fact I think you'll probably be better off without me there antagonising Jimmy at every given opportunity. I . . .' She broke off as the waiter, carrying a large silver platter returned to their table. Any further conversation was halted while they did justice to the special treat that lay before them. Finally, they pushed their empty plates away and surveyed each other, smiling fondly.

'I've really enjoyed myself today, Maggie,' Liz said softly. 'But more importantly, I'm glad that we've become friends. Mind you, it's taken long enough, hasn't it?'

'Liz,' Maggie started to speak.

'No, don't say anything, Maggie,' Liz interrupted her. 'I'm not going to get all mushy, I just thought I'd take this opportunity to thank you for all the help and support you've given me these past months, and to apologise for being such a bitch at times. Not that you're that easy to live with,' she laughed happily. Then her mood changing to a more sombre note, she continued.

'The change you've seen in me today isn't that sudden, it's been building for a long time. I don't know why I picked this particular day to speak out, it just happened. We all have to grow up and become independent sometime, and I suppose I realised I couldn't spend the rest of my life leaning on you. That and the need to feel some self-respect, because it's important isn't it, self-respect? You've always had it, even as a child. I don't know what I was more jealous of, that, or the fact that you were prettier than me.'

Leaning over the table she caught hold of Maggie's hand. 'You don't have to worry about me, Maggie, and I'm not going to hold you to the promise to stay until the baby's born. You see, I'm not afraid any more – I'll always love you, but I don't need you any more. Do you understand?'

A well of emotion was swelling in Maggie's chest, and desperate to bring some levity back to the conversation, she said shakily, 'Give over, Liz. You'll have us both bawling in a minute, and I don't think that would go down too well in a place like this. One must keep up appearances, mustn't one?' Again they were laughing, unheedful of the covert glances they were attracting.

'Look, Maggie, I want to get a bit more shopping before we go home. You wait here and have another cup of coffee, I won't be long.'

A startled look came into Maggie's eyes. 'Hang on, Liz. I'm not staying here on my own, I'll come with you.'

'I won't be a minute, I know exactly what I want to get. Here, I'll leave the money for the bill. By the time that waiter comes back and you've paid him, I'll be waiting outside. Won't be long.'

For a woman so heavily pregnant Liz was surprisingly quick on her feet, and before Maggie could make any further protest she had left the shop. Knowing there was nothing for it but to remain until the waiter returned, she sat uncomfortably in her chair, her face burning with embarrassment, wondering where Liz had rushed off to in such a hurry.

'Would you like it wrapped, Madam,' the saleswoman enquired, her nimble fingers folding over the fawn cashmere shawl on the counter. Liz thought for a moment. She was desperate to go to the toilet, and Maggie would be hopping mad if she left her on her own for too long. The pressure on her bladder decided her.

'No, thank you,' she replied, moving from one foot to another. 'Just put it in a bag and I'll wrap it myself.'

'Very good, Madam,' the woman replied. She could see the young woman's condition, and having had four children of her own sympathised with her evident predicament.

Lowering her voice she said *sotto voce*, 'If Madam would care to use our facilities, I could wrap the shawl while I wait.'

'What? Oh yes, thank you,' Liz replied gratefully. It would mean an extra few minutes, but she was sure Maggie would understand. Five minutes later she emerged from the shop, the gaily wrapped parcel firmly tucked under her arm. She hoped Maggie would like the shawl. It had cost her ten shillings, but she didn't begrudge a penny of it.

When Maggie had first offered to hand over the business to her, she had been dumbstruck by the generosity behind the thought, especially as she'd refused to take a penny in compensation. When she thought back over the years, and the hard time she'd given Maggie lately about paying back the money that had saved them from the workhouse, she'd been overcome with regret and shame. The knowledge of what Maggie had had to endure to obtain the money was pushed firmly to the back of her mind. She knew she could never fully repay Maggie for all she had done, the shawl was merely a token of her love and gratitude. Lord, she'd been gone longer than she'd bargained for. If she didn't hurry, they'd end up having a row and that was something she didn't want; she never wanted to argue with Maggie ever again. Some hope, she thought wryly as she quickened her step.

The coachman sitting atop the carriage smiled benignly as Liz hurried past. His wife was expecting their first child any day now, and the sight of the attractive young woman obviously pregnant reminded him once again that he was soon to become a father. His attention was drawn from the retreating figure by the arrival of his master who had emerged from the tobacconist shop. Jumping down from his perch he stood to attention while at the same time opening the carriage door.

For years to come he would never forget that day, or know why the horses had suddenly bolted. All he could remember was the door being jerked from his hand as the frightened animals had taken flight and mounted the pavement heading straight for the figure that had just passed him. Her mind preoccupied with getting back to the coffee shop Liz didn't realise the danger until it was too late. Everything happened so quickly. Suddenly people were screaming as they ran to get out of the horses' path, while the onlookers on the other side of the road stood rooted to the spot, unable to do anything except stare in horror as the two horses continued on their mad rampage along the pavement. In the mad scramble for safety, Liz was thrown against the wall, her eyes widening in terror as the frightened beasts bore down on her. Dropping the parcel she wrapped her arms around her bulging stomach, her lips moving silently in a desperate prayer.

'Please God, please, not my baby. Oh, God, no, not like this . . .' The horses and carriage smashed into the defenceless body, tossing it aside as effortlessly as a match, killing both Liz and her unborn child instantly, before careering on down the now deserted pavement. Liz lay sprawled on the ground, her eyes still wide, her mouth open, as if even in death she was protesting at the fate that had befallen her.

Maggie had just paid the hovering waiter and was wondering if the shilling she had left for a tip was enough. Shrugging her shoulders she was about to rise and go in search of Liz when the sounds of screams and the metallic ring of horses' hooves filled the crowded shop. Everyone seemed frozen for a split second, then chairs were pushed back as people rushed to the window to see what had happened. Only Maggie remained where she was. Her mouth had turned dry and she could feel her heart hammering against her ribs. Don't be stupid, she told herself calmly. Any minute now, Liz is going to walk through that door all agog and busting with information about the accident that had just happened.

'Oh, my God, there's a girl lying on the pavement, look at the blood. Somebody run for a doctor, she may be dying,' a stout, aristocratic lady was shouting to nobody in particular, while Maggie stood rigid, afraid to move, afraid to go out into the street for fear of what she might see. Oh, Liz, where are you? Hurry up, please. I don't care about you leaving me here on my own, even if I did feel angry at first. Just walk through that door, please.

'Are you all right, Madam? Can I be of any assistance?' the waiter stood by the table, his faced filled with concern.

Forcing a trembling smile to her stiff lips, she answered evenly, 'No, thank you, I'm fine. It's just my sister, you know the girl I was with. She hasn't come back yet, and I'm a bit worried. I'm sure she'll turn up any minute now.'

As the man made to leave her self-control broke, and grabbing his arm she said shakily, 'Look, I know you'll think I'm being silly, but would . . . would you go outside and see . . . see if . . .'

Patting her arm reassuringly the man said kindly, 'Of course, Madam. Now you wait there. I'm sure as you say your sister will be returning any minute.'

She didn't know how long she waited, and then he was back by her side. Fearfully she glanced up then felt her body jerk painfully at the look of compassion on his lined face. He stood awkwardly, not knowing how to break the news to this pretty young woman who only a short time ago had sat laughing with the other young girl who now lay in a broken heap on the cold ground.

'Oh, no, no, no. Liz', she whispered. Then as the truth hit her, her voice rose hysterically. 'Liz, Lizzie,' and then she was pushing her way through the crowd of curious onlookers, knocking aside two elderly women in her haste to get outside. On the other side of the road, a group of people were gathered, while a lone policeman tried to keep some order. Her footsteps faltering, she staggered into the road and joined the milling crowd. Through the legs of the men grouped at the edge of the pavement she saw the blue coat, the sight of which drove her into a frenzy. With a strength she didn't know she possessed, she cut a path through the crowd, not caring who she hurt in the process. And there she was, her Liz, lying as still as death, the front of her coat covered in blood, her eyes gazing sightlessly into space.

Dropping to her knees she gently lifted the blonde head and placed it in her lap, murmuring, 'It's all right, love, I'm here. You'll be all right now.'

The policeman moved forward, his face grave. 'Do you know this woman, miss?' he enquired, then cursed himself for asking such a stupid question. Still, it was his job and questions had to be asked. But Maggie was oblivious to all around her, as she continued talking to Liz, her hand tenderly stroking the ashen face.

'Do you remember when you had pneumonia, Liz? We all thought you were going to die then, remember. But I got you through it, didn't I? So it doesn't make sense that you should die now, not after all my hard work.'

'Miss, I'm sorry, but I have to ask you your relationship to this woman.' The policeman was kneeling by her side wondering where the hell the ambulance van was. Maggie looked up at him, her eyes glazed over, her mind refusing to believe what had happened.

'Of course I know her, she's my sister. Could you help me to get her home, please. I can look after her once I get her home.'

The policeman dropped his head. He'd seen it so many times, people refusing to accept that their loved ones were dead, retreating into a shell-like state until reality hit them.

Gnawing on his bottom lip he took a deep breath before saying as gently as he could, 'I'm sorry, miss, your sister's dead. There's nothing you can do for her any more. I've sent for an ambulance, it should be here soon. Is there anyone I can send for? Your mother perhaps, or a neighbour? What about your brother-in-law? He'll have to be informed.'

The words echoed round Maggie's head then seemed to bounce off again. It was all right, she told herself. Don't listen to him and it'll be all right. But she could do with some help. Not Jimmy, she didn't want him here, and Mrs Casey had moved to somewhere down south over a year ago. Well, she'd have to manage on her own, and there was always Mrs Simms, she'd help.

She didn't hear the ambulance arriving, it was only when two men dressed in short white coats tried to prise Liz from her grasp that she was galvanized into action.

Tightening her hold on the warm body she said gratefully, 'Thank goodness you're here. She'll be all right, but maybe it's best if you take her to the hospital. She's going to have a baby and . . .'

The elder of the two men took hold of Liz's upper body, while the other man held her feet.

'Careful!' Maggie cried out. 'I told you she's expecting . . .'

The younger man was tired. He'd been on duty for over sixteen hours and the long work load had taken its toll.

Taking a firmer hold on the woman's feet he said brusquely, 'She ain't gonna feel anything, she's dead. If you wanna come with us to the hospital, you'd better get a move on, we ain't got all day.'

The policeman started forward, his face a mask of anger at the cruelty of the man's words. But before he could reprimand him, another man had moved forward from the crowd, a bundle of parcels held carefully under his arm.

Going straight to Maggie's side he said kindly, 'You left these in the restaurant, Madam.' The stunned look on the girl's face was too much for him, and with a muttered, 'I'm so sorry,' he walked unsteadily away from her anguished gaze. Still in a daze Maggie stared down at the parcels she and Liz had spent the morning buying. Then out of the corner of her eye she spotted the gaily wrapped parcel lying at her feet. Bending down she picked it up. So this was what Liz had gone in such a hurry for. The wrapping had split open revealing the fawn cashmere shawl. On the top lay a small card. Her eyes blurred with tears as she tried to make out the writing. Blinking furiously she held it nearer to her face and read the gold lettering. It said simply, 'For Maggie, something new, Love Liz'.

'Are you coming, or not?' the ambulance attendant shouted. Startled, Maggie dropped the card. Stooping to pick it up she noticed for the first time the blood on her hands. Something seemed to burst inside her head, and then she was screaming, her wild anguished cries searing the minds of the people standing watching the spectacle. One by one they began to disperse, unable to witness the girl's agony, but even when they'd left the street the screams seemed to follow them. They quickened their steps, eager to get away from the pain and anguish that might one day be theirs.

The last of the mourners had gone, leaving Maggie and Charlie alone. Ethel Simms had been the last to leave. Her eyes red from crying, she had begged Maggie to keep in touch, then, with Jimmy holding her arm, she had gone. That had been over three hours ago and

Jimmy had yet to return. Maggie hoped he would spend the night with his mother, she didn't want any company tonight, certainly not his. Their bags were packed, and they would be leaving first thing in the morning. They would have to stay in lodgings for the time being until she found somewhere permanent for her and Charlie. The sound of weeping brought her eyes round to where Charlie sat hunched over by the dying fire, his thin shoulders shaking with sobs. She envied him his tears, for she had been unable to show any emotion since the day after the accident.

Touching him gently on the shoulder she whispered, 'Best get to bed, love. We've a long day tomorrow and I want to make an early start.'

Getting to his feet Charlie walked over to the bed. Sitting down on the worn mattress he looked up at Maggie and his voice breaking, he asked, 'Why don't people ever know they loved someone 'til it's too late?' Maggie could only shake her head in pity.

'I don't know, love. But don't torment yourself, Liz knew you loved her, you don't always have to say it, sometimes people just know.'

'But I should have told her and now I'll never have the chance.'

'Go to sleep, Charlie,' Maggie said wearily. 'There's nothing you can do about it now.'

Maggie knew that she should try and comfort him, but the effort was too much. Leaving Charlie sitting on the mattress, she sat down by the fire, trying to get some warmth from the dying embers. Her head dropped onto her chest, the trauma of the last few days catching up on her as she slipped into a fitful sleep. She was awoken by a hand on her shoulder, and jumped nervously, then relaxed slightly when she saw who it was.

'God, you gave me a fright, Jimmy. I thought we had burglars. I didn't expect you back tonight, I thought you'd stay with your Mum – she was very upset.'

As she went to rise, Jimmy pushed her back into the chair, and it was with alarm she realised he'd been drinking, heavily too by the look of him.

Careful to keep her voice steady she said, 'I was just going to make some cocoa, would you like some?' She shrank back in fear as he leaned over her, his beer fumed breath fanning her face.

'It isn't cocoa I want, Maggie. It's comforting I need, and plenty of it.'

'Now come on, Jimmy, you're drunk, why don't you go to bed?' she said, the break in her voice betraying her growing fear.

'That's a good idea, Maggie, a very good idea. We'll go to bed and comfort each other. You know how to comfort a man, don't you, Maggie? Course I can't afford no three guineas, let alone twenty quid, but seeing as I'm family you can do it for free.'

Maggie felt her mouth drop in surprise. He couldn't know about that, not unless . . . Oh Liz, how could you, how could you tell him?

Yet even knowing the horrible truth she had to ask,

'How did you find out? Nobody knew except me and Liz, and she wouldn't tell you.'

Letting out a loud laugh he threw his head back glee-fully, 'Course she told me. Wives don't 'ave no secrets from their 'usbands. Now don't give me no trouble, I've waited a long time fer this, and we don't want to wake Charlie up, do we?'

Jimmy leaned closer to her, his lips curved into a leer, a leer that changed to one of pain and surprise as Maggie's knee jerked up catching him squarely in the groin. With a howl of rage he grabbed her from the chair throwing her roughly to the floor. The fall knocked the wind from her body for a few seconds, and then she was fighting him. Fighting him with every ounce of her strength. Not again, she vowed, I've been raped once, never again, if I have to die to prevent it. Despite her efforts she was no match for the burly man, and once again she felt her skirts being lifted over her head and a hand pulling at her underclothes. His thick wet lips were clamped to hers making it impossible for her to shout out. She felt tears of rage and despair spurt from her eyes as his other hand fastened on her exposed breast.

Shutting her eyes tight she waited for the inevitable to happen. At the crucial moment the body lying on hers went limp. At first she thought he had passed out from the drink, then looking over her shoulder she saw Charlie's frightened face in the glow of the table lamp and the poker he held in his shaking hand.

Her mind suddenly clear Maggie said sharply, 'Don't just stand there, help me get him off.'

The poker fell from Charlie's hand as he rushed to help his sister. The task wasn't easy; Jimmy was a big man, and being unconscious made him a dead weight. After much pushing and pulling they finally managed to get him onto his back.

'Is he dead, Maggie?' Charlie whispered fearfully. Maggie stared down at the supine figure, her eyes filled with loathing.

'I don't know, and what's more I don't care.'

'But, Maggie, if he's dead, I'll have to go to prison – they might even hang me!' Charlie's voice rose as he considered the consequences of what he had done.

Chewing her bottom lip, Maggie reflected on Charlie's words. What if he had killed him? Even given the circumstances, the courts would take a dim view of murder no matter what the provocation. Steeling herself for the worst she bent over and placed a shaking hand on the wide chest, then heaved a sigh of relief when she felt the strong beating of his heart beneath her hand.

'It's all right, he isn't dead,' she told the frightened boy. Wiping the hand she'd touched Jimmy with down the side of her skirt she thought for a moment. He was all right now, but what if they left him unattended and he died as a result. Some one would have to see to him; but who?

Whirling round she grabbed Charlie by the arm and

said urgently, 'Quick, go and fetch Mrs Simms. She can sit with him until he comes round, just in case. As soon as she gets here, we're off.'

'But Maggie,' Charlie cried bewilderedly, 'She's his Mum – what am I going to tell her?'

'Don't worry about that, love,' she answered grimly. 'Just tell her I need her. I'll deal with the rest when she gets here. Now hurry, we haven't much time.'

As soon as the door had banged behind him, Maggie went straight to the scullery and removing the loose brick took her savings from the wall. Next she pulled up the rug and prised up the floorboard where they kept the takings from the stall. Lifting the tin box from its hiding place she opened it, her face falling at the sight of the empty box.

Damn it, she should have known he'd take the money the first opportunity he had. Sitting back on her heels she wondered if she had the courage to go through his trouser pockets. he couldn't have spent it all, not in such a short space of time. She didn't need the money, but she'd be damned if he was going to keep it. Taking a deep breath and praying he wouldn't come round yet, she gingerly felt in his pockets. Nothing. Her heart sinking, she was about to give up when out of the corner of her eye she caught sight of his jacket hanging over the arm of the chair. Getting to her feet, she felt around in the inside pocket, her mouth curving into a smile of triumph as her hand closed round a wad of notes. Hearing the arrival of Charlie and Mrs Simms, she hastily put the money with her own, stuffing it down the front of her blouse.

'What's up, Maggie? What's happened now?' Ethel Simms was the first to enter the room, her chest heaving with exertion, her face filled with worry. Then she stopped in her tracks as her eyes focused on the still figure on the floor.

'My God, Maggie, what happened to 'im. Is 'e drunk? Charlie said it was urgent, I thought for a minute . . .'

There was no easy way to say what she had to say. As much as she didn't want to hurt this kindly woman who had been her friend for many years, the words had to be spoken.

'He tried to rape me, and Charlie knocked him out with a poker,' she answered as evenly as she could, then averted her eyes as she saw the look of pain and sorrow contort the woman's face. Sinking heavily into the armchair she looked first to Maggie and then to the still figure of her son, all the while shaking her head.

'I'm sorry, Mrs Simms. I would have given anything not to let you know, but me and Charlie are leaving. We're not going to wait until the morning, not now, and I didn't want to leave him on his own, just in case. You were the only one I could think of to stay with him.'

'You get orf, Maggie, love,' the grief-stricken women said, her breath coming in short, painful gasps. 'I'll see ter 'im. Oh, don't yer worry abaht that. I'll see ter 'im all right.'

The bags were by the door and Maggie and Charlie

were dressed in their outdoor coats. Telling Charlie to take the bags outside Maggie walked slowly back to where her friend was sitting.

Putting her arms around the fat neck she whispered brokenly, 'I'm sorry, Mrs Simms. I wouldn't have seen you hurt for the world. You've been so good to us, I don't know how we would have managed without you at times.'

Patting the trembling arms, the bemused woman said abstractedly, 'Don't yer worry abaht me, love, nor 'im. 'E won't bovver yer again. I can promise yer that. But where yer going ter sleep tonight. It's gorn eleven, yer'll 'ave a 'ard time finding somewhere decent round 'ere. Look, 'ere's me key. I know me place ain't much, but it'll do for the night. At least yer'll both be safe there until mornin'.'

Maggie hesitated, she wanted to get as far away from Jimmy Simms as possible, but what her friend said made sense. She'd be hard put to find anywhere else at this time of night.

Taking the key she kissed the wrinkled cheek, 'Thanks, Mrs Simms, I'm grateful. We both are.'

Standing by the door, Maggie took one last look around her old home, then with a determined look on her face she left the room for the last time.

Left alone with her son, Ethel Simms put her hands over her face and cried. He'd been such a lovely boy, always helping out whenever he could, skipping off school to do odd jobs and then proudly handing over his meagre earnings to her. He'd been good with his brothers and sisters too. Playing with them for hours, and looking after them when she had a job to go to. How could such a lovely, good-natured child have turned into the brute of a man that now lay flat out, stinking of beer on the floor. And when she thought of those two lovely girls . . . Oh dear lord, how could he? It had been bad enough that he had let his wife support him, but to try and rape his own sister-in-law when his wife was barely cold! What sort of a monster had she bred?

'Ooh, Christ, me 'ead.' Jimmy had come round, his moans filling the room as he tried to sit up, his head held in his hands.

'Where's that little bleeder, I'll do fer 'im. . . .' He stopped suddenly. Shaking his head he looked to where the large bulk of his mother sat staring at him from the armchair.

'Ma . . . what you doing 'ere?' he asked in bewilderment. he was sitting up now, his face creased in pain. About to rise to his feet he sensed his mother moving towards him. Staring up at the face above him he flinched at the loathing in the normally loving eyes.

'What's up, Ma, why yer looking at me . . .'

Ethel Simms moved nearer. 'You bastard,' she spat at him. Then her huge fist shot out, catching him squarely between the eyes, and for the second time in less than an hour, Jimmy Simms' world went black.

CHAPTER FIFTEEN

Charlie was worried.

When they had made the hurried flight from their former home to Mrs Simms' for the night, Maggie had been full of plans for their future. Even when he had been trying to get some sleep on the sagging sofa in the overcrowded room, she had kept him awake going over and over about what they were going to do once she got them settled. She'd made no further reference to what had happened with Jimmy – it was as if the sordid episode had never occurred.

The following day they had risen early, but instead of going to the rooming house in Whitechapel as originally planned, they had walked the darkened streets until coming to a halt outside a large, Georgian house with a board advertising 'Lodgers wanted'.

Once installed in the two large, comfortable rooms, Maggie had resumed her feverish talk, the brown eyes glittering wildly in her flushed face. Charlie had listened in silence, his eyes widening, feeling a growing ache of dismay in his stomach as she'd ranted on about opening a coffee shop somewhere up the West End. When he'd feebly protested that he didn't want to work in a poncy coffee shop and would rather stay in the markets, she had rounded on him furiously, shouting that if he didn't like it he could get out and fend for himself.

As suddenly as her anger had flared it had died down, leaving her looking lost and bewildered. For a moment he'd thought she was going to cry, instead she'd closed her eyes wearily and fallen into a deep sleep. He could still remember the relief he'd felt, thinking that her rantings were merely due to lack of sleep; that was until she'd woken up some seven hours later, looked at him as if he were a stranger, then shaking her head made her way to the bedroom and stayed there until the following morning.

Then the nightmare had begun. For instead of waking refreshed, she had greeted him with dull listless eyes before slumping silently into the armchair. For over two weeks now he had watched with growing alarm as the once ebullient young girl wandered aimlessly round the two rooms with the same apathetic manner she'd displayed the first morning in their new home. Whenever he asked what they were going to do, she'd look at him abstractedly and mutter, 'Not now, Charlie, leave it till tomorrow.' He'd even said he wouldn't mind working in a coffee shop, if that was what she wanted, hoping that his offer would jolt her out of the trance she seemed to be in. But she'd only looked at him, her eyes puzzled as if wondering what he was talking about. Now he didn't know what to do.

Raising his head he looked over to where she sat slumped dejectedly in the armchair, then, almost fearfully he let his gaze drop to her lap. Oh, Gawd, she was at it again! Rubbing her hands up and down her skirt; hands that were red from constant washing, sometimes in water so hot that tiny blisters had erupted on the now raw skin. But her hands were the only part of her body she did wash, for the once fastidious Maggie had let herself go to such an extent that he hardly recognised her any more. He forced himself to look at her face and felt a gnawing fear clutch at his stomach. She looked awful. Her beautiful hair was lank and greasy; she was still wearing the black dress she'd worn for Liz's funeral, refusing to take it off even to sleep. And she smelt. Maggie, who was always so particular about washing, now looked and smelt like a tramp.

It couldn't go on like this. This wasn't the Maggie he'd known all his life. Even as a child he could remember her bustling around, looking after him and his brothers, helping their Mum with the never-ending washing that was always piled high in the scullery. The Maggie he knew could never sit still for long; she always had to have something to do, somewhere to go. His Maggie was nothing like the lifeless figure slumped opposite him. What was he going to do? He should be doing something instead of just sitting here day after day watching her slip further and further away from him, and worst, away from reality. He wasn't a boy any more, he was fourteen, nearly a man. But he didn't feel like a man; he still felt like the frightened young boy who had clung first to his mother, and for the past six years to his sister. Now it was she who needed someone to cling to, and he knew, deep down, that if he had been possessed of a stronger character he could have helped her.

Gnawing at his bitten-down nails his mind flew to the one person he knew of that might be able to bring Maggie out of the depression she had sunk into. Did he have the nerve though? He knew how Maggie felt about Mr Stewart. He didn't know why she had changed her feelings towards the man she'd once been so friendly with, but right now that didn't seem important. She'd probably go mad if he brought him back here, but he'd welcome her anger, at least it would show she still had some life left in her. Taking a deep breath he went to speak then changed his mind. Best get going before his courage deserted him.

Once out in the street he stood by the railings, his legs trembling. What if he refused to come? After all, he hadn't seen Maggie for nearly two years. Why should he drop everything and come running for someone who was no longer a part of his life? And what had caused the rift that sent Maggie into a rage whenever his name was mentioned? It must have been something serious. Oh, Gawd, what was he to do? In spite of the warm April morning he shivered as he debated about returning to the house. And then what? he asked himself furiously. Wait until she's carted off to a nuthouse? Because that's where she was heading for if she didn't get some help. Somewhere, deep within him, Charlie felt a strength growing. Strength born out of fear and desperation, but mostly out of shame, shame at himself for being so weak and indecisive. If he didn't do something now and anything happened to Maggie, he knew he'd never be able to forgive himself. Drawing his shoulders back he set off down the road, a determined look on his face. He knew where to go.

The new Stewart houses were sited only twenty minutes' walk away. He hadn't been there himself, but had heard about them from the landlady who was afraid of losing future prospective lodgers to the man who seemed determined to rehouse the whole of the East End single handed. When he arrived at his destination he faltered for a moment, then, his face set, he walked on.

In April 1851, Lord Shaftesbury, horrified by the living conditions in the East End of London, passed an Act urging the local councils to remedy the situation by buying empty land to build on and convert old buildings into suitable accommodation. The councils replied by declaring that such an undertaking could never be profitable.

The expansion of lodgings – or doss houses as they were better known – continued, financed solely by middle-class house buyers who employed warders to protect their property. Investors in lodging houses enjoyed regular returns on their capital, although the majority of them never came near their properties. It wasn't until 1888, when the Ripper murders were causing a sensation all over the world, that the appalling living conditions of the masses was highlighted. The sensational publicity led to the escalation of new housing policies by shame-faced councils, while leaving enough land and old properties to be purchased and used by those men and women in a position to buy them. The infamous rookeries slowly became a thing of the past, as the newly born London County Council and wealthy entrepreneurs vied to create a newer and healthier environment for the oppressed people of the East End.

One such man was Harry Stewart.

The two-century-old tenement buildings had been reduced to a heap of rubble. When Harry had signed the deeds, he had intended to restore them to their former glory. He had been greatly impressed by the size and location of the buildings. Unfortunately, he'd been in such a hurry to acquire his new property, he had agreed a price with the owner without inspecting the interior of the houses. That had been a grave mistake, and a costly one. Sadly, the interiors had been in such a state of neglect and dilapidation, he had deemed it wiser and more economical to demolish his latest acquisition and rebuild.

The knocking down part had been comparatively easy, with Harry stripped to the waist working side by side with his men, swinging a heavy pickaxe with the ease of one who was born to it. Now had come the hard part. Aided with the advice of architects, carpenters and plumbers, he estimated it would be a year before the new buildings were completed. Confident that the work would run to schedule, Harry had placed an advertisement in *The London Gazette* stating that the new homes would be ready for occupation by July 1894; he had already received over thirty applications for the planned two-roomed apartments.

The old houses had consisted of four storeys; the new ones would have five, thus giving an extra twenty-two rooms to let. It would be his biggest undertaking to date, a prospect that both exhilarated and frightened him.

Sitting behind an old, scarred desk in the hastily erected hut that served as an office, he surveyed the mountain of papers and documents that lay scattered before him and sighed. As his business had grown, so had the never ending mass of paperwork to be dealt with. Not for the first time, he pondered as to whether he should hire a clerk to deal with the irksome task of keeping his papers in order.

When he had mentioned his dilemma at dinner one night, Bella had immediately volunteered her services, an offer he had hastily declined. Giving one last despairing look at the desk, he leant back in his chair, his hands clasped behind his neck. From the open window he could see his men grouped around an open brick fire, upon which rested the biggest kettle he'd ever seen. Moments later the boiling water was poured into a teapot of equally large proportions, then left to brew while the men studied their tin boxes to see what their wives had prepared them for dinner. These were the men who had been with him from the start, men he could depend on and trust.

There were others, younger, single men who preferred to take their dinner at the nearest public house. Unhampered by wives and children to support, they could afford to pay for the hot, tasty meals provided by the pub landlord, unlike their married counterparts who had to be content with sandwiches and maybe a piece of fruit if they were lucky. The only drawback to the men visiting the pub was the consumption of beer that accompanied the meals. He'd had to fire three men in the past two weeks for coming back to work drunk.

It really wasn't good enough. Men should have a hot, nourishing meal during the day, especially men such as his who needed all their strength for the arduous job they performed. A rumbling in his stomach reminded him that he too needed to keep up his strength. Reaching under the desk he brought out a small, wicker hamper and lifted the lid. Inside lay two golden breasts of chicken, four red tomatoes, half a loaf of crusty bread cut in the middle and heavily spread with butter, two oranges and an apple, plus a bottle of white wine. The sight of the delicious food so lovingly prepared by Mrs Sheldon that morning brought forth the familiar feelings of hunger and guilt. Like a small boy fearful of being caught raiding the larder he picked up a piece of chicken and bread, all the while keeping an eye on the window lest one of his men should decide to come to the hut. His meal finished, he replaced the hamper, a wry smile on his lips. He'd better not mention the plight of his men regarding their meals at home. He wouldn't put it past Bella to suggest setting up a soup kitchen, with her in sole charge of course. Draining the last of the wine, he set the glass down on the desk, his expression thoughtful. Poor Bella. Memories of Christmas Day flooded back to his mind.

The day had started as normal, with presents exchanged from beneath the giant Christmas tree. Then, after the sumptuous dinner, the family had retired to the drawing-room, the men settling themselves in the high-backed leather armchairs, a glass of brandy in their hands to await the arrival of the servants.

Benson had entered the room first, then stood by the door while Mrs Sheldon, Gertie and Annie had received their presents from the mistress of the house. As was customary, Beatrice lavished praise on Mrs Sheldon for the excellent dinner and complimented the two girls for their help in the smooth running of the house. Once the women had left, their faces beaming with pleasure, Benson had stepped forward to receive his gift from the man he had served for over thirty years. The long, white envelope containing two five-pound notes was taken gratefully, and with much bowing and profuse thanks, the elderly man had left the room to join the women in the kitchen for their own private Christmas dinner.

A silence had settled on the room, until Hugh, throwing back his third brandy, had laid down his glass and announced his intention to marry. Lord, what a night that had been. Once the initial shock had worn off, the family had swarmed around the red-faced young man, asking questions, demanding to meet the woman who had captured the most eligible doctor in London. All the family that was, except Bella. Bella had remained seated, her face white with shock, her eyes filled with pain. There had been something else in her expression, something Harry hadn't been able to identify until later, and then it had come to him: betrayal – she'd worn the look of a woman betrayed.

It had occurred to Harry that maybe his brother was marrying out of desperation, and if that were the case, could he blame him? Bella had always been possessive of Hugh, but over the past two years, Harry had watched in alarm as Bella had slowly but skilfully adapted to the role of wife to the brother she adored. Hugh could no longer leave the house without telling her where he was going and with whom. Often she would insist on accompanying him, brushing aside his feeble protests as one would with a querulous child. She'd even started getting up early so they could breakfast together, and was always waiting for him when he returned home. Harry had pleaded with Hugh to tell her to go to hell, but Hugh would simply shake his head miserably, declaring that he couldn't hurt her feelings.

Bella's abnormal behaviour hadn't gone unnoticed by their parents. They too had watched and worried. Efforts had been renewed to find their ageing daughter a husband, but all to no avail.

Now at last Hugh had taken the first steps to a normal life, and this time next year, when he slipped a gold band on the finger of Miss Lotte Winters, he would finally break free from Bella's possessive hold. And once Hugh was safely married, he, Harry, would start looking for a place of his own.

Again the words 'Poor Bella' came to mind. He still didn't like the woman, but could now feel pity for her and the life that stretched before her. A life empty and devoid of any purpose. Twice in the last week, she had come to the site, purporting to have been 'just passing'. The first time he had taken her to luncheon at a nearby restaurant had been a mistake.

She had come again yesterday, but this time she hadn't made her presence known to him, preferring instead to wander among the men, chatting amiably as if attending a garden party. The men had been embarrassed, as had he – embarrassed and annoyed. Her unexpected arrival had meant him leaving his men, getting washed and changed and escorting her to the nearest hansom cab. He wondered briefly if her mind was becoming unhinged, then shook his head impatiently. She was lonely, desperately so, especially since Hugh had become engaged, thus depriving her of the only male company she'd had. Now she was trying to latch onto him and he wasn't going to put up with it. He felt sorry for her predicament, but any affection he may have once had for her had long since died. She was being pleasant to him at the moment, but he wasn't fool enough to imagine her change of attitude to him stemmed from rediscovered sisterly love. The only reason she had sheathed her claws was due to her desire to visit the site and mingle among the half-naked men. God! It had been pitiful to see her yesterday, smiling and attempting to make conversation with the embarrassed men while her eyes raked their sweating, dust-covered bodies.

Well, it couldn't be allowed to continue, she had made a spectacle of herself once; he would make sure it didn't happen again. He'd already had a discreet word with his mother last night, and she'd promised to speak to Bella, her face filled with sorrow as she realised the depths her daughter was prepared to stoop to in order to gain a husband.

The sounds of laughter brought him out of his reverie, and, glancing quickly at his pocket watch he hurriedly donned his jacket. He had an appointment with his solicitor at two o'clock. Luckily the offices were within walking distance. The laughter started again, louder this time, causing Harry to frown. He knew all too well the difference between natural mirth and drunken laughter. His face grim, he was about to open the door when out of the corner of his eye he saw Bella, her hand placed provocatively on her hip, while the other twirled a parasol casually above her head. Harry swore softly beneath his breath.

Damn the woman! Couldn't she see she was making a fool of herself? The two men with her were new, and obviously drunk. His regular men were watching the spectacle, their attitudes awkward as they witnessed the governor's sister's antics. Joe Pearson, the foreman, had sprung forward and was trying to get the two young men back to work, but they were having too much sport with the plain, middle-aged woman to take any notice. Harry watched in anger as one of the men began to make faces behind Bella's back, his antics making his companion roar with laughter. Furious now, Harry wrenched the door open, only to be knocked back as a tall, wiry figure burst into the hut.

'Charlie!' he exclaimed in surprise, the problem of Bella momentarily pushed from his mind.

The carefully rehearsed words Charlie had been repeating in his mind on his journey vanished. His whole face twitching in agitation he burst out, 'I'm sorry for disturbing you at work, sir, but Maggie's bad. Can you come, sir? Please, I ain't got no-one else I can ask.'

Harry's heart jumped painfully against his ribs at the sound of the anguish in the boy's voice. 'What do you mean when you say she's bad? Has there been an accident of some sort?' Fear made his voice harsh, and Charlie shrank back against the wall, his face blanched, his hands nervously pulling at the cap he held in his hands.

'Please, Sir, can I sit down? I don't feel so good; me legs 'ave gone all wobbly.'

The misery in his voice wasn't lost on Harry. Taking hold of the boy's arm he led him gently to a chair, then dropping to a kneeling position he asked in a steady voice, 'Now, tell me what's happened, Charlie.'

The worst part of his ordeal over, Charlie gave a shuddering sigh then as calmly as he could recounted the events of the past few weeks. When he had finished he bent his head to one side, hoping that Mr Stewart hadn't seen the tears that were burning his eyes. Harry remained in the same position for some time, his mind trying to digest what Charlie had told him. Straightening his legs he walked over to the window, his eyes clouded in sorrow.

That poor young girl, to be killed in such a way and her unborn child too. He had never met Lizzie, but that didn't stop him questioning the futility of her death. And what of Maggie? To have had to witness her sister lying dead in the street. God! It would be enough to turn anyone's mind. He must go to her immediately and see just how ill she was. Then if he deemed it necessary he would send for Hugh. This may be the one instance where his brother would be more equipped to deal with an emergency than he himself was.

Rounding on Charlie he barked, 'Come, we'll find a cab. It shouldn't take long to get to Whitechapel at this time of day.'

Charlie rose slowly from the chair. 'We . . . we don't live there no more, sir. We had to move, quick like, 'cos of Jimmy.'

Charlie saw Harry's eyes narrow, and wondered if he should have kept quiet about Jimmy.

'Jimmy?' Harry repeated. 'Would that be your brother-in-law?' He was remembering his last conversation with Maggie and her fears concerning the man. He felt his stomach contract in apprehension.

Wetting his lips he asked, 'What about Jimmy? Did he do something to Maggie? Answer me, boy, did that man hurt her in any way?'

Charlie was feeling sick. His head was pounding and his tongue seemed to be glued to the roof of his mouth. Should he tell? Oh, Gawd, he wished he hadn't come here now.

Harry saw the uncertainty on the boy's face and forced himself to remain calm. Taking a deep breath of air he said, 'It's all right, Charlie, there's no need to be alarmed. You have nothing to be afraid of. Now, take your time and tell me exactly what happened.'

Charlie's mouth opened and closed frantically, then in a rush of words he gabbled out the details that had forced them to flee from their home in such a hurry, his eyes glued to his shaking hands held in his lap throughout his stuttering explanation. When he had finished he glanced up at Harry then quickly dropped his gaze back down to his hands, unable to bear the look of anger that now consumed the man. He wouldn't like to be in Jimmy's boots if this man ever caught up with him.

Harry paced the floor, his eyes alighting briefly on the shotgun resting by the wall. Knowing that a large amount of money was delivered each week to pay the men's wages, Edward Stewart had insisted his son was protected against any would-be thieves. Harry had laughed at the idea. He couldn't see any man, however desperate, brave enough to attempt to take the hard-earned money of the burly men working right outside the door. He'd only agreed to take the gun in order to put his father's mind at rest; he himself hated any form of firearm. Now he had the strongest desire to pick it up and go looking for the man who had tried to violate Maggie. Any man who could act as that one had deserved to be shot.

'Can you come now, sir?' Charlie's voice broke into his murderous thoughts. 'I don't like to leave Maggie on her own for too long.'

Harry's head cleared. Shrugging himself into his jacket he picked up his walking cane, saying briskly, 'Of course, of course I'll come. And Charlie, let's drop the 'Sir' business, shall we? You used to call me Harry, and I'd feel more comfortable if you did so now.'

'Yes, sir . . . I mean, Harry,' Charlie answered, his lips stretched in a watery smile. Once outside the hut Harry placed his hand on Charlie's arm.

'Wait here a moment, Charlie, I won't be long.'

Charlie watched as Harry picked his way over the piles of rubble towards the woman standing among the debris. His eyes widened as he saw Harry pull her roughly away from the two men she had been talking to, then drag her protesting over the dangerous, uneven ground. Her two companions immediately made a great show of returning to work, their strong hands sifting among the rubble for unbroken bricks to be stacked and put aside for the new buildings.

'Really, Harry, how dare you humiliate me in front of your men.' The woman was nearly crying with rage as she struggled to break free from her brother's iron grasp. 'I only came down to see if you wanted to go to luncheon, you have no right to treat . . .'

'I know what you came down here for, and it had nothing to do with concern for my stomach,' Harry was shouting. 'Even if I had been planning to dine out, the spectacle I've just witnessed would have put me off eating for some considerable time.'

Charlie shuffled uncomfortably as they drew near, his face gloomy as he saw his secret plans dashed. So, Harry was married now, he thought miserably. Well, he didn't think much of his choice, she was an ugly old boot in spite of her fine clothes. His heart sank. Deep down he had been hoping that once Harry met Maggie again they would resume their friendship. He should have known that a man like Harry would marry. They were standing in front of him now, and Harry's next words sent Charlie's heart leaping with hope once again.

'I'm afraid I'll have to see my sister to a cab, Charlie, then we can be on our way,' Harry said, his voice clipped, ignoring the frantic struggling of the woman by his side.

'You'll regret this, Harry, I swear, you'll regret treating me like this. I'll tell . . .'

'*Shut up, Bella,*' Harry roared, his voice causing both Bella and Charlie to jump. An uncomfortable silence settled on the trio as they marched from the site onto the bustling high street. Ignoring the heavy traffic, Harry stepped into the road and waved down a hansom cab. Even before the horses had come to a standstill, he was already pushing Bella into the carriage, slamming the door on her.

Charlie shivered at the sight of the woman, her face white with fury, before the cab drove off into the stream of traffic. Then he was striding out, leading the way back home, the tall craggy-faced man beside him. Charlie felt his steps lightened by Harry's comforting presence. Maggie would be all right now. Everything would be all right now.

'Here's another cab.' Harry was extending his cane in the direction of the oncoming hansom cab.

'Hang on, sir . . . I mean, Harry.' Charlie clutched at his arm. 'It'll be quicker to walk. It ain't far from here, and I know a few short cuts.' Already he was walking across the road, with Harry striding briskly after him.

When they arrived at the house some twenty minutes later Charlie hesitated before saying, 'Maybe I'd better go up first. She ain't going to be pleased . . .'

Harry was tired and disgruntled; moreover he was desperately concerned about Maggie. Despite the fact that he hadn't seen her for nearly two years she had remained never far from his thoughts. Now that he was so near to seeing her again he wasn't going to let anyone stand in his way. Mindful of Charlie's nervousness he smiled encouragingly.

'I've had a lifetime of practice in the strange moods of women, as you witnessed a short time ago. Now, lead the way, Charlie, and once we are inside the room leave all the talking to me.'

Pulling a key from his pocket, Charlie unlocked the red front door. Once inside the lobby he said, 'We're on the top floor,' then fell silent, his long legs taking the stairs slowly as if reluctant to reach his destination.

Despite Harry's genuine concern regarding Maggie's health and mind, the businessman in him couldn't help but scrutinize his surroundings. The house was certainly a lot cleaner than some he had been inside. The walls had recently been painted a bright yellow, and the floor and stairs were covered in clean, if somewhat threadbare, carpeting. He wondered what the landlord was asking for rent, and just caught himself from asking the question of Charlie. Now was not the time for satisfying idle curiosity. They had reached the top landing. Charlie, anxious now to get the coming confrontation over with,

271

had already opened the door to the rooms he shared with Maggie.

With one last beseeching look over his shoulder he entered the room. 'Maggie? Maggie, I'm back,' he called out, his voice tinged with apprehension. Maggie was still sitting in the armchair, her hands rubbing against each other in agitation.

'Where've you been?' she asked dully, her voice betraying the fact that she didn't really care.

Harry stepped into the room, gently moving Charlie aside so that he could see Maggie more clearly. He felt the breath leave his body at the sight of the dishevelled, unkempt woman slumped in the chair. This couldn't be Maggie – it was some horrible joke. This wasn't the woman he had dreamed about, longed for. Then she lifted her head and he found himself gazing into the familiar brown eyes, and felt his heart melt with pity. With a bound he was across the room and kneeling at her feet. Ignoring the smell that was emanating from her he grasped her hands tenderly.

'Oh, Maggie, Maggie, what have you done to yourself?'

Maggie looked down at him, her eyes puzzled. Then the veil seemed to lift from her eyes, and with a loud shout she pulled her hands from his grasp.

'What are you doing here?' she breathed heavily. 'I told you I never wanted to see you again. Get out, get out. Charlie? Charlie, make him go, please, make him go.'

His face pale, Charlie ran to her side crying, 'No, Maggie, you need help, and I can't help you any more. Please, Maggie, don't send him away, I'm frightened. I don't know what do. You ain't well, Maggie, please, listen to Harry.'

With a strength that surprised both man and boy, Maggie threw Harry aside and jumped to her feet. 'I don't need help, especially not yours, Harry Stewart. Now get out of my house before I call for the police.'

Harry rose slowly to his feet, his face set with determination. 'You may call all you like, Maggie, but I'm not leaving you like this. Charlie's right, you're ill and need help, and if you won't accept it from me, then I'll have no choice but to have you admitted to hospital.'

Maggie shrank back from him, her eyes wide with terror darted around the room as if seeking some form of escape. Her face crumpled pitifully, then she was shaking her head wildly.

'No, no, not the hospital,' she whispered fearfully. 'Liz is there, she's all broken and bleeding. I tried to help her, but . . . but she wouldn't wake up, she . . .'

'Hush, my dearest, it's all right, everything's going to be all right now. You've been through a dreadful ordeal but it's over now. Listen to me, Maggie, please, you have to . . .'

With a cry like a wounded animal Maggie ran to the far corner of the room, her hands beating against the wall, then with a low moan she slumped down onto the floor. Instantly Harry was by her side, his face pressed against her hair, his voice soft as he endeavoured to calm her, but it was no use.

'It was my fault, all my fault. She went to buy me a shawl. I didn't know . . . I should have gone with her. Oh, Lizzie, Lizzie, come back, please come back.' Harry could only bend his head in pity as her anguished cries filled the room. Careful not to frighten her further he pulled the thrashing body into his arms. But when he went to take her hands she became hysterical. 'Not my hands, don't . . . don't touch my hands.'

Charlie stood by the door looking on helplessly. 'She's been like that since the accident. I mean, with her hands. She keeps rubbing them and washing them. Oh sir, will she have to go away? I mean to one of them nuthouses.'

Harry thought quickly. Hugh should be at home now. He and Lotte were going to the theatre tonight, and had arranged to dine at home before setting out.

Keeping a tight hold on the squirming body he shouted to Charlie. 'She needs medical help. Look, go to my home and ask for my brother. Explain what has happened and bring him back with you. Here, take this money and get a cab.' Charlie looked down at the sovereign lying in Harry's outstretched palm.

'Well, what are you waiting for?' Harry shouted. 'Here, here's my card, it has my home address on it. Hurry, boy, there's no time to lose.' Still Charlie stood transfixed, his legs refusing to obey him.

'But what if . . . if the servants won't let me see him?'

Harry whirled to face him, his face set like thunder.

'*Then bloody well force your way in, but get my brother here!*'

Charlie's feet seemed to leave the ground, and then he was running, running like he'd never run before, the memory of Maggie's pitiful mutterings ringing in his ears.

'I can't get the blood off, I can't get the blood off my hands.'

CHAPTER SIXTEEN

The long row of houses seemed endless to Charlie as he ran down the tree-lined street in Hackney, his eyes desperately searching for number twenty-three. Pausing for a moment he leant against a stone pillar, his breath coming in short, painful gasps. Pulling his cap from his head, he wiped his perspiring face along his sleeve then walked up the four deep steps and looked up at the number on the white painted door, then groaned loudly. The house he was resting at was number forty-one. Trust him to come into the street at the wrong end. His task wasn't helped by the fact that all the houses seemed the same. All the three-storey houses were flanked by chalk stone pillars with the front doors set back, the numbers hard to distinguish from the street. At last he came to the house he was looking for. Again he wiped his face, stalling for time while he thought out what he was going to say to whoever opened the door. Peering over the spiked railings down into the small courtyard he wondered if it would be better if he knocked on the servants' door. After all that's where Maggie always went when she came down this street on their rounds. It was a known fact that tradesmen and such like never approached the main door, it was the way things were done. Still he hesitated. If he went down to the servants' quarters and asked for mister Hugh it was doubtful he would be taken seriously.

'Oh Gawd, what shall I do?' he muttered under his breath, his fingers pulling at his cap. Out of the corner of his eye he saw a policeman coming his way, the burly figure strolling aimlessly along the quiet street, his wooden truncheon swinging gently from his hand as he patrolled his beat. The sight of the authoritative figure acted as a spur to the frightened boy; he couldn't hang around here any longer or he could be run in for loitering. Opening his mouth he drew in a deep lungful of air, then ran quickly up the stone steps.

Agnes was passing through the hall, her hands filled with a large silver platter upon which rested mid-afternoon tea, when the frantic hammerings on the front door began.

'Oh, lummey,' she exclaimed fretfully, looking from the door to the laden tray, then back to the kitchen from

277

which she'd come. She waited hesitantly, hoping Benson or Annie would come to see what the noise was, but the hall remained empty. The door chimes had now joined with the hammering and with an impatient 'tut' she rested the tray on the hall table and opened the door. At the sight of the gangly youth she opened her eyes wide.

''Ere, what you doing making all that noise, boy? The tradesman's entrance is below stairs. Now get orf with yer afore I call Mr Benson, he'll . . .'

'I've come for Mr Hugh. Go and fetch 'im, please, it's very important.'

Charlie pushed the startled girl to one side, striding past her into the hall, only to come to a standstill at the sight of the opulent splendour surrounding him. The plush blue and gold carpet seemed to spread like a river beneath his feet, running the length of the floor and sweeping up the curved stairway. A soft tinkling sound brought his eyes upward to the huge crystal chandelier that hung from the embossed ceiling above his head, and with a nervous start he darted out from beneath it, half-expecting the enormous creation to come crashing down upon his head.

Agnes had by now recovered her aplomb, and with arms placed squarely on her hips she faced the intruder angrily.

'Whadya mean bursting in like that? Now I'm warning yer, boy, you'd better get yer arse out of 'ere sharpish. People like you ain't allowed in the 'ouse.'

Charlie looked at the irate girl dressed in a black dress

with a frilly white apron with two large bows sticking out at either side of her waist and swallowed nervously.

'I ain't going nowhere till I've seen Mr Hugh. Mr Harry told me to come, and I . . . I ain't leaving, so you'd best go and get him.'

Amazed at his temerity, Agnes looked around her, uncertain of what to do next, willing Benson to appear and take the matter out of her hands, while Charlie stood his ground. As if in answer to her prayer, muffled footsteps sounded along the passage. With a great sigh of relief she turned to the elderly man approaching them.

'Oh, Mr Benson, I'm that glad ter see yer,' she began thankfully. 'This 'ere boy pushed 'is way in. I told 'im ter go but 'e won't take any notice of me, he says Mr Harry sent 'im.'

'Did he now?' Benson answered, his lined face thoughtful. He like the rest of the house knew of the young master's affinity with the lower classes. He studied the boy who had dared to intrude into his domain, his sharp gaze taking in the clean, long grey trousers and bright striped vee-necked jersey. The boy himself seemed to be in a state of agitation, his thick dark hair unruly as if fingers had been dragged through the curly mop. His hands held in front of him nervously pulled at the grey cap while his brown eyes stared back at him defiantly.

Benson thought quickly. There was a good chance the boy was telling the truth, and if that was the case he'd better not go too hard on him. However, he couldn't just bring the boy into the drawing-room unannounced, there were certain proprieties to be observed. He would take the boy into the kitchen and question him further, then, if he was satisfied with his story he would discreetly inform Master Hugh of the boy's presence. Clearing his throat he turned to Agnes.

'Take the tray in before it gets cold, girl. I'll see to our visitor,' he ordered grandly. Then stretching out his hand he made to take Charlie by the arm. Charlie, mistaking the man's intention pulled away, his hand fighting off the old man's grasp.

'No, you're not throwing me out, yer silly old codger. I want to see Mr Hugh. I told yer, Mr Harry sent me.' His voice was rising in fear and desperation. Harry's words echoed in his mind. Whirling round he ran to the foot of the stairway shouting wildly, 'Mr Hugh, Mr Hugh, it's me, Charlie. Please Mr Hugh, I need yer.'

Benson watched horrified as the boy ran up and down the hall, before bounding forward to drag the boy out of earshot of the drawing-room.

'Be quiet, boy,' he hissed frantically, 'I'm not going to hurt you, I merely want to . . .' When Charlie's boot caught him sharply in the shin he gave a cry of pain and quickly released his hold.

'Mr Hugh, help!'

Man and boy froze as the green baize door at the end of the hall flew open and a stout man dressed in a black morning jacket and dark grey trousers came storming towards them.

'What in thunder is going on out here?' Edward Stewart demanded, his black eyes sweeping over the startled trio. Charlie recognised the voice of authority, and felt his courage slipping away.

Then his arm was gripped once again as Benson tried to regain control of the situation.

'Begging your pardon, sir,' he began, 'but this here person forced his way into the house demanding to see Mr Hugh. He claims Mr Harry sent him. I was about to settle him in the kitchen, sir, while I . . .'

Edward Stewart waved his hand impatiently. 'Yes, yes, all right, Benson, I'm sure you acted correctly,' he interrupted the old man, his eyes fixed on the young interloper. 'You, boy, come here,' he ordered, and Charlie, his legs feeling like jelly, approached the imposing figure.

Wetting his lips he was about to explain his presence once again when a familiar voice cried out, 'Charlie? Charlie, is that you?' Charlie spun round, his body going weak with relief at the welcome sight of Hugh descending the stairs.

'Oh, Mr Hugh, Oh, crikey, I'm pleased to see yer. Thank Gawd you're here. Maggie's ill, really ill. Mr Harry sent me to get yer, he said I wasn't to take no for an answer. Can yer come now, Mr Hugh? Harry said . . .'

'Maggie ill?' Hugh repeated. The welcoming smile had dropped from his lips, leaving his face troubled. 'How do you mean, ill? Has there been an accident of some sort?'

Charlie felt as if he was back in the hut with Harry

listening to the same questions, and felt a rising sense of desperation.

'Please, Mr Hugh, I ain't got time to explain it all now. Can't you just get yer black bag and come with me?'

'I'm afraid it's not that simple, Charlie,' Hugh said gently. 'I have to know what the problem is so I can bring the correct medication with me.'

Casting an apologetic look at his father he asked, 'May I take Charlie into the library, Father? He's an old friend of mine and Harry's, and I'd like to help him if I can.'

All eyes were on the head of the household, not least of all Charlie, who still half-expected to be thrown out on his backside. Moving closer to Hugh he waited for the autocratic man to speak.

'Well now, seeing as this young man had stormed the barricades, so to speak, I'd be interested to hear the reason behind his action.' The voice, still authoritative, was now tempered with kindness. When the portly face creased into a smile, Charlie experienced an overwhelming sense of relief.

'You, girl, fetch another cup for our guest, and you, boy, come with me.'

Agnes and Benson watched in amazement as the boy walked with the master and Mr Hugh into the drawing-room. The elderly butler was the first to recover, and turned to the open-mouthed maid.

'Well, don't just stand there gawping, you heard the master, fetch another cup. And you'd better make a fresh pot of tea, that one will be stone cold by now.'

Agnes picked up the tray, her body bristling with indignation.

'Well! I never thought I'd see the day. A common barrow-boy being brought into the drawing-room for tea, just like he was a friend of the family. I bet Miss Bella'll have something to say about it.'

'That's as may be, girl, but this isn't Miss Bella's house. Now do as you're bid and look sharp about it.'

With a defiant toss of her head that threatened to dislodge her white, starched cap, Agnes cast one last disapproving glance at the green baize door before marching back to the kitchen.

Charlie's new-found confidence was short-lived. Flanked on both sides by these men of importance he had for a moment felt his courage returning, but when he saw the three, elegantly dressed women staring at his entrance he felt his face flame with acute embarrassment. Disconcerted, he vainly tried to shuffle his feet and found the reflex action hampered by the deep pile of the patterned carpet.

Anxious to gain a moment's respite, he let his eyes wander round the room he found himself in, his breath catching in his throat at the grandeur that greeted his gaze. Dusky pink velvet curtains with heavy betasselled pelmets hung on either side of the large bay window. Directly beneath lay a dark silver *chaise longue*, the bright threads of the material glinting in the sunlight that flooded the room. To the side stood a highly polished mahogany cabinet upon which rested numerous china ornaments. By the open fireplace, where a coal fire was burning brightly in spite of the mildness of the day, sat two black leather wing-backed armchairs. But it was the centre of the room that held Charlie's attention. The women were seated round an octagonal, spindle-legged table, their full skirts billowing over the tapestried chairs, obscuring the curved wooden legs from view.

They made an impressive trio. The eldest of the women wore a white lace cap on her fair hair. Her gown was of the palest blue and in her lap lay a piece of embroidery, her hand holding the needle momentarily stilled by his unexpected arrival. On her left sat another fair-haired woman. This one was younger, her plump figure highlighted by a maroon dress with the latest leg-of-mutton sleeves. Although both women were regarding him with curiosity, their blue eyes were kindly. Not so the third woman, who was glaring at him with undisguised hostility. He recognised her immediately as Harry's sister and without stopping to think said loudly, 'Hello, Miss. I hope you got home all right?'

All eyes turned towards Bella.

'You know my daughter?'

Charlie turned to the man by his side, his heart sinking as he realised the gaffe he had just committed. Shuffling his feet he murmured, 'Not really, sir. I met her at Harry's, I mean Mr Harry's site this morning . . .' His voice trailed off, uncomfortably aware of the tension his word had evoked.

'Did you indeed?' the gruff voice said ominously.

'Father,' Hugh interjected quickly, 'I really think we should listen to what Charlie has to say. Maggie, I mean his sister, may be seriously ill. I'd like to get to her as quickly as possible.'

Edward remained staring at his daughter, his black eyes filled with contempt. God! Even the commonest prostitute wouldn't stoop to plying for trade while their customers were at work. It wasn't to be tolerated. There was a way to put a stop to her antics, if Beatrice would agree. He had first thought of the plan last year when she had started her unnatural attentions towards Hugh. Then Hugh had announced his engagement and he had put the idea to one side. Now it seemed he had no option but to implement the plan. But first things first – he would listen now to what the boy had to say, and deal with Bella later.

'Mr Hugh . . .' Charlie implored, his voice cracking with urgency.

The plaintive voice brought Edward out of his reverie. Assuming a stance, he waved towards one of the plush covered chairs.

'Sit down boy, and let us hear what you have to say.'

Once seated, Charlie carefully kept his gaze on Hugh as he related once more the incidents leading up to Maggie's illness. This time, however, he was prudent enough to omit Jimmy's part in the story. He had hardly finished before Hugh was on his feet and heading for the door.

'She's obviously in a trauma brought on by delayed

shock,' he said to no-one in particular. 'I can sedate her for now with laudanum – that will give her mind a chance to rest. Together with the drug and plenty of care she may recover. If not, I'll ask Dr Hawkins to attend her. He's a good man, although I must confess some of his ideas are totally beyond my comprehension.'

Charlie leapt from the chair, the muscles in his face working furiously. 'We don't want no other doctor, Mr Hugh. You can make Maggie better, Mr Harry said so.'

Hugh looked at the agonized face and shook his head. 'Calm yourself, Charlie. I'll do all I can, but I may need some help.' Then before Charlie could answer Hugh had left the room.

'Now then, young man. What say you go to the kitchen and ask cook for some food to take home with you?' Beatrice was smiling kindly at him. 'Edward, ring the bell would you, dear? I'm sure Mrs Sheldon has plenty of pies and pasties in the larder.'

Charlie watched as the portly man pulled on a long, tasselled rope hanging by the door and protested indignantly, 'We ain't beggars, we've got plenty of money to buy food. Me and Maggie don't need any charity. I just need help to get her better again.'

Beatrice and Edward exchanged glances, a gentle smile hovering about their lips.

'I'm sure you are well able to fend for yourself,' Beatrice said kindly. 'But your sister is going to need nourishing food if she is to make a full recovery. It isn't charity to want to help someone. Ah, here's Agnes.'

Turning her attention to the maid she said, 'Take this young man to the kitchen and ask cook if she will pack a small hamper. I will leave the selection of food to her discretion.'

'Yes ma'am,' Agnes bobbed, then waited for the boy to follow her, leaving Charlie no option but to do as he was bid.

In the upper part of the house Hugh was busily checking his black bag, his actions mechanical as he tried to stem the wild beating of his heart. After all this time he was going to see Maggie again. Maggie with her lovely face and sweet smile. His mind went back to their first meeting. He had been shy at first, never wholly at ease with attractive young women, but Maggie had drawn him out and encouraged him to talk about himself and his work, showing a genuine interest in what he was saying. Not that there hadn't been plenty of young women who would have been only too happy to spend time with him, but he had never felt comfortable in their presence; not like he had with Maggie.

He had looked forward to their meetings at the park, eagerly counting the days until he would see her again. Never before in his life had he felt so relaxed and sure of himself as he had in those few precious months. Then Harry had started to discourage him from joining him on the Saturday excursions, but for once Hugh had ignored Harry's wishes. The desire to see Maggie had been too strong, over-riding the risk of annoying his elder brother. Then had come that Saturday when he had been called into the hospital and Harry had gone to see Maggie on his own. That had been the last meeting. When Harry had told him that neither of them would be seeing Maggie again, Hugh had felt an overwhelming sense of loss, and despite constant probing as to why, Harry had remained tight-lipped.

A few months later he had asked Lotte out to dine with him. He had known her a long time, but had never looked upon her as more than just a friend. That was until Bella's attentions had begun to suffocate him. In a desperate attempt to get away from her unwelcome and sometimes frightening ministrations, he had in a moment of recklessness asked Lotte to marry him. Snapping his bag shut he made for the door. He shouldn't be thinking like this. Lotte was a good woman, he felt safe with her, safe and secure. Not exactly the perfect recipe for marriage, yet he had been happy with the arrangement – until now.

'Come along, man, pull yourself together,' he said to the empty room. 'There was never anything between you and Maggie. She was kind to you, because that is her nature, but any real affection she felt was directed at Harry.'

Still he remained, his hand resting on the doorknob. What if when he saw her again, the old feelings came back. No! He mustn't think like that. Maggie belonged in the past – his future was with Lotte. Nodding to himself he left the room. He was a doctor about to attend a patient, that was all that need concern him. Why then did his stomach continue to churn at the prospect of seeing Maggie again?

When the door had closed behind Charlie and Agnes, Bella, unable to keep quiet any longer, burst out, 'Surely you're not going to allow Hugh to visit some dirty slut in her own home, Lotte? Women like that should go to the hospital and wait their turn with the rest of her kind. I've never heard of anything so preposterous – imagine a doctor of Hugh's standing making house calls to someone of her class. I certainly wouldn't allow my fiancé to go unaccompanied to examine a woman of dubious character.'

Lotte Winters rose slowly to her feet. 'But Hugh isn't your fiancé, Bella, he's mine,' she said steadily. 'And what you seem to be forgetting is that I am a nursing sister and well used to treating people from all walks of life.' Turning her back on the furious Bella, she turned to Beatrice and Edward.

'Would you both excuse me? I'd like to see if Hugh needs any help.'

'Of course, my dear,' Edward escorted her to the door. 'I'll instruct Benson to find you a cab to take you to your destination.'

Bella sat, inwardly fuming. How dare the woman talk to her like that?

After the initial shock of hearing that Hugh was to become engaged, she had visualised some pretty empty-headed chit of a girl whom she would be able to manipulate as she had done Hugh. But from the first meeting with her future sister-in-law she had realised with a shock that this woman was made of far sterner stuff than the man she planned to marry. The damned woman had even managed to instil some back-bone into the once weak, indecisive Hugh – a transformation the rest of the family had been delighted at. Not so Bella, who saw once again her plans crumbling into dust. Her chest heaving with frustration she made one last attempt to thwart the proposed visit.

'At least you've the sense to accompany him. Harry's probably rushed back to his precious buildings by now and you wouldn't want Hugh left to the tender mercies of a woman of the streets. If you ask me . . .'

Edward, his face dark with rage, went to speak, but Lotte forestalled him. Placing a restraining hand on his arm she stared across the room at her adversary and answered evenly.

'But nobody did ask you, Bella. However, since you have raised the subject, I'm neither insecure nor desperate enough to object to Hugh examining woman patients. I'm sure if it was up to you, he would spend his life dealing only with men. Fortunately the decision doesn't lie with you. After all, you are merely his sister, and as such have no say in how he conducts his practice – nor his life,' and with that last parting shot she left the room with Edward at her side.

'Why that jumped up . . .' Bella was on her feet, her hands clenched tightly by her side. 'Who does she think she is, talking to me like that. I've a good mind to . . .'

'To what, Bella?' Beatrice asked, her normally gentle voice hard. 'As I see it, Lotte was perfectly within her rights to say what she did, and if she hadn't, your father most certainly would have. And he wouldn't have been so polite. Now sit down and stop that pacing, it will do you no good. As Lotte has quite rightly pointed out, Hugh's affairs are no concern of yours, and the sooner you realise that the better it will be for all of us. Because I'm warning you, Bella, your father has had just about enough of your antics, as have I.'

Bella's agitated steps faltered as acute discomfort swept over her. Keeping her back turned to her mother she answered stiffly, 'I'm sure I don't know what you are talking about, Mother. Indeed, if there are any recriminations to be levied, they should be directed at your two sons. It is they who have sought to consort with the dregs of society. It's unfortunate enough they have to deal with these people without encouraging them to come to the house. All I have done is to show an interest in my brothers' work, I find no shame in that. It was bad enough that Harry's name is a byword in the East End; now he is seeking to drag Hugh down with him. If it wasn't for Harry's influence, Hugh could be practising in a private residence in Harley Street, instead of that disease-infested hospital. And what of Lotte? Spending her days looking at and laying hands on filthy men and women, performing tasks that no decent woman would consider doing. I suppose someone has to see to the wretches, but in my opinion, it should be people of their own class.'

Beatrice's eyes clouded over with compassion as she listened to her daughter ranting. How sad and how utterly tragic that a person could be consumed by so much hatred and jealousy. What a waste of a life, what a terrible waste.

The sound of the door opening brought both women's heads round. Beatrice quickly shot Bella a warning glance, but Bella, still smarting from the home truths she had endured this day, was desperate to justify herself and shift attention away from her deeds. Facing her father defiantly and jutting her chin out, she exclaimed loudly, 'Really, Father. How could you bring that urchin in here? It was bad enough that you allowed him entrance to the house, but to invite him to take tea with us was unforgivable. Goodness know what we might catch from him – he's probably crawling with lice. I really must protest at . . .' The words died in her throat at the steely glint in the black eyes regarding her.

'Pray continue, Bella,' Edward said, his voice deceptively soft. 'I'm sure your mother and I would be most interested to hear your views, especially those concerning the nursing profession. What was it you said? No decent woman would perform such menial, degrading tasks. And what of Miss Nightingale? Do you consider her to be a person unworthy to grace your presence?'

Bella could feel the situation slipping away from her, and anxious to keep face, she replied airily, 'Don't be facetious, Father. Miss Nightingale is a woman of breeding – she merely supervises her nurses, she doesn't actually take part in the unpleasant aspects of nursing.'

Edward stared at his daughter in amazement, then, shaking his head slowly he gave a mirthless laugh.

'My God, woman. Not only are you a thoroughly disagreeable individual, you're also a stupid one. Miss Nightingale endured horrific conditions during the Crimean War, conditions neither you nor I could even begin to imagine. She braved hardship and disease in order to bring comfort to the sick and dying, and worked side by side with her nurses until illness forced her to take a rest. But this isn't about nursing, is it? It's merely an excuse to vent your spleen on Lotte and disparage the excellent work she performs. You've never hidden your dislike, but then you would have found fault with anyone Hugh intended to marry. But let me tell you, Madam, all your sly innuendoes and vicious schemes will do you no good. Hugh will marry Lotte, and there's not a thing you can do to prevent it. If you have any sense at all, you would try and make friends with the woman if you wish to continue seeing Hugh after the wedding. But that isn't in your nature, is it? Well, I'm warning you, Bella, you had better take a long, hard look at yourself and change your ways, because if you don't, you're going to find yourself alone one day and you'll have no-one to blame but yourself.'

Bella flinched as the words found their way into her heart. This was her recurring nightmare, to be left alone with no-one in the world to care whether she lived or died. She had tried every trick she knew to turn Hugh against Lotte and she had lost. Her world was slipping away from her, but she would rather die than admit she was in the wrong. There was a painful lump in her throat and her eyes were dry and bright with unshed tears.

Swallowing hard she drew back her shoulders and said bitterly, 'It isn't my fault I'm the way I am. If I had been born pretty instead of being a carbon copy of you, I'd probably have been married and had children by now, instead of which I'm doomed to spend the rest of my life on the outside looking in. No-one likes me because I'm ugly, well, I don't care, do you hear me, Father, I don't give a damn, because you know something? I don't like you, so you can take your advice and in the colloquial expression of the East End, you can stick it where the sun don't shine.' The cockney accent sneeringly hurled at him through curled lips caused Edward to draw his shoulders back in surprise.

'Bella,' Beatrice cried, aghast at the contempt in the vicious voice. 'Don't upset yourself, my dear,' Edward said soothingly. 'Indeed, I'm glad we have finally come out into the open.'

Her chest heaving, Bella made to leave the room only to find her arm held in a steel-like grasp.

'Not so fast, Bella.' Edward's face wore a relaxed expression. 'There still remains the small problem of your visits to the building site. Harry won't tolerate much more, but I'm sure you are aware of that. You may have been able to coerce Hugh into letting you run his life, but Harry is a different kettle of fish. Now, I'm warning you for the last time; stay away from the site, and keep your nose out of your brothers' business.'

'Or what?' Bella glared up at him defiantly. 'I'm a bit too old to be kept locked in my room. I'm a grown woman, and can go where I like, when I like, and there's nothing you can do to stop me.' Pulling her arm free she walked unsteadily towards the door, anxious to get to her room before the threatened tears began to fall. She was about to leave the room when her father spoke again.

'There you are mistaken, Madam. While you continue to live under my roof and eat my food, you will do as you are told. If you persist in shaming the family I will have no option but to send you to your cousin Ethel in Wales. I'm sure she would welcome the company, even yours. It must be very lonely for her living in that god-forsaken valley miles from the nearest town. Maybe a few months spent living on a farm would help you appreciate the comfort of your home.'

Bella's hand froze on the door handle, her knuckles white as she squeezed the wooden knob. Turning slowly around she whispered hoarsely, 'You wouldn't . . . you wouldn't dare. She's mad, completely mad, and you've said yourself how the farmhouse isn't fit for human occupation. You can't send me there – I won't stand for it.'

Edward regarded his daughter and saw for the first

295

time the fear in her eyes. For a brief moment he felt a pang of pity for her, then swiftly brushed it aside.

'The matter is entirely in your hands. You have a choice: either act in a manner befitting the lady you purport to be, or spend the next six months in Wales with your cousin. Now, leave us, I wish to speak with your mother.'

Bella looked beseechingly at Beatrice, her eyes silently imploring her mother to intervene on her behalf. But Beatrice merely looked back, her eyes pitying as she shook her head slowly. Sounds from the hall penetrated the silence in the room, and throwing one last look of pure hatred towards her father Bella stormed from the room. In the hall, Hugh and Lotte were bent over the black medical bag, their faces earnest as they discussed the problem facing them. Seeing them so close, so obviously at ease and a part of each other brought forth her anger once again. She clutched the pearl necklace at her throat, her body shaking so violently she thought the raging turmoil inside her breast must surely tear her body asunder. The need to release some of the rage was overpowering, and she didn't have to look far for a scapegoat. Advancing on the unsuspecting Charlie, who was waiting by the door held open by Benson, she leant her body forward and hissed, 'You filthy little beggar. How dare you come sneaking into my home on the pretext of wanting a doctor. You're nothing but scum, you and all your kind. As for your sister and her mysterious ailment, well . . . If she's that friendly with my brother, then she is probably suffering from a dose of the clap. Harry never was that particular who he bedded.'

Charlie shrank back against the onslaught, then, the words penetrating his startled mind, he leapt forward shouting, 'My sister ain't like that, missus. And you can talk. Prancing about in front of Mr Harry's workmen. They was all laughing at yer, missus, yer made a right fool of yerself. My Maggie would never show herself up like that, she'd got more pride. Anyhow, she doesn't have ter chase after men, she can get 'em wivout even trying. But then I suppose wiv a face like yours yer got ter go touting for it – it won't come looking for you.'

When the hand came up and towards his face he flinched, then stood his ground, but before the blow could reach its target Bella felt her wrist grasped in a vice-like grip.

'Good God, Bella, have you completely lost your mind?' Hugh was staring down at her, his eyes horrified at the vicious, unwarranted attack. Pulling herself free Bella ran for the stairs. The undisguised loathing and shock on Hugh's face was the last straw. They were all against her, well damn them all, she'd get even one day, by Christ she would. Her voice thick, she muttered, 'Go on then, go. Harry's waiting with his slut and Harry must be obeyed, mustn't he?'

Benson coughed discreetly, 'The carriage is here, sir,' he said deferentially, his mind storing up the events he had witnessed to be retailed to the rest of the staff later that evening. When they were seated inside the cab,

Charlie squirmed on his seat, his face still flaming from the insults levelled at his Maggie.

'It ain't Maggie wot needs ter see a nutcase doctor, it's your sister. She's barmy, right off her trolley.'

'You may well be right, Charlie,' Hugh answered wearily, still shaken by the unpleasant scene. 'But Dr Hawkins is not a nutcase doctor, he is a psychiatrist.'

Charlie stared back at him stubbornly. 'I don't care what fancy name yer call him; he's still the sort of doctor the nutters are sent to.'

'You may be right, my dear, but forget about Bella, it's your sister we have to concern ourselves with now,' Lotte said softly. She felt Hugh's hand squeeze hers and smiled. When he had first asked her to dine with him, she had thought he was teasing her, as many of the younger doctors did. Even now they were engaged, she still couldn't believe he had chosen her. The hospital was full of younger, prettier women than herself, and she was forever fearful she would lose him. Even now after their four-month engagement, Hugh still treated her with the same respect and affection he showed his mother. There was no passion in their relationship, and she was wise enough to know that the love she felt for the man at her side transcended the feelings he had for her. But no matter how insecure she felt at time, she never let it show. She was glad she had been at the house when the young boy had called, for it presented yet another opportunity to work alongside the man she loved. That he obviously knew the girl they were going to attend didn't worry her – that was until they arrived at their destination.

The first sight of the unkempt girl, her greasy head nestled against Harry's shoulder, filled her with pity. It was only when Hugh fell to his knees by the girl's side, his eyes filled with tenderness, and heard the soft endearments tumbling from his lips that she felt the first pangs of unease. And when he gently pushed back the limp hair from the hot forehead, an icy hand seemed to clutch at her heart. Then the professional in her asserted itself, and walking to where the girl lay, she let her nursing instincts take over.

CHAPTER SEVENTEEN

For months Maggie hovered on the brink of insanity. It was only the constant attention and love showered on her by Harry, Hugh, Lotte and Charlie that prevented her from toppling into the dark abyss of the far corners of her mind. For months she had likened her state to being stuck down a dark well looking up at the sunlight at the top of the open mouthed circle. Some days she was content to remain in the dark where it was warm and safe, other days she would attempt to climb out of the blackness only to fall back exhausted from the effort, her chest heaving with dry, frustrated sobs.

She remembered dimly the presence of another man, a tall, sparse-looking man, his demeanour proclaiming him to be someone of importance. He had sat by her side speaking quietly to her, asking questions, but she had remained mute, her eyes fixed unwavering on the goatee beard that adorned his chin. Finally he had gone away, and she had never seen him again.

Slowly, very very slowly, she began to inch her way up the side of the black well until one morning she awoke to find herself out of the darkness she had dwelt in for so long. Further evidence of her return to reality was proven when she asked a startled Charlie, who had just laid a breakfast tray on the bed, to fetch her a mirror. Amazed and delighted at the request Charlie had dashed from the room, returning swiftly with the small, flyblown mirror that hung over the kitchen sink.

Maggie took the mirror with trembling hands, her eyes filling with tears as she looked at the stranger staring back at her. The face that had once been filled with life and vitality was now drawn and sallow. Her brown curly hair hung lifelessly over her cheeks and shoulders, and although it was clean, thanks to Lotte's administrations, there was no resemblance to the thick mane of glossy curls she had been so proud of. Laying the mirror down on the quilted coverlet she took a few moments to compose herself.

Her voice shaky, she whispered, 'What's happened to me, Charlie? How . . . how long have I been like . . . this?'

Charlie felt his legs go weak with relief at the normality of her tone. Sinking down onto the side of the bed he flashed her a watery smile. 'Blimey, Maggie, you've had me worried. I was beginning ter think you'd never snap out of it. But don't yer remember anything? I mean, well you must remember something; don't yer?'

Maggie looked into the anxious face and shook her head slowly. 'I remember that last night at our old place and . . . and Jimmy trying to . . . to . . .'

'It's all right, Maggie, don't upset yerself,' Charlie cried, hitching himself along the bed to be nearer to her. ' 'E ain't worth getting upset about, and besides, 'e won't bother yer again; Harry'll see ter that.'

At the mention of Harry's name, Maggie laid her head back against the pillows, her eyes closing as she struggled to remember. Through a misty veil of time she saw herself and Charlie tramping the dark streets before coming to a halt outside a large, red-bricked house proclaiming rooms to let. She recalled shouting at Charlie, why she couldn't remember, but the image of his face as he'd stared at her in hurt silence appeared in front of her mind, and she squeezed her eyes tighter in an effort to blot out the painful sight.

'Maggie? Maggie, you're not going again, are yer?' Charlie's voice cracked with alarm.

'No, no, love, I'm not going anywhere,' Maggie murmured soothingly. 'Just leave me be for a while; I've a lot to think about.'

'Thank Gawd for that. But look, yer breakfast is getting cold. Yer can think and eat at the same time, can't yer?'

The thought of eating was the last thing Maggie wanted to do, but she didn't want to disappoint Charlie. It was only when she bit into the cold, heavily buttered toast that she realised how hungry she was. Within minutes the plate was cleared, much to Charlie's delight; he immediately volunteered to cook her what he termed a proper breakfast. As soon as he had left the room, his face split into a wide smile, she sipped at the still hot tea and turned her face to the window, her forehead creased with the effort of remembrance.

There were so many images floating through her mind, vague, dim outlines of people coming and going. People talking to her, like the man with the beard. People coaxing her to eat, to walk, to rest, and even though the voices had been familiar, their outlines had remained a blur. In the back of her mind she'd known Harry and Hugh had been with her, but a part of her had refused to acknowledge their presence, preferring to think of them as just 'people'. And then there was the woman who had bathed her, sponging down her listless body and dressing her in clean clothing as well as holding her head over the sink in the scullery while gently scrubbing the long brown hair with carbolic soap. She'd been here a number of times, her long, full skirts swishing round the room as she'd helped Charlie fill the copper bath with hot, soapy water before shooing the boy from the room.

It was all coming back to her now. Harry and Hugh arguing as to the best treatment for her. Hugh insisting she be taken to hospital while Harry and Charlie remained adamant that she be kept at home. At these times, the unknown woman would hold Maggie's hand, her attractive, plump face filled with reassurance. Maggie could see her clearly now; the name 'Lotte' springing to her mind. But who was she? Obviously she was a very close friend of Harry and Hugh's, but which one of the men was she closer to? Suddenly it was very important that she find out exactly what had been happening to her since Lizzie's funeral. Sitting up in bed she gingerly swung her legs over the side. Then, very slowly she let her feet touch the cold linoleum and stood away from the security of the bed. The moment she let go of the coverlet she felt the blood rush to her head and her stomach lurch in panic. Before she could fall, she grabbed the bedclothes and pulled herself back to the safety of the bed. God! She was weaker than she'd first thought. How could she have been so ill with so little recollection?

' 'Ere you are, Maggie, a nice fry up for yer. This'll put the meat back on yer bones.' Charlie came into the room, his face still beaming with happiness and relief at having his Maggie back with him again.

'Look, Charlie, I have to talk to you. I need to know what's been happening. Everything's such a blur. I keep remembering bits and pieces, but none of it makes sense. Have Harry and Hugh really been here or did I imagine them coming to see me? And the lady; who is she, Charlie? Does she exist, or is she just a figment of my imagination?'

'Now don't go getting yerself all worked up, Maggie. I'll explain everything. You just eat yer breakfast and listen.'

Maggie started to protest, then the tiredness overtook her, and she did as she was bid. Carefully chewing the bacon and eggs Charlie had prepared for her, she listened in silence as Charlie recounted his visit to Harry's building site and the subsequent visit to his father's house.

'Lord, I was scared when that old geezer grabbed hold of me, I thought he was gonna throw me out. Then when Hugh came down the stairs I was so relieved I nearly kissed him.' Throwing back his head he laughed loudly as the incident came to mind. 'Anyways, his Dad came charging out of a room off the landing shouting his head off, wanting to know what was going on. I tell yer, Maggie, if I hadn't been that frightened of coming back here without Hugh and facing Harry, I'd have bolted for it. But he was nice, I mean Harry's Dad, once he'd stopped bawling that is. His Mum was kind to me too; she made the cook fix up a hamper to bring back to yer. I didn't want to take it, but she insisted and I didn't want to hurt her feelings. If it hadn't been for that old bitch of a sister, I'd 'ave felt quite at home. Coo, she went mad, yer should have seen her. Tried to hit me she did, and she would have done an' all if Hugh hadn't stopped her. I pretended I wasn't scared, but I was. She's mad, really mad. I wouldn't like ter meet her on a dark night.'

Maggie's head was spinning as she tried to absorb all that Charlie had told her. Pushing away the half-eaten meal she said frantically, 'Slow down, Charlie, I can't think straight with you galloping off from one thing to another. Now let's see if I've got this right. You went and asked Harry for help and he sent you to fetch Hugh?' She waited for Charlie to nod his head in confirmation before carrying on.

'And when you got to Harry's house, his Mum and Dad treated you nicely, but his sister tried to wallop you?'

'That's right, Maggie, I told yer, she's mad, barmy. Said if yer was one of Harry's friends, yer probably had a do . . .' His face reddened as he recalled the unpleasant scene.

'A what, Charlie? Come on, finish the sentence,' Maggie demanded, her voice weak but firm.

Hanging his head Charlie mumbled, 'She said yer probably had a dose of the clap.' When he saw the look that passed over Maggie's face he leant forward, his face earnest, saying quickly, 'Now, don't go getting yerself upset. I told her, she ain't right in the head. She's been hanging round Harry's building site playing up ter his men. Coo, yer should have seen Harry drag her away, I thought she was gonna claw his eyes out. There's no love lost between those two even if they are brother and sister, and I don't think the rest of the family likes her much either.'

Maggie's face bore a look of puzzlement, her fogged mind trying to digest what Charlie had told her. The picture Charlie had painted of the sister didn't match the woman who had been so kind to her during her illness, so who was the mysterious lady? She must be someone very close to Harry or Hugh to have taken on the task of ministering to a complete stranger. No woman would do all that she had unless it was on behalf of someone she cared deeply for. She felt her heart begin to beat erratically and plucking at the sheet she spoke softly.

'So who's the woman that's been looking after me. It can't be their sister, not after what you've said about her. Is she Harry's wife? Is that why she's been coming here? I mean I don't care, but . . .'

Charlie laughed delightedly. He'd been right all along – Maggie did care for Harry. Even during the times she didn't seem to know what was happening round her, she'd clung to Harry every time he'd called.

Grinning broadly he answered, 'She's Hugh's fiancée, they're getting married next year. She's lovely, she is, Miss Lotte. She's a nursing sister at the hospital where Hugh works. If it hadn't been for her, you'd have had to go into hospital, 'cos none of us men could have looked after yer like she did. Well, it wouldn't have been right, would it?'

Maggie felt a wave of relief flood through her body, then, realising she had given her true feelings away, she said dryly, 'You've got very chummy with them, haven't you? What happened to Mr Hugh and Mr Harry? It's all first names now, is it?'

'Aw, Maggie,' Charlie smiled at her, 'I couldn't keep on calling them mister, not after all the months they've been coming here. And anyway, they both asked me to call them by their first names.'

A jolt of surprise jerked Maggie's body upright in the bed, and her face ashen, she repeated, 'Months? You said they've been coming here for months? What . . . I mean how long . . . Oh God!' She suddenly noticed how hot it was in the bedroom, even though there was no evidence of a fire. Lizzie had been buried in April and judging by the warmth of the room it must be mid-summer now.

Her whole body shaking in alarm she whispered, 'What day is it, Charlie? I mean exactly what day and month is it?'

Charlie screwed his eyes up, trying to think.

'Well, I ain't sure exactly, but it's nearly the end of August.' When he saw the look of fear that came over her face he grabbed her hand, crying, 'Oh, don't look like that, Maggie. Who cares what month it is? All that matters is that you're well again.' Smoothing the coverlet into place he took the tray from her lap and walked towards the door.

'I can't wait ter see Harry's face when he comes round; he's been really worried about yer. Now, get some rest, I'll let yer know when he gets here.'

'Charlie, wait a minute. Do they all come round every day?'

'Gawd, no. Hugh and Miss Lotte work at the hospital all week, and they normally come round at the weekend. Although they do sometimes come in the evening, it all depends on how you've been. Harry comes every day though; he has his dinner here with me before going back to work. Now, get some rest; you want ter look yer best when he comes, don't yer,' he said gaily, a devilish smile playing round his lips.

Left alone Maggie sank back on the pillows once more, her eyes clouded with uncertainty. Did she really want to get involved with Harry again? That way lay only pain and disappointment, but could she live her life never setting eyes on his face again? God she was tired, but she couldn't lie here else she'd fall asleep, and she wanted to be up and dressed when he arrived. Taking a deep breath she got out of bed, careful not to move too quickly. She stood for a few minutes, then, when she was confident she wouldn't fall, she walked unsteadily over to the sideboard where the jug and pitcher stood and began to wash herself.

Later that evening when she was feeling more like her old self, Maggie again sat Charlie down to go over all that happened since her illness. Carefully hiding his impatience, the young boy repeated all he had already told her, adding bits of information he had earlier omitted. When he had finished Maggie shook her head in bewilderment, still not believing that such a lot could have happened without her being aware of it

'I've heard of people like me,' she said at last. 'You know, people who lose part of their lives. It's got a special name. Am . . .amnes, oh, something like that – but I never thought it could happen to me.'

'Hugh said it's quite common, especially if the person's had a bad shock.' Screwing up his face in an effort to remember Hugh's exact words, Charlie added, 'He said it's the mind's way of dealing with things that yer don't want ter remember. Like something really bad that's happened and yer mind can't cope with it, so it just sort of shuts off. Either that or yer go stark, raving mad.'

'Thanks, love, I really needed to hear that,' Maggie said wryly.

'But yer didn't go mad, did yer? You're too strong to let that happen. It must have been awful . . . I mean finding Liz lying in the road like yer did. And then that bugger trying ter . . . well, you know what I mean. It'd be enough ter turn anyone's brain. Anyway, you're better now, and you haven't got that amines . . . or whatever it's called. If you had you wouldn't be able to remember anything, and you are starting to remember, aren't yer?' he asked, his face anxious.

Waving a hand at him Maggie hastened to put his mind at ease, 'Don't worry, it's starting to come back to me, but in sort of fragments, like in a dream. Do you understand what I mean, Charlie?'

'Well, not really, Maggie,' he answered doubtfully; then, his face brightening, he added, 'But it doesn't matter, 'cos you're better now, and I'm gonna take care of yer, so you don't have ter worry abaht nothing.'

Maggie smiled tiredly, he was a good lad. Looking closer at him she saw suddenly that he was no longer a boy. What was he now? Thirteen, fourteen? Of course, he was fourteen, he'd left school just after Christmas – fancy her forgetting that.

There was something else nagging at her mind; then she remembered. 'Charlie.' She said his name almost fearfully. 'Charlie, love, what happened to the money? I had a lot of money with me when we left home, have you got it? Is that what we've been living on all these months?'

Charlie sprang to his feet. 'Gawd, I nearly forgot about that. Hang on, I'll get it for yer.'

He was only gone a few minutes before returning with a small, black tin box. Dropping to his knees he placed the box on the floor.

'It's all in here, Maggie,' he cried happily, his fingers turning the metal key in the lock. 'Miss Lotte found a wad of notes down the front of yer blouse when she undressed yer. She gave it ter me and Harry brought this box round ter keep it in. He asked me if I wanted him ter put it in the bank, but I said no to that idea. I'd rather have me money where I can see it – I mean your money, Maggie,' he added shamefacedly.

Reaching out her arm she gently stroked his hair. 'It's our money now, love, yours and mine,' she said softly, her eyes filling with tears as she recalled how carefully Liz had saved for the baby. The memory of Jimmy lying flat on his back sprang to mind and she shivered. Then straightening her back she stuck her chin out defiantly. She wasn't sorry she had taken the money from him. He'd never done anything to earn it, but there remained a small niggle of fear that he would come looking for her. Something Charlie had said earlier came back to her, and putting her hand under his chin, she raised his

311

face to hers. 'You said that Harry would see that Jimmy wouldn't bother me any more. Did you tell him what happened that night?'

Charlie lowered his eyes dejectedly, 'I didn't mean ter tell him, but he kept on at me. Yer know what he's like. He could worm the knickers off a nun if he wanted to.' Suppressing a smile she let her hand fall to her lap.

'It's all right, I'm not having a go at you. I just wanted to know exactly what you told him.'

Glad that she wasn't angry at him, Charlie fingered the box, wondering if he dared ask the question that had been preying on his mind since Lotte had discovered the money. His voice hesitant, he asked, 'There's a lot of money here, Maggie, over eighty pounds; I counted it. Is it all yours? I mean, that is ter say, I didn't know you had that much. Is some of it Lizzie's? Is that why there's such a lot?'

Maggie looked into the pleading eyes and said harshly, 'Yes, some of it belonged to Lizzie, and I'm not ashamed of taking it. That filthy swine had no right to it. I might have left him something if he hadn't . . . hadn't . . .'

Quick as a flash Charlie was on his feet, his arm going firmly round her shaking shoulder. Pulling her to his chest he said huskily, 'It's all right, Maggie, it's all right. I'm glad yer took it, yer deserve the money. And I'm glad I bashed the bugger over the head; pity I didn't do it sooner. Now, dry yer eyes, Harry'll be here soon, and I don't want him ter see yer looking upset.'

Giving her a final squeeze he picked up the box and walked with it into the scullery, there to put it back in its hiding place behind a loose brick under the stove, while in the other room Maggie sat waiting for Harry to arrive.

When Harry walked into the room, Maggie was sitting in the faded, embossed armchair, her hair tied back with a blue ribbon that matched the blue and white sprigged dress she was wearing. Charlie was standing protectively by her side, a soppy grin on his young face.

'Well, whadya think, Harry?' he asked of the tall, well-dressed man who stood open-mouthed in the doorway. 'Came round all of a sudden she did, just as I was giving her her breakfast. I told her ter stay in bed, but she didn't take no notice of me. Wanted to get herself pretty for yer, I expect, she . . .'

'Charlie!' Maggie admonished, her pale cheeks reddening in confusion. Trying to regain a normal attitude she turned to Harry, saying softly, 'Please come in and make yourself comfortable, Mr Stewart, Charlie was just about to make some tea.' Taking the hint, Charlie raised his eyebrows in Harry's direction and turned to leave.

'Just a minute, Charlie, I've brought some pie and peas,' Harry called after him. Then coming nearer to where Maggie sat, he leaned forward and said laughingly, 'I've become quite accustomed to pie and peas over the past few months, that and fish and chips. I've even toyed with the idea of opening a shop to cater for them. A person could make a fortune out of such an establishment, especially if that person had the foresight to provide tables and chairs where their customers could eat their meals in comfort instead of out of a paper bag.' The moment the words were out of his mouth he cursed himself for a babbling fool. The idea of setting Maggie and Charlie up in a shop near the building site had been forming in his mind for quite a while. He had long wished for such a place for his men, and of course having Maggie near would be a bonus. He had meant to wait until she had fully recovered before putting the idea to her, but the shock of seeing her waiting for him had caused him to act like an awkward child, blurting out the first thing that came to mind.

An uncomfortable silence settled on the room, broken only by the sound of Charlie whistling happily in the scullery as he busied himself making tea. Seating himself in the armchair opposite Maggie, he sat awkwardly on the edge of the seat, his fingers drumming nervously on his knees. Maggie saw his discomfort and relaxed her head against the back of the chair. The effort of getting herself washed and dressed had tired her, even her arms ached from the simple act of brushing her hair.

Anxious to put him at ease, she smiled at him, saying, 'I believe I owe you a great debt of gratitude, Mr Stewart, and your brother and his fiancée of course. Charlie has told me how you've all cared for me, and I can't begin to tell you how grateful I am. Without your help I would have ended up in a mental asylum, and you know yourself, once someone goes into one of those places they very rarely come out again.'

The sound of the formal, stilted words tore at Harry's heart, that and the fact she had gone back to calling him Mister. Her words were undoubtedly sincere, but there was no warmth in her voice. Obviously he was no longer wanted or needed, and the knowledge brought a great sadness on him. He had imagined that once she was recovered – and he'd had no doubt that she would recover – that they could pick up the threads of friendship once more, and in time . . . Well, clearly that wasn't going to happen. He felt hurt, hurt and angry. Angry with himself for expecting her to fall into his arms in gratitude, and angry that he had allowed himself to fall in love with her. Raising his eyes to hers he started to speak then stopped as his breath caught in his throat. There may have been no warmth in her tone, but it was there in her eyes, and once again a feeling of optimism rose inside his chest. Remembering their last meeting in the park he warned himself to go carefully; he didn't want to alienate himself from her again.

Clearing his throat he said cheerfully, 'Well, you're a sight for sore eyes and no mistake. You've had us all worried, I can tell you. Do you think you could manage more visitors? Because when I tell Hugh and Lotte you're up and about I doubt if I will be able to keep them away.'

Maggie too was trying to keep her true feelings under control. Part of her was saying that the man sitting opposite must care very deeply for her to have done what he had, but the cautious part of her mind told her to take one step at a time and see how things worked out.

'Please, I'd love to see Hugh and his fiancée. She must be a remarkable woman to have spent so much of her free time with a complete stranger. Charlie tells me that if she hadn't looked after my . . . well, my personal needs, I . . . I . . .' Her voice faltered, the blood rushing to her pale cheeks as she realised what she had said. Thoroughly embarrassed, she fixed her eyes on the empty fire grate, expelling a silent sigh of relief as Charlie came back into the room.

' 'Ere we are, grub's up,' he said cheerfully. 'It's still hot, I stuck it in the oven while I made the tea. Do yer want ter eat it at the table, Maggie, I can get yer a plate if yer wants. Me and Harry usually eat it outa the paper bag; it tastes better like that, don't it, Harry?'

Glad of the diversion Maggie looked up at Charlie and said dryly, 'Your grammar seems to have slipped while I've been lying idle. I'll have to take you in hand, young man. I don't want all my good work going to waste.'

'Aw, Maggie, now I know you're getting better.' Inclining his head towards Harry he said wistfully, 'She thinks I'm gonna end up being a lawyer or some sort of businessman. I keep telling her, my place is in the markets where I feel at home, but she keeps on at me.' Screwing up his face he mimicked her voice, 'Mind your aitches, Charlie, speak properly, Charlie.'

'And you can mind your manners as well, young

man,' Maggie retorted, enjoying the repartee. 'I'm not so weak that I can't clump you one.'

'Ooh, that's posh, ain't it, Harry?' came the sharp reply, causing them all to laugh loudly.

'Well, seeing as we're all being common, I'll have my dinner out of a paper bag. But don't think you've heard the last of this conversation, Charlie, me lad. I'll speak to you later.'

Again they all laughed before turning their attention to the appetizing wrapped parcels on their laps. When the paper bags lay screwed up on the floor and last of the tea had been drunk, Harry rose reluctantly to his feet.

'Much as I hate to leave, I'd better be getting back to the site. Most of my men will return to work after dinner without my presence, but it doesn't hurt to keep them on their toes.'

'Is the work on the buildings nearly finished?' Maggie asked, seeking some pretext to keep him with her a while longer. Indicating his fawn trousers and dark brown jacket she added lamely, 'What I mean is, Charlie told me you usually work alongside your men, and I don't think the clothes you're wearing are suitable for manual labour.'

Placing his shiny bowler hat squarely on his head he answered, 'Good Lord, no, I don't expect them to be finished before March next year – that's if my schedule goes according to plan. Then of course there's the windows and doors to be fitted, and the plumbing; that's always a major job. After all those jobs have been completed, I'll have the unenviable task of finding enough decent, second-hand furniture to fill the rooms I've so proudly boasted about.'

'We could help, couldn't we, Maggie? Well, I know a lot of blokes who deal in second-hand furniture. And I'd make sure it was decent stuff, no rubbish, and I'd get a fair price for you too.'

Charlie's face was alive with enthusiasm at the prospect of helping this man he had grown so attached to. Harry rubbed his chin thoughtfully. It wouldn't be a bad idea to get Charlie working for him. If his other plan didn't work out it would enable him to keep in contact with Maggie. Besides, he was genuinely fond of the young boy.

Holding out his hand he said briskly, 'I'll bear your offer in mind, Charlie. In fact you could say we have a deal. Now I really must be off.' Turning back to Maggie he asked, 'Do you really think you're well enough to see Hugh and Lotte tonight? I can always put them off until you're feeling stronger.'

'No, no, really, I'd love to see them. Please tell them they're welcome any time that's convenient for them.'

'If that's the case, I think I can safely say I'll be seeing you both later tonight.' Bending slightly from the waist he doffed his bowler in Maggie's direction. 'As for my clothes . . . well, I couldn't be seen visiting a young lady dressed as a common labourer, now could I? What would the neighbours think?' Chuckling softly he closed the door behind him.

'What are you grinning about?' Maggie demanded of her brother. 'You look like a Cheshire cat.'

Undaunted, Charlie picked up the grease-stained paper and laughed. 'He still fancies yer. And I'll tell yer something else, so does Hugh. I've seen the way he looked at yer when yer was bad, good job he's engaged, ain't it?'

Maggie felt the smile slip from her face. 'Don't say that, Charlie, don't ever say such a thing again, do you hear me?' she shouted wildly.

' 'Ere, don't go on like that, you'll make yerself bad again,' Charlie muttered uncomfortably. 'I was only saying as how . . .'

'Well, don't say it, you're letting your imagination run away with you. Now get this mess tidied up; if we've got company tonight I want the place to look nice.'

His face miserable now, Charlie put the screwed paper under his arm and picked up the three mugs. Biting back the retort that had sprung to his lips, he walked with heavy steps into the scullery. It wasn't fair, he thought with childish resentment. There was no need for her to go for him like that. As for getting the place tidy . . . He shrugged his shoulders defiantly. They'd all seen it in a worse state than a few bits of paper lying about. Biting on his lower lip he put the mugs in the wooden sink then gazed at the wall, his expression worried. He shouldn't have said anything about Hugh, it had just sort of slipped out. But it was true what he'd said, Hugh did fancy Maggie, and it wasn't just him that thought so.

Harry and Miss Lotte had noticed it too, although of course they hadn't said anything. All of a sudden he felt a deep sorrow for Miss Lotte, she was too nice to have to watch her fiancé moon over another woman. Still they'd be married next year, he hoped. But what if Hugh decided to go after Maggie instead?

Shaking his head he rinsed the mugs in the warm, soapy water. His earlier feelings of euphoria vanished as he realised for the first time the seriousness of the situation. Up until now Harry had watched with mild amusement his younger brother's tender administrations towards his patient, but now that Maggie was better Hugh might decide to dump Miss Lotte and make a play for her. And if that happened all hell would break loose. Sighing deeply, he put the mugs on the draining board. Why, when things were just starting to get better, did something have to spoil it? Why couldn't life be simple?

In the sitting-room Maggie was thinking along the same lines. If what Charlie said was true then she would have no choice but to sever all contact between herself and the Stewart brothers. The last thing she wanted was to cause trouble between the two men, and there was also Lotte to consider. Even though Maggie had never actually 'met' her, she felt a sense of loyalty towards the woman who had been so kind to her, and would do anything to prevent her from being hurt. Please, she prayed silently, let Charlie be wrong; please let him be wrong.

CHAPTER EIGHTEEN

Later that evening the room was once again filled with laughter. The men were grouped around the clean but scarred wooden table, their buttocks resting precariously on two, spindly legged, straight-backed chairs, while Charlie sat comfortably on an upturned orange box, his boyish face furrowed in concentration as he studied the cards he held in his hands. 'It's your bet, Charlie,' Harry said, his eyes twinkling with merriment at the young boy's earnest expression.

'Wait a minute, Harry, I ain't got the hang of this game yet,' Charlie cried plaintively.

Keeping a straight face Harry said solemnly, 'I'm sorry, Charlie, but you've had enough time to study your cards. Now you must either make a bet or fold.'

'I say, Harry, give the boy a chance,' Hugh interjected. 'It is his first time at poker after all.'

Harry leaned back in his chair and sighed. Poor Hugh, he had absolutely no sense of humour at all. Couldn't he see that he was merely indulging in a little harmless fun with the boy?

'I think I'd better fold,' Charlie said gloomily. 'I've got one of each suit and not a pair among 'em.' Laying his cards on the table he waited until Harry and Hugh finished the game before asking, 'How about a game of canasta? I know how ter play that.'

Harry swept the small pile of matches that represented his winnings towards him, saying cheerfully, 'Well now, that depends on your sister. It's been a long day for her, and she's probably wondering when we're going to leave but is too polite to say so.'

Harry turned his head to where the two women were chatting amiably, their bodies comfortably encased in the armchairs on either side of the empty fireplace.

'Oh no, I'm fine, really,' Maggie protested, endeavouring to keep her voice light. In actual fact she was tired and longing to go to bed even though it was only nine o'clock, but not for the world would she admit it.

'I was just about to make some supper,' Lotte said. 'Charlie cooked a chicken this afternoon, I thought we could have some sandwiches before you leave.' This offer was immediately accepted by the men, who then returned to the serious business of playing cards, leaving the women to make the refreshments. In the scullery that also served as a kitchen, Maggie began buttering the bread while Lotte carved the small chicken.

'Are you sure you're well enough to be entertaining?' Lotte asked, her keen glance taking in the fine lines of tiredness etched around Maggie's eyes. 'I can always tell them you've changed your mind and wish to retire. I know they'll understand.'

'Thank you, Lotte, but I'm fine, really. And besides I wanted the chance to be alone with you, to thank you properly for all you did for me while I was ill. To tell the truth, I feel a bit embarrassed . . . I mean, when I think of all you had to do for me, a complete stranger, especially a lady like yourself. It doesn't seem right somehow, but I'm grateful, you'll never know just how grateful I am. Saying thank you doesn't seem enough somehow, but I'll say it anyway.' Moving her head slightly she stared into the older woman's face and said awkwardly, 'Thank you, Lotte, thank you from the bottom of my heart.'

Lotte was forced to look away from the lovely face. She knew only too well how Hugh felt about the girl, and she knew also that Maggie had done nothing to encourage him. It was obvious she was smitten with Harry, any fool could see that. It was equally obvious that Harry had a great affection for her, but would he do anything about it? The question of class didn't enter into it, Harry didn't give a hoot about a person's origins, it was the thought of marriage he shied away from.

Careful to keep her feelings hidden, Lotte answered lightly, 'Good gracious, Maggie, there's no need to thank

me. You needed help and I was able to provide it, anyone would have done the same. As for me being a
lady . . .' She gave a short laugh. 'I'm a working woman,
the same as you, it is only our professions that differ.'

Picking up the plate laden with sandwiches she said
briskly, 'Now then, let us have our supper; then we can
leave you in peace for the rest of the evening.'

When the last of the sandwiches had been eaten Lotte
rose to her feet.

'We'll leave you to rest now, my dear. We should have
left it a few days before visiting, but we were both so
eager to see for ourselves how you were. I'm afraid our
common sense deserted us.'

'Oh no, really, I'm glad you came' Maggie rose to her
feet, her hand outstretched. 'I know I've already said it,
but thank you once again for all your kindness.'

'Hush dear, it is thanks enough to see you looking so
well,' Lotte interrupted gently. Turning to the men who
were in the throes of a new game, she said firmly, 'You
will have to leave your card game until another time.
It's been a long day for Maggie; she should be in bed
resting.'

'Oh, I was winning as well,' Charlie protested.

'Never mind, lad, there'll be other occasions – at least
I hope there will be,' Harry said, his eyes directed at
Maggie.

Smiling widely she replied, 'There'll always be a welcome for you here; for all of you.'

With much bustling and hand-shaking the guests left.

Harry was the last to leave, and as Maggie held the door open for him she asked hesitantly, 'That shop you were talking about earlier, you know, the one you planned to sell hot meals from. Would this shop be situated near the building site? And did you have a particular person in mind for running the place?'

Afraid to commit himself, Harry merely nodded his head, his chest swelling with hope at the look of suppressed eagerness on Maggie's face.

'I thought so,' she smiled back at him. 'When I feel more like my old self, maybe we can discuss the proposition further.'

'Whenever you're ready, my dear, whenever you're ready.' Taking her hand he kissed it lightly before bounding down the stairs.

'That was nice, wasn't it, Maggie?' Charlie was standing behind her.

'It's great having company and a good laugh . . . Oh, I'm sorry, Maggie, I didn't mean . . .'

'Don't worry, love, I know what you mean and I couldn't agree more. Let's hope it's the first of many such evenings.'

Bending over the arm of the chair she picked up the two books Lotte had brought for her to read. One was a copy of Walter Scott's *Ivanhoe*, the other was *Great Expectations* by Charles Dickens. Looking at the gold-embossed title she felt her stomach shift uncomfortably. Had Lotte deliberately chosen this particular book by way of a veiled accusation? Immediately the thought entered her mind she felt ashamed. Lotte wasn't the sort of woman to stoop to underhanded acts. Clutching the books under her arm she looked to the scullery where Charlie was happily washing the crockery.

Trust him to get the wrong idea about Hugh. For apart from enquiring about her health and making a brief examination – with Lotte present of course – he had shown no interest in her except that which one would show towards a friend. The knowledge that her brother had misinterpreted Hugh's intentions had come as a huge relief. Now all she had to worry about was recovering her strength and deciding what to do with her future. Sinking back down into the armchair she closed her eyes gratefully. In the days leading up to Lizzie's funeral she had tried to keep her mind occupied by thinking of different ways she could make a living for herself. She had toyed with the idea of applying for a job at one of the new telephone exchanges that were springing up all over the country, or maybe trying for a job in an office. She had never used a typewriter – indeed she had never seen one – but she was a quick learner, and the thought of working indoors and being able to wear smart clothes had seemed at the time to be just the sort of job she needed. She was tired of walking the streets and standing around in all weathers down the market.

Up until the late 1870s the only employment available to young women like herself had been either domestic service or factory work. Things were changing at last, and for the better too. Now she had another choice, and not only a choice but the chance to become a woman of business. if she accepted Harry's offer, she didn't intend to remain an employee all her life; oh no. She would work hard, and while she worked she would save until she had enough to buy the shop from Harry. A gentle smile played around her lips. Lord, she was getting beyond herself, wasn't she? The proposed shop was still a pipe-dream; even if Harry went ahead with his plans she might not like the work – and here she was already planning to buy him out. Still, she would see how things went. Before she made any plans she would have to talk them over with Charlie. She knew he would rather work in the markets, and she had finally stopped trying to persuade him differently. But if he would agree to help her get on her feet, then maybe one day soon she would be able to give him enough money to start up a stall of his own. He was quite capable of doing so now, but he was still young and hopefully would do as she asked for now.

The chair was so comfortable, she could feel her eyes growing heavier behind her closed lids and reluctantly heaved herself from its depth. Out of the corner of her eye she noticed something lying on the floor partly obscured by the chair. Bending over she picked it up and saw at once it was a man's glove.

'What's that, Maggie?' Charlie had come into the room, his eyes curious.

Clicking her tongue in mild annoyance she answered, 'What's it look like? Harry or Hugh must have dropped it when they came in. Although why they should want to wear gloves on such a warm evening is a mystery to me.'

'All the toffs wear gloves, it's part of the way they dress.' Charlie grandly imparted the pieces of information. 'Do yer want me ter run after them?'

'No, leave it. I don't suppose it's the only pair they have. Anyway . . .' A sudden sharp knock on the door brought both their heads round. Lifting her eyebrows Maggie said laughingly, 'Maybe it is the only pair they have.' Opening the door she saw Hugh standing in the hallway, a look of agitation on his flushed face.

Holding out the glove she said merrily, 'Is this what you've come ba . . .' She got no further. Before she could finish the sentence she found herself in a steel-like embrace, then Hugh was kissing her violently. She could feel his trembling body pressed against hers but before she could push him from her, he had vanished, his long legs taking the stairs two at a time in his haste to get away.

'I told yer, didn't I?' Charlie breathed worriedly, his eyes as round as saucers. 'I told yer, but yer wouldn't believe me. What yer gonna do, Maggie? It'll cause trouble, you mark my words, and if . . .'

'Shut up, Charlie,' she hissed between clenched teeth. 'Just shut up and leave me alone.'

Pushing past the startled boy whose eyes had begun to fill with tears she stormed into her bedroom slamming the door viciously behind her. Throwing herself face down on the bed she began to beat at the coverlet with clenched fists.

'Damn you, Hugh Stewart, damn you to hell,' she cried, her voice filled with rage and frustration. This put paid to her dreams of running Harry's shop for him, and the dream of one day buying it. Oh hell, hell, hell.

Hours passed, and still she lay not moving on the top of the bed. Charlie had long since gone to his own box-room, wisely deciding to leave his sister alone for the time being. Sometime during the night she fell asleep, only to wake with a start as the first rays of sunlight shone into the darkened room. Rubbing her eyes she stared around her, wondering for a moment why she was lying on the bed fully dressed. Then she remembered. Swinging her legs over the side of the bed she walked over to the window.

Her eyes bleak, she stared down at the cobbled pavement. The roads were already busy even at this time of the morning. Two carts rolled by on their way to Smithfield, their cargo of blood-stained carcasses piled high in the backs of the carts, the drivers weaving their way through the light traffic anxious to get to their destination before the daily commuters and horse-buses snarled up the roads. She remained at her post for some time, then throwing her head back she spread her lips into a grim line.

Why should she let Hugh spoil her dreams? She had done nothing to encourage his attentions, so why should she suffer for them? Sod it! She would take Harry's offer, and by doing so would be assured of seeing him daily. He was fond of her, more than fond. Perhaps one day he might even ask her to . . . Impatiently she shook her head. 'One day at a time, remember,' she chided herself. She would just have to make sure she was never alone with Hugh again. And if he persisted she would tell him in no uncertain terms that he was barking up the wrong tree.

Her face determined, Maggie flung open her door, calling out loudly, 'Charlie! Charlie, wake up, I have something I want to talk to you about.'

On a day in October when the autumn leaves of brown and gold and yellow began to tumble from the trees, Maggie and Charlie closed their front door behind them, ready to begin their new venture. It was still dark when they set off for Aldgate High Street, not yet six o'clock. The horse-buses were just starting to run, but they were too excited to wait for one to take them to their destination.

Stepping out briskly, their boots crunching the crisp scattered leaves beneath their feet, they skirted the main thoroughfare to arrive at the top of the high street some twenty minutes later. The street lamps were still burning, enabling them to see clearly the row of open-fronted shops that lined the road. Only one of the shops showed any sign of life at this early hour, this being the bakers owned by Mr Alfred Sutton and his wife Mabel.

Already the appetizing smell of freshly baked bread was wafting from the open doorway, causing Charlie to moan hungrily, 'Cor, Maggie, can yer smell that? It's makin' me mouth water. Can we get some bread an' cakes fer breakfast?'

About to say no, Maggie hesitated. It wouldn't do any harm to strengthen the acquaintance with her new neighbours, besides which her stomach was rumbling with hunger; she had been too nervous to eat any breakfast before leaving home.

'All right, but we'll have to be quick, we've got a lot of work to do before we open.'

They were greeted cheerfully by Mabel Sutton, her lower arms covered with flour, her round red face beaming a welcome at her early visitors. ' 'Ello there ducks, you're up nice an' early. We 'eard you was opening today, nothing much goes unnoticed round these parts. I've been meaning ter 'ave a word wiv yer, but yer was always in such a 'urry. Mind you, the place looks lovely, wouldn't recognise it from what it used ter look like. Yer name's Maggie, ain't it? You're a lucky girl ter 'ave a gentleman like Mr Stewart for a friend, he'll see yer all right.' Seeing the look that crossed the young girl's face Mabel Sutton threw back her head and laughed loudly.

'Oh don't yer go worrying, I don't mean nuffink by what I said, well, nuffink like that anyway. 'E's a good bloke is 'Arry, well-liked round 'ere. Still, a pretty girl like you and 'im not spoken for . . .' She let the words hang in the air, giving Maggie a broad wink. Maggie felt her face flush with embarrassment, yet the woman's face was so open and friendly she found it impossible to take

331

offence. Swallowing hard she smiled back at the woman, anxious to change the subject.

'We hadn't planned to stop for breakfast, but that delicious smell is too hard to resist. Could I have a loaf of bread and a couple of buns, please, Mrs Sutton?'

'Eh, there's no need ter be so formal, love. Me name's Mabel, now you just wait a tick while I pop out the back and see if me old man's got the first batch out of the oven.'

She returned a few moments later, an apologetic smile on her face.

'Sorry, love, they ain't ready yet. I've got some buns left over from yesterday if that's any good to yer.'

'Oh, yes, please,' Charlie interrupted greedily. The two sticky buns were eaten before Maggie had a chance to get her purse from her coat pocket.

'Charlie,' she admonished sternly, 'you'll make yourself sick. Honestly, anyone would think you hadn't eaten for days.'

'Leave 'im be, love,' the plump woman laughed. 'I've never known a youngster who wasn't always 'ungry. And yer can put yer purse away an' all, those are on the 'ouse.'

'Thank you, Mrs Sutton, I mean, Mabel. It's very kind of you.'

'Good luck fer today. I 'ope everything goes all right fer yer.' The friendly words followed them from the shop.

'She was nice, wasn't she, Maggie?' Charlie mumbled, his mouth still full. Maggie looked sideways at him.

'You'd think the devil himself was nice if he gave you something to eat. Honestly, Charlie, I don't know where you put it all. But you're right about Mrs Sutton, she does seem nice. Let's hope all the other shopkeepers are as friendly. It's a pity we didn't pick a market day for our opening, then again maybe it's better if we get into the swing of things gently. I don't think we could manage with a crowd of customers on our first day.'

'When is market day down 'ere?' Charlie asked, wiping his hand across his lips.

'I've already told you, Thursdays and Saturdays. Harry said that's probably when we'll get our best custom,' Maggie replied, her voice irritable with nerves. Although she would never admit it, she was secretly relieved and more than a little grateful that the building site was only ten minutes' walk away. If Harry's men were true to their promise, she was guaranteed steady custom until she could build up her own clientele. It shouldn't be too difficult, she told herself firmly. If she kept her prices reasonable and Harry's workmen spread the word, she should in a short time attract a steady stream of customers.

They passed the butcher's shop and the ironmongers, their steps slowing down as they approached their destination. As they drew nearer Maggie's heart began to thump loudly. She couldn't believe that it was really happening at last. The past couple of months had been fraught with anxiety, not least concerning Hugh. For weeks after the disturbing incident she had been on tenterhooks, expecting him to arrive alone and unannounced to declare his undying love for her. How she would have reacted to such a proposal she didn't truly know. Fortunately the need to dampen his ardour hadn't arisen. He still came round to see her, but always in the company of either Harry or Lotte, and never once by either word or deed had he made any reference to that night. So now at last she could breathe easily once again where Hugh was concerned, although she was careful never to let herself be alone with him; just in case he took it into his head to try his luck again.

Then there had been the troublesome task of finding a shop from which to run her new enterprise. When she had told Harry of her decision to accept his offer he had been overjoyed, promising to have her installed in her own premises within the month; but it hadn't been that simple. The high street was in a prime location and the owners of the sprawling shopping arcade were reluctant to sell, despite the lucrative offers Harry had made. Maggie had ventured to make the suggestion of trying somewhere else, but Harry had been adamant. He had even gone so far as to say he would build her the dammed shop if nobody would sell him theirs, so determined was he to have her near him. To Maggie's reasoning this was foolish, seeing as how he would be finished at the building site next year and his next venture could be miles away. When she had pointed this out to him, he had merely shrugged his shoulders saying that he wanted to see her settled before he moved on.

Just when she had given up all hopes of ever having her shop, an old couple who ran the haberdashery store decided to accept Harry's offer and retire. There had been a further delay while waiting for the old couple to dispose of their stock. They had no sooner handed the keys over to Harry when Maggie and Charlie had moved in. There had been a great deal of work to do as the shop hadn't had a good clean or a lick of paint for years, but with the help of Harry and a couple of his men after work, she was finally ready for business.

They were now standing outside the freshly painted shop, and as Maggie looked up at the sign hanging over the door she felt her body begin to shake.

'You nervous, Maggie?' Charlie asked, and Maggie was quick to notice the slight tremor in his voice. Putting the two heavy bags containing the meat pies she had made earlier that morning onto the cold pavement, she smiled at him.

'Of course I am, aren't you?'

'Well, I am a bit, but it'll be all right, won't it, Maggie? I mean we'll make it work, won't we?'

Her head snapped back quickly, then in a determined voice she answered, 'Don't you worry about that, Charlie, we'll make it work.'

Fumbling in her pocket for the key she found herself raising her eyes once more to the boldly printed sign that bore her name. Harry had wanted to call it Maggie's Restaurant, but Maggie had strongly opposed that idea. As she had forcefully pointed out, she was going to be catering for working men, men who didn't have time to get cleaned up before going for their dinner, and the very word restaurant would deter them from entering such an establishment. Besides, Maggie had very definite ideas about the type of eating house she was going to create.

The City of London and the surrounding areas were full of dining houses, beef houses, restaurants and coffee shops, all catering for the middle classes. The only recourse for working men such as labourers and dock workers was the pie and peas and fish and chip shops, not forgetting the traditional jellied eel stalls, all of which sold their produce in paper bags or cones to be taken away and eaten while walking back to work. It was Maggie's intention to continue the line of good solid belly timber, for apart from the fact such food was the type her potential customers would appreciate, it was also both cheap and quick to cook. She drew the line at jellied eels though – she couldn't bear looking at the slimy creatures, let alone come into contact with them. Her shop would also have the advantage of letting customers sit down and eat in comfort. The only other place where a working man could have this luxury was in pubs, and although many liked their beer, there were an equal amount who would prefer to settle for a strong mug of tea with their meal.

'Come on, Maggie, open up, I'm freezing,' Charlie moaned impatiently, then seeing her gaze fastened on the swinging sign he grinned widely.

'Looks good, don't it? Makes me feel sort of funny seeing your name up there, but yer deserve it, Maggie, and I'll help yer for as long as yer need me.'

Tearing her eyes away from the sign that proclaimed MAGGIE'S HOT MEALS: ALL WELCOME, she pushed open the door, then stood aside as Charlie, his arms filled with a large cardboard box piled high with vegetables and eggs, walked into the darkened shop, then to the nearest table to unload his burden.

'Coo, I'm glad to put that down, me arms are killing me.'

'Get away with you,' Maggie admonished gently, 'a big, strong lad like you moaning about carrying a few vegetables and eggs. What about me? Those bags weigh a ton; I hope I haven't made too many. Still, better that than not enough, eh?'

'Oh, don't you worry about that,' he reassured her. 'Once they're in the oven and the smell starts wafting out into the street, you'll have 'em breaking down the door.'

Maggie laughed loudly, then seeing her brother about to lower himself onto a nearby chair she said firmly, 'Now, come on, love, we haven't got time to laze about. Get yourself out of that chair and get the fire going. We want the place to look welcoming, so first light a few of the table lamps, then you can help me peel the veg and potatoes; come on, love, look lively, we open in half an hour.'

Leaving him to his task, she carried the bags into the kitchen. Turning on the lamps she stood for a moment surveying her new domain. The room was small, having been a storeroom for the previous owners, but Harry had skilfully used every inch to advantage. To her left was the double sink that was essential for the mountain of washing up she would have to do; 'I hope' was the silent plea she sent up. On her right stood the brand new oven range, its gleaming black surface reflecting the burnished pots and pans hanging from the wall rack. The middle of the room was taken up by an extra large square wooden table to prepare the meals on. Underneath the work surface were deep drawers to hold the cutlery and plates.

Putting the bags on the table she began to take the pies out, placing them neatly on the table, her forehead furrowing with worry as she looked at the rows of pies she had been up half the night making. What if nobody came? Her and Charlie would be eating meat pies for the next month. 'Oh, stop fussing about and get them in the oven,' she chided herself. Ten minutes later the pies were laid out on black baking trays ready to cook as soon as the oven was hot enough.

Next she took out a large parcel of bacon and sausages from the bottom of one of the bags and unwrapped them. Together with the eggs Charlie had carried they would make a filling hot breakfast for anyone either on their way to or from work.

While she waited for the oven to heat she prepared the ingredients for two pots of stew. This meal was also cheap and quick to make, and could be kept hot all day if necessary without spoiling its flavour. When the chunks of lamb and vegetables were nestling in the large pots of water she placed them on the gas rings on a low heat. Leaving them to simmer she then put the two trays of meat pies into the now hot oven.

She would see how today went, then tonight she would revise the menu, splitting the meals available into three categories: breakfast, dinner and evening meal; that way she wouldn't be faced with the prospect of being asked for a bowl of stew at eight o'clock in the morning. It was a good, nourishing meal but took hours to cook. Knowing she could do no more for now she took down two mugs and put the kettle next to one of the stewpots, then stood by the table waiting for it to boil. Biting her lip she drummed her fingers nervously on the wooden surface.

Maggie had so many plans for the place, but she could do nothing until she knew approximately how many customers she could expect, and at what time of the day they would arrive. It was no good baking meat pies and making a pot of stew in the mornings if she didn't get her first customer until lunch time. Then again, she couldn't not cook anything in case some of the numerous night workers decided to come in for a hot meal after their long night. And what about her idea to sell fish and chips? She would need a potato and fish fryer; they didn't come cheap, and they would also have to be kept on the boil all day – and that would put more money on her gas bill.

Suddenly the enormity of the problems facing her threatened to overwhelm her, and gripping the edge of the table she looked around her wildly. The sound of the kettle coming to the boil broke into her thoughts. Mashing the tea quickly she set the mugs on the draining board while she checked the stew, then sticking her chin out determinedly she walked into the other room.

'Thanks, Maggie, I could do with that,' Charlie said, gratefully taking the steaming mug from her hand. Easing herself onto a chair Maggie looked around the room. Harry had installed enough tables and chairs to accommodate twenty people; she hoped fervently he hadn't been too optimistic. On the far left of the room there were three steps leading up to a small landing. Harry had wanted to include the space in the main room but Maggie had asked him to leave it as it was for the time being. At the back of her mind she visualised using it as a coffee room for the sole use of any women needing some light refreshment. Again she would have to wait and see what kind of clientele she could expect to get; for now she would do well to concentrate on the main dining-room.

Sipping her tea she turned her head towards the blazing fire in the stone hearth and nodded in satisfaction. With the fire and the table lamps burning brightly the room now looked cosy and inviting.

'What time do yer reckon they'll start coming in?' Charlie asked.

Shrugging herself out of her green coat she answered

tersely, 'How do I know? There's no guarantee anyone will come, we'll just have to wait and see. I know Harry promised to bring some of his men in, but that won't be until dinner time, and besides, we can't keep depending on Harry. Him and his men alone won't keep us in business.'

'All right, there's no need to have a go at me.' Charlie shuffled on his chair awkwardly. 'Anyway, even if someone did come in now, we ain't got nuffink to give 'em yet.' Immediately contrite, Maggie leaned across the table and took his cold hand.

'Don't worry about that, love. It won't take me long to fry up some bacon, sausages and eggs if someone comes in. The pies should be ready soon too. The meat's already cooked, so I've just got to wait until the pastry browns. And I'm sorry I snapped at you, my nerves are a bit frayed at the moment. You always seem to get the brunt of my temper. Well, in future you'll have to start shouting back. You're not a child any more; you're nearly a man and you're going to have to start standing up for yourself. Start practising on me – I deserve it after the way I've treated you at times.'

Charlie smiled wanly. He could look after himself all right. What about that night he'd gone to fetch Hugh? He'd stood up for himself then, hadn't he? And he could handle himself if need be, but Maggie still thought of him as the shy, nervous little boy who had clung to her skirts for so long. But that boy had gone forever the moment he had faced Harry's father, standing his ground when every fibre in his body had urged him to make a run for it.

Lifting his head he looked at his sister, then rolling his eyes pitifully, he said, 'Gawd help us, I ain't that brave.'

The laughter that followed eased the tension between them, and draining the last of their tea they pushed back their chairs. Maggie was wearing a green-checked dress buttoned up the front and falling freely over her hips to the top of her boots. Around her shoulder lay the fawn shawl pinned together with a cameo brooch that Liz had bought for her. It was the first time she had worn it. It seemed somehow to bring Liz's memory close, not as she had last seen her, but buying the gift, her heart happy at the prospect of giving something special to someone that she loved.

'I've put the salt and pepper and sauce on all the tables, and laid out the knives and forks, Maggie. What shall I do now?' Charlie's voice called to her across the room.

Stroking the shawl tenderly she replied, 'There's nothing else you can do until we get some customers. You'd better get some rest now, just in case we do get busy – 'cos if we do there'll be no time for any dinner for us.'

Walking to the window she checked that the menu was clearly visible, and more importantly, the prices. Then carefully lifting up a corner of the starched white lace curtain she peered out into the street. Daybreak was dawning, and already some of the other shops were getting ready for business. She could hear the owners calling out greetings to each other as they prepared for another day, but her attention was fixed on the scattering of passers-by, willing them to stop and look in the window. Afraid her anxious gaze would put off any potential customer, she reluctantly let the curtain drop and returned to the table.

'Well me lad, all we can do now is wait,' she said gaily, trying to ignore the painful churning of her stomach, unaware that Charlie was experiencing the same discomfort.

The sound of the door bell made them both jump; then a gruff voice asked uncertainly, 'You open?'

Both Maggie and Charlie seemed to bound across the room, causing the roughly dressed man to start backwards.

'Yes we are, sir.' Maggie came forward, smiling eagerly. 'Could I take your coat, or would you prefer to keep it on? It's still a bit cold in here, as the fire hasn't been on long. If you'd like to sit down, I'll take your order.' She was babbling like a fool, but powerless to do anything about it. Holding her breath she waited until the man was seated, his cap held awkwardly between rough calloused hands, his gaze sweeping the empty room. The man's whole attitude had the look of someone getting ready to bolt.

Still smiling, she asked brightly, 'What would you like, sir?' while praying he would choose the meat pie or a fry-up. The stew wouldn't be ready for hours yet. Oh, dear . . .

Clearing his throat loudly the man said, 'I'll 'ave a mug a tea and a meat pie, ta.'

'Of course, sir. If you will make yourself comfortable, I'll see to your order.' Raising her eyebrows at Charlie as if to say, 'don't let him leave,' she walked quickly to the kitchen, her body slumping with relief as she heard Charlie drawing the man out about his job.

Opening the oven she breathed an audible sigh of relief at the sight of the golden brown pastry. Picking up the towel that hung on a hook by the side of the oven she moved the top tray down to the bottom of the oven, then put the middle tray up to the top rung. Placing the steaming pie on a plate she poured out a mug of tea from the still-hot teapot and began to walk into the other room. She hadn't taken more than a couple of steps when the door bell once again chimed and the sound of men's voices joined that of Charlie and her first customer. Closing her eyes for a second she swallowed deeply. 'Make it work out for us, God, please make it work out all right.'

Then smoothing the front of her shawl she strode from the kitchen, whispering silently, 'Wish me luck, Liz, I may need all the help I can get.'

CHAPTER NINETEEN

The landlord of the Black Swan in Stepney glared over the counter at the three men sitting in the middle of the tap-room. They had been there for over an hour nursing one drink, and by the look of them they wouldn't be buying any more. Swiping the counter with a dirty cloth he wondered if he should say something, then swiftly changed his mind. After twenty years of running a pub he could spot trouble when he saw it, and the three men looked as if they could turn nasty without much provocation. His attention was diverted by a customer calling for service. As he handed the man his tankard of beer he saw out of the corner of his eye the three men get up and leave, and blew out his cheeks in relief. That big, blond fellow had had the look of someone itching for a fight, and he'd only just cleaned up the mess from Saturday night's rumpus. Whistling under his breath he turned to his next customer.

Out in the street the men spoke for a few minutes, their collars turned up against the bitter January wind, their gloveless hands thrust deep into torn pockets.

'Well, I'd better be orf 'ome afore the missus sets the coppers out looking fer me.'

'Yeah, me too. Besides, it's too bloody cold to 'ang abaht in the street.'

Jimmy Simms said nothing, his blue eyes cold as he stared at his two companions. His unflinching stare unnerved the two men, sending them shuffling off down the icy road, their worn down boots making hardly a sound on the icy pavement.

Jimmy watched them go, his lips tight with anger. Bloody bastards, he seethed inwardly, they knew he had nowhere to go, yet neither of them had offered to put him up for the night. So much for friendship. They'd been chummy enough when he'd had a few bob in his pockets and could afford to buy them drinks. Now when he needed a favour in return they didn't want to know. God, it was cold. He had spent his last shilling on a room in a doss house last night, a room he had shared with half a dozen dirty, smelly vagrants; now he couldn't even afford that. A sudden gust of icy wind tore through his threadbare jacket, causing him to walk on, his head bent against the cold. Ducking into a nearby alley he leaned against the dirty wall, his face creased with anger.

What the hell was he supposed to do now? He had no money and nowhere to go. He'd spent the past three weeks shacked up with a barmaid from one of his local pubs. That little love-nest had been rudely interrupted by the unexpected arrival of her seaman husband. Gawd, that had been a hairy moment. He'd just about had time to get his trousers on and jump from the first floor window before the bearded giant had come crashing into the room.

Thinking his Mum would have forgiven him by now, he'd gone round to his old house, only to have the door slammed in his face. Despite his earnest entreaties, the familiar paint-peeled door had remained firmly closed. In a fit of rage he had begun to pound on the wood panelling, quickly taking to his heels as his Mum had come out after him, a heavy rolling-pin grasped in her fist.

Jesus, it was cold. He'd have to find somewhere tonight or he'd be frozen by the morning. The only place he could think of was the Sally Army, but he'd been banned from there after causing a fight a couple of months back. Maybe they wouldn't remember him – after all they must have seen thousands of men since he'd last been there.

A feeling of rage and helplessness swelled inside him. This time last year he'd had a cushy billet, plenty of food and a warm and loving wife. He'd lived the life of Riley, now he had nothing. Throwing his head back he looked up into the darkening sky. Why? Why had it happened?

Why did the silly cow have to go and get herself killed? Tears of frustration filled his eyes as he thought back over the weeks following Lizzie's funeral. He had managed to keep the rent man at bay by spinning him a tale about Maggie and Charlie coming back soon, telling him they had gone away for a few weeks to get over the shock and that when they returned the rent would be paid in full. It had worked too, until the rent man had become suspicious, demanding some back rent or a visit from the bailiffs. He'd left that same night, bundling up everything he could carry to sell at the nearest pawnbrokers. With the money he had received and the large number of acquaintances he had, he'd had no trouble in finding somewhere to stay, even it was sometimes only for a night.

Now the last of his so-called friends had deserted him, and he felt a tide of desperation rise within him. There must be someone, somewhere he could go to, but try as he would no-one came to mind. If only he had a few bob to get himself into a card game: he was lucky at cards most of the time. This pastime had saved him from having to find a job and work for a living. He clenched his fists inside his pockets, his teeth gritted in despair. Damn it, he was really in trouble this time, and it was all the fault of that bitch of a sister-in-law of his.

If she hadn't taken that money from his pocket he wouldn't be in this mess now. An image of Maggie swam before his eyes. Of course; that's where he'd go. He knew where to find her all right, news travelled fast in the East End. She'd landed on her feet all right, running a little gold mine by all accounts, or maybe it wasn't her feet she had landed on, more likely her back. Oh, yes, he'd heard about her new friend. Some toff who could afford her prices no doubt. Yes; that's what he would do. He'd go and see her; after all she owed him something, didn't she? He could have had the police on her for what she'd done, and that brat of a brother of hers. Bashing him over the head and stealing his money, oh, yes he could make trouble for her if he had a mind to. He forgot that the reason he hadn't reported her in the first place was because he was known to the police and knew he wouldn't be received with any sympathy. The only thought in his mind was to get some money, anyway he could.

Moving away from the wall he looked up and down the street wondering which way would be the quickest to take to get to Aldgate. A cold blast of wind prodded him on his way. He judged it to be around four thirty. If he walked fast he could be at his destination by five thirty at the latest. For a moment his footsteps faltered. The toff who had set her up was well-known around these parts. Those who had come into contact with Harry Stewart spoke well of him, and those that didn't, feared him.

Doubt once again assailed him, for he wasn't the bravest of men. Then the combination of the cold and hunger drove all other thoughts from his mind. If he didn't get some money from somewhere he would die, and with a bit of luck he would find her on her own at this time of day. Blowing hard into his hands he gave one last stamp of his feet before moving on.

'Maggie, Maggie, she's in here again.'

Maggie turned from the oven, her face flushed with the heat. Wiping a strand of hair from her forehead she asked impatiently, 'Who's in here again? What are you talking about, Charlie?'

Rolling his eyes in agitation he gabbled, 'Her of course, Harry's sister. She's up to no good, you mark my words, Maggie, she's not right in the head, I told yer, she . . .'

'Oh for goodness' sake, Charlie, she's not doing any harm,' Maggie snapped, brushing past him. 'She's probably just lonely and wanting a bit of company. She's been here a few times now and she's always been very polite to me. Now stop fussing about and do some of that washing up while I see what she wants.'

'But, Maggie, I told yer how she went for me that night, and what she said about you. I don't trust her, and Harry wouldn't li . . .'

'Now that's enough.' She whirled round to face him. 'I've had a long day and I'm too tired to listen to you babbling on. Ever since the first time she came here, you've been running round like a chicken with its head cut off. How many times have I got to tell you not to worry? I know she frightened you that night, but like I've told you a hundred times, people often say or do things they regret later. Lord knows I've said some spiteful things in my time, then wished I could take them back. How many times have I gone for you for no good reason? And what about me and Liz; God! If I had a pound for every time I've been nasty to someone I'd be a millionaire by now.'

Charlie stared at her, his face set. 'That's different and you know it. Why d'yer keep on making excuses fer her? Is it 'cos yer think she might be yer sister-in-law one day; is that it? 'Cos if that's the reason yer don't have ter worry. Harry can't stand her either, so there's no need to suck up ter her . . .' He broke off quickly, then backed away as Maggie advanced on him, her face red with fury.

'Don't you ever speak to me like that again, Charlie. You should know better than anyone else that it's not in my nature to suck up to people, whoever they are. And you don't have to tell me about Harry's feelings towards his sister, I know only too well what he thinks of her. That's why I feel so sorry for her. She's got no-one who cares for her and she knows it. So if coming here puts a bit of a sparkle into her dull life, I'm not going to deprive her of it.'

As suddenly as her anger had flared, it died down. Resting her bottom against the table she said quietly, 'Think about it, Charlie. Think about how miserable her life must be if the only thing she has to look forward to is coming to a working man's restaurant. It's pathetic; she should be pitied, not feared. As for me thinking she might be my sister-in-law one day, well . . .' She shrugged her shoulders. 'I'll admit I did hope once that one day me and Harry would . . .' Again she paused, her eyes filled now with sadness. 'But I've stopped hoping now. If he had any intention of asking me to marry him, he would have said something by now. Life's funny isn't it, Charlie? At one time I thought I had both the Stewart brothers clamouring for my affections and wished they'd both leave me in peace. Now they treat me as a good friend, nothing else. There's an old saying: beware of what you wish for, it may come true.' Smiling ruefully she added, 'And I certainly got what I wished for, didn't I?'

Charlie shifted his gaze, embarrassed at hearing Maggie talk so freely, while at the same time amazed that she should think that Harry didn't fancy her any more. Gawd, he was mad about her, you only had to look at his face whenever she was close by. Picking up a stack of dirty plates he walked over to the sink and plunged them into the warm soapy water.

'Yer must be mad if yer think that,' he said awkwardly. 'I mean I'm glad that Hugh changed his mind abaht yer, 'cos that would have caused trouble and I wouldn't have liked ter see Lotte getting hurt. But Harry . . . you just wait. He'll say something soon, I'll bet yer, he's probably waiting 'til the buildings finished, then he'll ask yer, you wait and see.'

The sound of the bell over the front door brought Maggie's thoughts back to her customers.

'Lord, I'd better go before all the customers start walking out. Now look, Charlie, about Harry's sister. Leave it, will you? She'll probably get tired of coming here soon, but until then I don't want you saying anything to Harry. I mean it, Charlie, not a word.'

At the mention of Harry's sister Charlie's face became sullen. Thinking back to what Maggie had said earlier he muttered, 'Just wants a bit of company. Huh! Wants to make eyes at the men that come in here more likely. Ugly old bat.'

Shaking her head Maggie smoothed down her apron and walked into the dining-room, then up the three steps to the landing she had made into a smaller dining-room for women only. Harry and Charlie had both ridiculed the idea, saying that no woman would come into a place that catered for working men. But here she had proved them wrong. There were many women who only wanted a pot of tea and cakes while taking a break from shopping, but couldn't afford the prices of the posher coffee houses.

Standing before the smartly dressed woman she experienced a moment's qualm. In spite of what she had told Charlie, the woman made her nervous. Was he right? Did Harry's sister mean her harm in some way? When she had first appeared some weeks ago Maggie's first thoughts were that the evidently well-born woman had wandered in by mistake. This impression had been immediately dispelled when the woman had introduced herself, saying that she had been curious to see her brother's new dining-rooms. The term dining-rooms was hardly applicable to the surroundings. Nevertheless Maggie had beamed with pleasure and set about making the woman welcome; that was until Charlie had seen her. Lord, what a fuss he had made, jabbering and shouting like someone demented. Anyone listening to him would have thought there was an armed gang ready to blow their heads off, instead of one lone woman. She could understand him being apprehensive after what had happened, but honestly, what possible threat could the woman pose to them? Swallowing her misgivings she took out her order pad and waited.

'Ah, there you are, Miss Paige.' Bella smiled up at her. 'I'll have a cup of coffee and some of your delicious scones, if you have them.'

'Yes, ma'am.' Maggie made a pretext of writing down the order on her notepad. She had to admit there was something about the woman that wasn't quite right, but as long as she remained civil she would continue to serve her and keep quiet about her presence from Harry.

The tinkle of the bell announcing another customer brought her head up, a welcoming smile on her lips. A smile that faltered when she saw who her customer was. She felt the blood drain from her face at the sight of her brother-in-law walking towards her, his face wreathed in smiles.

'Are you feeling well, Miss Paige?' Bella enquired, noting the sudden pallor in the young girl's face.

Before Maggie could reply Jimmy was standing directly in front of her.

'Hello Maggie love, long time no see, eh?'

Clutching her throat Maggie whispered hoarsely, 'What do you want? Get out before I call the police.'

The smile slid from Jimmy's face, to be replaced by anger. 'You do that, Maggie love,' he bluffed, 'you do that, and while they're here we can tell them about the little matter of some money you took from my pockets after your dear brother tried to cave me head in.' The tension in the air soon attracted the attention of the rest of the customers, not least Bella, who was watching the scene with avid curiosity.

Recovering her composure Maggie stared defiantly into the hated face. 'Get out of here, you snivelling, pathetic little man,' she hissed at him. 'That money I took belonged to Liz not you; you never worked a day while you were married, nor since by the looks of you. Well, there's no hand-outs here if that's what you've come for. You'd better try your luck somewhere else. I'm sure there are plenty of other gullible women you can try your luck on, just like my Liz. God, she must have been mad to have been taken in by you. And as for telling the police about me, well, go ahead, while we're slinging accusations around there's the little matter of attempted rape. I'm sure they'd be interested to hear about that. But you've no intention of going to the police, have you? If you had you'd have done it long before now. Now I'm warning you . . .'

A cry of pain escaped her lips as she found herself roughly grabbed by the arm.

'You little bitch.' The words were spat into her face while the unrelenting fingers dug deeper into her arm. 'I'm not leaving here until I get what's coming to me, do you hear me, yer dirty slut? I know what you've been up ter; got a fancy man now haven't yer. Not so fussy about spreading yer legs fer someone with a bit of money, are yer?' Maggie stared as if mesmerised into the hate-filled eyes, the pain in her arm making her feel faint. Behind them a concerted growl had erupted from the watching workmen, but both Maggie and Jimmy were too caught up in their own private war to hear them.

'How would he feel if I was ter tell him how yer got the money to start the stall, eh? Maybe he wouldn't be so pleased ter find out he's not the only one to enjoy yer favours.'

It was at that moment that Charlie decided to find out what was keeping Maggie. The sight of his sister being held against her will sent him bounding across the room, his young face filled with fury.

''Ere, what you playing at,' he shrilled loudly, then fell back a step when he saw who the man was. 'Bloody 'ell, it's you, yer cruel bugger. Let go of 'er or I'll bash yer face in.'

Jimmy threw back his head and laughed loudly, 'Piss off, yer little runt before I knock yer on yer back.'

With a strangled cry, Charlie flew forward, his arms flaying wildly, but before his outstretched fists could find their mark he found himself being picked up by the neck and thrown across the room. This act of brutality was the last straw for the watching men. Throwing back their chairs they advanced on the unsuspecting Jimmy.

'You wanna fight, mate, 'ow about trying it on with someone yer own size, yer bleeding bully?'

Jimmy swung round, his eyes rounding in fear at the sight of the angry faces surrounding him. 'Now look, this is private, it's a family matter, nothing ter do with anyone else,' he blustered, while letting go of Maggie's arm.

'Is that right, Maggie, love?' one of the men enquired of the ashen-faced girl. Maggie shook her head, 'No, he's no family of mine. Get him out of here, please, just get him out.'

'Right yer are, love, but before we do, there's something about what he said earlier, something about getting what's coming to 'im.' A wide grin on his face, the man's fist shot out, connecting squarely with Jimmy's jaw.

'I fink you just got it, mate.'

Jimmy's head rocked back on his shoulders; then he found himself being roughly carried from the warm room and out into the bitter cold evening.

'Don't show yer face round here again, if yer knows what's good for yer,' one of the men shouted at him, the warning accompanied by a hard kick to his side. Staggering to his feet he shook his head before lurching off down the road, the hatred he felt for Maggie increasing with every painful step.

Back in the dining-room Bella rose to her feet, a look of concern on her face. 'Dear me, Miss Paige, is there anything I can do for you?' she asked solicitously.

Maggie shook her head weakly. 'No, thank you. I apologise for the unpleasant scene, I don't often get any trouble in here. Now if you will be kind enough to wait, I'll fetch your order.'

Gathering up her gloves Bella adjusted her bonnet, saying quickly, 'Don't trouble yourself, Miss Paige. As a matter of fact I've just remembered I promised my mother I'd be home for tea, she had people coming round.' Picking up her bag from the table she nodded at the still shaken girl and quickly left.

'I'm sorry, Maggie, I wasn't much use was I?' Charlie was by her side, his hand holding the back of his head gingerly.

'You did fine, love,' Maggie reassured him. 'He's a big man; it was very brave of you to tackle him.'

The words did nothing to soothe Charlie's hurt pride, and with a shrug of his shoulders he returned to the kitchen to lick his wounds.

The men returned to their meal with much laughing and shouting. 'He won't be showing his face back here again, Maggie love,' one of them called to her. 'How's abaht a nice mug a tea, that's if you're feeling up ter it.'

Maggie looked at her friends and smiled gratefully. 'Oh, I'm up to it all right, Fred, and what's more it's on the house, for all of you.' Her eyes swept the group of men who in turn shuffled awkwardly on their chairs, their rough faces embarrassed at the look of gratitude on the young girl's lovely face.

Charlie jumped up from his chair when Maggie walked into the kitchen, his eyes bright with unshed tears of mortification. Bustling past him she set about pouring the mugs of tea for her saviours.

'You gonna tell Harry about what happened?' he asked querulously.

'Tell Harry, why should I tell Harry?' She looked at him in surprise.

'Well, I just thought . . .' he mumbled uncomfortably.

'Now look here, me lad,' she said brusquely, 'just because Harry owns this place, it doesn't mean I have to go running to him with every little problem. Besides, it's over now. Jimmy wouldn't dare come back here, not after what happened. And you can stop worrying about his sister as well. She's gone and I don't blame her. She's probably not used to witnessing unpleasant scenes. I doubt if she'll be back either.'

'Well, in that case, at least Jimmy's done something right for once in his life,' the boy muttered sullenly, although he couldn't see that spiteful old bitch being frightened off by a fight. In fact he would have imagined she would have enjoyed seeing men punching each other's faces in.

Sitting in the hansom cab, Bella sat by the window, her eyes scanning the pavement for the man who had just been thrown bodily from the dining-rooms. The idea to visit Harry's new establishment had been born out of a desire to see if she could find out something detrimental about his new lady friend, and in doing so bring him down from his high pedestal and smash his newly found happiness. Also of course it had given her the chance to mingle with the kind of men she liked the most, although she would never admit that, even to herself. Her plans had seemed doomed to failure at first. Everyone she had spoken to had a liking for the young scut that ran the place. But now, oh, yes, now she had finally got something on her, if only she could find the man.

Then she saw him. He was leaning up against a lamp-post, his arms wrapped around his body in an effort to keep warm.

Calling out for the driver to stop, she leaned out of the window and raising her voice to be heard over the milling crowd she called, 'You, you there, by the lamp-post, come here, I wish to talk to you.'

Jimmy heard the strident voice but paid no heed; he was too busy thinking up ways to get even with the Paiges. 'You, man, yes, you,' she added when Jimmy finally lifted his head to see who was shouting. His mouth dropped in amazement when he realised that the well-dressed woman was beckoning to him. Lowering his hands to his sides, he walked uncertainly towards her.

'You talking to me, miss?' he asked, ready to back away if she started yelling.

'Yes, I'm talking to you. Quickly, get in the cab, you're

attracting attention and I've no wish for my personal business to be voiced abroad.'

Hardly daring to believe his ears, Jimmy pulled open the door and settled himself nervously on the edge of the seat.

'I won't keep you from your business,' Bella started, her voice pitched high at what she had done in asking this man to sit with her. 'I was unfortunate enough to witness that unsavoury scene. Normally I wouldn't trouble myself with such matters, nor for that matter would I frequent such places, but my brother owns the so-called restaurant and I feel obliged to keep an eye on the place as he is unable to do so. From what I heard it seems the Paige girl isn't as innocent as my brother seems to think she is; if that is the case I wish to know. She has inveigled herself into both my brothers' affections, and obviously if there is any possibility of them being harmed in any way, it is my duty to prevent it. You are – or were – on intimate terms with her at one time and would know if there were anything in her past that my brother should be made aware of. Well, speak up, man, I haven't got all day.'

Jimmy licked his lips, his mind racing as he surveyed the woman seated opposite him. Gawd, but she must have been at the back of the queue when they were handing out the looks. Still . . . she wasn't short of a few bob, not if that brown outfit and sable muff were anything to go by. Those pearl earrings hadn't come from Paddy's market either. Taking off his cap he thought hard before answering. If there was one thing he was a good judge of, it was women, and this one for all her fine clothes was hungry for a man; it was there in her eyes, that unmistakable look. And if he played his cards right, he could be on to a good thing.

Assuming a wounded expression he said earnestly, 'I don't know if I should say anyfing, ma'am. I mean with her being such a good friend of your brother's an' all.' He waited for her reaction, then seeing her shoulders arch back with impatience he hurried on, 'But she's a bad 'un all right. I used ter be married ter her sister, God rest her soul.' Here he crossed himself piously. 'I was gonna look after her and her brother, but the pair of 'em did the dirty on me. Right after the funeral it was; my wife's that is. Anyway I'd just come in after seeing me Mum home safely, when that little brat bashed me over the 'ead as soon as I come in the door. When I woke up all me money had gorn, and them with it. I couldn't get a job, and then I was thrown out onto the streets. I've done all right up ter now, but . . . well to be honest, ma'am, I'm in a pickle. That's why I came here tonight, I thought as how she, Maggie that is, I thought she owed me something, after all I could 'ave 'ad the police on her and . . .'

'Why didn't you?' Bella interrupted sharply. 'Surely if what you say is true, the first action to take would be to inform the police. After all a crime was committed.'

Jimmy squirmed on the seat. Maybe he had been mistaken about her, maybe she was just looking after her brother's interests . . . Yet he had been so sure. Raising his eyes warily he felt a jolt of triumph run through him at the undisguised look of lust in her black eyes. Careful not to let her see his expression he kept his gaze lowered.

'I couldn't 'ave done that, ma'am, we are family after all's said and done, and yer don't drop yer family to the coppers. But there is something else you should know; she got the money for her first business by going on the game. She only did it the one night, but she done well. Three sovereigns from the first geezer, then twenty pounds from another one wot brought 'er 'ome in a cab. Gawd knows what she done for that amount, must 'ave been something special . . . begging yer pardon, ma'am,' he added hastily, afraid he may have gone too far.

Jimmy needn't have worried. Bella was far too busy assessing the potential of the man sitting so near to her. He was dirty and his clothes were threadbare, but clean him up and put him in fine clothes and . . .

Clearing her throat noisily she said, 'I may need to find you again. If all you say is indeed true, then of course I shall have to inform my brother. If you tell me where I can find you, I'll be in touch as soon as I decide what course of action to take.'

He had her; he bloody well had her. Brother's welfare, my arse – she was looking for a man, and what better man than himself? So what if she had a face like a bulldog chewing a wasp? As his old Dad used to say; you don't look at the mantelpiece when you're poking the fire.

Lowering his eyes once more he said shamefacedly, 'Lord, ma'am, but I feel embarrassed. The truth is I ain't got nowhere ter go. If I'd had the money ter find meself a place fer the night, I wouldn't 'ave gorn cap in hand ter that loose bitch . . . Sorry, ma'am.'

Bella waved his explanations away. Opening her leather bag she extracted a five-pound note. 'This should be enough to cover your expenses for the time being. I shall meet you at ten o'clock on the corner of Bright Road tomorrow. Do you know the place?' When Jimmy nodded eagerly she motioned to the door. 'Very good, until tomorrow then.'

Jimmy took the hint, and with one bound was out of the carriage and back on the pavement.

'By the way, I shall need to know your name, sir.'

'Jimmy Simms, ma'am, at your service,' he replied jauntily. He watched as the carriage pulled away, a huge grin engulfing his florid face. 'At your service indeed, ma'am,' he added beneath his breath before setting off for the nearest pub.

CHAPTER TWENTY

Beatrice Stewart took a sip of coffee, her eyes travelling the length of the long dining-table and sighed inwardly. Laying the bone-china cup back in its saucer she leaned back in her chair, her gaze settling on Hugh. Whatever was the matter with the man? He looked as if he had the weight of the world on his shoulders. Something was troubling him, that was certain, but what? Next to him Lotte sat quietly, a strained smile on her lips while her hands played nervously with a white table napkin. The sight of her future daughter-in-law struggling to put on a brave face caused Beatrice's heart to lurch against her ribs. Oh, dear. Was everything all right between Lotte and Hugh? Neither of them had said anything to the contrary, but it was painfully obvious that something was amiss.

Picking up her cup she took another sip, her mind wondering whether or not to risk taking Lotte aside and asking if there was anything troubling her. There was always the chance she would be told to mind her own business . . . No, no, Lotte was far too nice a person to be rude, even if she did think the person in question was interfering. She would wait until the men had retired to the study, then take Lotte to one side and ask her outright. Luckily Bella had taken to retiring to her room immediately after supper, so there was no need to worry about her unwelcome presence.

That was something else that had been troubling her of late. The change in her daughter over the past three months had been nothing short of miraculous. The once sullen, disagreeable woman had been transformed into a smiling, courteous person that bore no resemblance to the Bella they all knew. Edward had put the sudden change of character down to the threat of being sent to Wales, but Beatrice wasn't convinced. If she didn't know better she would swear her daughter had fallen in love. The thought brought her head back with a jolt. Could it be, could Bella possibly have met someone? She had been going out a lot of late. Oh no, she couldn't have, the idea was preposterous. Sneaking a glance at her daughter sitting beside her she noted the smile hovering around the thin lips and noticed for the first time the softness in the plain face. Again she felt a lurch of fear. Whoever had said that motherhood was the fulfilment of a woman's dream must have been a man. The moments of joy were far outweighed by the burdens of worry, even when the children in question had reached adulthood.

Sighing gently she turned her attention to Harry. Even he had seem preoccupied of late, but then he was worried about the new buildings being ready on time. Yet it wasn't like Harry to bring his troubles home with him.

'Cyril Jenkins has asked if we would like to accompany him and his wife to Ascot at Easter. What do you think, my dear, would you like to go?' Edward's voice broke into her thoughts. Thankful of the diversion Beatrice turned her attention to her husband.

Hugh stared into his half-filled wine glass, his face drawn and pale. What was he to do? He couldn't go on like this any longer. From the moment he had seen Maggie lying so ill he had been forced to admit that he loved her, and had loved her from their very first meeting. Yet what could he have done? It had been obvious from the start that Harry looked on her as his own property, and whatever Harry wanted, Harry invariably got. The idea of trying to take Maggie away from his elder brother had never crossed his mind; until now.

With his impending wedding only a few months away, he had become more agitated with each passing day. He had hoped the feelings he had for Maggie would eventually fade, but that hadn't happened; he knew now with increased certainty that it never would.

'Are you feeling all right, dear?'

He jumped guiltily at the sound of Lotte's voice by his side. Turning his head he looked into her concerned face and quickly lowered his gaze, muttering, 'It's nothing to be concerned about, I'm feeling a little off colour that's all. As a matter of fact I think I'll retire early if you don't mind me escorting you home now.'

Before Lotte could reply Harry pushed back his chair and said, 'What's up, Hugh? Are you feeling rough, can I do anything for you?'

'Is everything all right, Hugh?' Beatrice joined in the conversation.

Hugh looked around at the worried faces surrounding him and had the sudden urge to scream at them, at all of them. His stomach was churning painfully at the knowledge of what he was going to do. His family would be shocked to the core, and Lotte . . . Poor Lotte. She didn't deserve to be jilted, but better now than at the altar. Because he knew in his heart that he could never go through with marrying her. Oh why had he ever asked her – it had been a mistake from the start. If only he had been born with some gumption, then he wouldn't have had to contend with Bella's unnatural attentions and be forced into a hasty proposal to a woman he didn't love in order to get away from her. Yet he could have been happy with Lotte if Charlie hadn't arrived that night and reopened all his old feelings . . . If only, if only . . . God, what a mess!

'I can escort Lotte home if you're not up to it, old man,' Harry was saying, already on his feet.

'Nonsense, she can stay here tonight,' Beatrice interjected, 'You get off to bed, dear, we'll take care of Lotte.'

'No really, I'd rather go home, thank you all the same,' Lotte too had risen to her feet, her face pale and set.

'What's all this, who's going home?' Edward blinked his eyes rapidly, emerging from his brandy induced nap.

Hugh remained seated, his hands held to his head as the babble of voices flowed around him. He couldn't take much more. If they didn't stop fussing he'd go mad. All he wanted was to get away from the house, from all of them. But first he had to take Lotte home and once there . . . He shook his head. Don't think about it, he told himself. Just take her home and then tell her. She half suspects anyway. She'll be hurt and upset but not overly surprised. Lotte was a very intelligent and observant woman, he only hoped she would be understanding.

Scraping back his chair he rose unsteadily to his feet. 'I said I was feeling a bit off colour,' he shouted above the voices, 'I didn't say I was at death's door. Now if you'll excuse us, Lotte and I will take our leave.'

Ignoring the shocked faces that accompanied his outburst he took Lotte's arm and led her from the room. When the door had closed behind them, an uneasy silence settled on the room. Harry was the first to leave the table, followed closely by Bella. Left alone with her husband Beatrice felt her eyes fill with tears and didn't quite know why she was crying.

In her room Bella sat before the ornate dressing table smiling at her reflection. Lord, what a fuss they had all made about Hugh, and only a few short months ago she herself would have been the most worried. But things had changed, oh indeed they had, and all for the better. Before meeting Jimmy she had lived her life through others, but no more. Now she had a real life of her own, a life that had suddenly taken on new meaning.

Every morning when she awoke she imagined for a brief moment that all that had happened was merely a dream and then she would remember Jimmy. Jimmy with his strong arms holding her, his solid body pressed tight against her own. Jimmy with his whispered words of love and promises, his voice thick with emotion as his lips travelled down her throat towards her upturned breasts. The image her mind presented her with brought out beads of sweat on her brow. God, how she needed him, wanted him right now, this minute. Wiping her forehead with a white handkerchief she leaned back on the plush, red upholstered chair.

If only Jimmy wasn't so concerned about the differences in their social status they could be married, but the dear, sweet man was worried that he wasn't good enough for her. He was trying desperately hard to set up his own business, but every time the impending deal came near to fruition something happened to send his dreams tumbling down around him. Only two weeks ago he had cried on her shoulder, telling her to forget him and find someone who was more worthy of her. The sight of the big, proud man so obviously distressed and humiliated had filled her with a fierce protective-ness for him.

Giving a small sigh she removed her pearl necklace and earrings and opened her jewel box. Biting on her lower lip she stared down into the nearly empty box. For the past six weeks she had been selling her jewels in order to finance Jimmy's endeavours into the world of business. Only the other night her mother had asked why she wasn't wearing the emeralds with her green evening gown. It was only a matter of time before she was found out, and then what? Closing the lid of the box she thought hard. It wasn't Jimmy's fault his ventures kept failing, he just wasn't used to dealing with men of business. Now if they were married, she could help him. They could build a future together. If only she could persuade him that she didn't want or need a big house and servants to be happy, that all she wanted was him. If she could make him believe that she would be happy sharing two rooms as long as he was in them with her, then maybe he would forget all this nonsense about their social differences and marry her.

A desire to see him swept over her. Glancing at the mantel clock she saw that it was only eight o'clock. Would he be at home? Could she take the chance of arriving unannounced? She experienced a feeling of unease and quickly shook it off. Of course he would be pleased to see her; he loved her. Swiftly now she donned her outdoor coat and made for the door. Stopping only to tell her mother she was going to visit a friend she left the house before any protests could be made. Ignoring Benson's offer to get her a cab she walked to the corner of the street and hailed a passing hackney carriage. Once inside she sat on the edge of the seat clutching her leather bag. He would be pleased to see her, of course he would. The sound of the horses' hooves clipping along the uneven road echoed in her ears as her mind kept repeating over and over: he loves me, he loves me.

'Lotte, there's something I wish to talk to you about.'

The unmistakable sound of bad tidings in Hugh's voice set Lotte's heart beating wildly. They had hardly spoken on the ride home, and now, standing outside her modest one-bedroomed house in Plaistow, Lotte knew with certainty that the moment she had been dreading for months had finally arrived. Determined to keep her dignity she walked into the darkened hallway, lighting the table lamp before turning to face Hugh. He was still standing in the street, the light from the lamp showing clearly his discomfort. Placing her bag and key on the table she walked back to the door.

'There's no need to say anything, Hugh, I already know and have done for some time now. You want to call off the wedding, don't you?' Miserably Hugh nodded his head, unable to look into Lotte's face.

'I thought so,' she said quietly. 'Well, at least it's out in the open now. Is it Maggie; is that the reason you've decided against marrying me?'

'Lotte, please. I never wanted to hurt you, you must

believe that,' Hugh answered, his eyes pleading with her to understand. 'Maggie's never given me any encouragement, so you mustn't blame her. I . . . I know she doesn't care for me and that there's no future for me with her, but I couldn't marry you knowing how I feel about Maggie, it wouldn't be fair. I wouldn't blame you if you hated me, but could we . . .'

'Why don't you go to her and ask her how she feels - you may be surprised at her answer.'

Hugh's head jerked up in alarm. Wetting his lips he looked closely at Lotte searching for signs of ridicule but found only sympathy in the dark eyes. A deep sense of shame rose within him.

'Don't, Lotte, don't be kind, I don't deserve it. As for going to Maggie . . . You know as well as I that it's Harry she cares for.'

Desperately trying to appear calm, Lotte fought back the threatened tears to say steadily, 'Don't be such a defeatist, Hugh. You don't know that for certain, and besides, if you want something badly enough you must be prepared to fight for it and take the chances of rejection.'

Still he stood staring at her, looking for all the world like a child who had lost his mother. Unable to bear the hurt any longer she made to close the door.

'Goodbye, Hugh, and good luck.'

'Lotte, please . . .'

The door slammed shut in his face, but not before he had seen the tears glistening in Lotte's eyes. Alone and bewildered he looked up and down the street as if seeking inspiration, then thrusting his hands into his overcoat pockets he walked aimlessly along the pavement.

Maggie finished the ironing and sighed with relief. She really would have to teach Charlie how to iron, that is if she could ever catch him at home. For the past couple of months he had taken to going out in the evenings saying he was going to see some mates, but she wasn't convinced. Boys of his age didn't usually bother to wash and change just to go out with their friends. Smiling gently she put the clean clothing in the ottoman, then sat down by the fire, an open book on her lap. When the knock came on the door she jumped slightly, her heart beginning to beat with expectation. Could it be Harry? He hadn't been here for weeks, and when he did come he did nothing except sit and talk about the work on the buildings, the weather, the dining-rooms, in fact he talked about everything under the sun except the one thing she wanted to hear. Smoothing down her navy wool skirt she checked that the top button on her white blouse was fastened, then walked to the door.

'Hugh!' The name came out as a gasp. 'Wh . . . what are you doing here, what do you want?'

Hugh heard the fear in her voice and felt his heart skip a beat. In normal circumstances he would have made his apologies and left, but now, fortified by five brandies drunk hurriedly at the pub on the corner of the street, he brushed past the startled girl and lurched into the room.

'Hugh, what is it?' she cried out, the fear rising in her at the unmistakable smell of alcohol that was emanating from the staggering figure. 'What have you come here for; what do you want?'

Hugh spun round unsteadily, his eyes glazed. Then summoning up all his courage he sprung forward grabbing her around the waist.

'Oh, Maggie, Maggie, my love. Please don't turn me away, I need you; God, how I need you,' he gabbled into her ear, his voice slurred. This was all he wanted, to hold Maggie in his arms, to have her near to him. Mistaking his intentions, Maggie held herself rigid with fright. Once again she felt the unwelcome presence of a man's hands upon her person. Good Lord! Was it her lot in life to be continually manhandled and abused by every man she came into contact with? Did she have an invisible sign around her neck saying 'help yourself'?

A rising surge of anger overcame her fear, and summoning all of her strength, she pulled at Hugh's hair, forcing his head backwards. Ignoring his cry of pain she jerked her knee upwards, catching him squarely in the groin. The clutching hands immediately released their hold on her as Hugh sunk to his knees, his cries echoing in her ears. She watched without pity as he crawled away from her towards the armchair.

When he had heaved himself into the chair she cried

out, 'You can get out of there, Hugh, you're not stopping. Now get out before I start screaming. I will, I'm not joking, if you don't go I'll raise the whole house. Are you listening, Hugh? I mean it, I . . .'

'No, no, not again, please God, not again.'

Maggie stood by the door, ready to run if he made any sudden moves, but he remained in the chair, his head in his hands while he continued to cry piteously, 'I'm sorry, I didn't mean it . . . forgive me, I didn't mean to hurt her, it was a mistake, it was all a mistake.'

His anguished cries filled the room while Maggie continued to watch him suspiciously. Very carefully she moved away from the door, her face wary. 'What are you talking about, Hugh? Who did you hurt, what girl? Answer me, damn you, what have you done?'

Hugh raised his head wearily, his face streaked with tears. The effects of the brandy had worn off the moment Maggie had started to fight him, her struggling body reviving the memory of the darkened alley and the girl he had raped. The ugly word brought his body upright while his head shook wildly in denial. No, he wasn't guilty of rape, it had been a genuine mistake. That area of London was notorious for prostitution, which was why he had gone there, but the girl . . . For years now he had tried to suppress the memory of that night and the unknown girl's struggles to get away from him. If only he had been able to share his nightmare with someone it might have helped to assuage the guilt and shame that had racked him ever since. He had tried to speak to

Harry about it, but the fear of seeing the disgust and contempt that would surely have followed had stopped him from unburdening himself.

Now he could keep quiet no longer. He needed to share his shame, needed to hear someone tell him he had nothing to reproach himself for, and what better person to confide in than someone he would never meet again. And after tonight, he would never see Maggie again; that he knew with painful certainty. The knowledge that he was about to ease the burden that had weighed heavily on his conscience for so long sent a wave of relief through his body. Relaxing back in the chair he began to speak, stumbling at first, then gaining strength as he reached the climax of his story. So intent was he, he failed to notice the look of horror that had come over Maggie's face. When he had finished he leaned back tiredly, a look of relief on his smooth features. Then he saw Maggie standing before him, the look of disgust and rage in her eyes making him flinch. Averting his gaze he rose unsteadily to his feet.

'I don't blame you for reacting in this way, but let me tell you, you can't feel any more loathing for me that I haven't felt for myself over the years. I'll take my leave now and never bother you again. I had no right to assume you would welcome my advances, clumsy as they were, but . . . but all I wanted was to hold you in my arms, to feel you near to me. I'll admit that if you had been willing, if you had shown some affection for me, I might have been tempted to press my attentions further.

A few kisses perhaps, I would never have expected anything more, that I swear to you. I have no excuse to offer
in my defence except to say that I love you, and have
done since the first moment we met. You may well think
I have a strange way of showing my love, but . . . but I'm
a weak man, I always have been, and the only way I
could find the courage to come here tonight was to forti-
fy myself with drink. I never intended to harm you in any
way, you must believe that. I'll understand if you decide
to tell Harry about my visit . . .' – he gave a short, nervous
laugh – '. . . and prepare myself for a sound thrashing. It's
no more than I deserve after the way I've behaved
tonight. Goodbye, Maggie. I hope you find happiness
one day, I'm only sorry it couldn't have been with me.'

Maggie stood by the table, her fingers gripping the
rough edge as her mind tried to digest what she had just
heard. It couldn't be true, it was some horrible joke. Yet
even as she tried to deny it, she knew deep down that
what Hugh had told her was the truth. Still she remained
silent, unable to utter a word in the face of the horrific
revelation. It was only when Hugh brushed past her, his
face flushed with embarrassment and shame that she
found her tongue.

Grinding her teeth together she said harshly, 'Did
Harry ever tell you how we met?'

Hugh stopped in his tracks, his forehead wrinkling in
bewilderment at the unexpected question. Turning
slowly he raised his gaze to her face, then stepped backwards, alarmed at the fierce rage burning in her eyes.

Swallowing noisily he stretched his neck up from his collar, and with as much aplomb as he could muster he answered warily, 'He told me you were a friend; he didn't go into detail and I didn't ask. Why? What earthly reason has that to do with what has transpired here tonight?'

Maggie let go of the table, her hands clenched into tight balls as she advanced upon him. 'I'll tell you how we met, shall I? He found me lying on the ground in a dirty, backstreet alley after some filthy bastard had raped me. Oh . . . you can look shocked, Hugh; after all, it was you, wasn't it? Well! Answer me, damn it, say something, you gutless bastard.' Her chest heaving, she fought to control her rage, fought to control the urge to leap at this man, to tear at his face and body; to hurt and inflict the same measure of pain that she had suffered at his hands.

'Was that the only way you could get a woman, by forcing yourself on her? Still, I did very well out of it, didn't I? Three sovereigns, that was very generous of you, and of course there was the twenty pounds that Harry gave me, after he had seen me safely home. Oh he didn't get anything in return – you had that pleasure all to yourself. Didn't you think it strange when he gave you your wallet back; you must remember the wallet you dropped when you ran off leaving me with my skirt up around my waist like a common whore. I gave it to Harry, more fool me. I should have pocketed it, but then I'm not a thief, I . . .' The importance of what she had just said suddenly dawned on her. The wallet she had picked up and handed over to Harry had belonged to Hugh. The implication was so horrendous she doubled over as if she had been violently punched in the stomach. Oh, dear God! Oh, no, no . . . no!

Screwing up her eyes she thought back to that night. She saw herself giving the wallet to Harry and remembered the look on his face as he'd stared down at it. She hadn't thought anything of it at the time, but now . . . God, she felt sick, sick and betrayed. He must have looked inside the wallet, must have found something to show who it belonged to. No wonder he had given her such a large amount of money, and she had imagined he was just being kind. Christ! What a fool she had been. The only reason he had been so generous was because he had hoped she would keep her mouth shut about what had happened . . . And yet, if that were true, why had he given her his name and address?

Whirling round she stumbled blindly to the armchair and flopped down heavily. It was over. All her hopes and dreams shattered beyond repair. Squeezing her eyes tightly shut she rocked back and forth, her arms tightly wrapped around her body in anguish. She had loved them; loved them both in different ways, and they had used her in the worst way imaginable. Hugh, unwittingly, and Harry . . . Harry had known exactly what he was doing.

She thought back to the days spent walking in the park, her tortured mind conjuring up visions of the three of them talking and laughing as if they were all of one and the same class and background. She saw herself puffed up with self-importance at being seen in the company of the two men who were obviously of the gentry, and shuddered with humiliation at the memory. She should have listened to Liz. She should have kept the money and steered well clear of Harry after that first meeting in the park. But she hadn't heeded her sister's advice, and now she was paying the ultimate price for her foolishness.

Why? Why hadn't Harry told her about Hugh? She knew it wouldn't have been an easy thing for him to do . . . but to carry on the pretence, to let her go on believing they both cared for her, that she was someone special was much, much worse. She didn't understand, didn't understand any of it. Another shuddering tremor attacked her body. She had imagined she'd known them so well; when in truth she didn't know them at all; neither of them.

Hugh too was in a state of severe shock. If what Maggie had said was true, and he had no reason to doubt her, then Harry had known all along. The wallet had had his initials engraved inside – there was no way Harry couldn't have known who it belonged to. His mind reeling, he walked over to where Maggie sat hunched in the chair.

In a voice choked with tears he whispered, 'I'm so sorry, Maggie. You'll never know how sorry I am. I don't know what you were doing there that night, but I do know it was for an innocent purpose.' When his hand tentatively touched her shoulder Maggie jumped violently. Her eyes swimming with unshed tears she glared up at him in disgust.

'Don't touch me,' she hissed, her voice filled with contempt and hatred. 'Don't ever touch me or come near me again, you pathetic miserable little man.'

Hugh's face blanched, his whole body quivering at the venom in her voice. For a brief moment Maggie felt a spark of pity for him, then swiftly squashed the feeling. He didn't deserve her pity. She hated him; hated both of them. Yet even as she silently berated the two men, part of her longed for Harry's presence. Her body seemed to be crying out for his strong arms to hold her, to comfort her. Disgusted at her weakness she dropped her face into her hands and sobbed quietly.

Unable to witness her distress any longer, Hugh gave a strangled cry and fled from the room. Once out in the street he started to run, his feverish thoughts racing round and round inside his head. There was only one purpose in his mind now: to confront Harry. Harry whom he had loved and looked up to all his life. Harry, whom he would have done anything for. Harry, who had deliberately brought him face to face with the girl he had raped. Harry, his beloved brother who had betrayed him with his machiavellian games. For the first time in his life, Hugh felt the emotion of hate, and with every step he took the feeling grew stronger. Hansom cabs passed him by, the drivers looking down at him hopefully, but he ignored them all. He had to keep walking, keep moving, keep alive this burning hatred until he reached his home, and the person who had destroyed his world.

At the same time that Hugh was with Maggie, Bella was knocking on Jimmy's door. After the third knock she prepared to walk away when the door was pulled roughly open to reveal Jimmy, bleary eyed, wearing only a grubby, grey singlet. The sight of him sent a momentary shudder of distaste down Bella's spine, a feeling that quickly passed when he reached out and pulled her to him.

'Belle, darling, what are you doing here at this time of night?' Jimmy cried, trying to inject some enthusiasm into his voice. Keeping her held tightly against him he stared over her shoulder, his face worried. Bloody hell, half an hour earlier and she would have met Doris on the way out. During the months he had been courting Bella he had spent many a night entertaining other young ladies, such as the plump barmaid from The Crown in Stepney.

'Look, Belle, I wasn't expecting company,' he said quickly. 'Give me a minute ter get some clothes on, and I'll be right wiv yer.'

Going into the small adjoining room, he pulled on a pair of brown trousers and a grey shirt. Pulling his braces up over his shoulders he waited a few more minutes while he got his thoughts into order. She'd given him a fright turning up like that. Maybe now was the time to play his final trump card.

For weeks now he had become increasingly bored and impatient with the middle-aged harridan he had so cleverly seduced. It had been fun at first – after all, he had never had a virgin before. She'd been a willing pupil too, eager to learn all he had to teach her. He still couldn't believe that she'd swallowed his tales about broken business deals, bringing him more jewels to sell each time a 'deal' fell through. It was hard to credit that an educated woman like her could be so gullible, but he wasn't complaining. For the first time in his life he had more money than he knew what to do with, but still he wanted more and was determined to get every last piece of jewellery from her before disappearing from her life. He had planned to wait a couple of weeks before spinning her another tale, but after the unexpected visit and the consequences it might have had he decided to bring his plans forward. Giving a small shake of his head, he hunched his shoulders and walked back into the bedroom and sat down on the bed, a worried expression on his face.

'What is it, darling; is something wrong?' Bella ran to his side.

Shaking his head mournfully he waited a minute then, his voice heavy, he said, 'Something's happened, Belle, something terrible, I'm gonna 'ave ter leave the country unless I want ter spend the next ten years in jail.' He saw Bella move nearer to him and quickly buried his head in his hands.

'Don't, Belle, don't come any nearer. There's nothing you can do for me now and I care too much for yer to drag yer down wiv me. Go home, Belle, go home ter your family, and try ter forget all about me. I've brought yer nuffing but disappointments and lost all yer lovely jewellery into the bargain. But you'll get every penny back, darlin', that I do promise yer. I don't know when, but one day when it's safe ter come back ter England, I'll find a way to get back all the money I lost. Now get out, Belle, please. I feel so ashamed and frightened. If yer don't go soon I'm gonna make a fool of meself and start blubbering, please . . .'

Thoroughly frightened now, Bella leapt the few short feet that separated them and pulled roughly at his hands, crying, 'Darling, darling, don't talk so. Tell me what has happened, there must be something I can do to help. Please, Jimmy, confide in me, don't shut me out. I can't bear to see you so miserable. Please, whatever you've done, whatever's happened, we can work it out between us; please, Jimmy, please.'

Pulling her roughly into his arms, he rocked her back and forth, his mouth split into a wide grin as he gazed over her shoulder. It was going to work. The stupid cow was so desperate to have a man, she'd believe anything he told her. Another man might have felt some pity for such a woman as Bella, but Jimmy felt nothing but contempt, and a rising desire to get away from her as soon as possible. Composing his face once more into a solemn expression he drew away from her.

Then, taking hold of her hands he said earnestly, 'All right then, Belle. I didn't want yer ter hear the sordid details, but I suppose I owe yer the truth, 'specially after all we've been ter each other. Promise me though, that you'll let me say me piece wivout interrupting, now promise me, love.' Bella nodded, her throat too full of fear to utter another word.

Letting go of her hands Jimmy rose to his feet. Then, running his fingers through his unruly hair he said awkwardly, 'It's like this. Do yer remember that first time we met at Maggie's place? Well of course yer do. What I meant was, did yer hear her saying that I'd tried ter rape 'er? You've never mentioned it, and I didn't know if you'd 'eard or not. There was a 'ell of a lot a noise going on at the time. I didn't take no notice of her, I thought she was just saying it, you know, making out I was the villain 'cos she felt guilty abaht what she'd done. Then her "friends" threw me out into the street, and . . . well, the rest yer know.'

Stopping for a moment. he looked down at Bella sitting on the grubby bed, and putting what he hoped was a loving smile on his face he said softly, 'If it hadn't been fer you, darlin', I'd 'ave frozen ter death that very night. 'Cos I had no-one else ter turn to. You saved me life, Belle, and you've given me every opportunity ter make somefing of meself, and I've let yer down time and time again. That's why it's so 'ard ter tell yer about what's happened, and it's even 'arder to know that after tomorrow it'll be years before I see yer again; if ever.'

Wiping his brow with the back of his hand he took a deep breath, 'Well, here it is, Belle, I 'ad a visit yesterday from that little brat Charlie, you know, Maggie's brother. He gave me a message from 'er. She says that if I don't leave the country, she's gonna go ter the police and tell 'em I tried to rape her. I couldn't believe it at first, I mean, why should she do such a thing? And it's not true, Belle, you've got ter believe me, I never laid a finger on her, well, no decent man would touch 'er after what she done, going on the game like she did.

'And you know something funny, Belle? She even told my Liz she was raped that night an' all, she must have it on the brain. Anyway, like I said, I thought she was just trying ter scare me, to get back at me like. 'Cos she never liked me, not from the start. Thought her sister was too good fer me, she did. Then I gets ter thinking. She's probably worried I might tell her fancy man . . . Oh Lord, I'm sorry, Belle, I keep forgetting he's yer brother. But it's the only reason I can think of why she's so anxious ter get rid of me. Maybe he's asked 'er ter marry him and she's scared I'll put a spanner in the works, so she wants ter make sure I'm put out of the way permanently. And if she gets your brother on her side, well . . . what chance would I have wiv the coppers? They'd never take my word against theirs, would they? And I've been in trouble wiv the Law before. No. . . . it's no use, Belle, she's got me over a barrel, there's nothing I can do except make a run fer it.

'But oh, Belle, darlin', I had such plans for us. Not the

sort of ones I've made such a mess of, but plans of us being together. I . . . I thought that if we got married, well, you coulda helped me get a decent business going, not the pie in the sky sort that I've been daft enough ter be taken in by. Oh, I know yer too good fer me, but I thought, well, if yer don't ask, yer don't get.'

Shrugging his shoulders he walked towards the door. 'I'll be leaving tomorrow night. I've got a mate who can get me a ticket on the next boat heading fer France. 'Cos, you know, Belle, if I don't go straight away, I wouldn't trust meself not ter go down ter that place Maggie runs and bloody doing 'er a real mischief. And I ain't gonna take the chance of swinging at the end of a rope, not for a no-good slut like 'er.'

Turning his head away from Bella's anguished gaze he waited for her to speak, but no sound came from the direction of the bed. His heart kicked hard against his chest. Had he spun her one tale too many? What if she walked out now without offering to help him as she'd done so many times during the past months. As the silence grew he gave a silent sigh of resignation. Oh, what the hell. He'd had enough money out of her to last him a good few years without working, and when that ran out, well, there were plenty more elderly, gullible women in the world; the proof was sitting on his bed. He heard the bedsprings squeak as she stood up, and felt his stomach muscles tighten.

'Take me with you, Jimmy. Don't leave me behind, I'd die without you, I would, I would.' Her voice was beginning to rise, and fearful someone would hear her and come to investigate, Jimmy quickly grabbed her to him, stifling any other sound she could make.

'Oh darlin', darlin', don't yer think I don't want yer wiv me. But I've only got enough money fer me own ticket and a few days' lodgings while I try and get some sort of work. I couldn't put yer through that kind of life, not a lady like you. And don't go offering me any more of yer jewels, Belle, yer can't have many left. I feel bad enough as it is. Keep what you've got, you'll probably need it for a dowry one day.'

Bella stared into the face of the only man who had ever loved her and fought down the rising tide of fear that was threatening to engulf her. He couldn't leave her, she wouldn't let him. Somewhere deep down in her subconscious she knew she had been made use of, but her mind refused to believe the truth. All that mattered was that she stay with this man, and if money was the way to keep him, then she would get him money, enough money to keep him happy for a long, long time.

Grabbing hold of his arm she gabbled feverishly, 'I'm coming with you, Jimmy. There's nothing for me here, not without you. And you're wrong about my not having many jewels left. I have plenty. Enough to enable us to live comfortably in France for many years. Look, I'll meet you here tomorrow afternoon with the money for the tickets. We can sell the rest of my jewellery once we're safely in France; say yes, Jimmy, please say yes.'

'Belle, Belle, are you sure? I mean, it won't be easy. I

might not be able to find any work. And what about your parents? How yer gonna get out of the house wiv a suitcase wivout anyone seeing yer?'

Bella's body slumped with relief. It was going to be all right. He wasn't going to leave her. Oh thank you God, thank you. Picking up her gloves and leather bag from the table she made to leave.

'Don't you worry about me, Jim, I'll manage to get out without being seen. As for my parents . . . I imagine they will greet my departure with great relief. I've been a disappointment to them for years; they will be glad to be rid of the embarrassment of having an unmarried daughter of my age still living at home.'

Bending down to kiss her lips, Jimmy asked softly, 'Are yer sure, Belle? It's a big step to take. What if yer don't like it over there, and . . .'

Placing a gloved finger on his lips Bella smiled tremulously. 'I would be happy anywhere as long as you were by my side, darling. Now I must go. I don't want to arouse my parents' or brothers' suspicion by staying out too late. There's just one thing. We will get married, won't we? I . . . I know it's not a lady's place to ask, but. . . .'

Jimmy nuzzled her cheek affectionately, ' 'Course we will, just as soon as we get settled. Now you get orf 'ome. I don't like yer being out on the streets this time a night. I'll see yer tomorrow at about two, all right?'

'Yes, darling. Tomorrow at two. Goodnight, my dear, I love you.'

Jimmy waited until he heard her footsteps going down the stairs, then punched the air in delight. He'd done it; he'd pulled it off. When she arrived tomorrow, he'd wait until she'd handed over the money and jewellery, then tell her to wait with the cases while he went for the tickets. Just in case she got suspicious, he'd pack his battered case with all his clothes while she was there. Of course he wouldn't be back for them. Why should he, when he would be able to buy a complete new wardrobe with the valuables she would bring to him?

Walking over to the grimy window he looked down onto the busy street. This time tomorrow he would be comfortably settled somewhere in Devon. He'd only been there once with his Mum and Dad when he was a kid, but the memory of the green fields and hills had remained with him ever since. Once there, he'd change his name, make a complete new life for himself. Turning away from the window he pulled a half-empty bottle of whisky from under the bed.

Lifting the bottle in the air he said gleefully, 'Here's to you, Belle, darlin'. I'm about ter become a new man, and it's all thanks to you; yer stupid old bitch.' Taking a deep swallow, he sat down on the only chair in the room and began to go over his plans for the last time.

CHAPTER
TWENTY-ONE

Harry closed the heavily bound ledger and sighed with relief. Thank goodness that was done for the month. It seemed that lately all of his spare time was taken up with bookwork, a task that had always irked him. Going over to the walnut cabinet he took a bottle of brandy from the silver tray and poured himself a large drink. When the glass was empty, he refilled it and carried it back to his desk. Slumping down into the comfortable high-backed chair he stared into the crystal glass, his eyes thoughtful. With a bit of luck and hard work, his new buildings should be completed on time, and after that he had promised himself a few months' holiday; if his luck held he wouldn't be spending it alone. A slow smile spread across his face. Reaching into his inside pocket he drew out a small, black box and opened it. There nestling on a bed of blue silk lay a diamond ring, a ring he hoped that very soon he would be able to slip onto Maggie's finger; that was if she would have him.

Snapping the box shut he returned it to the safety of his pocket while at the same time throwing off the remainder of his brandy. Setting the glass down he drummed his fingers on the desk top, debating whether to have another drink before retiring. No, he'd better not, there was yet another long day ahead of him tomorrow and he needed a clear head to get him through the last few months of work. But when August came and the buildings were finally ready for the waiting tenants, the first thing he planned to do was take Maggie out somewhere nice for the evening, maybe to Maxine's, and afterwards he would ask her to marry him. It had taken him a long time to win back her trust after his blundering attempt to make her his mistress, but now he was sure she had forgiven him and wanted him as much as he wanted her.

Lord, it had been hard though. Being so close to her at times and not being able to tell her his true feelings for fear of frightening her off again. He had been sorely tempted to propose months ago, but had deemed it too soon after her illness to place such an important decision upon her. Then there was the pressure of work to contend with; it would all have been too much too soon. No, it was better this way. Better to wait until he could spend more time with her, to be able to bestow all his attention upon her instead of having to split himself in two. He didn't plan on a long engagement; what was the point? They had known each other long enough to be sure. No, a month's engagement, then the wedding, maybe in September. His mother could make all the arrangements. A sudden frown crossed his face. What would his parents' reactions be to the idea of him marrying someone like Maggie? Oh, they weren't snobs, neither of them, but still; people could be very strange where their own family were concerned.

Oh, what did it matter? They wouldn't be living here anyway. As soon as Maggie said yes, he would start looking for a suitable house for them; that was if she said yes. What if she refused him, what then? Giving a shaky laugh he turned the gas lamp down and walked to the door, then paused. What would he do? He didn't honestly know, he'd never been in this situation before. One thing he was sure of was that he wouldn't be able to shrug off Maggie as easily as he had done with the numerous women who had preceded her. Giving himself a mental shake he turned his head to make sure the lamp was safely extinguished, then turned the door handle. He was just about to leave the room when he heard the front door burst open, then Hugh's voice, shrill with anger, filled the house.

'Harry, Harry, where are you, you dirty swine. I know you're here, it's no good hiding.' Then he was bounding up the stairs towards Harry's room. Kicking open the door he looked wildly round the room, then like a man possessed he began pulling out drawers, tossing Harry's clothing onto the floor in a desperate attempt to find the evidence that would prove his brother had made a fool of him. Downstairs, Harry stood rooted to the spot, his face stunned with disbelief at the hatred he'd heard in Hugh's voice. What in God's name had happened to make him behave so?

'Is anything amiss, sir, I thought I heard shouting?' Benson had appeared by his side, his lined face worried.

'No, it's all right, Benson, I'll handle this, you get off to bed.'

'Thank you, sir, but the Master and Mistress aren't home yet from the Thompsons and I never go to bed until I see the Master settled for the night,' Benson answered, his eyes staring up at the ceiling. Harry didn't answer, for he too had his eyes riveted upwards. Without a word he began to climb the stairway, slowly at first, then quickening his steps as the noise from his room became louder.

'Hugh, what the devil's going on?' he cried in bewilderment at the sight of his brother kneeling on the floor surrounded by piles of his clothing. Walking into the room he looked down on the wild-eyed figure and felt a shiver of fear run up his spine.

'Have you taken leave of your senses, man? What the hell are you playing at? Are you ill? Hugh, answer me for God's sake, you look like . . .'

Hugh rose slowly to his feet, one arm hidden behind

his back. Stepping over the debris he advanced towards Harry. Then, without warning he thrust the brown leather wallet in Harry's face. Harry's eyes widened, his mouth dropping with shock at the sight of the wallet held in Hugh's trembling hand.

'Do you recognise this, Harry? You should do, you bought it for my birthday, remember. Only I lost it a couple of years ago, I told you about it at the time. So what's it doing hidden at the back of your drawer, Harry? Well, I'm waiting. It's not like you to be at a loss for words. No? Still no answer, no ready quip or plausible reason to explain why the wallet I lost should be hidden in your room. Well, let me make it easier for you, shall I? I didn't come straight here after seeing Lotte home; I went visiting. Do you know who I went to see? Why, it was Maggie, and we had a long talk, did Maggie and me. It was a very enlightening conversation. We discovered we had more in common than either of us had ever realised.'

'Hugh, please, listen to me, I . . .' Harry's voice was barely a whisper.

'*No*, Harry, you listen to me for a change. I went to see Maggie in an attempt to get her away from you. Oh, yes, I know it was a pathetic attempt, because let's face it, what woman would have me if she could have you instead. You've always got whatever you wanted, haven't you, Harry? But it wasn't enough for you, was it. There's no excitement when everything falls into one's lap without any effort. So you went down to the East

396

End looking for some excitement, just like I did. It was only the one time for me, but then you know all about my night out, don't you, Harry? You've known from the start but you said nothing. Even though you must have realised I was going through hell at the knowledge of what I had done, you did nothing to alleviate my suffering. I could have forgiven you for that, but not for what you did later. When did you first get the idea of introducing me to my "victim"? Was life getting a little dull for you, Harry? Is that why you took me along to meet Maggie, in order to get a cheap thrill out of our misery. I . . . I . . .' He broke off, his voice choked with tears.

'Hugh, oh God, Hugh. It wasn't like that, please, please listen to me, I can explain. If you'll only . . .'

'Get away from me, you bastard,' Hugh snatched Harry's hand from his arm. With tears coursing down his cheeks he screamed at the stricken figure. 'I loved you, Harry. I loved you more than anyone in the world. I would have done anything for you. And all the time you were laughing at me, holding me up to ridicule. How could you, Harry, how could you be so . . . so cruel. I never did anything to . . . to deserve the way you've tre . . . treated me.' Flinging himself round he buried his face against the wall, his body shaking with sobs.

Harry stood helplessly watching his brother's anguish, knowing there was nothing he could do or say that would ever make things right between them again. Still, he had to try, he had to make Hugh understand. God damn it. Why had he kept that blasted wallet? He'd meant to throw it away countless times, but had never got round to it. Now it was too late.

Tentatively placing his hand upon the shuddering arm he said softly, 'Hugh, Hugh, I . . .'

'Get away from me, you stinking bastard!' Hugh's shrill cry split the air, his arm coming up and round to catch Harry a violent blow around the side of his face. Unprepared for the attack Harry staggered backwards, his foot catching in one of his shirts, sending him crashing back against the corner of his dressing table. He lay stunned for a few moments, then Hugh was standing over him, his mouth working furiously as he spat at him.

'I'm leaving now and I never want to see you again for as long as I live. From this moment on, I have no brother. As far as I'm concerned you're dead; as dead to me as you are to Maggie. You've lost her, Harry, lost her forever. You betrayed and abused her trust, just as you did mine. May you rot in hell for what you've done to us.'

'Hugh wait, please wait,' Harry struggled to his feet, his hand holding his forehead. 'I had to make sure you didn't recognise each other. Hugh, you know how I feel about Maggie, I had to make sure. That was the only reason I brought you face to face. As God is my witness, I would never deliberately hurt you. I love you, you're my brother. Hugh . . . *Hugh*!' Staggering out onto the landing he rested his hands on the balustrade and watched helplessly as Hugh ran down the stairway, his long legs taking the steps two at a time.

It was at that moment that the front door opened to

admit Edward and Beatrice, the laughter they were sharing abruptly stopping at the sight of their son, his
distress painfully evident.

'Why, Hugh, whatever's happened, dear? Is something wr . . .'

'Not now, mother, please, I have to get out of this
house, or I won't be responsible for my actions.' Exerting
his last piece of self-control, he gently moved his mother to one side before bounding down the stone steps and
out into the dark night.

Edward and Beatrice looked at each other in bewilderment, but before either of them could speak Benson
came rushing from the kitchen. 'Oh sir, sir, I'm that glad
you're home. There's been ructions upstairs, sir. Mr
Hugh was shouting at Mr Harry, well . . . screaming
would be a better word, then they started fighting. Lord
sir, I never thought I'd see the day when the two masters
fell out. It was terrible to hear, sir. I tried to . . .'

'Yes yes, that will be all, Benson,' Edward snapped
impatiently. Quickly handing over his top hat, coat, and
cane he mounted the stairs, his face worried. Beatrice
didn't bother to divest herself of her outdoor wear, she
was too busy following her husband, as anxious as he to
find out what had been happening in their absence.

When they reached Harry's room, they both stopped
in surprise, their eyes taking in the shambles that littered
the floor and bed. And Harry, oh, Lord, Harry who sat
among the debris, his face a mask of pain and misery. So
shocked were they by the sight of their strong son

reduced to such a state they remained silent, each of them too stunned to speak. Edward recovered first.

Clearing his throat he said in bewilderment, 'What the bloody hell has been going on, Harry?'

And Harry raised his head wearily and answered, 'We had better go downstairs. There is a lot I have to tell you. After you hear what I have to say, you may well ask me to follow Hugh from the house and never return.'

Like a man who had lost everything he valued in the world, he rose to his feet. Brushing past his parents he walked down the stairs and into the dining-room. After a few moments Edward and Beatrice joined him, their faces drawn with anxiety.

When the door closed behind them, Bella stepped out of the library into the hall. She had arrived home soon after Hugh and had heard the altercation that had followed from the bottom of the stairway. When she had heard Hugh coming down the stairs, and the sound of a carriage drawing up outside the house, she had quickly hidden in the library. Stepping nearer to the dining-room she leaned forward trying to hear what was being said, but heard only muffled voices. Her face thoughtful, she moved away from the door. Walking quietly she made her way up the stairs. Pausing briefly to stare at the wreckage of Harry's room, she passed by to her own.

Once there she made straight for her jewellery box, panic mounting in her breast at the sight of the contents. What was she going to do? There wasn't enough here to satisfy Jimmy. She'd led him to believe she had plenty of jewels to bring to him tomorrow. She couldn't go to him with this paltry handful. Biting down on her bottom lip she continued staring into the box as if willing it to bring back all the precious pieces that had once adorned the red-lined interior. Slumping down onto her bed she listened out for any sound from below, but could hear nothing. Dimly she wondered what had happened between Harry and Hugh. She'd heard Maggie's name mentioned during the quarrel, but hadn't been able to hear everything that had been said. Not that she gave a damn about anything that happened in this house. Her only concern now was to get away, but she needed money, money and jewels.

A crafty look came over her face. Of course, her parents' room. Her father always kept some money in his wall safe, along with her mother's jewellery. Creeping along the landing she carefully pushed open the door leading into the master bedroom. Once inside she made straight for the wall safe hidden behind a landscape painting. Within minutes she had the safe open, and five minutes later she was back in her room, her heart beating wildly as she stared down at the wad of notes and the pearl-encrusted box she held in her shaking hands. To her great surprise, a feeling of guilt swept over her. She couldn't do this, not steal from her own parents. But how else could she be with Jimmy? Stifling her conscience, she put the money and the box into her bag, then quickly undressed for bed.

It was nearly two hours later when she heard the

footsteps on the stairs and the muffled voices on the landing. Her door was pushed open slowly and she quickly closed her eyes as the light from a lamp was shone on her face. Then the door closed again and she heard her mother crying. Turning her face into the pillow she stared into the darkness. It wasn't too late to change her mind. She could easily put back the money and jewellery tomorrow before their absence was discovered. Her father only kept the money for emergencies, and her mother rarely used the jewellery in the safe, preferring to wear her pearls and garnets which she kept in a trinket box on her dressing table. No, the theft wouldn't be discovered immediately; in fact it could be weeks before either of them opened the safe. Flopping over onto her back she tried to get some sleep; she had a great deal to do tomorrow. A picture of her parents floated in front of her eyes, then the guilt assailed her once more.

Blast it! They had plenty, it wasn't as if she were leaving them penniless. Giving up all notion of sleep, she padded across the thick carpet to her window. This time tomorrow she would be in another country. In all probability she would never see her parents or brothers again. Once she left this house, she could never come back, not after what she had done.

Lifting her head, she stared up into the cloudy sky. She didn't care; she didn't. So why did she feel so bad? This was the first time she had experienced guilt, and she didn't like it; she didn't like it one little bit. Damn that little slut. It was all her fault she was in this position.

Not content with trying to tear her and Jimmy apart, the little trollop had also wreaked havoc between Harry and Hugh, the result of which would surely reflect on her parents. How the hell could one chit of a girl cause so much destruction?

An image of a smiling Maggie appeared in the window. Bella felt her hands curving towards the long neck, then quickly dropped her hands to her side. For a brief moment she had imagined the young girl was in the room, laughing at her, taunting her. God! She must get some sleep, she must. Tearing her eyes away from the window she walked back to her bed.

When the frantic hammering started on the door, Lotte rose slowly from the armchair, her footsteps steady as she walked to the front door. Pausing for a brief moment, she took a long, deep breath then opened the door.

'Oh Lotte, Lotte, it was terrible, terrible. I've left home, Lotte. And Maggie hates me now . . . It was Harry's fault, Lotte. I hate him, I do, I do. Let me stay, Lotte, please let me stay with you.' Hugh fell against her, his arms clutching at her desperately while he sobbed on her shoulder. Pulling him gently into the hall, Lotte closed the door and led him into the living-room.

Pushing him down into the chair before the blazing fire she said softly, 'Hugh dear, it's all right now. Everything will be all right now.' Kneeling down by his side she laid her head in his lap and closed her eyes.

She had known when she sent him to Maggie that she was taking a risk. Nevertheless, she had taken the gamble. It had been the biggest gamble of her life, but it had paid off. He was back, and this time he would stay; she would make sure of that. Tears of relief slid silently down her face; then she closed her eyes and slept.

CHAPTER
TWENTY-TWO

'What's up, Maggie? You've hardly said a word all morning, and yer don't look too good neither.'

Maggie stood by the stove vigorously stirring a large pot of lamb stew with a wooden ladle. Careful not to burn her lips she tasted a drop of gravy from the spoon. Deciding it needed more salt, she threw a liberal sprinkling into the simmering pot before turning to Charlie.

'Nothing's up, as you put it. Now get on with those potatoes – they won't peel themselves.'

'All right, I'm doing them, ain't I?' Charlie replied defensively. He looked after her retreating back as she walked through to the dining-room and sighed deeply. Cor, she was in a mood and no mistake. Best if he kept his head down for the rest of the day, and hope she cheered up before going home tonight.

In the dining-room, Maggie bustled round the tables enquiring as to whether her customers were enjoying their meal. When this simple exercise had been completed she walked up the few steps into the ladies' quarter and sat down. The space she had reserved for her women customers was empty at this time of day, and taking the opportunity for a moment's respite she stared dejectedly into space.

Charlie was right when he said she didn't look too good; she didn't feel it. She'd hardly had a wink of sleep last night, and when she had woken this morning, she had imagined for a moment that the previous night had all been some horrible nightmare. It had been a nightmare all right, but a nightmare from which she would never awake. The hurt and shame she had felt had now turned into a slow, burning anger. Not against Hugh, oh no. He had been as much a victim as she was. In the cold light of day she had been able to see Hugh's side of the story. After all she had gone to that particular part of the East End that night for one purpose. It wasn't Hugh's fault he had mistaken her for a prostitute and had taken her before realising his mistake. No, it wasn't Hugh she blamed for the shame and misery that was filling every part of her body, nor even Harry; it was herself she was angry with. Angry that she could have been so stupid as to believe that a man like Harry would ever look on her as anything else but what she was: a common working girl who could be manipulated into believing she was something special.

At what point would Harry again have put his proposition to her – because that was what he had been leading up to – to try and make her his mistress? And if she had succumbed, how long would his interest have held. Not long she was sure. For men like Harry the excitement was in the chase, the conquest, after that they invariably moved onto the next woman. She was glad now that Hugh had confessed to her, for if he hadn't she would probably have joined a long line of women in Harry's life. At least she had been spared the final humiliation of being used and tossed aside by a man she had grown to love and imagined one day would marry her.

When she heard the footsteps on the wooden stairs, she remained motionless, not daring to look up. The shiny, black polished boots planted themselves in front of her. Above them loomed a pair of grey and black pin-striped trousers, the crease down the front sharp enough to cut your finger on. She didn't have to look up, she knew who it was; she had been expecting him all morning.

'Hello, Maggie.'

Her face and neck grew hot at the familiar sound of his voice, a voice now tinged with uncertainty.

'What do you want?' she said dully, her heart racing at his presence.

Harry looked down on the shining brown hair and coughed nervously. 'We have to talk, Maggie. Could we go to the kitchen where we can have some privacy.'

'Very well.' She stood up slowly, then still not looking at him she made her way to the kitchen.

''Allo, 'Arry,' Charlie beamed at him cheerfully.

'Charlie, could you leave us for a few minutes, please?' Maggie spoke tersely, trying to hang onto her self-esteem. Whatever happened she mustn't give way, mustn't let him see just how much he had hurt her. Harry smiled at the bemused boy as he passed him.

Turning back to Maggie he again gave a small cough before saying solemnly, 'I've come to apologise, Maggie, and to tell you what I told Hugh. That is that I never meant either of you any harm. You were, and still are very dear to me. I know my actions may appear to have been malicious, but you must see how I was placed. How could I tell you the truth, or Hugh? I was in an impossible situation from the very beginning.

'Then, when I met you again and continued seeing you, I realised you had become very special to me. I should never have brought Hugh along with me. I was still angry with him for the way he had behaved, unreasonably so, for he had suffered enough. Still I wanted to punish him. I don't know what I expected from your first meeting, all I can remember is the relief I felt when you failed to recognise each other. I know you were fond of Hugh, I thought at one time . . .' He shrugged his shoulders. 'Suffice it to say, I became jealous of the attention you gave him. All that is academic now. Hugh no longer acknowledges me as his brother, and my parents are distraught at all that has transpired. I feel I have been punished enough.'

He looked appealingly into the dull eyes, then cried, 'Maggie, please, don't turn your back on me too. I couldn't bear it. Say you'll forgive me. We could start afresh, put all this sordid business behind us and begin again.'

Maggie heard the pain in his voice but could only shake her head. 'No, Harry, I'm sorry, but it would never work, not now.' She gave a hiccup of a laugh. 'It's funny, you know, because if you'd come round earlier you'd have been met with a barrage of abuse, and maybe the sharp end of a kitchen knife. Even up to the moment you arrived I was feeling a lot of anger and hate towards you, but not any more. Now I just want to get on with my life. I don't want to give up working here, I like it and the people who come here, but I don't want anything more to do with you. If you'll promise never to come here again, I'll carry on running the place for you and Charlie can bring you the rent every month. If you can't give me your word you'll leave me in peace, then I'll leave, it's as simple as that.'

Harry stared into the unflinching brown eyes and knew he had lost her. God! What had he done to deserve this. He should have known the past would catch up with them one day. If only Hugh could have been content with Lotte, he would never have gone to Maggie and the truth would have remained buried. But then life never works out as you would want it to. His motives may have been selfish at the beginning, but ever since, all he had tried to do was to protect the two people he cared most about. And this was his reward, to be shunned by both of them. He wondered how she would react if he were to take her in his arms. Would she relent, or push him away? As much as he wanted to try once more, his pride prevented him from moving towards her.

Drawing his body up to his full height he said stiffly, 'If that is the way you feel, then you have my word I will never trouble you again. Good day to you, madam.'

Maggie watched him go with tears in her eyes. Why had he given up so easily? From the moment she had heard his voice, all anger had left her. She also knew that nobody was to blame for the disaster that had left their lives in tatters. A chain of events had begun the night she had left her home, with no-one being able to foresee the outcome. She should have given him the benefit of doubt, but had been too proud and afraid to take the chance of being hurt any more.

' 'Arry gone then?' Charlie's voice broke into her thoughts. 'I didn't see 'im leave. Is he coming back?'

Maggie turned to the stove, lowering the flame beneath the cooked stew. In a voice far from steady she replied, 'No, Charlie, he won't be coming back; he won't ever be coming back.'

Bella heard the town clock chime and moved uneasily on the bed. It was now four o'clock, and Jimmy had been gone for nearly two hours. Glancing down at his suitcase she felt a moment's reassurance. He had packed while she was here, putting all his worldly goods into the battered case – he wouldn't have done that if he wasn't coming back. Why wouldn't he, her mind shot the question at her. He has enough money now to buy whatever he likes, so why should he come back for you?

'Because he loves me, he loves me. He wouldn't leave me, he wouldn't,' she cried to the empty room.

Getting to her feet she looked down into the street, willing him to appear, to see him running down the street, anxious to get back to her, full of explanations as to why he had been so long. He would too; any minute now, he would be standing in this room full of apologies, his dear face worried. And she would laugh with him, tell him it didn't matter, and he'd be all smiles again. Yes, that's what would happen, any minute now.

She was still telling herself that when the clock struck five. When the six chimes echoed in the room she rose slowly to her feet, her face ashen. Something had happened, maybe he had been involved in an accident; or maybe he had never had any intention of coming back for her. She shook her head wildly. No, something had prevented him from returning, that must be the reason, it must. Turning to the window once more, she caught sight of herself in the flyblown mirror over the bed and stopped dead in her tracks. The reflection showed an anxious, middle-aged woman dressed in a deep blue dress, a navy cape trimmed with sable draped round her shoulders. Well-dressed certainly, but also middle-aged; middle-aged and ugly. With an anguished cry she threw herself down on the bed and sobbed, deep heartrending sobs that seemed to tear her body asunder. When the paroxysm of tears finally passed she rose unsteadily to her feet.

What was she to do? Jimmy wasn't coming back, he'd left for good, his pockets lined with her money and possessions and probably laughing his head off at the gullible woman he had so easily duped. With shaking fingers she opened the door and left the house, her mind reeling at the enormity of her situation. All she had in the world were the two suitcases she held in her hands, and a few sovereigns in her purse.

Standing in the noisy, bustling street she stared aimlessly into the crowds. Dear God! What was she to do? She couldn't go home, not after emptying the safe. There was no way her parents would believe the servants capable of stealing from them, Lord! the idea was preposterous. Nobody in their right mind would imagine Benson capable of theft; the old man would rather die than steal from his beloved employers, and neither he nor the rest of the staff knew the combination. It would be impossible for any of them to have opened the safe, and there was no sign of forced entry so burglary would be instantly ruled out. That left only herself, Harry and Hugh. Her brothers had no need to steal, so the finger of suspicion would rest solely upon her.

A wave of dizziness swept over her as the milling

crowd jostled her trembling body. The only solution that came to her troubled mind was to go home and fling herself on her parents' mercy. Almost immediately she dismissed the idea. Her mother would in all likelihood be shocked but forgiving, but her father! She shivered involuntarily. The idea of facing those piercing black eyes, filled with contempt, was too much to contemplate in her present vulnerable state.

As if in a dream she staggered on, her mind frantically trying to find a way out of the horrendous mess she now found herself in. Then it came to her. Her footsteps slowed as she considered the idea that had sprung into her mind. She could go to Harry and ask him to intervene on her behalf. She was well aware that her brother strongly disliked her, but in spite of his feelings, he was a fair man and a compassionate one. She had nothing to lose by asking him, and everything to gain, for if anyone could win her parents round, he could. The thought of humbling herself before Harry turned her cold, but she had no choice. Worst of all, she would have to be completely truthful with him. Attempting to lie would be a fruitless exercise where Harry was concerned. Looking up at the church clock she saw it was now six thirty. He would still be at the building site. He and his men had been working late these last few months in an effort to reach the August deadline. Swallowing down the bile that had risen in her throat she hailed a passing hansom cab and climbed in.

When she reached the building site she went directly

413

to the wooden hut but found no sign of Harry. Lowering her suitcases to the floor she pondered what to do next. Maybe he was at the dining-rooms, making sheep's eyes at that little whore of his. A look of rage passed over his face. This was all her doing, the spiteful little bitch. if she hadn't threatened Jimmy with the police, he would still be here and she wouldn't now be in this position of having to crawl to Harry to beg him for help. Indeed, with each passing minute the idea of having to humble herself in front of her brother grew more intolerable.

Walking slowly round the desk she sat down, her eyes alighting on the shotgun standing by the wall. For a long time she stared at the gun, her tortured mind whirling round in circles. Her future loomed desolately ahead of her. Even if Harry agreed to help, she was doomed to a life of emptiness. There were to be no more 'Jimmy's', she wasn't so stupid to be taken in twice. So what was the purpose of her life now? To remain at home ostracized and unloved for the rest of her days, while the person who had caused her misery may well discover that her scheming had paid off. If Harry married the Paige girl, he might bring her home to live with them, and she would be forced to watch their happiness every day. In time there would be children, her children. Little brats running all over the house with her parents doting on them and herself ignored and forgotten. The images brought her to her feet, the chair crashing to the floor.

No; it wasn't to be borne, she'd rather die than let that happen. A red mist descended over her eyes. Every slight, every humiliation she had suffered since childhood rose to the fore. All the hate and frustration now focused on one person, and one person alone. The trembling left her body leaving her calm and determined. Picking up the shotgun she left the hut.

Three men emerged from the houses opposite. One was Joe Waite, newly appointed foreman, anxious to reach home and tell his wife and four children the good news. He couldn't wait to see their faces when he told them about the extra two pounds a week he would now be earning, money which could now be spent on a holiday for them all, the first holiday they had ever had. He was in the middle of sharing a joke with his companions when he saw the woman he knew to be the governor's sister walk away from the hut, the shotgun resting under her arm.

Darting forward he shouted, ' 'Ere, Miss. Whadya think you're doing? Yer can't . . .'

Bella turned slowly her eyes as cold as stone. Raising the gun she aimed carefully and fired. Joe Waite felt a dull thud hit his chest – he was dead before he hit the ground. The two men looked down at the crumpled figure, their faces a mask of disbelief, then they began shouting wildly. One dropped to his knees to aid his stricken friend while the other ran to find the governor.

Bella walked on.

'That's the last of 'em gone, Maggie,' Charlie yawned loudly. 'I've put the "closed" sign up.'

Maggie was in the kitchen putting some left-over pies into her basket. They would do for tea, and it would save her cooking again when she got home. She was about to answer Charlie when she heard the tinkling of the door bell.

'Oh no,' she groaned. 'Quickly love, tell whoever it is we're closed, then clear the tables. And lock the door,' she called after him.

Laying a cloth over the pies she glanced around the kitchen and nodded. Apart from the few plates and knives and forks left outside all the washing up was done. Minutes passed and still Charlie hadn't returned. Giving an impatient sigh she walked into the dining-room. He was probably having a chat with the unwelcome customer. Normally she didn't mind staying open a bit later, but tonight she couldn't wait to get home.

'Have you cleared the tables yet, Charlie, I want to . . . Oh my God!' Her hand went to her throat at the sight that met her eyes. Charlie was standing transfixed by the far wall, his terrified gaze on the woman holding the shotgun. Maggie's legs turned to jelly at the awesome sight.

Struggling to remain calm she said hoarsely, 'Miss Stewart, whatever's the matter. Wh . . . what do you want?'

The gun turned from Charlie towards Maggie.

'What do I want, Miss Paige? That is very simple, I wish to be rid of you, and I fully intend to do just that.'

There had been many times in her life when Maggie had experienced fear, but never fear like this: stomach-churning, gut-wrenching fear that had left her limbs paralysed, unable to move.

'B . . . but why? What have I done? It . . . it doesn't make sense.'

The gun was now levelled directly at her chest.

'Sense! You talk about sense. Don't you know there is no sense to life. One is born, lives a short time, then dies. A fortunate few enjoy their brief time in this world, while others . . .' A faraway look came into Bella's eyes, but almost immediately it was gone, to be replaced by an empty, dead expression that sent a further chill of fear to Maggie's heart. Remembering what Charlie had told her about the woman's fierce possessiveness towards her brothers, she started forward, her hands held out in supplication.

'Please . . . if this has anything to do with Harry or Hugh, you don't have to worry. I . . . I won't be seeing either of them again. Honestly, I . . .'

'I have no doubt about that,' Bella's clipped voice interrupted her. 'You won't be seeing anyone again, not after today.'

Desperately Maggie tried once again to reason with the woman. 'Please, don't. Don't do this . . .' The words died in her throat. It was no use. The woman was deranged, her face and eyes devoid of any emotion. Closing her eyes she began to pray.

Bella stared for a moment longer at the girl she had

grown to hate. She knew that time was running out, Harry would know by now what had happened and realise she had come here. Still she waited, savouring the trembling girl's fear, relishing the sense of power the gun gave her.

She had forgotten the boy. Charlie watched in mounting horror as the woman's finger tightened on the trigger. With a strangled cry he ran forward, throwing himself between Maggie and the gun.

'You're mad, barmy,' he screamed hysterically. 'I told yer, Maggie, I told yer she wasn't right in the 'ead, but yer wouldn't listen ter me.'

'Get out of my way, you snivelling little brat!' Bella's composure snapped. Rage gave her strength, and with a violent shove she sent the boy spinning across the room. The sound of running footsteps in the street brought her head round, her eyes narrowing. Turning back to Maggie she aimed the barrel carefully. A movement close by caught her attention. Charlie was trying valiantly to get to his feet. Keeping a watchful gaze on him she squeezed the trigger. Harry and his men had just reached the door when the shot rang out. The sound froze them in their tracks. Then, with a loud cry they put their shoulders to the door and crashed into the room.

Harry was the first into the room. The first person he saw was Bella standing straight, her chin jutting out defiantly.

'You're too late, brother dear, but don't fret too much.

I'm sure you will find another whore to take her place.'

Harry looked frantically round the room; then he saw her, slumped down by the wall, half-hidden from view by the cash counter. With an almighty roar he snatched the shotgun from Bella's hands and upended it, savagely bringing the butt crashing down on the sneering face.

'Harry, Harry, don't. I'm all right, I'm all right.'

Harry's head jerked back at the sound of the whispered voice. Then he was bounding across the room to where Maggie was attempting to rise from the floor.

'Oh Maggie, Maggie, my darling. I thought . . . Dear God, I thought she had . . . Oh Maggie.'

Looking up into the rugged face Maggie smiled weakly. 'I fainted. When she started to pull the trigger, I just fainted. I never was very brave.'

'*Maggie, Maggie!*' Charlie's voice filled the room. Too weak from shock to stand, he crawled towards his sister, tears running down his pale cheeks. Maggie put out her arms and gathered him close, rocking him back and forth as she had done when he was a baby, while Harry looked on, his face wreathed in a huge smile of relief. The men who had come with Harry moved forward, crowding around the trio, punching and slapping each other in delight. No-one noticed Bella.

Careful not to attract attention she pulled herself to a sitting position, groaning quietly. Her face felt as if it were on fire. Gingerly she touched her smashed lips and winced. Looking down at her hand she saw the blood and wondered dimly where it was coming from. Then she remembered. Craning her neck she stared at the crowd of men and the young girl in their midst. The sight enraged her. She didn't stop to wonder how she had missed Maggie at such short range. The only thought in her crazed mind was to finish what she had started. Turning her body round, she reached for the table, her fingers coming into contact with something sharp. Grasping the knife by the handle she slumped back onto the floor and waited. Like a wounded animal deprived of its quarry she remained motionless, ready to strike at the first opportunity.

'Come on, men, give her some air,' Harry cried jovially, his broad frame quivering with emotion.

'Righto guv,' The man neared to him replied.

Then, shuffling his feet he asked awkwardly. 'What abaht 'er, guv? Yer sister I mean, what yer gonna do abaht 'er?'

The smile slipped from Harry's face. 'One of you go and fetch the police,' he said grimly. 'The rest of you stand guard over her until they get here.'

The men parted to let Maggie, supported by Harry and Charlie, through their ranks. No-one saw Bella get to her feet until it was too late. Her screams split the air as she ran up behind Maggie, the knife held high in the air. Caught by surprise, Harry vainly tried to ward off the blow with his arm, but he wasn't quick enough. The blade flashed by his ear before embedding its cold steel into Maggie's neck.

A moment's silence filled the room, then pandemonium broke out. Men ran forward and grabbed Bella, pulling her roughly away, their gazes averted from the smashed, bloody face and the mangled lips from which undistinguishable sounds were coming. Harry and Charlie gently lowered Maggie to the floor, their horrified eyes staring at the hilt of the knife protruding from the bloody white flesh.

'Is . . . is she dead, Harry?' Charlie asked, his voice choked with tears.

Harry hung his head helplessly. What had Hugh told him about knife wounds? Damn it, why hadn't he listened to his brother's teachings. Then he remembered.

Twisting round on his knees he shouted, 'Fred, run for a doctor, tell him we need an ambulance cart, quickly.'

The man he had called to was out of the room before Harry had finished the sentence.

'One of you fetch a clean cloth from the kitchen; I'll have to staunch the flow of blood until help arrives, hurry, man, hurry.'

Within minutes the man had returned, a small towel in his calloused hands.

' 'Ere yer are, guv. Gawd! She don't look too 'ealthy, does she?'

Harry bit down hard on his bottom lip, then set to work. As gently as he could, he wrapped the towel around the knife, then held the cloth in place and pressed down firmly.

'Ain't yer gonna take the knife out, Harry?' Charlie pleaded anxiously.

'No, Charlie, it's dangerous to remove a knife from a wound. If I pull it out it will cause more bleeding. Best to wait until a doctor gets here.'

Charlie's hand rested on his. 'Yer didn't answer me, Harry; is she . . . is she dead?'

Harry felt his body jerk painfully. Aware of the numerous eyes upon him he took a deep breath and bent his head to Maggie's chest. The sound of the heart beating against his ear was the sweetest sound he had ever heard. Blowing out his cheeks he raised his eyes to Charlie and smiled, 'She's alive, Charlie, she's alive. Here, hold the cloth in place, firmly now, I'll be back in a minute.'

Getting to his feet he faced his sister. His voice cold and deliberate, he bent his head towards her and snarled, 'You evil bitch. You couldn't stand to see me find happiness, could you? You never could bear to see anyone happy. Well, your pleasure is going to be short-lived, because you're going to hang for this. Do you hear me, Bella? You're going to hang. Even if Maggie survives, you'll hang. The man you shot is dead. He was a good man, ten times your pathetic worth. Don't think because father is a judge you'll get away with your evil actions, he'll have no more pity for you than I have. And I'll tell you something else; the day they take you to the gallows I'll be there, and when the trap door is sprung I'll cheer.' His lips curled in distaste. 'I hope the hangman is inept at his job. I hope you die slowly and painfully, you vicious, evil bitch.'

Bella glared back at him, her black eyes filled with hate. Gathering up the blood that filled her mouth she spat at him, then started to laugh. She was still laughing when the ambulance cart came for Maggie. She was still laughing when the police bundled her unceremoniously into the police wagon.

CHAPTER
TWENTY-THREE

The trial of Bella Stewart sent shock waves throughout London. Every day saw a queue of people waiting to be let into the High Court eager to see the woman who had murdered a man in cold blood, and then attempted to kill a young woman who was rumoured to be Harry Stewart's mistress. Members of the press joined the spectators with pencils sharpened, their notebooks resting on cramped knees. The front row was left free for Joe Waite's widow and four children. Not one day did they miss, determined to be present when the verdict was handed out.

There was much speculation abroad as to whether the honourable Judge Edward Stewart would attempt to exert his influence in the hope of saving his only daughter from the gallows. Here they were proved wrong. Apart from engaging a solicitor for the defence, the proud autocratic man stayed firmly in the background, content to let justice take its course.

On the last day of June, Beatrice, Lotte and Hugh sat high in the gallery, with Harry and Charlie seated a few rows in front as the jury filed out of the court to deliberate their verdict. Many saw it as a fruitless exercise; the woman was guilty as hell. The evidence against her was damning. Two men had seen her shoot Joe Waite down like a mad dog, and the attack on the Paige girl had been witnessed by half a dozen men, including the girl's brother and Mr Harry Stewart himself. After three long months it still wasn't known what had provoked the murderous attacks, for not one word had the Stewart woman spoken in her defence. The evidence of the stolen money and jewellery together with the two suitcases packed with the accused's belongings led the court to believe that she had been about to run away with a lover. The jewels and money had never been recovered, thus leading to further speculation that the man in question had absconded with the valuables, leaving his ageing mistress behind.

Theories abounded, but nothing came to light to explain the woman's behaviour. Even if there had been a lover, why would the woman want to kill Joe Waite, a man she didn't even know?

When the judge had left the court, the spectators began to move towards the heavy, wooden door, their necks craning to catch sight of the Stewart family sitting high above them. If any were hoping for some signs of distress or anxiety they were disappointed. The faces of the well-dressed men and women remained dispassionate.

'Come on, Mother, it's time to go,' Hugh said quietly, his hand resting gently on his mother's elbow.

Beatrice shook her head at him impatiently. 'I'm well aware of that fact, Hugh, and I'll thank you not to continue treating me like a child.' Hugh dropped his hand, then stood awkwardly as his mother swept by him, her head held high.

'Don't take it personally, dear,' Lotte said tenderly, 'she's very distraught, although one would never know to look at her. She's a remarkable woman. I could never show such restraint if I were in her shoes.'

Hugh nodded absently, his eyes resting on the two figures directly below him. Lotte followed his gaze, her blue eyes clouding over in pain.

'Hugh, dear. Why don't you speak with him? He is your brother after all. I know you want to see an end to this squabble. Harry's done all he can to make peace, it's up to you now. Please, darling, for my sake and that of your mother, bury the past and go to him before the breach becomes too wide to bridge.'

Hugh swallowed nervously. Lotte was right, but as much as he wanted to talk to Harry, something deep inside him prevented him from doing so. They had reached their carriage when Harry's voice called out to them.

'Hey Lotte, Hugh, wait a moment.' Harry came running to their side. Panting for breath he waited a minute before saying, 'It doesn't look too good, does it? Not that I'm surprised. The Queen herself wouldn't get off with that much evidence against her.'

He heard himself talking and winced with embarrassment. He'd been saying the same thing every day for weeks now in a desperate attempt to break the ice between himself and the brother he cared so deeply for.

The stony look on Hugh's face prevented him from saying anything further. God! It was infuriating. He'd never imagined Hugh could be so stubborn; bloody-minded would be a more apt name for the way his brother was behaving. They were both miserable with the situation that existed between them, but still the man refused to budge. Well, damn him. He'd done all he could, he wasn't going to continue to humble himself day after day only to be met by a frosty silence. If Hugh wanted to end the argument, then he could make the next move, because he, Harry, had had enough.

Lotte looked on exasperated. Lord, but she was strongly tempted to knock some sense into the man by her side. Didn't they have enough trouble to contend with? If only Hugh would swallow his stupid pride. But no, he was too busy playing the martyr. Well she'd had enough of it. She'd been understanding at first, hiding her initial shock as the sordid story had tumbled from Hugh's sobbing lips, but now her patience was fast running out.

Glaring up at Hugh she turned to Harry, 'Please forgive my husband's rudeness, Harry. I for one am always pleased to see you.'

The tension eased from Harry's taut face. Taking Lotte's hand he placed it to his lips.

'And I you, Lotte. I count myself fortunate to have acquired such a delightful and compassionate sister-in-law. It is a great pity you can't instil those attributes into your husband.'

Lotte smiled, one hand tightening on Harry's. 'How is Maggie? I'd very much like to see her, but I'm not sure if my presence would be welcomed.'

Harry lowered his eyes for a moment before answering gravely, 'She's still the same, quiet and withdrawn one minute, angry the next. Oh, not like she was after her sister died, she's well aware of all that's happened; too much aware, that is part of the trouble.'

'It's understandable, Harry, she's been through a terrible ordeal. When I think of what Bella did . . .' She shook her head sadly. 'Do you think there's any truth in the rumours, I mean about Bella having a lover that deserted her?'

'I honestly don't know, Lotte. It would explain a lot. If she had been planning to run away with a man and he let her down, she would have had to take her rage out on someone. Knowing how much Maggie means to me made her the obvious target. Poor Joe just happened to be in the wrong place at the wrong time.'

Hugh listened to the conversation, his heart pounding

against his ribs. Why couldn't he say something? He wanted to, so why couldn't he speak? Then Harry was beside him, his strong hands resting on the open window as he said his farewells to their mother.

'Goodbye, Mother. Tell Father I'll call round one evening when this business is over. If either of you wish to get in contact with me, you have my address.'

Beatrice nodded briefly, her mind too filled with concern for Bella to worry herself over the estrangement between her sons. There would be time for them later.

'That goes for you too, Lotte. If ever you need me, you know where I am.' Then doffing his hat he strode off, his footsteps taking him to where Charlie was patiently waiting by the corner. Hugh watched him go, his stomach churning with mixed emotions. Helping Lotte into the carriage he was about to follow her when he stopped. Slowly stepping back onto the pavement he hesitated for a few seconds, then he began to walk after Harry.

'Harry, Harry, wait a minute.'

Harry's steps faltered as he heard the familiar voice. Turning on his heel he waited for Hugh to catch up with him.

'Harry, I . . . I'd like very much if you . . . if you would care to visit us. Would tonight be convenient?' His voice was stilted and unsure as if fearing a rebuff.

Harry saw the red flush spreading over the thin cheeks and held out his hand. Hugh hesitated for only a second; then their hands joined together, and they were smiling inanely at each other.

'I'd like that, Hugh. I'd like that very much. And look, if you and Lotte are thinking of buying a larger house, I know of a few that would suit you both perfectly.'

The smile on Hugh's face broadened. 'Thank you, Harry, but that won't be necessary. Lotte's house will do us for now. Mother has asked us to move in with them, Lord knows there's enough room, especially as you're no longer there . . .' His voice trailed off.

Shuffling his feet he added shamefaced, 'Harry, I'm sorry, sorry about everything. I think I must have gone mad that night. It was the guilt you see. Guilt and shame that made me act as I did. I've told Lotte everything. She's been marvellous, I'm a very lucky man, Harry. And, Harry, I wish you and Maggie well. I've been all kinds of a fool. I don't know what possessed me to go . . .'

'Let's forget the past, Hugh,' Harry interrupted him quickly. 'Once this trial is over, we can all start to rebuild our lives. It won't be long now, the jury has already made its mind up. I think they decided Bella's guilt before the trial started. It's not every day they get the chance to send one of the upper class to the gallows.'

Hugh's head snapped back on his neck. 'Don't you feel any pity for her, Harry? She is still our sister when all's said and done.'

Harry gave a mirthless laugh. 'No, I don't. Nor do I believe in the preconceived notion that blood is thicker than water. Even as a child she was spiteful and malicious, those childhood traits turned to evil. She murdered a man in cold blood, without turning a hair, and if she'd had her way Maggie would be lying alongside him in the graveyard. So no, Hugh, I don't feel any pity for her. She's brought all this upon herself, and now she has to pay the price.'

Hugh saw the steely glint in his brother's eyes and quickly sought another topic of conversation.

'She was very lucky, Maggie I mean. A fraction either side and the blade would have severed the jugular vein. It's a miracle there wasn't more damage. If the blade had been longer it would surely have sliced an artery – it could even have permanently damaged the voicebox. All in all, Maggie was very fortunate.'

'I doubt she would see it that way,' Harry said dryly.

'No no, of course not,' Hugh answered hastily. 'I'm afraid my professional interest sometimes clouds the personal issue.'

'You'd better go, Mother is getting impatient. I will be seeing Maggie tonight, but I'll come by later if that is all right.'

'Oh, absolutely. And Harry, I'm glad we are friends again. I've been so miserable, you can't imagine just how miserable I've been.'

'I can, Hugh, indeed I can.'

Charlie walked over to them, his face agitated. 'I'll 'ave ter go, Harry. I don't like leaving Maggie fer too long.'

'I'm coming now, Charlie. Good day, Hugh, I'll see you later this evening.'

Hugh shook his brother's hand vigorously, then headed back to the carriage.

Half an hour later Beatrice was standing in the study, her hand twisting nervously as she waited for Edward to look up from the letter he was writing.

'Edward, the jury is out. It won't be long now. Won't you change your mind and visit Bella? It may be the last . . . the last chance you get.'

Edward laid down the pen and leaned back in his chair, his face impassive. 'No madam, I have no intention of visiting our daughter. If she had killed someone by accident, that would be different. Then I would move heaven and earth to save her. But that isn't the case. She knew exactly what she was doing and has so far shown not the slightest remorse for her actions.'

Sighing heavily he stood up and took Beatrice in his arms. 'She went bad, Beatrice, somewhere along the way her mind turned to evil. What we must never do is to blame ourselves. I consider myself to be a good judge of human character; Lord knows I've seen enough human deprivation and wickedness in my courtroom. I firmly believe that the traits of good and evil are born within us, and there is nothing anyone can do to alter that fact.'

'But, Edward, she's going to . . . going to ha . . . hang. You must do something . . . you must.' Her body heaving with sobs, she leaned against his broad chest. Edward stared over her shoulder, his eyes bleak.

'There is nothing I can do for her now, my dear. There's nothing anyone can do for her now.'

*

'Maggie, Maggie, the jury's out, it won't be long now.' Charlie ran into the room eager to impart the news.

'Calm down, Charlie. I keep telling you, they won't hang her, no matter what she's done. She's one of them, isn't she? One of the gentry. Her Dad's just biding his time, making it look as if he isn't interfering, but you wait and see. He'll step in at the last minute. The judge at the trial is probably a friend of his; they'll cook something up between them, you mark my words.' Maggie sat by the empty fireplace, her fingers busily sewing a three-inch frill collar onto a white blouse.

'There, you are wrong, dear. My father has no intention of intervening. If he had he would have done so by now.'

Maggie's hand went automatically to her neck then relaxed. The blue dress she was wearing had a high neck, the starched cotton resting just below her ears. The blouse on her lap was the last item of clothing to be altered to hide the jagged scar on the left side of her neck.

'You would say that, wouldn't you? Well, I won't believe it until she drops through the trap door.' Aware of Harry and Charlie's scrutiny her cheeks flamed. 'I know that sounds vindictive, but I don't care. She's not safe to be let out onto the streets again. Even now, knowing she's locked up, I'm still afraid of her. Afraid she'll come into the dining-room one day looking for me.'

Maggie shuddered. 'I'll never forget those black eyes; there was no life in them. Beady, glittering black marbles of death, that's what I'll remember, it's what I'll always remember. That day I had to give evidence, I could feel those eyes boring into my skull, I thought I was going to pass out.'

'It's nearly over, Maggie. You mustn't let it get to you, if you allow that to happen, then Bella will have won. Don't you see, you have to return to normal, you mustn't let what happened affect your life any more.'

Maggie heard the earnest appeal in Harry's voice and nodded grimly, 'Oh, don't you worry about me, I'll be all right. I'll never let anyone get close enough to hurt me, not any more.'

The determination in her voice caused Harry to step backwards. Wetting his lips he tried to alleviate the tense atmosphere.

'There is some good news. I met Hugh outside the court, he's asked me to visit him and Lotte this evening. You know they were married last month, don't you?'

'I know, you told me. It's the only good thing that's come out of this whole rotten mess. I'm glad for Lotte's sake, she's a good woman. I wish we could have stayed friends, but that's impossible now.'

'No, it isn't, she wants to see you, but is afraid she won't be welcome. May I tell her to visit, she'd be so happy, and . . .'

Maggie stood up quickly, 'No, there'd be no point. As soon as the trial is over, me and Charlie are moving. I don't know where yet, but it'll be far away from this place and all the memories it holds.'

Charlie was just coming from the kitchen, a tray of tea and cakes in his hands when he heard Maggie's words. 'What! Whayda mean we're leaving? It's the first I've 'eard of it.'

Maggie turned her head towards him. 'I'm sorry, love, I keep forgetting you're nearly grown up now, I should have talked it over with you. But, Charlie, I can't stay here, I have to get away, I have to. If you want to stay I'll leave you enough money to see you all right until you can get another job. You'll give him one, won't you, Harry, and keep an eye on him?'

Harry could only nod mutely, too stunned by the unexpected announcement to utter a word.

'Now, 'old on, Maggie. Yer can't just leave. What about the business and all our customers. They think the world of yer, yer can't walk out on them, it ain't fair.'

'Look, I'll leave you two to sort out your plans. I'll come back tomorrow to hear your decision.'

Raising his eyes in despair at Charlie he left the room, his mind whirling. She couldn't go, he wouldn't let her. Stopping on the stairs he pulled himself up straight. No, by God he wouldn't. No matter what lengths he had to go to, he wasn't going to lose her again.

Five days after Bella was sentenced to hang, a message came for Edward Stewart to attend the home of Jeffrey Bellingham, the High Court judge. He returned ashen-faced and trembling. Beatrice was waiting anxiously for him in the parlour.

'What is it, dear? What did he want?' she cried, her arms going out to him.

Sinking into his chair he wiped his forehead with a large white handkerchief, then in a voice barely above a whisper, he said, 'She is going to have a child, Bella is going to have a child.'

Beatrice sank back in the chair, her face a mask of disbelief. Not daring to look at her, Edward fixed his gaze on his trembling hands.

'That's not all. When the doctor informed her of her condition she said nothing, just stared as if she hadn't heard him. Then a few hours later the wardress heard her screaming. When she opened the cell door, Bella attacked her. It took three wardens to restrain her.'

Wearily he lifted his head and swallowed deeply. 'All this happened early this morning. In view of her condition and the obvious state of her mind, Jeffrey has decided to revoke the death penalty. Instead she will be committed to a mental institution for the criminally insane, to remain there for the rest of her days.'

A tear trickled from the corner of Beatrice's eye as she went to her husband. Kneeling down by his side she took his hand and put it against her cheek. So there had been a man. Her poor Bella had finally found a man – that was all she had ever wanted. Now she was doomed to spend the remainder of her days locked up in a cell, never to see the light of day ever again. Beatrice shivered. Far better to have been hanged than to suffer the horrors of a lunatic asylum. And what of the child, their grandchild; what would become of it? Would Edward allow her to take it into their home and bring it up as their own? She shook her head. There would be plenty of time to consider what had to be done. For now, her duty was to comfort her husband.

The newspapers had a field day. Copies of the local paper trebled over the next few days. When the people of London read the news they shook their head wisely. Well, what had they expected? She was one of the gentry, wasn't she? They stuck together, that lot. If it had been one of them they would have been dangling from the end of a rope by now. And as for that tale of being sent to a loony bin, that was a laugh. Some cushy hospital room more likely, being waited on hand and foot, and her bastard too when it arrived. Some people weren't content to sit and speculate. A mob gathered outside the law court protesting at the verdict. Scuffles broke out, leading to the arrest of many men and women, decent people outraged at the revoking of the death penalty. It was two weeks before Harry went to see Maggie.

Standing outside her door on this sunny July afternoon he waited for her to answer, his mouth dry, as he pondered on the reception that would greet him. Maggie opened the door and stared at him. Not saying a word she turned and walked slowly to the centre of the room then stopped, her back towards him.

'So, she got off, I knew she would.' Her voice, dull and lifeless sent a shiver up his spine.

437

'Maggie, I know what the newspapers are saying, but it isn't true, none of it. There was no conspiracy. Bella is expecting a child. You know a pregnant woman cannot be hanged, whatever her class. As for the story about her languishing in luxury . . . Oh Maggie, you've no idea, no idea at all.'

Pulling her round to face him he said urgently. 'I've just come from the asylum. I didn't want to go but my mother insisted on visiting Bella and my father refused to have anything more to do with her. I couldn't let her go alone, but dear God, I wish I had. The luxury room the newspapers are shouting about is a tiny cell. A cell with dirty straw littered on the floor, a wooden plank for a bed and a tin bucket for a toilet.'

Letting go of her arms he walked over to the mantelpiece and rested his elbow on the shelf.

'The bucket is never used, because Bella prefers to squat on the floor like an animal. The stench of the place is with me now. I should never have taken my mother there; it was a pointless visit. Bella didn't recognise either of us – she's completely insane. If you could have seen her, Maggie, you would know you have no need to fear her. She sits on the floor talking to the unborn child. Her hair and body are matted with her own filth. My mother is distraught and my father hasn't been to court since she was committed. That's why I haven't been round before now, I've been staying with them, trying to persuade them to go away for a while, without much success until today. I think now my mother may take my advice. Now that she has seen for herself that Bella is beyond help, I hope she'll start thinking about herself and my father. My uncle has a chalet in France; we've been there many times for holidays. It is situated in a very peaceful spot and would be the ideal place for them to go.'

'It sounds lovely,' Maggie said bitterly. 'It must be nice to be able to escape to a chalet in France when things get too much for you.'

Harry bent his head in despair. He couldn't cope with this, not today, not after the horror he had witnessed this morning.

Angrily picking up his hat and cane he said abruptly, 'I'd hoped you would understand. I never expected to feel pity for Bella; I never did and I'm her brother. But after seeing her in that place . . .' He drew himself up. 'I won't trouble you with any more distressing details. I will tell you this before I go. If I were in Bella's place and had the choice between what she has now and the rope, I know what I'd choose.'

Maggie remained standing until the door slammed before letting the tears fall. Why had she acted like that? It wasn't his fault. She shouldn't have been so hard on him. Hot tears splashed the back of her hands as she listened to his footsteps clattering on the stairs and pleaded silently.

'Oh, Harry, I'm sorry. Come back, please come back.'

Charlie came running around the corner, a newspaper-wrapped parcel under his arm.

''Ere, watch it, mate . . . Oh, it's you, 'Arry, you been ter see Maggie?'

'Yes, I've had that pleasure,' Harry answered, his face grim.

Charlie saw the look, his heart sinking. 'Look, 'Arry, yer don't want ter take any notice of Maggie. She's got a rotten temper, but she doesn't mean 'alf of wot she says.'

'That's as may be,' Harry said stiffly, 'but I'm in no mood for her tantrums today. I'll come back when she's in a better frame of mind.'

'Now, 'old on, 'Arry,' Charlie protested indignantly. 'She got a right to be in a tantrum. It wasn't right, 'er getting off like she did, yer sister I mean. I'd be bloody angry an' all if I was Maggie.'

Harry shifted impatiently. 'I'm sorry you feel that way, Charlie. Now if you'll excuse me, I have business to attend to.'

Charlie watched Harry go with mounting panic. What if he didn't come back? Him and Maggie were as bad as each other. Why couldn't one of them tell the other how they felt? Maybe he should say something, but what?

''Ere, 'Arry, I've got some pie and peas for dinner. Do yer fancy sharing 'em wiv us? Yer know, like we used ter in the park.' Harry looked over his shoulder and smiled weakly, then shaking his head he walked on.

Clutching the grease-stained parcel tighter, Charlie took a deep breath, then shouted loudly, 'She loves yer, 'Arry. She won't admit it, but she loves yer.'

Harry stopped in his tracks. Hardly daring to breathe

he spun round on his heels and marched back to where Charlie was standing, his eyes seeming to stand out of his head. Taking the boy by the arm Harry's grip tightened.

'What's that you said, Charlie? Are you sure, are you absolutely sure?'

Charlie winced as the pressure on his arm increased.

' 'Course I'm sure. She won't say anyfing, 'cos she thinks you just want ter make 'er yer fancy bit. Yer don't do yer, 'Arry,' he pleaded, ' 'cos if that is all yer want, then don't bother coming back. I like yer, 'Arry, I like yer a lot, but I love Maggie, and she deserves better than ter be some rich man's bit on the side.'

Harry's eyes lit up. Grabbing the startled boy around the shoulders he pressed him to his chest before running into the house.

' 'Ere, you've squashed me dinner,' Charlie called out ruefully. Then, hunching his body, he followed Harry into the building, his face troubled. Those things he'd told Harry were merely his own interpretation of how Maggie felt. She'd never said anything to him. What if he was wrong?

Maggie heard the door opening and said listlessly, 'You took your time. Anyway I'm not hungry any more. I don't feel like eating now.'

'How do you feel about having this instead.'

A small black box was thrust under her nose: a diamond ring set in the middle of blue silk sparkled up at

441

her. Unable to believe her eyes she stared at the ring, her heart racing. Then Harry was on his knees, his eyes gazing into hers.

'I love you, darling. I think I've loved you from the first time I set eyes on you. Will you marry me, Maggie?'

Out in the hallway Charlie hovered, his fingers tightly crossed as he waited for Maggie to reply. The silence from the room lengthened as he prayed silently, 'Say yes, Maggie. For Gawd's sake, say yes.'

Peeping around the door his heart leapt with joy at the sight of the couple closely entwined in the chair. Forgetting the parcel tucked under his arm, he threw his hands in the air with delight, sending the contents spilling out onto the cold floorboards. Grinning broadly he bent to pick the squashed pies and peas from the floor, then settling himself on the stairs he began to eat his dinner.